THE SHADOWS LENGTHEN

THE SHADOWS LENGTHEN

Lucinda Hart

Copyright © Lucinda Hart 2025

All rights reserved. No part of this publication may be reproduced, stored in or introduced into a retrieval system or transmitted in any form or by any means, electronic, mechanical, photocopying, recording or otherwise without prior written permission from the publisher.

This is a work of fiction. Names, characters, places and incidents are either the product of the author's imagination or are used fictitiously, and any resemblance to any person or persons, living or dead, events or locales is entirely coincidental.

Published by Vulpine Press in the United Kingdom in 2025

ISBN: 978-1-83919-667-6

www.vulpine-press.com

For Alfred William Matthews
1923 – 2020

My grandad Alfred was – like Ivor – a Shropshire lad who ended his days at the far tip of Cornwall. Alfred was an industrial chemist, not an artist, although he loved galleries and private views, and became friends with several of the St Ives painters. Ivor's independence, intelligence, perception and kindness come from Alfred. As do his peppermint-green eyes. Alfred loved the landscape and geology, the art and nature of Cornwall, but his heart was always with Housman's blue remembered hills in those dreamy and uneasy borderlands.

Cornwall Mourns Local Artist
(*The West Briton*)

~

Tributes Paid To Penwith Artist
(*The Cornishman*)

~

Cornwall Art Community in Shock
(*The Times*)

I shuffle the flimsy articles on the table like I'm doing a card trick, but there's no magic to make the headlines vanish. No trickery to hide the pixelated images of his face, his paintings.

I should have spent more time with him. I should have known him better. The girls should have known him better. If I could take back this summer I would make time for him, instead of wasting it on someone not worthy of my breath.

There are so many questions that will never be answered, moments never shared. So much I want to say, now that I can't say anything to him.

~

The light is fading fast as afternoon smudges into evening. An inky bloom of rainclouds rolls in from the northern horizon. Ivor Martin glances through the studio window and rinses his brush at the sink.

He's stayed working longer than he intended to but, at his age, he figures he does not have time to waste. He has so few hours left and, suddenly, so much work to do, so much love and longing to pour and scrape and etch into his canvases. This will be his last series of paintings. Not through choice – no, never that – but, like the swollen clouds outside, Ivor senses darkness rolling in quickly to his own horizon.

He dries the brush and winces at the gout in his knuckles. Dark red shiny joints like cherries. The pain locked itself away as he worked but now it burns once more in his bones. He replaces the brushes in their tin, gives the tap a final firm twist which jars his hand further.

The canvas glints with tacky acrylic paint. Thick clots and runny streaks. The colours and landscape of Ivor's youth, so many miles from this windy outpost of west Cornwall. For his last work, he's returning to his roots. Earth to earth.

He struggles into his jacket, his hand finds the familiar smooth curve of his walking stick, and he shuffles towards the door. Cold air hits him in the face as he steps carefully out of his studio and onto the flagstone path. He swaps his walking stick to the other hand so he can turn off the light and lock the door. Hot pain throbs in his knuckles.

It's only a short walk between his garden studio and the back door of his bungalow. The path is edged with daffodils, now ghostly white horns in the dark. Rain freckles Ivor's head as he starts towards his house and the warm light of the living room window, stained red through the curtains.

He must get Stefan to clear this path. It's slimy in the wet. He doesn't know if his foot slides from under him, or whether the walking stick misses its purchase on the stone, but suddenly he is going down, down, and his knee, his bad left knee, explodes in a burst of pain, and his head hits the cold wet path.

He cries out and swears.

Smoke-dark clouds billow over his head, spewing rain onto him. At the edge of his vision he can still see the red light of the living room and the shapes of his furniture beyond: the bookcase, the standard lamp, his chair.

He tries to sit but his knee screams like Munch's dark figure. His swollen legs are clumsy as logs. A daffodil brushes his cheek with a wet kiss. He walks his gouty fingers across the flagstone to find his walking stick but it's skittered out of reach.

~

It only takes one drink.

Tansy slides her hand up and down the cool bottle. It's a Chilean Merlot. Her mother must have been given it as a present as she'd never have chosen it herself. Tansy would have though. And over ten years ago she chose such a wine often, and too often. During the last decade she's handled many bottles, wrapped them for gifts, poured from them at parties, and never wavered. But now, this February evening, two weeks after her thirty-eighth birthday, and ten years and five months since that last gin, she finds her fingers reaching for the screw top.

There's no reason for this to happen tonight. No reason at all. It's not an anniversary, good or bad. She's not had a shock or a fright. Maybe it's simply because it's a quiet evening. Her mother is away in Plymouth for the night, and the girls are actually silent. When she looked into the living room a few minutes ago Scarlet was still watching CBeebies on iPlayer, and Amber had fallen asleep on the sofa, her face flushed, her hands balled into little fists. If Tansy holds her breath she can just hear the murmur of her laptop, spurting out the Christmas play that Scarlet still wants to watch every evening but, other than that, there's just the soft grumble of the boiler. A quiet evening.

The bottle is cool in her hands. Forest green glass, darkened by the wine. Black and red label with a gold font. Decadent. A tiny twist on the lid is all she needs. A second or less. She places the bottle on the worktop and takes a tumbler from the cupboard.

There's no reason to do this tonight.

There is every reason.

The seal breaks with a crack. Tansy glances around as though someone might have heard. The cooker clock changes numbers. Another minute of her sobriety.

She lifts the bottle and pours. Ruby-black fluid falls into the glass. She screws on the lid again. Checks the cooker clock. Yet another minute has gone by.

At last she lifts the glass to her lips. The first taste is bitter as bile. Did I really crave this every day, she wonders. She takes another sip, and another. Each sip is less acid, more smooth. She takes a bigger mouthful and turns her back on the clock. She doesn't want to know the exact moment she broke her vow.

She tops up the glass. The wine is thick and heavy with South American fragrance. Like perfume, ink, blood.

Ivor shivers as he finally extracts his mobile from his trouser pocket. He doesn't think about what he'd have done if that, like the walking stick, had slid away from his grasp. The screen lights up and rain speckles the photo of Scarlet and Amber. He clicks his contacts, but his fingers are swollen and wet and it takes him several goes to get through. Emmeline is away, he remembers, visiting friends in Plymouth. Tansy will be at home with the girls. She must be. He hits green and winces at the pain in his knee. His breathing sounds ragged to his own ears, crumpled as he is, in this half-sitting, half-lying heap.

Tansy has drunk half the bottle. She should feel something, she thinks. Guilt, anger maybe, at her weakness, her stupidity, her downfall. Or elation at the embrace of her old poisonous friend. But she feels nothing. Nothing at all. She drinks and feels nothing.

The hall phone rings and she jumps. It must be her mother. Only her mother and her grandad use the landline. Her grandad. Scarlet calls something to her, but she ignores her daughter, runs into the hall.

Why didn't she call him? Her mother spoke to him before leaving and said he was fine. But no one was going to him today. She should have called him. She should have arranged someone to go. She should have gone.

"Tansy. I need help."

Ivor's voice is thin and cracked. He sounds breathless.

"What's happened?"

"Fall. Fell down."

"Where are you?"

"Studio. Outside the studio…on the path."

"On the path?" She glances through the front door panes. It's dark. Rain hits the glass like gravel. "I'll call an ambulance," she says.

"Can you come?" Ivor gasps.

"I'm on my own," she starts. "With the girls. I'll have to…" She's wasting time. "Yes," she says. "But I'll call Mel too. After the ambulance."

"What ambulance?" Scarlet grabs her by the leg. "Who's got an ambulance? Are we getting an ambulance?"

Tansy gently knocks Scarlet aside as she dials 999.

5

Melanie Atkins hardly hears the ring of her mobile over the TV and the shouts of her four children. She snatches it from her handbag which someone has kicked under the table and sees Tansy's name.

"Tansy, hi." She puts her spare hand over her other ear. Jamie seems to be beating up Thomas in the living room.

"Mel, it's Grandad."

The TV, the kids, it all swoops away into white noise. Mel's heart rushes under her ribs.

"Is he OK?" Then, "I wasn't supposed to be there tonight, was I?"

"No, no. He's had an accident. I've called an ambulance. I've got to get the girls sorted and get them there. Could you please go to him? You'll be so much quicker. Please?"

"I'm on my way."

Mel is about to hang up when Tansy says, "He's in the garden by the studio. He'll need blankets."

"I'm going." Mel snaps off the phone.

She grabs an armful of blankets from the airing cupboard, and cannons into her husband as he slouches into the kitchen.

"What you doing?" Joe asks, nodding at the sliding pile in her arms.

"Have to go. Ivor's had a fall." She strides into the hall and unhooks her jacket. "Can you get the girls to bed soon please? Read them a story."

She's out of the door and into the rain before Joe answers.

Tansy shakes three-year-old Amber more roughly than she usually would.

"Amber, Amber, please wake up darling, we have to go out."

"Where are we going?" Scarlet wails again.

"To Grandad's. I told you. Come on, Scarlet, can you get your coats for me while I change her nappy?"

Amber scowls as Tansy hauls her half upright on the sofa. Her leggings are wet – they would be, wouldn't they? – and there is a dark puddle on the cushion she was lying on. Tansy throws the cushion to the floor and peels off the wet trousers.

"Mummy, Mummy, I'm tired."

"I know, sweetheart, I'm sorry. I need you to be very grown up for me tonight."

"What about me?" Scarlet is sullen. "Can't I be grown up too?"

"You're always grown up," Tansy mutters automatically. "Scarlet, could you grab me some trousers for her from the washing? That pile there on the chair. Yes, those jeans are fine."

Scarlet lobs the jeans towards Tansy.

"I'm grown up too," Amber shouts.

"No you're not. You're only three. You're a baby. I'm the grown up. I'm five."

"I am not a baby."

"Are."

"I'm not a baby."

"Shut up, both of you."

Tansy tugs the jeans onto Amber's furious little body. Oh fuck, socks, they'll need socks. One glance at Scarlet. She's not wearing socks either.

Please let the ambulance come quickly, Tansy mutters to herself. She told the operator Ivor was ninety-five and had fallen in the cold and wet. She told him that Ivor had arthritis and cellulitis and would not be able to get himself up unaided. She also knows people wait hours for an ambulance.

Mel. Mel will be there soon. That's something she can guarantee. Capable, quick-thinking, practical Mel, who manages her husband, four children, and two guinea pigs without ruffles or stress.

It's only as Tansy is finally strapping Amber into her car seat that she remembers the half bottle of Merlot she's drunk. She's probably over the limit. She shouldn't be driving.

She closes the back door and slides in behind the wheel. The interior light dies a few seconds after her own door closes. The car is very cold and very dark.

"I'm cold," Scarlet starts.

"Tiger, I haven't got Tiger. Mummy, I need Tiger."

"We have to go now. Tiger will be waiting for you here, Amber."

Tansy revs the engine and flicks on her headlamps. A swipe or two of the wipers and a wipe with her cloth. She puts the Golf into reverse and rolls down the drive.

She's driving out into the night with two children. She's probably over the limit. And Ivor is in great danger, alone and injured in his dark wet garden.

Like Tansy, Mel is only a few moments' drive from Ivor's. His bungalow is in a country lane winding out of the village of Gerent's Cross. She roars down the narrow road, watching her rear mirror for an ambulance's blue lights, but sees nothing.

She parks in the muddy layby opposite the bungalow, leaving Ivor's drive for the ambulance and Tansy. There are lights on in the kitchen and, beyond that, the usual warm glow from the living room. It looks just like it does when Ivor is at home, waiting for her to come and prepare his dinner, wash his legs, sort his laundry.

"Ivor," she calls out as soon as she goes in, but of course there is no reply.

In a couple of strides she's out of the back door and onto the flagstone path and there he is: a dark shape just outside the studio.

"Ivor, it's Mel. I'm here."

She crouches down beside him and wraps him in the blankets. He is freezing cold, and his eyes, behind his glasses, are dazed.

"There's an ambulance coming," Mel says, "and Tansy and the girls."

"Sorry," Ivor mutters. "So sorry."

"Ssh. Don't be silly. It's not your fault. Can we shuffle you back into the studio?"

"So cold...my leg."

"Where's the key? In your pocket?"

Mel fumbles in Ivor's pocket – he's wearing his jacket at least, she thinks – and finds the studio key. She opens the door and snaps on the light. For a second she just stares at the canvas. She's only been in here a couple of times before. This is something new. It still looks wet. It looks full of memories and yearning. Times lost. People lost.

~

"They say it's coming." Tansy snaps off her mobile.

She and Mel between them managed to haul Ivor into the studio. He cried out a lot, and Tansy was frightened of hurting him further, but he couldn't stay out in the icy night another moment.

"You stay with him and I'll go and look for them." Mel squeezes her arm as she slides past.

Scarlet and Amber are sitting on the floor at the far end of the studio. Amber's falling asleep again, despite the hard floor, and the cold, and the situation. Scarlet has found a stick of charcoal and is

9

covering her palms in black dust, but Tansy can't be bothered to say anything.

She feels the weight of the painting behind her. She didn't even know Ivor was working again. It looms with the weight of a life lived, of people lost.

Suddenly over the bungalow roof the sky pulses blue and a moment later Mel leads two paramedics through the back door and over to the studio. Tansy exhales and wonders why the painting makes her feel so unhappy.

After Ivor is put on a gurney and the ambulance leaves, Tansy and Mel stand side by side on the front step as the ambulance pulls out onto the lane. The girls are in the living room, tired and squabbling.

"I can go if you like," Mel offers once more.

"You've done enough. I'd go, you know I would, but with them, well, I can't, can I?" Tansy worries at a broken nail miserably. She should go. She should be with Ivor, but she can't take the girls up to A & E for God knows how long in the middle of the night. And there's the other thing too. The wine thing.

"Have you called your mum?"

"Christ. No. I'll do it when we go home."

"Is there anything I can do?" Mel asks as they go back indoors.

"No. Really. Thank you. I'll call Mum. I'll text Carol and Stefan too. I'll ring the hospital later, see what's happening. They were pretty positive, weren't they, the paramedics?"

"He certainly brightened up." Mel clicks off the kitchen light. "He must have been scared to death out there. I know I would be. Please let me know what the hospital says, won't you?"

"Of course."

"Any time. I mean it."

Tansy shepherds the girls out to the car. As she bundles Amber into the travel seat she can feel a very swollen nappy again. Mel locks up the bungalow. It looks bleak and empty with its dark windows.

"There's not a lot you could do at A & E at the moment," Mel says, reading Tansy's stricken thoughts.

"No, I know." Tansy shivers. Alcohol on an empty stomach, alcohol for the first time in over ten years, the cold night, the shock, the terror. "I'll get the girls home before they fall asleep in the car. Before Amber floods the seat."

Mel gives her a quick hug. Tansy turns on her lights so Mel can see the way to her own car in the lane. When she gets home she has to carry Amber into the house. She takes both girls to her own bedroom and leaves Amber on the quilt while she runs for wipes and a nappy. Amber doesn't stir as she changes her. Scarlet stumbles out of her boots and collapses down next to her sister.

~

Tansy tries to call her mother in Plymouth, but it goes straight to voicemail. She leaves a message asking Emmeline to call her back. The half bottle of Merlot is still where she left it on the worktop, the glass beside it. She picks up the glass, studies the purple stain at the base. She can't go to the hospital tonight. Not with the girls. She unscrews the metal lid and sloshes out another inch.

Her mobile is almost out of charge. She types a quick message to Ivor's other two carers.

Carol/ Stefan – Grandad had a fall in the garden tonight. Mel and I went up.

He's gone to hospital in an ambulance. Will update you when I know more. XX

When the ambulance arrived Ivor was freezing cold, even with Mel's blankets. The pain in his legs made him breathless, and there was blood in the white wisps of his hair. By the time he was bundled into a wheelchair he was talking more, aware of what had happened.

"So sorry, so sorry," he kept saying to Tansy and Mel. "Don't want the girls to see me like this."

Tansy plugs her phone in to charge. It's too soon to call A & E. There won't be any news for hours. There never is.

~

Carol Allen doesn't look at her phone until she goes to bed. She usually leaves it on her bedside table where it won't disturb her. Jeff is still downstairs watching some ghastly film with guns and men shouting. Carol opens the bedroom curtains and peers out into the slice of night beyond.

Their cottage is down a narrow lane to a farm. This, and its riding stables, are their only neighbours. She can see the gold haze that marks the lights of Penzance to the west, and a few isolated windows from other remote dwellings. A helicopter pulses across the sky. Carol often hears owls and foxes at night. She sees hedgehogs on the lawn and, in the summer, giant hawk moths come to her scented plants.

She draws the curtains and pads over to the bed. The side lamp is on. She has her cup of tea and her novel waiting for her. And her phone. She swipes the screen quickly. There's a new message. It's probably from Louis, she thinks. He uses her mobile to talk to her as he and Jeff do everything they can to avoid each other. Carol and Jeff have been married five years now, and it doesn't look like the situation will get any better with Louis.

Carol clicks, expecting news of her son's life in London, his job, his flatmate, some girl, whatever. But it's not from Louis, it's from

Tansy, and Carol's heart rate soars before she even reads it because she knows, she just knows, it's bad news.

~

Tansy jumps as her mobile rings. It's still charging on the table beside her. She must have dropped off.

"I'm so sorry," Emmeline starts. "Bloody thing was off. What's happened? You all OK?"

Tansy's mouth is dry and sour. She needs water. She explains about Ivor, Mel, the ambulance.

"I called the hospital about midnight," she says. "He's on a ward. He's doing all right. They're giving him antibiotics. His cellulitis is bad again, and his chest."

"No bones broken?"

"No. Shock, I think. Cold."

"Christ yes. Look, I didn't realise this thing was off. Couldn't sleep, went online and saw your message. I'll leave first thing, OK? And we'll have to sort out something better for him. I think he should have someone come in every day now, d'you agree?"

"Yes, yes, sorry, my throat's really scratchy. Yes, we'll sort it out. And go and see him."

"See you soon," says Emmeline, "and well done for tonight. You and the girls. Well done."

~

Carol cannot sleep. She knows from Tansy that Ivor is on a ward and that he is safe for now, but the story could so easily have had a different ending. In fact, the ending is still uncertain.

Beside her Jeff snores and coughs. She wonders, as she has so many times, if it would have been easier if she'd been open about Ivor to him. It's too late now. Whatever happens.

~

Stefan Rose wakes just a moment before his alarm goes off. Strange that, but he often does it. Like he often wakes at 4.33 on the morning of his birthday: the very time he was born. He stumbles out of bed, the quilt trailing behind him, and ducks his head to look out of the attic window. Wet grey roof tiles in the half-light, stained with patches of gold lichen. A flickering street lamp. Steely sea. The cries of seagulls. St Ives in winter.

Stefan rents a tiny attic flat at the top of town. He waited months to find a place he could afford and somewhere with street parking. As it is, he often has to leave the car miles away and sometimes, in summer, he keeps it at the hotel car-park where he works. This morning he'll be OK: late last night a space came up in front of the house next door and he ran down the street in the rain without his jacket to move his little hatchback closer.

He's going to Ivor's this morning, before the hotel. He prefers the morning shifts where he wakes Ivor with a cup of tea, if he is not already awake and helps him to the bathroom. While Ivor washes and dresses, Stefan pours milk on cereal, and chops a banana or pear, makes another cup of tea. If there's any washing up from the night before he'll do that too, and anything else Ivor might need, like emptying the bin or sorting the washing.

He makes himself a quick coffee and takes two chocolate digestives for his own breakfast. Rain clatters against the kitchen window. Stefan looks round for his mobile. He can't see it anywhere obvious, like on the breakfast bar, or near the charging socket. It must be in his jacket pocket, the jacket he didn't bother with when he went racing out into the downpour late last night to move the car.

His fingers find the cool slim object in the pocket. When he turns it on, it vibrates immediately, warning him of missed messages.

Tansy, Tansy, Mel, Carol, Tansy. All last night. Shit. What the hell has happened to Ivor? He opens the texts, fearing the worst, the very worst, the same fear that stalks him each time he opens Ivor's door. Ivor had a fall and is in hospital. He should be home soon. Stefan exhales, feeling the rush of his heart. He hasn't known Ivor long, just a few months, but he's become fond of him, dreads the day that cannot be far off.

—

They're asleep in a damp tangled knot on the bed – Tansy, Scarlet, Amber – when Emmeline strides into the bedroom in her coat, dangling her car keys.

Tansy stirs at the sound, jumps awake, thinking her mobile is ringing, that someone has something terrible to say. Before she trailed into the bedroom with the girls she stuffed the empty wine bottle in the recycling box and rinsed the tumbler.

"I'm here. Any news?" Emmeline perches on the edge of the bed, her pale hair in a messy bun, her glasses pushed up on her head.

Tansy's throat feels thick from the alcohol and she has cramp in her leg where Scarlet sprawls over her. She scrabbles for her mobile. Texts. One from Emmeline to say she's leaving Plymouth, one from Stefan – *So sorry I didn't get these last night. How are things?* – one from Mel – *How's Ivor today?* – and a missed call from Carol.

Nothing from the hospital.

Tansy manoeuvres her arm from under Scarlet and slides off the bed.

"Come on. Let's have some tea," her mother says. "Then we'll ring the hospital. The girls are staying home today, yes?"

Hell. It's a Friday morning. School. Nursery.

"Uh, yes, probably better they do."

In the kitchen Emmeline clunks mugs onto the counter, drops in tea bags. Tansy leans against the worktop, answers her mother's questions as best she can. She suddenly sees a dark red wine stain on the granite and spits on her finger to wipe it away.

"We need to sort out something better for him," Emmeline starts. "He can't go on like this now. He needs more supervision."

"It's my fault. I should've checked up on him. It's just he was fine when you left."

"We certainly should have insisted someone went to him last night."

"He doesn't want to lose all his independence."

"I know," Emmeline agrees. "But sometimes people have to if they're not safe. Even if you'd checked up on him he could still have gone to the studio later. What was he doing in there anyway?"

"Painting."

"I thought…"

"He'd given up?"

"Well, with the gout and that."

"He says he was doing a last series of paintings. Going back to his youth. Like a full circle."

Tansy rubs at a tear, imagining Ivor knowing his life is coming to an end, that he will never return to those fields and orchards of Shropshire where he grew up, married, became a father to Emmeline. Those times live only in his memory. She pictures him in his studio, mixing colours with an unsteady hand, seeing those places one last time on the canvas before him.

"If he's going to paint, we need to get his stuff indoors. Set up a corner of the living room or something…" Emmeline trails off, then, "It's my fault too. I shouldn't have gone away like that."

Tansy drinks tea, shrugs. "You have to have a life. How are Jane and Bob anyway?"

"Oh, fine. Fine."

"Mel was brilliant last night. I knew it would take ages to get the kids ready. She just shot off straight away."

"We must do something to say thank you. Give her a bottle." Emmeline puts down her mug and goes to the wine rack. "There's a bottle of Merlot somewhere here. I got it on that meal deal thing from Sainsbury's. We'll give her that." She slides out a bottle, then another. "That's weird. I'm sure I put it in here."

Sweat prickles on Tansy's back. She's still got to tell her mother what she's done. The damage she's done.

"No," Tansy says, and her voice sounds weird. "No, it's not there. The wine. The Merlot."

Emmeline replaces a bottle of prosecco. "Oh, where did I put it?"

Tansy blurts out "It's just not there any more. It's gone."

She hesitates. It would be so easy to say *Mel came back here and I gave her the bottle of wine.* But that bottle, that empty bottle, is in the recycling box. It was a really stupid place to put it. She should have stuffed it right at the bottom of a bin bag, and prayed the bag didn't burst, spilling her secret onto the tiles with a crack.

Emmeline is looking at her strangely. Tansy's sure her mother has realised what's happened but her brain can't quite make that final terrible connection.

"The wine's not there," Tansy explodes. "It's in the recycling. The bottle. It's empty."

"Who had it then?"

"Me."

"You?"

"Yes. Me. I drank it. Last night." Tansy looks out of the window at the damp grey garden. She doesn't want to see her mother's face. The anger, the shock, the disappointment.

"You drank it?"

"I'm sorry. I'm so sorry."

"But all those years…Was it the first time?"

"Yes, it was the first time."

"Was it the stress, being alone with the girls and then…"

"It was before. It was before he fell. I don't know why. I was looking at it, and I realised I was bored not doing it any more. I just wanted that taste, that feeling again."

Emmeline crumples down on a dining chair. "You wouldn't have done that if I'd been here."

"Probably not. It's not your fault. None of it's your fault. It's my fault. I knew what I was doing. I kept thinking *do I really want to do this?* And I could have changed my mind so many times. But once I'd made up my mind, I'd made it up. Once the thought was there, that I could open it, I could drink it, then the thought just wouldn't go away. It was like a collision course."

"You had all of it?"

"Yeah, I finished it when we came back. I was cold and stressed. The only thing that upset me about it was that I couldn't drive up to the hospital, but I couldn't have with the girls anyway. Mel said she'd go if I wanted her to, but I said she didn't have to. She could have been there hours."

"Christ," Emmeline mutters. "My friends ask me up for a night and every fucking thing goes wrong."

"I'm sorry," Tansy says.

"How did it make you feel?"

"The wine? Nothing. I felt nothing."

"If you felt nothing you won't want to do it again, will you?"

"I don't know," Tansy says. "Sometimes nothing is what you need most."

~

Ivor has the cubicle curtains pulled out on both sides so he can see as little as possible of the ward and the other inmates. His bed is in the middle of three, the worst position. The man on his left by the window shouts a lot and groans, so much that the nurses now ignore the noises. To the right, the patient seems to be having trouble with his catheter, from what Ivor can hear through the stained fabric. When the nurses visit his neighbour the curtains bulge into his space and he can see scuffed black shoes at the bottom.

His nurse this morning, a young man with tattooed arms, has told him that his family have called the ward for an update and that they'll be in to see him that afternoon. Another caller, a lady by the name of Carol Allen has also been asking after him, but of course she couldn't be told anything because of confidentiality.

"It's fine," Ivor says as the nurse inflates the blood pressure cuff. "Tell Carol anything."

"BP's good now." The nurse slides an oximeter onto Ivor's finger. "You'll be out of here before you know it."

"Can't wait," Ivor grimaces.

When the nurse has gone Ivor considers his words. He can't wait to get out of this noisy, smelly, suffocating place, where he can't sleep, the food is vile, and the other patients gruesome. He wants nothing more than to be home in his bungalow with the daffodils tossing their blonde heads outside his window. He wants to be in the studio, working on his last paintings, as this fall has emphasised his fears that his hourglass is draining fast.

But it isn't that simple. Something else has changed in him now. He is afraid. Ivor has never been afraid, but he was the previous night, shaking with pain and cold under the rainy sky. He is afraid to return home because he no longer feels that he is safe there with just occasional visits from Carol, Mel, and Stefan.

One of them comes most mornings to get him up and dressed and to make sure he has anything he needs for the day. Usually three or four nights a week he'll see one of them, who will cook his dinner – nothing fancy: eggs maybe, sardines, jacket potato, cold meat – help him wash and shave, and get ready for bed. Emmeline and Tansy are around too, visiting and ringing every day, but now, half-propped up on this uncomfortable bed, in this ghastly printed gown, all those lonely hours at home seem beyond him. He will have to talk to Emmeline and Tansy about having more visits. Every morning without fail, and every evening too, at least until his confidence returns. If it ever does.

Being ninety-five is wonderful, but also painful. The gout swells his hands and makes him clumsy with a brush or pen, a knife and fork. Arthritis in his left knee has twisted his posture and he can't walk without his stick. And the renal failure that has been ever creeping on lately causes his legs to swell and become infected. He is back on antibiotics now, for his legs and for his chest.

He closes his eyes against the ward, slides back through time to when he cycled the lanes of Shropshire almost a century ago, when he crept into the forge down the lane to talk to the blacksmith at work, when he hitched a ride on the undertaker's huge dog. He hasn't been back to the village for twenty years. Some of the old buildings were still there then. The undertakers' shiny new premises still bore the old name, although it's owned by the Americans now; the forge had long since been knocked down and a community hall erected on the site.

The parish church remained of course, as churches do, and the ivied gravestones of his forefathers.

Undertakers, gravestones. Soon he'll be sliding into the earth. Not in the soft green pastures of Shropshire, but the ravaged windy moorland of Penwith, united for ever with Sylvia.

"Cup of tea, love?"

Ivor opens his eyes. The tea lady has parked her trolley at the foot of his bed. He asks for tea, just a splash of milk. As he drinks from the sticky cup he takes his mobile off the cabinet and tries again for a signal. He really needs Emmeline and Tansy to bring some things for him. He only has the small bag Tansy and Mel threw together the night before. Pyjamas, toothbrush, mobile, charger, glasses, book, socks. He wants more novels, humbugs, a sudoku book, a copy of *The Times*, and some fruit juice – but his signal bar remains blank.

He wonders idly if he should always have a hospital bag packed now in case something like this happens again. That's what pregnant women do. He remembers Tansy telling him that when she was expecting Scarlet. Ivor swipes through the gallery on his phone. Some of his garden, some of his drawings and canvases, but mostly Scarlet and Amber. Every day he wishes Sylvia had lived long enough to meet these funny, loving great-grandchildren of his. He'd love to draw them if they'd keep still long enough. Scarlet with her long gold tresses, and Amber's strawberry blonde pixie-cut that she did herself with kitchen scissors, to Tansy's horror. He checks his watch. It's after school and nursery. Scarlet and Amber must be coming to visit him too. He wishes he could change into something other than this green gown, stained with his breakfast coffee, wishes he could freshen up. He rubs his eyes, tries to look more alert.

Noise and clattering on the ward, then Emmeline appears round the curtain, and Scarlet rushes up to him, almost knocking the teacup from his hand. Tansy pushes Amber's buggy into the cubicle. Amber is eating Pom Bears, dropping crumbs on the floor.

"How are you doing?" Emmeline asks. "We've brought you some things." She plonks a black holdall on the bed. "Have they said when you'll be coming out?"

"Not yet," he says, as he struggles to open the zip.

Emmeline and Tansy exchange a glance, which he does not miss.

"We need to rethink things," Emmeline says. "For when you go home."

"I know."

~

Jake Gregory's studio is down an alley off Causewayhead in the centre of Penzance. He's been working there since he returned to Cornwall when Tansy was nine, when she found out that he was her missing father. The lower floor soars to a high whitewashed roof, and Jake stores his largest canvases there. Shafts of sunlight stream through the tiny back window onto a row of ragged houseplants. A frail staircase leads to the upper level, which is a riotous jumble of paint pots, torn newspapers, broken easels, and stained mugs. The walls are patchworked with posters: his own exhibitions, and those of other artists, including several of Ivor's, postcards from friends, band flyers, photographs. Above his desk is a large glossy photo of Tansy and her daughters. The pictures on either side irritate Tansy: Jake's two sons in London, and his other daughter in France, all conceived while he was out of Cornwall.

Jake hands Tansy a tea in one of his ghastly mugs. The inside is dark with tannin stains above the liquid level. She shoves some of his papers aside and puts it on the table.

"So, any luck finding anywhere?" Jake asks, waving a box of Maltesers under her nose.

She takes a handful. "Yeah, looks like they've got a space at Lanyon House, you know it? Just out of St Ives?"

"On the cliffs?"

"That's the one. Mum's going to look round this afternoon."

"How long will he be there?"

"Couple of weeks probably. Just to get him more confident on his feet. We're going to find someone else, another carer, to add in. Get people in twice a day at least when he goes home."

"Give him my best."

"Of course."

"I'll go and see him when he's there."

"He'd like that. How's the work going?"

"I'll show you in a sec. Most of it's downstairs. There are those small ones."

Jake points to two abstract canvases on the wall. Dark and ethereal at the same time, a palette of indigo and violet and white, with scratched markings, almost runic, and sudden surprising inserts of collage.

"When are you going to paint again?" Jake asks.

"With two small children? I don't think so. We do a few things off Mister Maker."

"Amber's at nursery now. Sure you could have a go."

Tansy hesitates. "Grandad's going to need more time from us all now. And, to be honest, it's been so long I hardly know what to do. Where to start."

"Start with anything. Draw the girls, your mum, start ripping up paper for a collage. Anything."

"Maybe."

Tansy finishes her tea. She watches Jake, looking once more for any sign of the girls in him, but she can't see anything. At sixty his dark hair has turned grey, but is still thick and curls over his collar. There are lines round his eyes, of course, and a thickening of his jaw. The marks of a lifetime of drinking. It's where Tansy gets it from. She knows that.

"Jake, I need to tell you something."

"Shit, sounds heavy."

"Fell off the wagon."

"Oh." Jake obviously doesn't know what to say. Perhaps he's pleased, Tansy wonders. Perhaps he'll suggest they go for a drink again.

"The night he fell."

"Well, it was the stress. You were responsible for him and the girls."

"It wasn't really like that. I chose to. Before the accident. I decided to do it."

"I bet Emmeline went ballistic."

"She wasn't too bad really. She was upset, but, you know, it was too late."

"Are you still drinking?" Jake asks.

"Sometimes. Not every day."

Not yet.

"You know I've always admired you for what you did. I couldn't have done it."

"Admire me? Why? What did I do? Ten years, all for nothing."

"Not for nothing. Not at all. You can do it again. If you want to."

"I don't know if I do. Show me the pictures, then I'm off to see Charlie."

People often talk about getting together with their best friend and how wonderful it turns out, but for Tansy it was the opposite. She and Charlie had been friends since primary school. They'd never gone out together as teenagers, had gone their separate ways, met other lovers, but somehow seven years ago they ended up kissing after a mutual friend's party. Tansy couldn't even blame the drink, not on her part anyway, as she was already sober. Soon afterwards she and Charlie found a flat together. He had just opened his shop in Chapel Street and Tansy was working in a gallery and at a holiday camp.

By the time Amber was born she and Charlie were driving each other crazy. If asked, she couldn't even name the things that irritated her so much, and she guesses it was the same for him. She knows he was relieved when she and the girls moved in with Emmeline. He gave notice on the flat and found somewhere cheaper for himself.

But now, they get on well again. They're back to their factory settings, old friends. Tansy believes her mother's calm acceptance of Jake's disappearance, other children, drinking, and general flakiness, has helped her to form a civilised partnership with Charlie, and a fairly stable home life for the girls.

She runs across the zebra crossing and starts down Chapel Street. Charlie will close the shop for half an hour or so and go for a coffee with her, as he often does. They'll talk about his business in second-hand records and music memorabilia, she'll show him pictures of the girls and tell him what they've been doing at school and nursery. She'll check he is still OK to have them at the weekend. And then they'll kiss each other on the cheek and she'll drive home to Gerent's Cross. By the time she gets home her mother will have left to visit the care home in St Ives where Ivor is planning to go for a respite stay after leaving hospital, and it will be time for her to collect Scarlet and Amber from school and nursery.

Carol misses going round to Ivor's. Of the three carers she knows him the best and understands him. Obviously. She has been to see him on the ward a couple of times, taken him fruit and newspapers, books and a large piece of home-baked lemon cake. She was scared to see him the first time, afraid he would have diminished in those few days.

The ward is noisy and smelly. There are tea trolleys, nurses, other visitors. The patient on one side of him shouts and moans. He wanders at night sometimes too, Ivor told her. Once, security had to come at three in the morning.

"It'll be much better at Lanyon House," she tells him now. "You'll have your own room. You can get away from it all." She hesitates, not knowing whether to proceed. "You could have some drawing stuff, get your eye in again."

"Maybe," he says.

She lifts the grimy jug of cordial on his table. He nods and she pours into a plastic beaker.

"Emmeline's gone to look round this afternoon," she says. "And if it's OK she'll get things moving and we'll get you there in a day or so. And if it's not good, she won't let you go there, you know that."

Ivor drinks the cordial and grimaces.

"We'll all come and see you there. You're only a stone's throw from Stefan. And you know I'll come."

Ivor reaches for her hand. She squeezes very gently, aware of the crimson knots of gout still under his skin.

"How are the legs?" she asks.

"Bit better actually, with this rest, I suppose. They get me up in the chair every day but I like to put them up properly, let the fluid drain."

"You were lucky. Lucky Tansy and Mel came so quickly. Lucky you only cut your head."

"I've had a lot of luck," he says. "It'll run out soon."

"Ivor."

"Carol, don't. I'm ninety-five. I'm falling to bits. I just wanted to do those last paintings. Full circle, you know."

"You'll be home soon. It's only a respite stay. Just a week or so."

Ivor's green eyes are clouded and distant. Carol is frightened. Everything he says is true. Time is running out for him. She's known him so long, so very long, she doesn't know how she'll fill the gap he will leave one day.

~

Tansy often sees Mel at the primary school in the afternoons. Not so much in the mornings as she and the girls always seem to be late and rushing. There's only a ragged handful of parents and children saying their goodbyes when she finally drags Scarlet and Amber into the yard.

She sees Mel's pale hair and distinctive green coat and jogs across the yard towards her. To the left of the school is the nursery building and its fenced yard. There's a lot of squeaking and shouting coming from behind the nursery fence. A few small shapes move around behind the glass door. Tansy glances at them but she can't see Amber. She's probably out the back getting muddy.

"Does your mum like the place?" Mel asks. "Today, wasn't it?"

"She's there now."

"Do let me know."

"Of course. And tell Joe I'll be getting in touch for an MOT soon."

The infants' door bursts open and the kids come running out. Scarlet trails her coat along the ground, looks like she's about to drop her lunchbox. Beside her, Mel's daughter, Sophie, looks neat and clean, her hair still in two perfect plaits, her coat zipped up.

Mel still has to wait for eight-year-old Megan to come out; Tansy and Scarlet join the queue at the nursery door. The glass window is splattered with the children's stained glass pictures: black card and sweet-wrappers. Tansy remembers making the same when she was little, the intense vibrancy of the coloured cellophane, the smell of the Pritt Stick. She sees Amber whizzing about inside, one of the nursery teachers running after her with her coat. Scarlet's muttering something about one of the kids in her class and what he said to someone.

Two little boys come shooting out of the nursery and into the arms of their mothers, then Amber, her coat splodged with mud and paint. She's even got a green streak in her hair.

Tansy hugs her close. She is so lucky to have these two in her life, so lucky really to have Charlie too. He's no good as her boyfriend, but he's great as her friend, and he adores the girls. Mostly she's happy with her lot in life. Just sometimes, occasionally, she wishes she had experienced the crazy, overwhelming kind of love people talk about, the stuff of songs and poems, the kind of love that blasts all reason from your brain. She never has, and she wonders if she ever will.

With a sticky hand in each of hers she starts walking back to the car.

~

Stefan is only thirty, but sometimes the prospect of the rest of his life feels insurmountably long. He's been alone for the past two years, but hasn't regretted it because to do anything else would be obscene, immoral. He has a vague idea that at some point in his life he might fall in love again and, above all, he must protect himself from that. He doesn't even want to be fond of anyone, to care about anyone, in case they too are taken from him. This is why he has been so frightened for Ivor. He didn't realise how much he cared about the old boy. In fact, now he'd count Ivor amongst his closest friends, and there aren't many of those. Keep people away, he tells himself. Don't let them in. Then it can't hurt when they go. As they undoubtedly will.

Tansy has told him that Ivor is moving into Lanyon House some time today for a couple of weeks. While he's there she and her mother are going to rearrange his house for him. Ivor'll love that, Stefan grinned to himself, when Tansy told him. They are going to get him a reclining chair, raised feet for his bed, take up the carpet in the living room to expose the parquet beneath so he doesn't catch his feet or walking stick in the fabric.

Stefan doesn't know how much of this they've told Ivor. He thinks he'll call in and see him at Lanyon House in the next day or so. It's only a few minutes' away by car. He'll give him time to settle in, then go round. Take him some chocolates or fruit or something. He's missed his chats with Ivor.

~

Ivor is alone at last. For the first time since he fell in the garden, finally, he is alone. He exhales with relief.

He's been given a room at the front, on the first floor, overlooking the narrow, churning beach below. Lanyon House was once a luxury hotel and this room, with its high ceiling, wide windows and view must have been one of the very best rooms.

There is a hospital-style bed with a small locker beside it, and a table and two chairs in the window. He can eat his meals up here if he prefers, the matron – or whatever she's called – told him. There are some hideous pictures on the wall: crude watercolours of tin mines, a print of ugly flowers in an ugly vase. On the wall by the bathroom is an old black and white photo of Lanyon House in its heyday as a hotel.

Ivor rearranges his possessions on the little table. Mobile phone, glasses, humbugs, book. The matron has looped the red emergency cord around his chair so it's within his reach, and left an anaemic cup of tea for him. Using his stick and the windowsill he hauls himself upright and gazes out at the view.

It's a steely winter's day. The sea surges up the beach, leaving foam pouring down the rocks. It must be nearly high water as the breakers have almost reached the scraggy dunes. A few tiny Lowry figures move on the strip of sand. Under his window the old hotel lawn slopes gently down to a flat oblong area, now grassed over. Swimming pool, he thinks, or tennis court.

The window rattles as a squally fist of rain hits the glass.

Different noises tonight. The rattling old window, maybe the surge of breakers below. But no shouting through the curtain, no hoarse whispers, no telephones, or the squeaking wheels of trolleys.

A knock on the door. Ivor sighs, his peace already interrupted. It'll be Emmeline and Tansy.

"Hello," he calls.

The door opens and a carer comes in. She has shiny dark-brown hair in a ponytail, and freckles across her nose.

"Hello Ivor," she says. "I'm Vicky. I'm on your floor until dinner time tonight. Just wanted to see if there was anything you needed. If you've settled in OK."

"I'm fine, thank you," he says.

"Enjoying the view?"

He realises he's still propped up against the windowsill.

"It's very hypnotic."

"You've got the best room," Vicky grins at him. "Perhaps you could do some painting while you're here."

No, Ivor thinks, when she has gone with a promise to see him again later. He doesn't want to paint the view from this window, this room. He doesn't want his last work to be painted in confinement. He wants to get home before the daffodils have died to brown paper twists and get into his studio again. He needs to walk that path and up that step again. He needs to leave the studio and lock up, walk carefully and safely to his back door. He will ask Stefan to clear the path for him and make it safe. That was the last thought he had before he fell. He'll ring Stefan while he's at Lanyon House and ask him to do that.

He finishes the cup of tea. His hand shakes and the cup clatters onto its saucer. More rain on the windowpane. The sky is now swollen with blue-black clouds. Ivor shivers, checks the radiator is on. There's no point asking Stefan to clear the path. He won't work in that studio again. His legs are too heavy and clumsy with fluid, his hands too gouty. He'll leave behind him an unfinished canvas, showing how his story was ruptured. For the first time in years, decades, Ivor feels tears burning his eyes.

—

"You'll never guess who came in today." Vicky Baxter heels off her shoes in the hall and hooks her coat up.

It's eight o'clock. She's just finished a twelve hour shift at Lanyon House. There's no smell of dinner cooking. So nothing different then. Sixteen-year-old Harry will have cooked himself a pizza to eat in his room. His younger sister, Skye, won't have had anything because she's so desperately trying to lose weight. And Kevin? Well, Kevin is home because his van is outside, but he'll be watching TV with a beer or two. So, yes, situation normal. And no-one has acknowledged her return or responded to her comment. Situation normal again.

Vicky pads into the kitchen in her tights. Her feet are both cold and clammy, and the tiles feel icy. Skye is sitting at the breakfast bar, scrolling through her phone.

"Guess who came in today," Vicky says again.

"What?"

Vicky swallows her irritation. "New resident. Temporary resident."

"So?"

"Ivor Martin."

"Ivor Martin? You mean *The* Ivor Martin?"

"That's the one."

Vicky thaws a little as Skye beams. She dumps down her empty water bottle and food bag. "He's been in hospital. He's staying at Lanyon for a couple of weeks' respite care."

"What's he like?" Skye actually puts down her phone.

"Lovely guy. He's nearly a hundred. So bright, so with-it. He'd have some stories to tell."

"Could I meet him? Could I show him my artwork?"

Vicky swills out her Tupperware bowls. "I don't know. Let him settle in a bit. I'll talk to him."

"That'd be awesome." Skye's hand itches for her mobile again.

"Have you eaten?"

"Not hungry."

"Skye."

"I'll have something later."

"The others?" Vicky asks, though she can see a pizza tray dumped by the sink and its box crammed into the bin.

"Harry cooked pizza. Dad…he's waiting for you."

Skye slides off her stool and slips out of the kitchen. Vicky watches her. She's probably lost more weight, but it's so hard to tell under the enormous jumper. Surely she must nearly be at her target. It's a prickly subject. Skye pretends she isn't dieting so no-one else is allowed to acknowledge it. An elephant in the room.

Vicky turns her back on the pile of washing-up and junk in the kitchen. She needs a shower and a change before she can think about dinner. Kev could at least have washed some potatoes or something. She stamps upstairs, conscious of the sweat and grime on her carer's dress. It's only as she steps under the hot jet that she realises she hasn't even said hello to Kev. She's never done that before. Situation not normal.

Tansy tops up her glass. It's an Australian Shiraz this time. Emmeline doesn't say anything. She's drinking too: hers is a Chardonnay. Tansy screws the lid back on and waits for her mother to speak.

"Are you going to see him tomorrow?" Emmeline asks.

"Yes."

"Bring back any washing and we can do it. He said today he wants orange juice. Buy some on the way over. Those little ones with straws."

"Yes, I know."

"And I'll go and see that guy with the reclining chair. He says he's got a van so if I buy it he can take it up for us."

"OK."

Emmeline isn't going to say anything. Tansy doesn't know if that's better or worse.

Tansy herself feels strange, like she's leaning over a cliff, into a vortex, a black hole. She knows that, in the future, she'll look back on this time, and know that it was when something happened. She's not sure if the drinking is the something or whether there is some other event waiting to trip her or startle her onto a foreign trajectory.

~

Stefan swings into the car park by Hayle estuary. The tide is receding, leaving silver sand flats and cold pools of stagnant water. There are wading birds. He doesn't know their names. Ivor would. Ivor knows all about birds and plants, geology and weather, the lore of the countryside.

It's early morning, the time he'd be at Ivor's if he were getting him breakfast. When he gulps the salty air the cold stings his throat. He fingers the ring he always wears on his left hand, where a wedding band would rest. He's constantly afraid he'll lose the ring, but if he leaves it on his bedside table his hand feels naked. Once he almost left it at Ivor's on the windowsill above the sink. He'd taken it off for the washing-up, and to put the bins out. When he came back in to wash his hands Ivor called him from the dining table. Stefan ran to him. Ivor had upset his cup of tea, was wiping at the table with a cotton handkerchief.

"Don't worry. I'll sort it out and make a new one," Stefan said.

It broke his routine and he forgot to put the ring back on. Only as he was grabbing his jacket did he notice the pale band of skin.

The ring is everything. If he lost it, truly lost it, he'd be lost too.

~

The glass electric doors unfold and Tansy steps into Lanyon House. There's a lounge area straight ahead, with rows of high-backed armchairs. Some residents sit in these, with Zimmers beside them or walking sticks propped alongside, others are in wheelchairs. Tansy walks through the lounge, avoiding anyone's eyes. An old woman calls out to her – well, she thinks it's to her – but she walks on to the reception desk to sign in.

She takes the stairs to the first floor. A carer is shoving a trolley with the remains of meals stacked onboard. The place smells of institutional food. Somewhere a resident has a TV on very loud behind a closed door. Tansy knocks on Ivor's door and goes in.

He's sitting at the window watching the surf.

"How you doing? Brought you some orange juice. And a couple of books. And a paper."

"I want to go home," Ivor says.

Tansy slides a straw from its cellophane sheath and pierces a box of juice for him.

"I know. We're working on it."

"What does that mean?"

"Mum's got some guy to come and take up the carpet in the living room."

Ivor closes his eyes and sighs.

"So you don't fall again. She's found you a reclining chair. Someone was selling one in the village."

"A chair someone else has died in."

"If you like we can get you a new one. Oh, and we've ordered some feet for your bed to raise it up a bit, should make it easier to get up. And we've got to arrange that physio the hospital promised."

Ivor looks defeated. Tansy wishes she hadn't said it all like that, so baldly.

"We also want to sort out more visits for you."

"Carol would come more often. She said so."

"We still need another person, or even two."

A knock at the door.

"Hello Ivor. Sorry, I didn't know you had a visitor."

"Vicky," Ivor smiles at the carer. "This is my granddaughter Tansy."

"Can I get either of you a drink?"

Ivor holds up his juice; Tansy shakes her head.

"I'll advertise on Facebook again. There are loads of carers around. I'm sure we can get someone quickly."

Tansy watches Vicky folding some of Ivor's clothes that were on the bed. She stops in the middle of smoothing down a jumper, as if she were going to say something.

~

Vicky leaves Ivor with his granddaughter and shuts the bedroom door carefully. The corridor is empty for a moment. She wanders down towards the staircase, past all the closed white-painted doors. There's shouting behind Mrs Trewin's: she's so deaf everyone has to yell. Ivor has told Vicky about the carers that come to him at home, how desperate he is to be there again with them getting him up and cooking his dinners. He's told her his family want to get another carer to add to the rota. Vicky lives between Lanyon House and Gerent's Cross. She has grown fond of Ivor over the past few days, and he was quietly happy that she knew who he was and could talk about some of his paintings. She'd love to be that extra carer on the days she's not working twelve-hour shifts, and it'd get her away from Kev. She might mention it to Ivor when Tansy's gone, see what he thinks first.

~

A couple of days later and Tansy has just come back from dropping the girls at nursery. She has bags of shopping from the Co-op: fruit, bread, milk, eggs, strawberry jam for Amber, and another bottle of

Australian Shiraz. The hall phone startles her as she kicks the front door closed. Still shaken from the night of Ivor's fall, her first thought is that it's Lanyon House. She drops the shopping with a thunk of the Shiraz.

"Hello, is that Emmeline or Tansy Martin?"

"It's Tansy," she says sharply.

"Hi. My name's Vicky. I'm one of the carers at Lanyon House. I think I met you the other day."

"What's happened?"

"Happened? Oh. Ivor. Nothing. I'm not at work. I was talking to Ivor the other day and he said you were looking for someone else to look after him and I'd be really interested. I like him very much and I've got a lot of experience."

"But aren't you working at the home?"

"Not every day. I'd be able to tell you in advance when I'm there."

Tansy tugs out the milk and puts it into the fridge. She scoops up an out-of-date yoghurt to dump.

"That could be great. But I'll have to discuss it with my mother," she says. "You know it's only an hour or so, morning and evening. We are hoping to get every morning and evening covered. And we're here as well, of course." She's aware of her mother, still in pyjamas, standing quietly in the doorway giving her a thumbs-up. "Let me talk to her and we'll give you a call."

Tansy writes Vicky's number on the pad and hangs up.

"Vicky from Lanyon House."

"I know her."

"She's talked to him already. He's happy."

"Sounds good," Emmeline says. "Let's get back to her, ask her to meet us."

When Scarlet stumbles out into the playground, her teacher Miss Carey comes with her.

"Tansy," Miss Carey starts.

Tansy appraises Scarlet. She doesn't seem to be hurt or upset. Oh hell, perhaps she's beaten up someone else.

"Um. Am I right that your father is Jake Gregory, the artist?"

Scarlet thrusts her lunchbox towards Tansy, who grabs it automatically.

"Yeah, that's right."

She likes Miss Carey. She's young and kind to the kids, with a scribble of auburn hair in a top-knot.

"It's just we're planning an arts week, and want to get some local artists in to work with the children. I wondered if he might be persuaded to come and do a workshop. What do you think?"

"I think he'd love to," Tansy says. "He has got a show coming up but he's worked with schools before and really enjoyed it."

"That would be wonderful." Miss Carey beams at her. "Shall I email you the details?"

"Definitely."

Tansy takes Scarlet's wrist and they start towards the nursery door.

"You in trouble, Scarlet?" Mel appears and ruffles Scarlet's hair.

"I am not," Scarlet says crossly. "But Sophie got told off today, didn't you, Sophie?"

"You never said," Mel teases her daughter.

"Miss Carey wants my dad to come and do an art workshop," Tansy tells Mel.

"Oh wow, brilliant. With Miss Carey's class?"

"I don't know. She might just have asked because she's the one who knows me."

Amber barrels out of the nursery with arms full of blobby paintings and some tangled weaving on a card.

Stefan was never a surfer. He liked the odd lunchtime game of football when he was at school, and even joined a cricket team for a while in his teens. He preferred sports on dry land. He wasn't a strong swimmer, hated water getting into his ears, and the huge waves that broke on the north Cornwall coast terrified him. He'd go to the beach, of course, everyone in Cornwall went to the beach, and he'd see the surfers out beyond the foam, often just waiting there for a wave. Stefan couldn't think of any other sport where you had to actually wait for something else to happen, something beyond your control.

So it surprised him to fall in love with a surfer. He met Nina through a friend of a friend in St Ives. She was the same age as him, with sun-bleached blonde hair, and the day they met her face was burnt pink.

Sometimes he'd go to the beaches with her and her twin brother, or her and her friends. He never told her but he was afraid every second she was in the sea. The waves curled in huge and high, foam surged around rocks and, though he never ventured in, he knew about the dangers of rip currents. Nina and her brother George were fearless in the water, vying with each other, always competing.

One day there was only one winner.

Vicky drives past her own road and on to Lanyon House. She's not working but she wants to visit Ivor and tell him the news.

She has just met Tansy and Emmeline at Ivor's house. It's a large bungalow on the very edge of Gerent's Cross with a studio in the garden. Tansy showed her the path where he fell, where this all started. There are daffodils in the garden, and fruit trees, the lawn is wild and overgrown.

"He did all the gardening himself until a couple of years ago," Emmeline said. "Stefan mows the lawn sometimes for him. He's one of the other carers. Nice young guy. Works at a hotel in St Ives."

"Ivor wants to get back in the studio," Vicky said. "My daughter's a big fan of his. She couldn't believe it when I said I'd met him."

"Is she studying art?" Tansy asked.

"It's her favourite subject. She's fourteen. I know she's angling to meet him. I mean, if I do end up helping him."

"I think you'd be great," Tansy said. "And you already know him. Welcome to the team."

~

Vicky parks at the staff end of the car park and opens the driver's door. The wind nearly wrenches it from her hand. It's so exposed on the headland. When it's really stormy they have to lock the front doors to stop any of the residents wandering out. On calm days the able-bodied sit on benches in the grounds; a couple have sneaky cigarettes in the open air.

Vicky hardly glances at the residents in the lounge. She knows Ivor prefers to stay upstairs on his own watching the sea and sky outside. She bounds up the stairs, nodding to a couple of staff and residents, knocks sharply on Ivor's door and swings it open.

There's a woman sitting at the window with him. She looks about sixty, with dark hair to her shoulders and large silver hoops in her ears.

She's wearing some kind of long patchwork dress. She must be one of his arty friends, Vicky thinks, and opens her mouth to apologise.

"Carol, this is Vicky, one of the ladies here who look after me." Ivor says. Then to Vicky, "I thought you were off work today?"

"Yes, I am," she says. "I came to see you. To tell you that Emmeline and Tansy and I have had a chat this morning, and they're happy for me to muck in. When you go home."

The woman, Carol, starts a little. Of course, Vicky realises. Carol. Emmeline told her the names of Ivor's carers: Mel, Stefan, Carol. This must be Carol.

Ivor beams. "So glad you passed their tests," he says. "Carol here has been helping me for a while."

Carol fingers some beads at her throat.

"She's an old friend of mine," Ivor explains. "And she's been a godsend to me lately."

"I'll leave you two then," Vicky says. "I just wanted to tell you. See you tomorrow, Ivor."

~

"I'd come more often, you know that," Carol says, when she's sure Vicky has gone down the passage.

"Of course I know."

"You'll feel safe once you're back." Carol reaches for the pack of cards on the table, and moves Ivor's tea tray onto the floor. "Shall we have a game?"

"You deal. I'm going to the bathroom."

Carol helps Ivor to his feet. He grasps his walking stick.

"Shall I come with you? To the door?"

"It's only a few feet away, woman." Ivor clumps heavily to the bathroom door.

He does not shut it fully, and Carol can hear his laboured breathing. She shuffles the cards slowly. Ivor is diminished. She can see that now. His skin looks pale and grey, his legs are causing him pain and, most of all, he has lost all confidence in himself. Carol wonders, as she has for some time, how long Ivor can continue to live alone and what other option there is for him. He told her he would stay in his bungalow until he's carried out feet first, and Carol knows how much he'd hate being stuck somewhere like Lanyon House for ever. She wonders how to broach the subject with Ivor's family. She knows they think about it too, and that none of them wants to be the one to bring it up.

~

Stefan kissed Nina long and hard.

"Don't be too long," he said.

He squeezed her bottom, tried to lighten his words, but he was scared.

"We'll be home by lunchtime," Nina said.

"Yeah, well, the weather's coming in, they said."

He and Nina had moved into a tiny flat in Carbis Bay near to her parents and brother. Stefan had just got his job at the hotel and she was working as a dentist's receptionist. They'd even started talking gently, carefully, about having a baby.

"I'm off." Nina skipped out of the flat. Stefan listened to her feet running down the stairs.

She stored her board in the ground-floor lobby. The two guys in the bottom flat, also surfers, let her keep it with their kit. Stefan heard the slamming of the front door, George's van approaching, and Nina was gone.

The cove was known as Amity. It had another name from before but everyone called it Amity after the coaster that went down on the skerries decades ago. Stefan, superstitious and edgy about the sea anyway, never liked the deep, remote beach up the coast, with its rocky reefs and rip currents. He particularly hated Nina and George surfing there. Even the name – Amity – felt ominous.

Stefan checks once more that Ivor has everything he needs to hand: his mobile, a beaker of water, a couple of humbugs, his book, and the red emergency cord looped round his wrist. It's boiling hot in Ivor's room, but he still insists on wearing a heavy jumper. Stefan's back is sweaty under his work shirt. Below the window the breakers cream in gently, pouring foam over the rocks. Stefan watches the tiny people on the sand, wonders if they ever look up to this turreted Gothic building high above them, if they ever wonder about the residents trapped inside, wonder at their stories. He picks up his jacket from Ivor's bed.

"I've got to get to work now. Next time I see you, you'll be back at yours. I'll get that path tidied up for you as soon as I can."

"Thanks."

Stefan closes the bedroom door behind him and strides towards the stairs. One of the carers is leaning on a trolley marking things off on a sheet of paper. Ivor has told him one of the girls here is going to help look after him at home. Can't be this one: she's tough-looking with ragged hair, and Ivor said the girl – Vicky, that's it – is very pretty with a long ponytail. He signs out quickly in the visitors' book on the desk and jogs through the lounge area.

Glassy-eyed residents appear to watch him and ignore him at the same time. Someone is groaning. A male carer is squatting down beside a woman in a wheelchair. Even the air is stale. No wonder Ivor prefers to hide upstairs. Stefan would too. It's soul-destroying down here. Imagine spending your last days on earth jammed into a chair, staring fixedly at a magnolia wall.

The electric doors whoosh open and he inhales the cold salty cliff air. Two elderly women are sitting on a bench smoking. Stefan gets into his car and guns out of the car park. The road is a narrow tarmacked track clinging to the cliff's edge. He averts his eyes from the gaping bay on his left, the turquoise arches of the waves, the exploding spume.

He chose a blue-green glass for his ring, because it reminded him of the sea.

~

Tansy has come into Penzance to look for birthday presents for Charlie. Not only does she have to choose something from herself, she also has to find things the girls can give him. Because she and Charlie have been either friends or lovers all their lives it is getting harder and harder to think of interesting things to give him. She hasn't called in at Jake's studio, nor at Charlie's shop, because both of these visits would waste time, and she just wants to get on with the job. She has found a mug, a pack of mismatched socks, a key fob, a T-shirt, and a stained glass mobile, which she'd really like to keep for herself. She'll just go into the bookshop and see if she can find anything he might fancy, then call it a day as she has a couple of weeks before his birthday.

The bookshop is in Market Jew Street, on the higher landward side. The uneven paving slabs still glisten from an earlier shower, but the sun splits through the clouds, and the light, a dazzling lemon-white shaft, momentarily blinds her.

It takes her a moment to adjust her vision to the darker interior. There are a few single shoppers, and a young woman trying to move a buggy round the central table before the child swipes a pile of books to the floor. Tansy squeezes past local interest and biography to the fiction section, and scans the shelves for titles and authors she thinks Charlie might like. The bookshop makes her light-headed, as it often does: the soaring shelves of tightly-packed volumes, the rainbow of their spines, the sheer number of words there to be let loose.

She flicks through a couple of novels and wonders what Charlie will be doing on his birthday. There's one area of life that she and he rarely speak about. Last year she assumed that she and the girls would see him on his birthday and then, at the last minute, he told her he was spending the evening with a woman he'd met online. Tansy didn't care, not for herself, she knows things are better now than when they were together, but Scarlet was heartbroken and little Amber sulky when Tansy made some excuse for their father. The only guilt she feels about breaking up with Charlie is how it might have affected the girls, but surely it can't be as harmful as being in an unhappy family?

She slides a book back into the shelf and gathers up the three she's going to buy. As she waits at the counter for the man in front to pay she glances round the shop. In the art alcove a young man reaches for a hard-backed book with a distinctive cover. A very distinctive cover. A cover she knows like the back of her hand, because it's the reproduction of one of Ivor's paintings.

The man in front shoves his books into his rucksack and moves on. She puts her purchases down and finds her card in her wallet. The guy in the art section turns slightly. He's probably a bit younger than her, with dark hair in a stubby ponytail. He's wearing a long coat over faded jeans. Tansy realises the shop assistant is waiting for her card. As she packs away her books she looks back at the man. He's still rifling through *Ivor Martin: A Shropshire Lad*.

Instead of leaving the shop Tansy walks over to him. He doesn't look up. She's only done this a few times in her life, and mostly when she was younger and possibly drunk, but she knows, she just knows, it's important this man realises who she is.

"He's my grandad," she begins.

The guy looks up. Mint-green eyes.

"What? Sorry?"

"Ivor Martin. He's my grandad."

"He's…" the guy jabs a finger at the title of the book. "*He's* your grandad? Wow. Bloody hell."

"Yes. Give it to me."

Tansy drops her bags and takes the book. The guy has a single blackened nail on his left hand as though he's shut it in a car door or hit it with a hammer. She flicks through to the double pages she's after.

"That's me. A long time ago."

Two charcoal drawings of Tansy face each other across the book's spine. In one she's sitting cross-legged on the floor, dark hair slung over one shoulder, looking at something the viewer can't see. In the second she's leaning against a wall with a glass in her hand. Cut off denims, bare feet.

The guy looks at the pictures and then up at Tansy.

"*Tansy I* and *Tansy II*," he reads. "That's you then. Tansy?"

"That's me. I was eighteen. He did a lot more of me, but it's mostly landscapes in this book."

"Is he still painting?"

Tansy pulls a face. "That's a long story. He's not so well at the moment."

"I'm so sorry to hear that. I love his work. How old is he now?"

"Ninety-five. He's been in hospital. Anyway, look, I'm sorry to interrupt you. I just like showing off." She gathers her bags again. "Well, bye then."

As she steps out into the bright rainshine of Market Jew Street she hears a voice at her shoulder.

"Tansy."

She stops in the middle of the pavement. The sun glints on puddles. A seagull shrieks from a rooftop. She inhales a breath of tobacco from a passing smoker.

"Tansy. Do you have half an hour for a coffee?"

She has that same lightheaded spinning sensation she had in the bookshop only – what? – fifteen minutes ago. She knows, just as she knew she had to speak to this man, that this is the something she has been waiting for, the thing she's been searching for each time she stared into the vortex of her future.

"Yes," she manages at last. "That'd be…lovely."

"D'you know Samarkand?"

"I don't even know your name," she laughs.

"Sorry. Gareth. Gareth Crane."

"Tansy Martin. But you know that."

"Samarkand?" Gareth waves over the street. "Haven't you been there?"

"I hardly have time for coffee shops. Except –" *with Charlie.* She swallows the words.

"You've already said you have time today. Come on." He runs down the steps to the road. "It's under new management. Fairly new anyway. It used to be a dive. That's probably why you never went there."

~

Isobel Macauley gathers sticky cake plates and coffee cups from the corner table and wipes down the surface. She straightens the chairs and makes sure the glass vase with its single rose is central. She glances round the ground floor but no one signals her over for a refill or to place an order so she takes the crockery upstairs to the kitchen. It's been a busy morning in Samarkand – poached eggs on toast, full English, blueberry pancakes, waffles, cakes – and now it's almost lunchtime. She exchanges a few quick words with Tye and Jordan in the kitchen, then goes back down.

Her mother Holly is at the till, chatting to a couple while they settle up. Another table for Izzy to clear in the window. Izzy's stepfather Aidan squeezes behind Holly with a tray of drinks. Izzy intercepts him and takes the tray.

"Table six," he says.

They've been running Samarkand for almost a year now. When they took over the place was run-down and dismal, a time-warp tea room. They stripped everything out, Holly and Aidan, helped by Holly's daughters, Izzy and Abi. The walls are a soft sage green, the tables scrubbed wood, and the chairs mismatched with patchwork cushions. Holly has hung patterned paper lampshades up which cast soft coloured glows, and strung fairy lights over mirrors and picture frames. Beside the counter there is a dresser displaying speciality teas – Aidan's passion – wrapped in bright metallic paper.

Izzy finishes wiping the window table. The front door opens, and a man stoops under the low lintel, followed by a dark-haired girl with shopping bags.

"Hello Izzy."

"Hi," Izzy says, recognising the guy, but not the girl, as a previous customer. "Would you like this table? Or one at the back?"

He looks at his companion who smiles and shrugs.

"This'll be lovely," he says to Izzy. "People-watching."

"I'll come back in a few minutes," Izzy says.

"I like this place," Tansy says, as she settles onto a heap of striped cushions, and curses herself for sounding so lame.

"Yeah, I come in often when I'm in town."

"Where do you live?"

"Hayle. Here, what would you like?"

The girl who greeted Gareth at the door, the one he called Izzy, comes over to the table. She's young with short choppy red hair and a row of silver hoops in each ear.

"You said your grandad was ill? Not serious I hope?" Gareth says as Izzy glides away with their order.

"I don't think so. He fell over. In the garden on his own at night. He was leaving his studio." She still tastes the guilt of not going to see him, not even calling him, of opening and finishing the wine.

"Is he OK?"

"He had his mobile with him. He called me and I went up and got one of his carers to come up too. Together we managed to get him back into the studio out of the rain until the ambulance came."

Tansy has kept something back. She's kept two people back. Scarlet and Amber. They were there too.

"Did you go to the hospital with him? Did he break anything?"

"No luckily. No breaks. I didn't go, no." She glances up as Izzy arrives with a tray.

"One Earl Grey." Izzy places a clear glass teapot and a mug in front of her. "And a cappuccino."

"I couldn't go," Tansy says when she has gone. "I was on my own with the kids. I've got two girls. One's at school, one's at nursery."

She watches Gareth across the table, expecting to see the light turn off behind his eyes.

"Hospital's not the place for kids," he says.

"I blame myself," Tansy rushes on. "I should have checked he was OK. My mother was away for the night and the girls' father and I have separated so I was alone with them."

"Is he around? Their father?"

"Yes, he's in Penzance. You might even know him. He owns the record shop in Chapel Street."

"Oh bloody hell, yes. I know the place." Gareth drinks cappuccino, and Tansy twists her neck to look out of the tiny window at Market Jew Street. The café is down some steps, below the level of the pavement, and all she can see is a fractured slice of shoppers walking past.

"Is he back at home now? Ivor, I mean?"

"He's at Lanyon House. It's a care home. Just to get him back on his feet. He's going home this week." She picks up her mug and inhales sharp bergamot. "I don't know where we go from there. How he'll get on."

"I love his work," Gareth says. "I love how he doesn't just paint the coast like so many of the guys here do. He paints the inland places, the fields, the farms, all that. Yes, it's west Cornwall, of course, it is, but it isn't all the sea."

"Part of his heart's still in Shropshire."

"Where he grew up?"

"Yeah. Mum was born there. They came down when she was little. He was working on a Shropshire painting the day he had the accident. Anyway, look, I'm going on about myself. What about you?"

"What about me?"

"I don't know. You live in Hayle. Are you an artist?"

"Only on the side. I have sold a few. I moved down last year. My family's in the south east. I wanted to live in Cornwall."

"Are you working?"

"Bits and bobs," he says. "Bits and bobs. D'you fancy some lunch? I'm starving and they do amazing sandwiches."

Tansy checks the time on her phone. "I have to be back to collect the girls," she says. "But I can stay for a bit – yes, I'd love to."

"Great." Gareth plucks the menu from its stand and slides it over to her. "My treat."

"No, no, I..."

"You can get it next time."

"Is there going to be a next time?" Tansy grins.

"I hope so."

"So do I."

—

Carol opens the oven door and slides out the cake tins. Sweet vanilla scent swirls round her face. She carefully wiggles the cakes out of their tins. When they're cool she'll spread them with cream and jam, stack them together and sprinkle on icing sugar. Ivor's always liked her baking. It'll be a treat for him to come home to.

Her phone rings. She checks her hands for stickiness and wipes them quickly on her jeans.

"Carol, it's Emmeline."

"I'm just making a cake for Ivor," she says. "What time is he back tomorrow?"

"About lunchtime they say. Are you still OK for the evening shift?"

"Absolutely. Can't wait to see him."

"Great. Great. I've asked Vicky, the new girl, if she could meet you there at six, so you can show her what you do, then Tansy can get her on the rota."

"Have we got one sorted?"

"Not yet. You're doing tomorrow night, and Stefan the next morning. I'll get Tansy to sort it out when she gets back. She's disappeared into Penzance. I thought she'd be back by now."

"No worries. You know you can always ask me."

"I know. Thanks."

"Do give Ivor my love when you see him. Will you be there to welcome him home?"

"Yes, both of us."

"I know he'll be so happy to be back."

"Yes." Emmeline sounds tired, worried. Not surprising, Carol thinks. She and Tansy – and Ivor – have difficult conversations ahead, difficult choices to make.

She hangs up the call, and tries to swallow the resentment she feels at having to show the rookie around.

~

Tansy checks the time on her phone.

"I'm so sorry. I have to go. The girls need collecting from school."

"It's OK. No worries. I'll settle up."

Gareth takes his wallet out and goes over to the till. An older woman with faded auburn hair takes his card, exchanges a few words. Tansy nibbles the discarded crust of her sandwich. She hasn't drunk alcohol – she can't, she's driving – but she feels heavy and lethargic, like she could stay here all day, talking to this man who only a couple of hours ago she never knew existed.

She stands reluctantly and slides her arms into her jacket. Gareth's having a joke with the waitress and the woman on the till. Tansy wonders if she is Izzy's mother, their colouring and eyes are so alike.

"So can I have your number?" Gareth asks when he returns, folding a receipt into his pocket. "And I'll give you mine."

Tansy swipes her phone open and taps it in.

"Are you on Facebook?" he asks. "I'll add you. Can we talk later?"

"Of course."

Tansy stands watching him over the remains of their lunch, the scrunched-up paper napkins, the crusts, the few spiky chips left in the bowl. She wants to remember everything about him: the stubby dark ponytail, the seawater eyes, the silver hoop in his ear, the blackened fingernail.

He taps on his own mobile.

"Done," he grins. "Come on, then. Can't have your girls waiting." He waves to the two women behind the counter. "Bye Izzy, bye Holly," and ducks under the low lintel and onto the street.

It's rained again and the sun flashes in the puddles underfoot.

"I'm just going to finish my shopping. We'll speak later, yes?"

"Definitely."

"Till later then, Tansy Martin."

In the car on her way home Tansy turns up the radio and sings along. She puts on her sunglasses against the glare of the wet sunlight. This man, this Gareth Crane, is her collision course. She's waited for the moment of meeting someone and simply knowing – *knowing what?* – and it has happened today, this wet March day in Penzance.

"You could have told me you were going to be this long," Emmeline says when she arrives home. "I thought I'd have to pick up the girls. You know I want to go to Dad's and get everything ready for tomorrow."

"I'm sorry," Tansy says, dumping her shopping bags. "I was birthday shopping for Charlie."

Emmeline eyes the bags. "You haven't got that much. Did you see your father?"

Tansy tosses her car keys hand to hand. There's no point keeping silent. "I met someone. I had lunch with him."

"Who was that?"

"I'll tell you later." Tansy can't stop grinning. "I have to get ready to pick the girls up."

She locks the bathroom door behind her and swipes her phone on. A notification from Facebook and a new text. A friend request from Gareth Crane. She accepts instantly. She wants to trawl through his profile and look at his pictures and see who his friends are, but she hasn't the time now. Instead she opens the text.
I really enjoyed today. Can't wait to talk to you. G x

Once she's collected the girls and got them both into the bath she goes back to Facebook and opens up Gareth's page. He stares back at her from his black and white profile picture. Behind him is a dreamy pearlescent view of Hayle estuary. She can't see any of his friends because he's kept that private but he has some photos. She clicks through them. Him in a bar somewhere with a blonde, beers on the table in front of them; standing on a beach with his arm around another girl. Their faces are tagged and she goes through their pages, desperate for information, but they too keep private profiles. Back onto Gareth's again and she is surprised that the page has only been open for a few months. He doesn't write much on his wall. A comment about an exhibition he went to, a joke here and there, a link to a news site. Messages, one from each of the blondes, and he's put hearts underneath, Tansy sighs. Of course he's had a life before her, before today.

It strikes her how little she knows about him. He told her he had inherited some money and was using that to start his life in Cornwall, while he did odd jobs here and there. He said he did some modelling for an art class because he knew the teacher. He mentioned a younger sister, but not her name.

The sound of surging water tugs Tansy back to the bathroom. The girls have turned the taps on and filled the tub to the very top. A tsunami has broken over the edge, saturating the bath mat and leaving pools on the tiles. Amber is shrieking at Scarlet, something about the rubber duck, and Scarlet is wringing out a sponge over Amber's head. Tansy shoves the phone into her pocket and grabs their towels. He said he enjoyed having lunch with her; he said he wanted to see her again. *Concentrate on that, and ignore the blondes.*

~

When Mel arrives at Ivor's bungalow she parks in the layby again. Emmeline's car is on his drive, leaving room for the Lanyon House ambulance to stop by his steps.

Mel takes the apple pie off the passenger seat and locks her car. The front door is open and she calls out.

"Hi, it's me."

Emmeline is in the kitchen with the fridge door open and a couple of bulging carrier bags on the floor.

"Restocking the fridge," she says. "Oh, that looks lovely. Thanks Mel."

Tansy is arranging some daffodils in a vase on the table. White frilly ones, bold yellow ones, jonquils with orange hearts.

"From his garden?" Mel asks.

"Yes." Tansy gives a white daffodil a final tweak and glances at her phone on the table.

"Here he is," Emmeline calls from the kitchen.

Tansy throws the door wide open and the three of them stand on the steps watching as the driver opens up the back and brings Ivor out in a wheelchair. He is muffled up in a heavy jumper and his green padded coat, and has his walking stick across his knees.

"I'm *walking* in," he says. "I'm walking in to my own house."

Mel glances at the steps, slippy with damp moss, but she's not sure how they'd manoeuvre the wheelchair up them anyway.

Ivor is standing now, hunched over his walking stick. Mel's heart squeezes for this man, this extraordinary man, whom she has grown to love. Emmeline takes his other arm, and the driver from Lanyon House guides him from behind. Up one, up two, up three steps and into his house. And he's home before the daffodils have all died, Mel thinks.

"I'll put the kettle on," she says. "Welcome home, Ivor."

~

On the drive home Tansy checks her phone yet again. "For God's sake," Emmeline says. "Give the man a chance to have a life."

Tansy tosses her phone into her bag on the floor. Nothing from Gareth today. But she has kept the half-dozen texts they exchanged last night. When she was curled on the sofa with a glass of Merlot the little red dot jumped on the screen to show a new message. The red dot had never been so exhilarating, she thought.

~

Carol arrives at Ivor's early and is taken aback to see a car already on the drive. When she opens the door into his tiny hall she can see him and the carer from Lanyon House, Vicky, sitting together at the dining table talking. It looks like Vicky has been there a while. She's taken her coat off and has made them both a cup of tea. Carol hesitates, irritated with Vicky and also irritated with herself because why does it matter so much having another person on Ivor's rota? Carol should not feel so possessive of him.

"I've made you a cake," she says, and comes over to kiss his cheek.

"I am being spoilt," he says. "Mel brought me an apple pie at lunchtime."

Carol goes into the kitchen and puts the cake down on the worktop beside the uncut pie. Again she is angry with herself for caring that Mel got there first. She rolls up her sleeves and washes her hands at the sink and wonders what Ivor will have for dinner.

"Emmeline's dropped off some food," he calls to her as she opens the fridge.

"What d'you fancy? There are some ready meals. Tikka masala, steak and kidney, chilli...or some ham?"

"Just some ham please and a bit of salad. I don't feel hungry."

"Vicky," Carol calls out. "Let me show you what I do."

It's been a while since Ivor was at home, but Carol knows the routine. First she gets Vicky to fill up the water bottles he keeps at different places in the house: on the table, by his armchair, beside the bed. She tells Vicky to draw the curtains in the bedroom and anywhere else, to turn down the bed and to bring his pyjamas and dressing gown to him. Carol chops up tomato and cucumber and, when Vicky comes back, shows her where the bowl and towels are kept for washing Ivor's swollen legs and feet.

Carol lets Vicky wash him and change him into his pyjamas, while she finishes the meal and makes him a cup of tea. Of course Vicky has done this kind of work for years, with many patients. Carol glowers to herself and watches Vicky dry Ivor's legs and smooth in moisturising cream where his cellulitis has cracked the skin.

When Ivor is seated back at the table and pecking at his meal Carol turns to Vicky in the kitchen.

"I do the washing up after the meal. I might start the washing machine or empty it if it's been run in the day. On bin days there are bins to take out or fetch back. Are you doing breakfasts or just evenings?"

"I can do either. I'm not far away. As long as I'm not working those days. I mean I could do an evening in an emergency but it would be later than this, when work finishes. And I'd rather not because of the family."

"OK."

"But I would help out if needed. Obviously."

"That's pretty much it really. In the mornings it's to help him up and into the bathroom and make him some breakfast. He doesn't eat much."

"I know." Vicky glances at Ivor, who's shoving a piece of ham round the plate with his fork.

Of course she knows. Again Carol has forgotten that Vicky knows more about this new Ivor than she does.

"Do you care for anyone else?" Vicky asks.

"No. Just Ivor." Carol takes out a plate and cuts a small piece of her cake for pudding. Vicky must wonder why she only cares for Ivor. "I have a couple of cleaning jobs too," she says quickly. "They're in the daytime so they fit nicely round this. Ivor, have you finished that ham?"

"Thanks. Yes."

"Here's a piece of cake. Shall I cut you a piece for a snack?"

Damn. She's forgotten to tell Vicky about the snack plate of biscuits and fruit, in case Ivor is hungry, or in case the next carer is late. Angry with herself yet again Carol peels a satsuma and snaps open a pack of digestive biscuits.

~

Izzy and Abi live at home with their mother and stepfather in Penzance. Izzy has the whole top floor as an open-plan room, to Abi's envy. She's decorated it herself in shades of lilac and blue and has found a few strange and interesting pieces in junk shops to brighten it: old bottles, Delft tiles, a bright rag rug. She kneels on her bed and gazes out into the dark. The streetlights and lit windows of Penzance, the sparkles of ships in the bay below.

She can hear Abi's voice, a fast metronome, loud with anxiety, quickly hushed. Abi's in her room on the floor below with that idiot Rick. Abi's convinced Rick is The One. Izzy isn't, but Izzy is not convinced of anything at that moment. Holly and Aidan aren't keen on him, Izzy does know that, but Abi won't have a word said against him, so they all have to put up with him coming round, staying late or overnight, taking over Abi. He crushes Abi. What little confidence she has left, he is eroding.

"Rick, please just…what is it? Tell me. This isn't fair."

Abi sounds like she's about to cry. Izzy hopes her parents are still watching TV downstairs, that they haven't heard. She slides off her bed and pads to her open doorway and the narrow stairwell leading down to the landing.

"Look, I'm going."

"Please stay and talk to me. I don't understand. How can I do anything when I don't know?"

Izzy shrinks back as Abi's door slams open. Rick jogs down the lower stairs. Abi shoots out of her room, calling after him. Rick doesn't bother to shout a goodnight to Holly and Aidan; Izzy hears him slam out of the front door, Abi crying behind him.

When Izzy arrives in the hall the door is open and Abi is standing halfway down the path in her pyjamas. Rick has disappeared.

"What was all that about?" Holly comes out of the kitchen and glances between Izzy and the open door. "Was that him leaving? Has he upset her?"

"I think so."

Izzy steps out onto the path. Abi is hunched over, hands on knees, like a marathon runner. Her feet are bare. Izzy puts an arm around her.

"Come on. Come back inside. It's cold."

Abi stumbles upright, lets Izzy guide her into the house.

"What's going on?" asks Aidan.

"He's gone," Abi whispers. "He wouldn't say why."

"Has he left you?" Holly reaches for Abi's hand.

"Yes. No. I don't know. I think so. He said he's not happy and he wouldn't say why."

"I'll make us all some tea." Aidan escapes back to the kitchen.

"Abi, come up to my room," Izzy says.

"I'll bring the tea in a minute." Holly looks lost in the hall as Izzy gently pushes her younger sister first up the stairs.

"My feet are muddy," Abi says as she crumples down on Izzy's bed.

"It doesn't matter. Here, have a tissue."

Izzy sits beside her, gently rubs her back. Abi has the same red hair as Izzy, but long and straggling, bound in two skinny plaits. Izzy offers to unbraid them and brush her hair. Abi shakes head and hunches into Izzy's pillow, crying again.

An hour later, Abi has fallen asleep on Izzy's bed. Izzy drapes a patchwork throw over her and picks up the dirty tea mugs to take downstairs.

"So what's he done?" Holly asks as she goes into the kitchen.

"I don't really know. It seems to have come out of the blue. Said he wasn't happy with things and they should split up. She wanted to know what the problem was. He refused to say. She asked if there was someone else and he said no. He's not on Facebook or Instagram so she can't look on there. I don't know."

"I never liked him," Aidan says as he opens the dishwasher and a cloud of steam escapes into the kitchen.

"Nor me." Izzy takes a stack of plates from him and puts them in the cupboard. "How long's he been around now? Almost a year, isn't it?"

"Do you think she asked to move in with him?" Holly wonders.

"She didn't say. I don't know. It'll probably blow over."

"How is she now?"

"She's asleep in my bed."

"You take her room if you like," Holly suggests.

"No thanks. He's been in there. I'll sleep on the floor up there with her."

Izzy fills two glasses of water and heads back upstairs to her attic. Abi is still asleep, the blotches paling on her face, one plait hanging off the side of the bed.

"You could do so much better," Izzy whispers to her.

She never mentioned the unmentionable to Holly and Aidan, and they never mentioned it to her. If Rick has left Abi, just walked out of the house without a word of explanation, it could be the very thing to make it happen again. Izzy strokes Abi's forearm, traces her fingers over the knotted scars.

"Don't go there again, Abi, please."

—

So would you like to meet up?

Of course.

Let me know when you can. Really looking forward to it.

Me too.

Goodnight Tansy Martin xxx

Goodnight xxx

Tansy waits a moment or two, the icon fizzing before her eyes, in case it flares with another tiny red dot. When nothing comes she flicks onto Gareth's Facebook profile and swipes through the blondes again. They're both busty with the eyeliner flick that she can't do. She looks at Gareth's latest entry on his page, a link to a video about ley lines. She doesn't watch the video, but notes one of the blondes has put a heart under it.

She'd turn her mobile off so she doesn't keep refreshing it, looking for a red dot, but she daren't because of Ivor.

~

Stefan unlocks Ivor's front door and calls out as he always does. Ivor rarely hears him as he is pretty deaf and is probably still asleep anyway, but Stefan feels the usual twist of doubt in his guts. One morning someone might open the door and go through to Ivor's room, and find him cold and unresponsive. That someone could be Stefan.

His boots click loudly on the newly exposed parquet flooring. He glances at the reclining chair and smiles wryly, knowing Ivor will hate the dark red flowery swirls of the fabric. The remains of a snack are on the side table – a couple of biscuits and the crust of a slice of cake – which he must have eaten before bed.

Stefan knocks loudly on the bedroom door, but his heart rate has already calmed because he can hear Ivor snoring in the room beyond.

He wakes Ivor with a gentle shake, helps him to sit in bed, asks after him.

"So good to see you home again," he says, as Ivor judders to his feet.

"Can you walk with me to the bathroom? Some physio person is coming later to give me a Zimmer or something."

Stefan grabs the overnight urine bottle by the bedside to rinse out and eases Ivor into the bathroom.

"OK." Ivor hooks his walking stick on the towel rail. "I'm all right."

"If you're sure. Leave the door open, OK? Just in case."

Ivor agrees and Stefan goes to the kitchen to make breakfast. He sees the cake and the pie on the worktop and curses himself for not doing something for Ivor. He doesn't start work until noon. He could spend an hour or so in the garden, tidy up that path to the studio.

The kettle boils and he makes tea. Ivor has fresh fruit in the bowl and he chops up a banana to add to the cereal. When he's carried the breakfast to the table he goes back through the house and finds Ivor moving stiffly into his bedroom. Stefan helps him dress and takes his spare arm to lead him to the dining room.

"I can stay on a bit and sort out that path, if you like," he offers.

Ivor takes a small mouthful of cereal. "Have those women of mine asked you to keep an eye on me?"

"No more than usual. But I have got some time and I can get that path safer for you. Then when you get the Zimmer or whatever you should be able to get out there again. Back to painting. What you were doing when you were so rudely interrupted."

Ivor smiles. "Thanks Stefan. Now go and make yourself a drink."

Back in the kitchen Stefan makes coffee for himself and sends a quick text to Tansy to tell her what he's going to do. Then he takes off his ring and puts it on the windowsill and squirts washing-up liquid into the bowl.

~

"Hey, that's my backpack. Stop fiddling."

"Move it, move it, I want to put my drink there."

"Mumma, Amber's shoving my backpack so she can put her water bottle there."

"No, I am not."

"Yes, you are."

"Oh stop it, please." Tansy wriggles the keys into the ignition. "Just be nice to each other."

"She started it."

"You started it. Mummy, Scarlet hit me."

"I did not."

"Enough." Tansy turns round. "I can't drive with you two going on like that. Come on now."

She's just about to start the ignition when her phone beeps in her pocket.

Gareth, is her first thought. Then, Grandad.

"Mumma, Amber's water bottle's leaking on me."

Tansy snatches the phone from her jacket pocket. That little red dot again. She hits it. Stefan. No, no, please no. The screen freezes before the message comes up.

Hi Tansy. All OK with Ivor. Going to stay on and do some gardening for him.

"Put the lid on."

"I can't."

"I'm wet."

Tansy fires the engine and the radio comes on with a blast.

"It's *Shotgun*," shouts Scarlet. "My favourite song."

She warbles along tunelessly as Tansy reverses down the drive.

~

When Tansy has dropped Scarlet – still mumbling the lyrics to *Shotgun* – at school and Amber at nursery, she drives the few yards to Joe Atkins' garage. JRA Autos is on a tiny industrial estate at the opposite end of the village to Ivor's bungalow. Mel's car is parked on the forecourt and she pulls in next to it.

Inside the workshop a red hatchback is up in the air on the hydraulic lift. The same radio station that Tansy has in the car is playing quietly. Joe and Mel are in the office talking. Tansy sidesteps a puddle of oil on the floor and takes her keys to Joe.

"How's Ivor today? Mel asks as Joe takes the keys and puts them in the ice-cream box he uses.

"Stefan texted me. Said he was fine. He's going to tidy up the garden and the path."

"The studio path?"

"Yes."

"He shouldn't go there on his own. Not yet."

"We were going to bring him some stuff in. Art stuff. But he'd go nuts if we interfered. He's getting a Zimmer later on."

"You might be needing one if you fail today," says Joe.

"Every chance of that, I think," Tansy grins.

"Come on, I'll give you a lift home," Mel offers.

~

Mel opens the passenger door of her people carrier for Tansy and quickly checks for sweet wrappers, dirty tissues, and spillages. Joe waves them off and Mel turns down the radio.

"I wanted to ask you a favour," she says.

"Sure, what's that?"

"Would you or your mum write me a reference please?"

"Well, sure, you mean as a carer?"

"Yes. I'm applying for a job."

"Are you leaving us?" Tansy asks, and Mel hears anxiety in her voice.

"No, no, not at all. I wanted to get back to caring in a home just a couple of days or even nights a week. There's a vacancy at Lanyon House."

"What about the girls? I mean, that's brilliant, and of course I'll write you one, or Mum will. I just wondered about Megan and Sophie."

"It'd only be a day or two a week. Joe's Mum said she'd be happy to help. There's the after-school club too. I don't know. Maybe it wouldn't work. I'd just like to try. Anyway, I haven't got the job yet. I'm sure they'll want someone younger with more recent experience."

"Not necessarily."

Mel shrugs. She hasn't worked as a carer in a home for some years. Now all her children are at school she realises she can have some freedom, and the money would help, there's no denying that.

"Come back for a coffee?" she asks as the road forks, one way for her house, the other for Tansy's.

"Ah, why not?"

Mel notices Tansy checking her phone as they walk to the front door.

"He'll be fine," she says, unlocking the door. "Just relieved to be home,"

"Oh. Yes. Of course." Tansy pockets the phone and Mel realises she wasn't thinking of Ivor. Tansy looks awkward. It must be a man, Mel thinks. Tansy doesn't elaborate and Mel doesn't ask.

Loud squeaking comes from the living room as they hook up their coats in the hall. Maggie May and Ruby Tuesday are scampering round their pen, sending hay into the air.

"They only had breakfast before school," Mel laughs, and gestures to the trodden-down spinach and half-eaten carrots the guineas have abandoned.

"Scarlet's still asking for a guinea pig," Tansy says, reaching in and scratching Maggie's soft head. "I said we'd have to wait till Amber's a bit bigger."

"Probably a good idea," Mel smiles, thinking of angry, temperamental Amber. "Come on, let's have a drink."

In the kitchen she fills the kettl e and finds two of her best mugs. Tansy's jumpy, she notices, and wonders if her friend will say anything about the call or text she's clearly looking for. They drink coffee and talk about Ivor and the children, the coming summer and Mel's job application. Tansy says nothing about the person she's hoping to hear from and after half an hour says she'd better be off.

"Lift?" Mel asks. "It's no trouble."

"No thanks. The walk'll do me good." Tansy gives the guineas a goodbye stroke each, and puts on her jacket.

Mel watches her from the doorstep. As soon as Tansy reaches the pavement she checks her phone again.

~

Tansy leaves early for school pick-up and calls in at Joe's first. Her Golf is parked in a different place, so she knows the MOT has been done.

"Sorry, Tansy," Joe says with a rueful grin. "Tyres. And a couple of advisories. I can get the tyres done tomorrow if you can leave it with me."

"How many?"

"Both front. One's really bad. You shouldn't be driving on it."

"OK. Thanks Joe. Let's do it tomorrow."

She wanders off towards school and nursery, nodding and waving at some of the other parents. She stands by the gate, as there are still a few spare minutes, and taps out a text.

Failed the MOT. Having the tyres done tomorrow. Could meet the next day if you are free? X

Mel's people carrier swings into a parking space and Tansy puts her phone away hastily.

"How did you get on with the occupational therapist?" Mel asks, jogging towards her.

"She was bossy. Aren't they all? Anyway he's got a Zimmer frame now and a stool to rest on in the kitchen. She was a bit snotty about some of the things we've done, you know, like the chair, going on about a hospital-style chair with a straight back. We said, OK, if she can get one."

"What did Ivor think?"

"Oh, he left us to do the negotiating," Tansy grins. "He was just pissed off with it all."

Mel checks the time. "Come on, we'd better go down."

Tansy's phone beeps in her pocket but she can't look, not now, not in front of Mel and the other parents. The girls will be here any minute and she's got to tell them they're walking home. They will dump all their gear on her: backpacks, water bottles, lunchboxes, coats.

Scarlet comes first holding a bright flapping sheet of paper. Bloody hell, thinks Tansy. A painting to carry home too.

—

Izzy and Abi are working together in Samarkand. Abi is on the till, Izzy on tables. Lunch has finished, and most of the orders are for drinks and cakes, maybe a round of toast or an ice cream sundae.

Izzy plumps up a pair of patchwork cushions on one of the wooden settles and glances over as Abi laughs happily with a man settling up. Things have settled with Rick, Abi told her that morning. It was a mistake. He was under stress. He didn't know what he was saying. Everything is fine.

Izzy loads a tray with dirty cups and glasses. Abi looks over and grins at her. She looks happy, Izzy admits grudgingly, but for how long?

Abi's wearing a short-sleeved T-shirt, and the scars aren't noticeable unless you know. If you did know though, you'd see her golden freckles do little to disguise the knotted lines and shiny jagged marks. Izzy fears those lines are constantly screaming to Abi: cut here.

~

It's been a fairly quiet night in the bar. Stefan has swept and mopped up, checked the newly-washed glasses for smudges, and dismantled the coffee machine. He turns off the music and dims the lights. The last remaining couple are already getting ready to leave. Stefan busies himself at the bar while they gather bags and phones. He wishes them goodnight as they walk past.

The hotel bar is licensed twenty-four hours a day, but after eleven the night porter takes any orders. He doesn't mix cocktails like Stefan does, only serves beer, wine, and spirits to the late-night drinkers. Stefan grabs his jacket and glances around one more time. He'll hand the keys to the night porter and be off.

Every night he has to make a decision about whether to leave his car in the hotel car park or try to find a space near his flat. When he steps outside it's drizzling. He can hear the rush of the waves and shivers. Tomorrow is the anniversary of Nina's death. Two years since she ran down the stairs from their Carbis Bay flat and into the sea.

George sent him a message on Facebook earlier, asking if he wanted to meet for a drink on the anniversary. Stefan wrote back: no. It's not that he doesn't like George – he does – but every time he sees him, he sees Nina in their identical eyes and colouring. He remembers George urging Nina to compete with him all the time. George could have saved her. Not once she got into the rip current perhaps, but he should have looked at the wind and the waves and told her they weren't going in after all, and she would have listened to him.

Stefan twists his ring and unlocks the car door. He'll find somewhere to park. He usually does.

As he drives down the darkened streets he wonders how Ivor is. It's too late to ring him and check. He'd have loved a grandfather like Ivor. Growing up it was just him and his mother. He saw her parents occasionally, but they both died before he was twelve. Shortly after, his mother married his stepfather, and now he is all Stefan has in the way of family. Breast cancer took his mother eight years ago. And then he lost Nina. Now he truly is alone. Sometimes he wonders if he should jack it all in here and go travelling or move to London but, in his heart, he knows he needs to be by the sea, who gave Nina her last embrace, whose sounds and moods she so loved.

He also knows that he has to move forward without her, and he wonders if he will ever love another girl.

~

Mel hits submit and her application to Lanyon House whizzes off into the ether. Caring for Ivor has made her realise how much she misses working with older people, people who need support. She's spent all the recent years on her family, and she loves them all to distraction, but she would like to find herself out there again.

She clicks off her laptop and puts it away. Probably she won't even hear from them. The guineas squeak and rustle in their hay. She stoops over the hutch and gives them each a stroke before turning off the light.

"Look again." Ivor indicates the cards Carol has laid down on the table.

"Oh. Yes. The run. I always miss runs. Especially low numbers." Carol moves her tiny silver peg along the cribbage board. "You're still going to thrash me."

Ivor gathers the cards awkwardly. His gout has flared up again, and he's on the Colchicine to relieve it. Carol knows better than to offer to shuffle and deal for him. He drops cards slowly, one by one, in front of her.

"I missed this," she says, gathering up her hand of six. "When I was away."

"I missed it too. I missed a lot."

"Do you remember when you taught me to play?"

"Of course."

Carol meets his clear grey-green eyes. He's taken off his glasses to play. His eyes have lost none of that extraordinary colour. She never knew how to describe it: peppermint, seawater, mistletoe.

"When I had that scare."

"I wanted to take your mind off it."

"Thank you." Learning a card game had not taken her mind off the possibility of cervical cancer, but it had helped.

"Just think, Carol." Ivor drops two cards for the box. "If things had been different…"

"Please don't. I know I fucked up. Then and now. Most of all then."

"Are you going to stay with Jeff?"

"I don't know. It seems so much hassle at our age."

"At your age? Come on, girl. You've got years on me. Decades."

He reaches out, grasps her hand as firmly as he can. "Please don't waste the rest of it. When I'm gone…"

"Don't say it."

"You know I haven't long. I can't bear to go and think you're unhappy. If it couldn't be me, then at least don't let it be him. If he is upsetting you."

"I wish I could go back," Carol says, and how paltry the words sound to her ears, so what must they sound like to Ivor's?

"So do I, girl. So do I." He releases her hand and looks down at the cards he's holding. "Come on, let me win, and then you can find what I'm having for tea."

The moment has gone, and Carol swallows the hardness in her throat. Life could have been so different, be so different. She thought she was doing the right thing, for herself, for Louis, and for Ivor. But running away is not the answer, she has come to realise.

One day Carol will have to come clean.

―

Emmeline has gone to see Ivor, and the girls are at school and nursery. Tansy is alone in the house, and ricochets between her bedroom and the bathroom, brushing her hair, re-lining her eyes, changing her earrings from simple silver hoops to her lucky amethysts. She checks the time again.

Gareth is modelling at an art class in Redruth this morning and suggested they meet at the Costa at the traffic interchange. She isn't sure where this is exactly, and spent ages the night before looking at Google maps, and working out where to come off the main road. Emmeline has agreed to fetch the girls at home time.

She's blotting her lips when her mobile rings.

"Charlie. Hi." She exhales with relief that it's not Gareth cancelling their meeting.

"How are you all? Thought I'd see how Ivor's getting on."

"Yeah, he's doing fine."

"Oh good. It's quiet in the shop today. Don't suppose you fancy coming into town for lunch?"

"I can't," she says. "I'm just on the way out."

"Anything nice?"

Tansy hesitates. "I'm meeting a friend."

"Ah. Right. OK."

He knows it's a man, Tansy thinks, as she hangs up. He knows it's a man who matters to me. Quite why Gareth Crane matters so much to her she can't answer. All she knows is that this is the crazy rush, the endorphin overload, she's craved.

In the car she turns up the radio and sings *Friday I'm in Love*. She can't be in love, not really. Surely. Soon the uneven surface of the A30 grumbles over the radio. The sun splits through the clouds. It's another sunny rainy day, the kind of day that makes her think spring can be beautiful, the kind of day for hope and new adventures. A day for endorphins and craziness.

She leaves the A-road and gets lost amongst the roundabouts and traffic lights. Jagged ruins of minestacks loom over the road. Under the tarmac and pavements are the old tunnels and holes of the county's past. This is a broken and bruised landscape, scoured of its seams of copper and tin. There's a giant piece of mining machinery on one of the traffic islands, and Tansy realises she's gone down this stretch of road once already.

She imagines the landscape as a painting. The old crumbling stones of chimneys and engine houses, the new roads as dark brushstrokes. Traffic lights glowing through the sudden splatter of drizzle. She flicks on her wipers and sees the sign for Costa down a road to the left.

She's early. Traffic rumbles past on the artery road beyond the wall. She checks her face, her phone. Lemon-white sunlight makes the cars and damp tarmac glitter. Tansy's never liked this time of early spring before, but now, this year, it is swollen with expectation.

At last she gets out and wanders over to the glass entrance. As she paces up and down a muddy hatchback comes into the car park. She starts walking towards it. The driver's door opens and Gareth gets out. Tansy skips the last few steps towards him. He opens his arms to hug her and she grazes his stubble with her lips.

In that instant her head swims. She should feel embarrassed at the kiss, and embarrassed at their late-night texts and how the little red dot lit up more than her mobile screen, but she's not, and he's locking his car and taking her arm, leading her to the door.

There's no-one queueing. They order quickly and take their drinks to a table in the window.

Gareth shrugs off his jacket. His hair is loose today, tumbling on his shoulders. He's wearing a small silver dreamcatcher in his ear. Tansy meets his eyes, notices a fine dark outline to his irises. His eyes are the same colour as Grandad's, she thinks, irrelevantly.

"Tell me about the art class."

"It was portrait today. So I kept my clothes on. I do life modelling there too."

"Is it students?"

Tansy knows lots of girls would giggle and blush at the thought of life drawing. People like those blondes. But life drawing is nothing to her. Her grandfather and father are artists. She's been to life classes. It's nothing, it's normal.

"Housewives and a few guys. A couple of students on gap years who want to keep their hand in."

"Did you like what they did?"

"Yeah, some of them. One gave me a massive nose."

"I never get the time to do art these days."

"I'll have to model for you."

Tansy doesn't know what to say and drinks her Earl Grey. She wants to ask who the blondes are. She knows their names, she's searched as far as she can on their Facebook profiles, but most of the details are private. What she does know is that they are both in Cornwall. So they're still around. And they're nothing like Tansy. She's tall and dark haired, thinks of herself as a Modigliani girl; those two are busty bleach-haired clones.

"What are you thinking?" Gareth grins at her.

"How little I know about you."

"Plenty of time to change that. Tell me what you'd like to know."

She can't ask. She can't even ask *do you have a girlfriend?* Because, if he does, why the hell is he sitting here with her in Costa, watching her like that?

So she asks him about books and films and artists. She tells him more about Jake and Ivor. She says maybe he could meet them one day. He talks about his design degree and how he ditched it and worked in seedy city bars and shops instead. He tells her a little about his grandmother who left him the money for his move to Cornwall.

When he goes back to the counter for refills Tansy gazes out of the greasy window, and marvels that this grimy Costa on little more than a traffic island even exists, and that it is now a special place. She watches a seagull stalking through the car park, she hears the rumble of a heavy truck going by. The sunlight and the rain are blinding through the glass. She wants to paint this place, she wants to keep this dismal Costa in her heart always.

"Shall we go on somewhere else after these?" Gareth has returned with a glass of tea and a mug of froth sprinkled with chocolate flakes.

"Like, for a proper drink?"

"I'm driving."

"So am I. We could have one. Anyway, we could go somewhere better than this."

"OK. Let's. Mum's picking up the girls today. Do you know anywhere?"

"Not really," he grins. "We'll see where we end up."

I don't care where I end up, Tansy thinks, and finishes her tea. She wonders what the other people in Costa think, whether they assume she and Gareth are together. It feels like they are, like they've known each other for ages, and yet if that were the case, there wouldn't be this tension, this atmosphere, this whatever the fuck it is. And whatever the fuck it is, she wants to bottle it and keep it safe and inhale it for the rest of her life.

It's raining when they leave. Pewter clouds have smudged out the sun.

"Shall we go together?" Gareth asks. "If you're OK with that?"

"I'm OK with that."

Tansy's car is nearest. She unlocks the doors and they dive in. The windscreen is speckled with huge raindrops. The car suddenly feels small. When she reaches out for the gear stick, her arm brushes his.

"A mystery tour," Gareth says.

"Hope you know how to get back here. I got lost this morning."

"Ah, we'll be fine. Let's go through town and see what's on the other side."

Tansy drives. She doesn't know where they're going. They get lost in an industrial estate. At last they're in the country.

She indicates left and pulls into a pub car park edged with trees. She shouldn't drink. Not on an empty stomach. Not when she's driving. She hasn't even told Gareth how she gave up alcohol for ten years.

The bar inside is so dark it's disorientating. No-one else seems to be there. Gareth orders a bottle of lager. Tansy asks for an orange juice. She'll tell him. She will. They take their drinks to a corner table on a raised dais. Their eyes meet and they laugh and laugh, and can't stop. The darkness of the pub, the grimness of the worn-out barmaid, the yellowed tourist information leaflets in a wall rack.

I can't remember laughing like this, Tansy thinks, gasping for breath.

~

Vicky is at home trying to get on top of a vast heap of washing. There are the bins to take out, the bathroom to clean, and all kinds of general tidying to do. Kev is also at home. His job got postponed at the last minute as the supplies hadn't arrived. Vicky asked him an hour ago if he'd run the hoover round the house while the kids are at school but he's still lying on the sofa in his slippers, watching YouTube videos of cars.

Sometimes Vicky really hates him. In October he forgot her birthday. He actually forgot it completely. She hasn't had a Valentine's card for years. She can't remember the last time he kissed her or touched her, other than to draw her attention to something. She does remember when he moved in to the spare room though. That was two years ago. You deserve better, the little voice whispers inside her head. Maybe when Skye has left school, Vicky tells herself again. It's a date to look towards. A date when she can make a decision about her life because she's only thirty-nine, and she can't bear the thought of spending the rest of her days with a man who so clearly dislikes and despises her, a man who – if she is honest – she also dislikes and despises.

They are driving back to Costa. Gareth has turned up the music and is singing along with Bruce Springsteen. Tansy struggles to concentrate on the road, about who to give way to, how to negotiate a parked car, because of the enormous, swooping energy surge inside her. The roundabout with the mining machinery appears ahead and she sails round it, and immediately realises she's taken the wrong exit again. When she laughs it bubbles like lava.

"I've really enjoyed our second date," Gareth says.

"And me," she says, this time taking the right road. Is it a date? Is it really a date?

There's the Costa sign coming up. It's nearly time to say goodbye. She parks in a vacant spot next to his car and turns off the ignition.

"Can I kiss you?" he asks.

She isn't expecting that, but she nods dumbly. He's the first man to kiss her for so long, the only man other than Charlie for years. She's intoxicated, reaches up to wind her hand into his hair.

"Next time we'll go somewhere quieter?" he asks.

"Where?"

"My flat?"

"Yes," she breathes.

He kisses her again. Let's go to your flat now, she thinks, but at last he releases her.

"Until next time then."

"Next time."

He opens the car door, stands out into a sudden shaft of sunlight. Tansy watches him unlock his car, flick open a pair of shades, tug out his seatbelt, and all the time she wants to jump out and run back to him. He fires his ignition, and waves, and she follows him out of the car park.

Driving home, she cannot stem the glorious effervescence in her veins. Through the splintered sunlight a rainbow arcs across the washed-out sky.

~

"This is my daughter, Skye," Vicky says to Ivor that evening. "She's a huge fan of your work. I hope it's OK for her to come."

"Of course," Ivor says.

Skye beams shyly.

"Have a chat with Ivor while I get things sorted in the kitchen," Vicky says.

Skye perches on the edge of a chair at the dining table. Vicky goes into the kitchen and turns on the oven, puts a ready meal onto a baking tray and pierces its film lid. As she comes out again to bring Ivor's night clothes from the bedroom, she hears him telling Skye to bring her art portfolio round one day and he'll have a look and see if he can advise her. Skye glows with happiness and reaches over to hug him.

~

Tansy opens a bottle of Merlot. The girls are playing quietly together. Emmeline went round to Ivor's while Tansy was with Gareth. She took him up a prescription from the chemist, and some strawberries.

"Can we have a talk please?" Emmeline starts.

Tansy clutches her wine glass. It'll be about the wine, or about the crazy ebullience she's had after Gareth's kiss.

"About Dad."

"OK." Tansy slides onto a chair.

Then, a shriek from the other room.

"No, no, you *did*!"

"I *did not*!"

"Mumma! Mumma!"

"Mummy!"

"Quiet, you two," Tansy calls. "I need to talk to Granny."

"He's not going to get any better," Emmeline says. "He'll probably get worse. I think we need to get another carer in."

"As well as Vicky?"

"Yes. Especially as Mel is applying for other jobs."

"Oh. Yes. Of course."

"I thought maybe ask any of our lot if they know anyone, ask around for a few days, then put it on Facebook again."

That was how they found Mel, Carol, and Stefan. Tansy put an advert on the Gerent's Cross village page. Mel responded straight away; someone else tagged Carol. Someone from St Ives tagged Stefan because he was looking for a few extra hours' work a week. In fact Tansy had many other responders. She wonders if she still has that list of people, if any of them might still be interested. She's sure she has it somewhere.

"Let me see if I've got the list of the other people," she says.

"We need to get on with it straight away. I can see he may need more than two visits a day as well as us. And if the carers can do all the things he needs like the meals and the washing and so on, it means when we see him we can actually talk to him. And the girls can see him without us racing about doing the jobs."

"I'll go and look now." Tansy tops up her glass and heads off to her room.

Before she searches for the list she checks her messages. Nothing new. She re-reads the ones Gareth sent earlier.

I meant what I said. I really enjoyed today. X

You're a beautiful girl, Tansy Martin. X

I loved kissing you. X

I can't wait to see you again. X

She digs out her diary from the year before. Yes, on the inside cover is a list of names. The first on the list is Izzy Macauley. Tansy types that name into Facebook. Instantly she recognises the girl in the profile picture. It's the waitress from Samarkand. The one who knows Gareth. Would she really want to be a part-time carer if she's working there? Tansy hesitates a moment then types her a message.

~

"Who's it from?" Abi asks.
"Someone called Tansy Martin. I know that name. Let's look."
Abi shuffles along the bed to see Izzy's phone.
"D'you remember I saw an ad for a caring job? For an artist? And they'd filled the positions. She says they're looking for an extra person and I was top of the reserve list."
"A caring job?"
"You remember?"
"Vaguely. Why d'you want that? You've got Samarkand?"
"Yeah, I know. I just fancied something of my own, away from Mum and Aidan. Not for any reason. Just to give me some space. It's only an hour each time. A few shifts a week."
"Well, could you work it round the café?"
"I don't know. I think I'll ask some more about it. And the artist, the guy. He's pretty famous, you know. I googled him last time."
"Did Mum know about this?"
"Yeah, she didn't mind."
"Oh well, go for it then. At least find out. Where is it?"
"Gerent's Cross."
"That's easy enough."

Izzy taps out a reply to Tansy Martin. She thinks she has seen her somewhere. Perhaps she came in to Samarkand. She tells Tansy she's not working the next day; she could drive up to Gerent's Cross and meet her.

~

Tansy creates a Facebook group called *Ivor* and adds her mother, Mel, Carol, Stefan, Vicky and Izzy.

Hello everyone. I thought this would be the best way for us all to stay in touch about the rota and so on. This morning Mum and I met Izzy who would like to join the crew. We felt we needed another person as Grandad might need more help in the future. Izzy's family have a lovely café in Penzance called Samarkand which I can thoroughly recommend!

~

It's your own fault, Carol thinks. If you'd only been honest from the start, then they might not keep adding in all these other people. Izzy Macauley. Samarkand. Carol thinks she knows the place. At the bottom end of Market Jew Street. She looks young, probably only in her twenties. Carol sighs. Tansy and Emmeline are only doing their best for Ivor. She shouldn't be so hard on them or the new carers. It's her fault for keeping quiet.

"OK. I'm off now." She scoops up her car keys and heads for the door.

"See you soon," Jeff says. "You won't loiter at the Robinsons' place."

Carol ignores the barb. Lately Jeff has made snide remarks about the extra time she spends at Ivor's, either going early in the evening for a game of cards, or staying on a bit to chat. No, she doesn't stay longer at her cleaning jobs. But the Robinsons are usually out and she lets herself in with a key; Susie Walker is aloof and unfriendly; and the Cowles are far too busy with their children and their dogs and their marathon-running to talk to her.

But Jeff knows Ivor is different.

~

"Shall I wash up?" Izzy asks Stefan.

"No, you go and talk to Ivor. Get to know each other. There's not much." Stefan nods to the meagre pile of plates and mugs. Ivor eats very little these days. Tonight he only asked for crumpets and Stefan's sure it wasn't because Izzy was there too.

Stefan twists off his precious ring and drops it on the windowsill. It needs a clean up there, he thinks, squirting washing up liquid into the bowl. There are some dried up leaves from a long-dead plant, a sharp flint of cracked soap, a Biro, a bottle of Baby Bio caked with dark brown crystals. And dust all along the windowsill. He takes the sponge and starts on the glasses. Ivor has a dishwasher, of course, but there's never enough to fill it, and Ivor isn't sure if it still works. Perhaps Stefan should take a look.

Izzy and Ivor seem to be getting on OK next door. He glances towards them, sees Izzy helping Ivor to his feet, adjusting his dressing gown, and guiding him to the TV with his Zimmer. She seems a nice enough girl, he thinks. She should be fine. She's been working in a café, so she is good with people. Perhaps she can entice Ivor to eat some better food. He knows Samarkand but he hasn't been in. Maybe he'll call in next time he's in Penzance. It occurs to him often that the people he works with, both at the hotel and Ivor's carers, are his substitute family. When Ivor dies he knows he wants to stay in touch with Tansy and Emmeline, and the other girls. He still hasn't met Vicky yet, just seen some of her comments on the Facebook group chat, but everyone seems genuinely fond of Ivor and wanting to make his life as happy and comfortable as possible. Stefan hopes this strange fellowship will hold when the inevitable happens.

"Stop it," he whispers aloud. "Don't even think it."

He stacks the last plate, pours away the dirty water and rinses his hands. Izzy's calling him from the living room.

"Coming."

He races through. Ivor is settled in his chair with the lamp angled over him as he likes.

"Sorry, didn't mean to scare you," Izzy says to Stefan. "Ivor wants a couple of books off the top shelf and I can't reach them. I think you could."

Stefan reaches up to get the hardbacks for Ivor – one on Shropshire, and the other on the geology of west Cornwall, and puts them on the chair arm. He glances round quickly. He hasn't forgotten anything. Water bottles changed, bedroom ready, cup of tea made, snack plate of fruit and biscuits wrapped in foil, the Zimmer right by Ivor's feet.

"I think we're done. Got everything, Ivor?"

"I think so, yes. I'll have a read and then watch the news and get off to bed."

"Mel's coming in the morning, I think," Stefan says.

"Lovely. Thank you. And lovely to meet you, Izzy. Do you think you can put up with me?"

Izzy grins. "I think so. I'd like to."

"OK, we'll leave you in peace, then."

Stefan grabs his coat and ushers Izzy out first.

"He's a great guy," he says, as he locks the front door. "I hate seeing him…go downhill. I don't know what he'll do in the long term. I know he doesn't want to go into a home. I think his family need to talk to him, but it's hard, isn't it?"

"So hard. I completely get that he wants to stay here. He's lucky because he's so switched on. Perhaps with all of us looking after him he can stay here."

"Let's hope so. If you want to ask anything just Facebook me."

"I will. Thanks. I'll let Tansy know I'd like to do it."

~

Izzy unlocks the butter-yellow Fiat she shares with Abi, and waits for Stefan to roar off. She glances at Ivor's darkened kitchen window. A faint blue haze from the lights beyond, and the spilling leaves of an orchid. She wants to fumble the spare key from the keysafe and run in again, check Ivor really is all right on his own. That's silly. Ivor would think she was fussing. She turns on her headlights and noses out into the lane.

It doesn't take long to get to Penzance, which is one reason why this job is suitable. It gives her a bit of space from the family, and she can work it round her shifts. Tansy told her that Stefan works at a hotel and Carol has a couple of cleaning jobs, that Vicky is a carer at Lanyon House and Mel is hoping to join her there. Between them all they can look after Ivor, surely.

She's surprised to see lights on in the house. Holly and Aidan are at Samarkand as there's a gig tonight, and she thought Abi was out with Rick. Perhaps they're both here, Izzy supposes, locking the car and shouldering her bag.

"Hi, it's me," she calls out.

A grunt from the living room. Izzy throws her bag over the newel post and hooks her coat on a peg.

"I thought you were with Rick," she says carefully.

Abi's on the sofa, with her shoes kicked off. She's been crying again. Her face is puffy and blotched.

"What's happened now?" Izzy asks.

"He wouldn't speak. I don't know."

"Wouldn't speak?"

"Yeah, that. We just sat in the pub and he was silent. Every time I tried to say anything, start a conversation about anything, he wouldn't answer. Or just one word or whatever. He wouldn't talk to me at all."

"Is he on drugs or something?" Izzy doesn't know anything about drugs but she wonders if this sudden change could be because of some new influence. "Or…he isn't…?"

"What, seeing someone else? I don't know. He says not. But he doesn't like me. I don't know what the hell I've done." Abi scoops up her phone, swipes it to life, casts it aside.

"I thought you two had sorted out whatever it was?"

Abi shrugs. "Obviously not. How can I when I don't know what it is?"

"How did you leave it?"

"I just said I wasn't sitting there being ignored, that people were looking, and if he couldn't talk to me I'd go home. And he just shrugged and said OK, and I went. I had to. I couldn't stay when I'd said that, could I? I kept looking behind me, thought he might follow me, but nothing."

"You need to think about this." Izzy says. "He's not good for you. He's hurting you. And I'm scared you'll hurt yourself again."

She doesn't hear Abi's reply, doesn't ask her to repeat it. As Abi shuffles on the sofa, her sleeve rides up. No smudged blood, no fresh lacerations. Izzy tears her eyes from Abi's skin.

"Fuck," Stefan says aloud.

He's just closed the flat door behind him and realised he left his ring on Ivor's kitchen windowsill, along with the dust and the Baby Bio and the papery leaves. He wonders how the hell he didn't notice, didn't feel the exposed skin against the gear lever on the way home. He must be tired. Izzy distracted him, of course, calling for him like that, and he thought Ivor had fallen or something, and then he was escorting Izzy out, and locking up, and talking to her.

"Fuck."

He isn't going to drive back now. He's got a parking space outside, and Ivor would wonder who the hell was unlocking his door on a Saturday night. He could call Ivor, tell him the ring is there. No. Firstly, it's not fair to disturb Ivor. Stefan knows exactly where the ring is. And secondly, knowing Ivor, he'd haul himself up with that Zimmer and tap-tap-tap his way into the darkened kitchen to look for it and put it out on the table, because he's so kind and polite and old-school thoughtful and, in doing that, he might hurt himself.

Stefan knows the ring is safe. He'll collect it tomorrow evening after his shift at the hotel. Now he's realised it's not there, his finger feels naked and newborn, unprotected. In a way he is unprotected, he thinks, without that ring to anchor him. He's cut adrift, caught in a rip, being pulled farther and farther out.

―

Amber is awake at dawn on Sunday as usual. Tansy only gets a lie-in when the girls are with Charlie. She changes Amber's saturated nappy, cleans her bottom and legs with wipes, and gets her into fresh clothes. There's no chance of Amber dozing off again, so Tansy deposits her on the sofa in front of CBeebies, and pours her a bottle of milk. Tansy makes sure she has her phone with her, and snuggles under a blanket on the sofa, half awake and watching Amber slurp, half drifting through a fantasy of *Gigglebiz* and *Bing*.

Her mobile rings at the same time as Amber shouts," More milk."

"I'm really sorry," Mel says. "Sophie's been sick a few times. She's not well at all. I can't leave her, and I wouldn't want to pass it on to Ivor anyway."

"Oh no, poor Sophie."

"I know it's late notice."

"Don't worry, Mel. I'm sure one of the others will be around. Or one of us can go."

"More MILK," Amber throws her empty bottle towards Tansy, and it sails over the back of the sofa. "NOW."

"OK, OK." Tansy stretches for the sticky bottle.

She could put a message on the group chat and see who responds but, because it's so early, they might not be looking. Carol. She's the one. Tansy knows Carol doesn't do her other jobs on Sunday, she's always helpful if there's a problem, and is very fond of Ivor. As Tansy hands Amber a refill she's already dialling Carol's number.

~

Carol sets off for Ivor's early. Jeff is still asleep. She thinks he's aware that she's going, but she's not going to bother to shake him alert and make sure. She's secretly pleased that Tansy called her straight away, asked her first, didn't offer the morning shift to one of the new girls.

Ivor is sleeping and she stands a moment in his bedroom doorway watching him. Remembering and regretting. His breathing is harsh and ragged. There's a blood smear on his chin from a razor cut. *What the hell am I doing, just standing here?* Carol jumps alert. His chest is bad. She gently rouses him and adjusts the pillows so he can lean back. He hacks and hacks, and coughs up phlegm.

"I was expecting Mel," he manages at last, wiping his mouth on a tissue.

"Her daughter's poorly. You've got me. I don't like that chest. I think you need antibiotics."

"It'll clear in a day or so." He coughs again and again.

Carol finds a stray humbug on the bedside table and unwraps it for him. They ease his throat, he always says, and clear his airway.

"I shall tell Tansy and Emmeline you need to see the doctor tomorrow."

"Don't fuss."

"You need antibiotics."

"Give it a day." He crunches the sweet, and starts to swing his legs over the side.

Carol glances to where his pyjamas have twisted. His bad leg is swollen and red, the skin stretched taut.

"Your leg looks swollen too. How long has it been like that?"

"It wasn't so bad last night. Stefan and I thought it was a bit pink."

"It's hot to the touch. Some antibiotics will really sort you out. You know cellulitis and your chest don't clear without them." She moves the Zimmer so Ivor can lever himself up and decides that, whatever he says, she will tell his family he should get a home visit from the doctor as soon as possible.

~

"Come on, you two." Tansy holds Amber's coat open for her. Amber runs away, chased by Scarlet, who still hasn't got her socks on.

"Shall I just go?" Emmeline asks, tossing her car keys hand to hand.

"No, I want to come." Tansy steps out in front of Amber and grabs her, stuffs her arms in her jacket. "Now shoes. Scarlet, pick up those socks and get them on. We're leaving now."

"Don't go without me," Scarlet wails, hopping on one leg, ineffectually flapping a mermaid sock. "Don't leave me."

"I'm not leaving you. We want to see Grandad. He's not so well. He might need a doctor tomorrow."

"Can we go in his garden?" Scarlet sits down with a thump and tugs the sock on, twisted and lumpy.

"If we get going now. Ready?"

Emmeline unlocks the front door and they file out into a pale sunny morning. Scarlet stops to fiddle with a cobweb. Emmeline is tense. Tansy knows her mother is getting edgy and worried about Ivor's long-term prospects, and so is she. Daily visits from them and from his carers still leave him hours without help, and he's alone every night. Tansy and Emmeline have talked about him moving into their house, but there isn't a suitable bedroom. He wouldn't manage the step into the shower, and he'd need a raised seat for the lavatory which would be difficult when the girls need to go. Tansy inhales the fresh spring air, and smiles because she'll send Gareth a message later.

Ivor is sitting in his usual dining chair at the table. He has some papers spread in front of him, and he's taken off his glasses. Accounts, bills, something like that. Under his diary are some loose papers. Pen drawings. Tansy pulls them out as he greets the girls. Drawn on pages from an old notepad with a Biro, his lines are shakier than they were. The view through his window, the patterned jug on the sill, a tea mug and a sprig of grapes. There's something fresh about them, something innocent almost, but they're not the definite and confident strokes of the artist she knows. She slides them back under his diary and swallows a tear.

"Your chest is bad," Emmeline says.

"Bloody Carol making a fuss again."

"She cares, Dad."

"Yes," Ivor says quietly. "I know."

"Can they have a run outside while we have a cup of tea?" Tansy asks.

"Course they can." Ivor coughs again. "Stefan's tidied up a bit out there."

Tansy unlocks the back door and the girls rush out into the garden. The daffodils are dying back now, their golden hearts paler and papery. The bluebells will come soon. Ivor has huge drifts of them under his fruit trees. Already spring green shoots are searching for the light.

Tansy turns back to Ivor. He's trying to get up. His hands on the Zimmer handles are tense and taut, but the Colchicine seems to be knocking back the gout a bit.

"Sit down."

Ivor crumples back down again.

"You don't understand. You don't know what it's bloody like. I can't do anything these days."

"I do understand," Tansy says. "It's early days. And Carol's right. You need the doctor. We'll call them first thing tomorrow."

Emmeline comes back from the kitchen with a tray of tea mugs and chocolate biscuits, asks Ivor if she should get something out of the freezer for Vicky to cook that night, and starts folding his clean washing into piles.

"I'll make you a sandwich for lunch," Emmeline says, pairing up the last two socks.

"It's fine, I can –"

"Just let me as I'm here. It's no problem."

Tansy watches the girls race round the garden. Amber disappears behind the corner of the studio, and Tansy's heart jumps, even though she knows there's no secret tunnel from the garden, no broken glass, nothing that could harm her or spirit her away. Scarlet has found a branch and is waving it over her head. Ivor turns stiffly to watch them. Tansy knows how much it means to him to have these two in his life, and how precious he is to them too. Not many children know their great-grandparents, or even their grandparents, come to that. It seems a lifetime ago that she lost her grandmother. Sylvia's photograph is still high on the wall beside the window. It was taken when she was a young girl, before she'd had Emmeline, probably about the time she and Ivor met back in Shropshire.

"I've put it in the fridge," Emmeline calls through. "It's cheese and cucumber."

"Thanks, love."

"I'll get these two in now." Tansy opens the door and shouts for Scarlet and Amber. "Come in and wash your hands, girls."

Scarlet runs up and hugs Tansy's legs with muddy hands. Amber sits down on the grass and starts howling.

"Let go, sweetheart. I'll have to get her."

Tansy unhooks Scarlet and strides across the lawn. Amber scrabbles to her feet again and shoots off behind the studio, but she's forgotten it's a dead end. Tansy grabs her and scoops her up. There's a leaf in her bright hair, mud on her face.

"We need to clean you up."

"I don't want to go in. I want to stay here."

"We need to give Grandad a bit of peace. Let's wash these grubby hands."

She takes the girls into the kitchen to wash at the sink. Scarlet studiously squirts liquid soap onto her palms and scrubs them together, peering out of the window at the front garden. Amber tries to escape by hiding under Ivor's stool, and Tansy has to squat down to coax her out and to the sink. Scarlet has left splashes everywhere and a streak of green handwash over the tap. Tansy works a lather onto Amber's fingers, and gives the bowl a quick wipe.

—

Stefan is on a short day at the hotel bar. He goes home, showers and changes, still conscious of the coldness on his finger. As he drives to Ivor's he realises he'll probably end up being there at the same time as the evening carer.

Yes, there is a car on the drive. Not the yellow one Izzy came in. He knocks on the front door and calls out as he opens it. Ivor is on his stool in the kitchen wearing a pyjama top. A girl with long loose brown hair squats on the floor gently washing his swollen leg. They are talking about something and don't even notice Stefan until he speaks.

"Sorry to interrupt. Hi Ivor."

The girl glances up. She has a scatter of freckles over her nose and earrings made of bright feathers.

"This is Vicky," Ivor says. "She's new today."

"Are you Stefan?"

"Yes." Stefan looks at Ivor's leg. "That's worse today."

"Ivor was telling me his family want him to see the doctor tomorrow. He's had some trouble with his chest too."

"Good idea. Get them to look at that leg."

Vicky moves the bowl of water away and towels Ivor's stretched pink skin. He winces a little. She scoops out moisturising cream from the large plastic pot and smooths it on.

"I left my ring here last night," Stefan explains. "I took it off to wash up and forgot it."

"I haven't seen a ring." Ivor feeds one foot then another into his trousers. "Where is it?" The exertion makes him cough again.

"On the windowsill."

Stefan picks up the bowl to pour down the sink, then wonders if he should have left it. Vicky might not like him interfering, but she is busy helping Ivor to his feet, hauling the striped trousers over his bottom. Stefan tips away the soapy water, rinses the bowl and his hands, goes to pick up his ring.

It's not there. Everything else seems unchanged. The brittle leaves, the shard of soap, the Baby Bio. But the ring has gone. He looks in the sink, on the drainer. He can feel his heart rate soaring.

"It's not here," he says.

"What's that?" Ivor calls.

"My ring. I put it there on the windowsill. It's not there."

"Are you sure you put it there?" Ivor asks. "Thank you, Vicky. I can walk from here."

"I always put it there when I wash up. Remember, Izzy took you down to the TV and she called me to reach the books for you. I never picked it up."

"Vicky, would you help Stefan look for it?"

Ivor taps away on his Zimmer. Vicky washes her hands, glancing around the sink.

"I'll just put this in the microwave and I'll have a look."

Stefan stands there in the middle of the kitchen searching for a glint of blue and silver. Vicky starts Ivor's meal with a series of beeps.

"What does it look like? Is it silver?"

"It's silver, with a blue…blue glass."

Vicky moves aside the dirty washing up. Nothing. Stefan drops to his hands and knees.

"It was on the windowsill. With the Baby Bio and that. I don't see how it could have fallen anywhere." He's going to cry in a minute. He knows it. He straightens up.

"It's very special, isn't it?"

"It is. It really is." He looks down at Vicky. She hardly comes to his shoulder. He can smell whatever fragrance she's wearing. He feels like he's going nuts. Ivor won't have nicked it. Was it Mel this morning? Surely she wouldn't have. Was it Izzy? No, they were together from when she called out to him till they left.

"If you see it…" Stefan starts. "Please tell me. It's got ashes in it. The glass. It's got my girlfriend's ashes in it."

~

Vicky can't settle. She has served Ivor his meal of microwave macaroni. He's eating it at the table, and she's chopping up strawberries and raspberries for his pudding, but her eyes keep darting round the kitchen. She drops her knife, sure she's seen a metallic flash on the floor by the fridge, but it's a tiny curl of foil.

"Poor Stefan," she says when she takes the dish of fruit through to Ivor. "The ring has his girlfriend's ashes in it, did you know?"

"No, I didn't. Could I have a top-up please?" Ivor holds out his glass for a refill of lemon squash. "I knew he lost his girlfriend, before he started coming here. He doesn't talk about her."

"But he's so young."

"Thirty."

Vicky wants to ask Ivor what happened to Stefan's girlfriend, but she doesn't like to. She takes his glass to the kitchen, pours a splash of squash and tops it up with lemonade.

"I know," Ivor calls.

She takes the drink to him. "What?"

"Emmeline and Tansy and the girls were here earlier. I bet they took the ring. The kids, I mean. Amber was being tricky. They washed their hands in the kitchen."

Vicky feels huge relief.

"That must be it."

"Let's find out before we say anything to him, yes?"

"Shall I ring them or do you want to? He lives in St Ives, doesn't he? I could drop it off."

"I'll call them when I've had this." Ivor spoons up a raspberry. "I'm sure that's what's happened."

"I hope so," Vicky says.

Why are mealtimes always like the zoo? Tansy wonders. Why is it that, whatever the girls eat, they end up with sticky and greasy fingers, and more food on the floor than in their mouths. Scarlet has eaten one of the thin slivers of pizza on her plate, but Amber has pulled the greasy cheese topping off hers and is rolling it in her fingers. Tansy swipes up a cup of milk before it goes over. The landline rings and she hears Emmeline answer, saying, *"Everything OK, Dad?"* Immediately Tansy runs into the hall still clutching a lime green beaker of milk.

"All right, we'll have a look," Emmeline says, making calming gestures to Tansy. "We'll call you."

"What's up?" Tansy asks when Emmeline hangs up.

"Stefan left a ring by the kitchen sink. He came back for it and it's not there. Dad thinks the girls might have nicked it earlier."

"Oh shit."

"Worse. It's got his girlfriend's ashes in it. So we must find it."

"Mumma. You've got my milk," Scarlet calls.

"Coming. And I need to ask you something." Tansy returns the drink to Scarlet who slurps it loudly. "When we were at Grandad's, did you take a ring? It was by the kitchen sink? It's really important because it belongs to one of his carers and it's very precious."

As she speaks, Tansy can tell from the way Scarlet's shoulders stiffen that she knows about the ring.

"Where is it, Scarlet?"

"It's really pretty. I knew it wasn't Grandad's."

"Where is it?" Tansy asks again.

"I don't know." Scarlet puts the beaker down. "Amber took it from me."

"Oh Christ," Emmeline mutters.

Amber drops a moulded ball of pizza dough on the floor.

"You've obviously finished dinner." Tansy grabs the plates. "Now, Amber, please tell us where the ring is."

"Don't know." Amber slides off her chair.

"Please sweetheart." Tansy knows she mustn't make Amber shout or cry. If she does, they'll never find the bloody ring. What the hell can she do if they don't find it? Stefan will go nuts. Oh fuck, fuck, fuck.

"Amber. You're really naughty," Scarlet starts. "Tell Mumma where the ring is."

"Umm, in the bath?" Amber asks.

"I'll look," says Emmeline.

It won't be there, Tansy knows and in a moment Emmeline is back, shaking her head.

"Amber. I told you. You're naughty. You've lost it."

"You took it." Amber jabs Scarlet in the chest.

"Oww. Mumma, she hurt me."

"You, you!" Amber shrieks, pounding Scarlet.

"Please! Please, stop it. I need your help. This is so important."

Amber's already going purple, swiping greasy hands through her hair. The tears will come any second.

"Amber, darling," Tansy says. "Please think where it might be."

"I shall look in our bedroom." Scarlet sidles past Amber and is about to thump her, but Tansy grabs her.

"I'll look where they've been," Emmeline says. "Jeez, It could be anywhere."

"Amber? The ring? You wouldn't want someone to take Tiger and not give him back, would you?"

"Scarlet took it, not me."

"Scarlet says you were looking at it. Where is it?"

"In Scarlet's bed?"

~

Vicky takes her time settling Ivor in front of the TV. She makes up another glass of cordial for him, and a cup of tea. He has his phone and the remote to hand. She rinses his support stockings at the sink, peering everywhere for Stefan's ring, and hangs them to drip-dry. Emmeline has not called back to say they have the ring. Slowly Vicky puts her coat on and finds her keys.

"If those kids have got it…" Ivor says.

"It could be anywhere."

"You get off. Don't hang about for this."

"I don't mind. If they find it, I can collect it and take it to the hotel tomorrow for him. He'll really want it back."

"He should have called me when he knew he'd left it, and I'd have found somewhere safe for it."

"He wouldn't want to bother you."

"I'm not dead yet."

"Far from it."

"Make yourself a drink if you're hanging on. Won't your family want you back?"

"Not really." Vicky sits on the sofa opposite Ivor. "The kids will be on Facebook or whatever, and Kev…well, he doesn't notice if I'm there or not. Unless I've done something he doesn't like."

"He doesn't hurt you, Vicky?"

"No. Not like that. Oh, never mind me. It's just…bad times, I suppose."

"I'm sorry. If you need an ear I'm here. Though I'm a bit deaf."

Vicky smiles, embarrassed she said anything. They both jump as the phone rings on Ivor's side table. He squints at the screen.

"That's wonderful," he says. "She's still here. We're just having a chat…if she can, that would be great. Yes, he's at work tomorrow. Where was it? Where? Oh, those kids."

Vicky exhales with relief.

"They found it," Ivor says, clicking off the receiver.

"I'll collect it on my way home. Where was it?"

"In Tansy's slipper."

"God, that was lucky. OK, if you're all settled, I'll go and get it."

Vicky locks the front door behind her and puts the key away in the safe under the kitchen window. Tansy said something about getting keys cut for her and Izzy. She won't nag about it; she's happy to use the spare.

"Thank you so much," Emmeline says, handing over a folded envelope on the doorstep. "I can't think what we'd have done if we hadn't found it. Tansy's having words with them right now."

"They're only kids. They wouldn't have done it to be nasty."

"No, of course not. It's just nothing's safe from little eyes and little fingers especially when it's glittery. Will you ring Stefan and sort out a handover?"

"Yes. He'll be so pleased."

"Thanks, Vicky."

Vicky puts the envelope on the passenger seat and drives home. Perhaps she could drop it off now before she goes home, if she can get hold of Stefan. She doesn't know where he lives, but she does know the hotel. It would be easier going to the hotel tomorrow, easier than trying to find somewhere to park in the back streets of St Ives. And she is late. What with staying late at Ivor's and then collecting the ring.

She parks in her usual spot on the road and turns off the ignition. People have ashes put into jewellery, and paper weights, and sewn into cuddly toys, she does know this. She unfolds the envelope. It's not properly stuck down. She lifts the gummy flap and tips the ring into her palm. Silver, with a blue-green crystal. Tiny shards flicker in the stone. Vicky turns it this way and that, starts to slide it onto her finger and stops herself. The ring is Stefan's and it contains all that is left of a girl he loved. Who he still loves. She wraps it once more and takes out her phone and hits Stefan's name, but it goes straight to voicemail.

"Hi Stefan, It's Vicky. I've got your ring. I'll bring it to the hotel bar tomorrow. I think you said you were working. I won't leave it with anyone else. OK. See you."

She presses red and stuffs the ring into her bag. It'll be an event to go to a posh hotel, she thinks. Might take a book and have a quiet drink. Escapism.

~

Izzy leaves Ivor's on Monday morning. She's got him up and dressed, given him his breakfast, ironed a few shirts for him. It is a refreshing change, talking to just one person, a person with a lifetime of stories, no rushing about with menus and damp cloths and trays of drinks. She's told him she agrees with everyone else that he needs some antibiotics and promises to be in touch later to see how he gets on.

When she gets home Abi is alone in the kitchen with her phone on the table in front of her.

"How did you get on?" Abi asks.

"Good." Izzy knows Abi isn't interested in her or Ivor at the moment. "Any news?"

"Nothing. I've sent texts and left voicemails. Nothing. Should I go and see him at work?"

"No. That wouldn't be a good idea."

"It's only a builders' merchant."

"Even so. It's not private. Other guys will be there. You don't want them saying things, do you?"

"If he's left me he could at least say so."

"Well, yes."

"It's all right for you. You don't care about any of this. You don't get affected."

Izzy waits a moment, her hand on the kettle.

"You don't know what affects me," she says, speaking calmly,

"You're not bothered about relationships and that, though, are you?"

Izzy decides not to answer. It's not the time.

"What time are you starting?" she asks instead.

"Twelve."

"Have some breakfast with me, then. Bacon sandwich?"

"OK." Abi swipes her phone again. "I'll just send one more message."

Izzy knifes open a packet of bacon.

~

When Tansy gets back from dropping off the girls, Emmeline has already booked a home visit from the GP for Ivor. The surgery won't say what time it will be, but Emmeline says she will go and see him, and tell him in person.

"Find out how Izzy got on," Tansy asks. "Her first time."

When her mother has left, Tansy heels off her boots and sends a message to Gareth.

The girls are with their dad this weekend for his birthday. Would you like to get together? X

Definitely! X

Tansy smiles and scrolls through their conversations on text and Facebook. He doesn't update his profile much, but he has put up photos he's taken of some run-down buildings in Hayle. Both the blondes have liked the pictures, along with some other friends whose names she recognises from his profile.

Shall I come to yours then? X

I'd love that. X

Vicky loves the times she's alone in the house. Kev left early to get on-site near Truro where he's fitting kitchens into a couple of holiday lets. Harry and Skye have gone to school. Vicky inhales the house. The charred smell of Harry's burnt toast, the sweet breath of Skye's perfume, some over-ripe bananas in the fruit bowl. She wonders if she should try to get in touch with Stefan again or just turn up at the hotel. She's on a long shift at Lanyon the next day and wants to return the ring as soon as she can. When she's made herself a cup of tea she checks her phone and finds a voicemail from Stefan. She must have missed the call getting the kids ready. He tells her he'll be in the bar from noon; he sounds so happy.

Vicky chooses an Aztec patterned day dress and black suede boots. She can't turn up in the shabby leggings she stumbled into at seven that morning. She dusts on a little make up and leaves her hair loose. The ring is safe in her bag where she left it overnight. There didn't seem any point in telling the others about it. Kev would probably say something shitty about a man wearing a ring of ashes.

~

It's the longest Stefan has ever gone without the comfort of Nina's ring on his finger. He does wonder if a day will come when he should remove it, keep it in a drawer somewhere, take it out every now and then to turn the ocean-blue crystal to the light to catch its sparkles. When, if, he meets another girl, he'll have to do that. In the early days, raw and ragged with grief, he swore he'd never replace Nina, never give his heart to anyone. But time has blunted the angles of his pain.

He glances up every time someone walks into the bar. The sea beyond the huge windows is the colour of his ring. Spring is on the way. Another year spools out behind him. Nina wouldn't grudge him happiness.

He's been gazing out of the window at the rippling ocean and doesn't realise someone is standing at the bar.

"I'm so sorry," he starts.

Vicky holds out a folded envelope. "For you," she smiles.

~

"I've got some antibiotics," Ivor says. "They'll be ready at the pharmacy shortly."

"I'll get them on the way to school this afternoon." Tansy says. "Who came?"

"Some locum," Ivor sniffs and coughs again.

Tansy hates the sound of his cough down the line. It sounds like fluid is bubbling up his throat. It hits her suddenly, as it occasionally does, that he really is almost a hundred, that he is frail and getting frailer all the time. There are stories he won't see through to the end. The world keeps turning but one day it will spin on and Ivor Martin won't be there.

~

"Thank you so much. I really appreciate it. You bringing it here."

"No problem," Vicky smiles as Stefan slides the ring on. "Feel better now?"

"Yes. Look, let me get you a drink. On me."

"I'm driving," Vicky says, thinking how much she'd love a gin and tonic. "Can I just have a juice please?"

Stefan fills a tall tumbler with pineapple juice, adds ice and a straw, wedges of orange.

"Wow, that's amazing. At mine I'm lucky to find a clean mug to put juice in."

"I don't go to all this trouble at home," Stefan grins. He twists his ring and the blue crystal sparkles.

Vicky plays with the lime-green straw in her drink. "I'm so sorry about your girlfriend," she starts. "I know no words help, but I am. Really sorry."

"It's been a couple of years now. I don't know where the time goes."

Cancer, Vicky thinks. Breast cancer maybe, or cervical. Young girls get those, and they don't have enough screening. Or a car accident. Or, oh fuck, was it suicide?

"She must have been so young."

Why must she? Vicky corrects herself. Stefan might have had a girlfriend twenty years older. Stop assuming things.

"Yeah, twenty-six. She drowned. Just up the coast. At Amity Cove, you know?"

"Yes, yes, I know the place."

"She was a brilliant surfer. She was there with her brother. They were fearless. Unlike me. I don't like the water. Anyway, they were surfing there one day and Nina...got into difficulties...a rip. Her brother couldn't get to her. They found her straight away. Luckily. I mean, it would have been even worse if, well, you know."

"Oh Stefan, that's terrible. Is your family local? Have you got anyone close?"

"Hardly. Mum died years ago. I've got a step-father, that's all. I don't see him. I'm still close to George, that's Nina's brother, and her parents, but it hurts. And I have to break away really. The people I work with are more my family. The guys here, and you lot. Ivor's lot. Sad, isn't it?"

"Well, if you need a friend, I'm here," Vicky says. "If you ever want to come over for a drink or a meal or whatever, just say so. The kids are doing their own thing most of the time, same with my husband really. So just give me a shout."

"Thank you."

"Perhaps we should all get together one day. All Ivor's people."

"That'd be good."

"Yes, we could all go up to his, and have lunch with him or something. Have you known him long?"

"Since last summer. I had fewer hours here then and I'd done a bit of caring work in the past. I never thought I'd get so fond of the old bugger."

"The nature of the beast when you look after people."

"I'll be devastated when..."

"Yeah, we all will." Vicky drinks juice, wonders whether to ask about what's on her mind. "You know Carol? I did get the feeling she wasn't too happy about me coming along. I met her at Lanyon House when Ivor was staying there. Maybe I'm being over-sensitive. What do you think? I don't mean to put you in a position."

"Carol's very…protective of him. She's known him years. I mean, really years. Twenty odd years or so. She tore strips off me once when I did something wrong."

"Ah, that explains it then. If they're old friends."

"Would you like another?" Stefan nods at Vicky's empty glass.

"Go on then."

Vicky gazes out of the huge windows while Stefan gets her drink. The sea shifts imperceptibly: green, grey, deep purple. She's never been one for sea swimming. It frightens her. The power of the water is beyond the power of any human. She wonders if Nina knew, in her last moments, that she was dying, that her brother could not help her, that she would never see Stefan again. What happens in those last flickering seconds? Vicky has sat with the dying many times; she has held dried-leaf hands, wiped dark spittle, waited, her own heart seemingly halted, for the next shuddering breath. She likes to believe the patient is far, far away, reliving happier, sunnier days, memories stored in some ancient part of the brain. But what if it isn't like that? What if it's a jagged chaotic darkness of pain and anger and terror?

"Vicky, you OK?"

"I'm sorry. I was miles away."

"I could see. Oh, hang on." Stefan turns to a couple approaching the bar. "Good afternoon. What can I get you to drink?"

Vicky half listens to him listing the South American reds available, and wonders if she should take her drink to a table in the window and watch the ocean. Stefan won't want her hovering round the bar all the time. She slides off her stool and chooses a squashy leather chair beside a glass-topped table. Stefan is talking to the couple at the bar, about the Tate and the harbour, the beaches. Vicky takes out her phone and swiftly googles *Amity Cove drowning*. As soon as she hits search, she remembers the beach has another name, Amity is only the moniker given to it by the locals, but the screen fills with links, and there she is. Nina. A head and shoulders photograph of a young laughing girl with sun-streaked hair wearing a wetsuit. Vicky shields her phone from the light and scrolls down. It's coming back to her now. She does remember something about the incident, and how it sparked an online debate about beaches without lifeguards. She wonders if Nina minds that tiny molecules of her are forever trapped in a crystal on Stefan's finger.

~

Tansy googles Gareth's address in Hayle as soon as he sends it to her. It looks like an old warehouse or something converted into flats. She checks where she can park. She wonders now why she suggested the weekend. It's days away. Yes, the girls will be with Charlie, but surely she could have sorted out something with Emmeline before then. She could text him again and suggest meeting earlier. Her finger hesitates. No, that looks so desperate. She hardly knows him after all. She doesn't know how he spends his days.

~

There are more people in the bar now. Skinny girls in tight black dresses bring trays of lunches to tables. Vicky feels out of place alone at her table. It's always the same. She envisages herself in an arty coffee shop or a wine bar, sitting comfortably alone reading or people-watching, but the reality is that she feels awkward, like an unsightly boil.

When she looks at the other drinkers she knows she looks more dishevelled, more dull, more *wrong*, sitting there alone, looking as though she's putting a brave face on being stood up.

She finishes her drink. Too much pineapple juice really. Her stomach feels tight and wrinkled inside. As she puts on her jacket Stefan appears beside her and scoops up her empty tumbler.

"You didn't have to move."

"I was looking at the sea."

What a stupid, thoughtless thing to say. But Stefan lives in St Ives on the ferocious north coast; he works in this bar with its huge windows to the ocean. He must be aware of the sea and the tides all the time. He must watch the changing skies over the bay. He will see surfers, tiny black seal-heads in the water, and remember or, worse, forget and think one is Nina.

"Come over again. It's a lovely spot to sit and think."

"I will. Yes."

"Thanks so much for the ring. I'll take better care of it next time."

Vicky taps her pocket for her phone. "OK, I've got to make a doctor's appointment now. I'll see you."

"See you soon."

Stefan takes the glass back to the bar. Vicky walks out to the car park. The wind scrabbles at her hair, flicks it into her eyes. She might as well call the surgery from here. Her contraceptive implant is almost due to come out and, as Kev hasn't been anywhere near her for two years, she can't see the point of having a new one fitted. It's making her fat. Better off without it. Now she sounds like Skye, fussing about a few pounds. There's a difference though, between a woman of thirty-nine and a girl of fourteen. She'll be better off without the damn thing pumping hormones into her. Get back to being natural again. Feel the pulse of her body, its own song.

It's still a bleak admission, she thinks once more, tapping the number into the keypad. That part of her life is over. No, she corrects herself. It's over with Kev. Not forever. Surely not.

~

"Are you going to be there?" Jake asks Tansy.

Tansy glances at the clock. It's almost time to go. She's collecting Ivor's prescription on the way to fetch the girls. Jake always rings at inconvenient times. But then, he was never a proper father, so school collection times won't mean anything to him.

"I doubt it. Too embarrassing."

"It's not just me. There's half a dozen or so. Ted McKinnon, Anita Ford, Matt Tyler, Jason Stein. Christ, he'd better be sober at a primary school."

"I think I'll stay away, thanks. Scarlet would be embarrassed. Mel's helping, I think. You know, one of Grandad's carers. She does lots there. Christmas fairs, raffles, all that. Sure she said she was doing the art week. Which year have you got? You haven't got Scarlet?"

"No, I think they're a bit older. Not sure."

"Well, don't embarrass Scarlet, whatever you do."

Or me, Tansy thinks, as she hangs up.

~

"He had a problem with his phone," Abi tells Izzy. "He didn't get any of my messages."

"Right." Izzy casts her eyes round the café. No one raises a hand or nods her over. "He has now then."

"Yes." Abi swipes her screen with a sticky finger. "Dammit, got cake on it." She wipes the glass on her apron, then reads the message aloud: "Sorry Abi, not ignoring you. Didn't get your messages. Yes, everything's OK. Catch you soon. Kiss kiss kiss."

"See, it's all fine," Abi says.

Oh come on!, Izzy wants to shout. *He's pissing around with you.* Izzy has no idea what Rick's problem is. Probably just that he's met a girl he fancies more than Abi, or that Abi's neuroses and stress have been too much for him to handle. If he were a real man, a kind man, a man who loved Abi, he'd handle it. He'd kiss the bumpy scars on her arms, and would do anything, anything at all, to protect her from ending up in that place again. Izzy shivers with a sudden chill, remembering the things Abi has done: the streamers of blood from her arms, the time she thought she'd overdosed on paracetamol, but was too drunk to realise she hadn't taken any, the nights she'd lie curled up beside Izzy sobbing and sobbing until Izzy thought her own heart would break. *Don't you dare hurt her*, Izzy almost says it aloud.

Instead she says, "Well, as you're feeling better now, can you give me a moment? I want to call Ivor and see how he got on with the doctor."

—

Vicky lets herself into the house. Her visit to see Stefan has bitten hours off the day. Soon the kids will be home, Skye from school, and Harry from the sixth form. And then Kev at some time. She'd better sort out what they'll have for dinner.

She writes her appointment time on the kitchen calendar as simply *Vicky Dr.* The house is quiet but for the odd whoosh from the boiler. Empty. Skye has been asking for a new kitten since the death of their cat, Schrodinger, last year. Vicky has stalled because she realises that, even subconsciously, she knows times are changing. Just the word divorce looks like a sword thrust through the family home, but surely the kids won't be that surprised? Surely they have noticed their parents don't sleep together or even talk to each other most of the time. Surely they know that's not how a marriage should be.

"I don't want this," Vicky says aloud to the calendar, the boiler, the ghost of Schrodinger.

She has no idea what will happen. Will Kev shout and sulk and blame her, or will he be secretly relieved she's brought it to a close? They'll have to sell the house, she'll need somewhere smaller for her and the children. The children will want to be with her, won't they? Does she nag Skye too much about her dieting? Harry will be off to uni in no time. Will she be left completely alone like Stefan?

He's stuck in a terrible rut too. A young guy like him, a nice-looking guy, with a good job, he shouldn't be tied to a dead girl. Not two years later. But Stefan's grief is real. Even so, Vicky thinks, he should be looking, even gently, for a girl, someone to share his life with, have a family with maybe. He can't spend his life in mourning. It's not living.

~

Izzy runs down the stairs, retying her apron behind her. She's called Ivor from the quieter upper floor and he's told her the doctor has given him antibiotics. Izzy's relieved. She waits at the bottom of the stairs for a couple to leave their table, noticing that a string of pink fairy lights has a couple of dead bulbs that need replacing, then she gathers together their teapots and cups. Her mother is back from her foray into town and is talking intensely to Abi behind the counter. The couple from the table hover at the till; Holly breaks away from Abi to take the man's card. Izzy loads up the dirties onto a tray to take to the kitchen upstairs.

When she comes down again Holly is wiping the table with furious strokes of the cloth.

"Mum?"

"She's invited that twat over tonight," Holly whispers. "I told her I don't want him there the way he's going on."

"That must have gone down well."

"I said Aidan and I would probably go out for a drink if he's going to be there. I don't really want to go out. I'm tired when I'm done here, but I'm so angry. Come with us, if you like?"

"Maybe. You can't be booted out of your house because of him."

"No, but I just don't want to see him today. She's all happy now because he's texted her with some crap about his mobile not working. I don't believe it."

"Nor me." Izzy doesn't think Abi looks happy now, tugging at her plait and scowling at the cappuccino machine.

"I can't have her ill again," Holly says. "I can't go through that again."

"No," Izzy agrees. "If only she'd go back on her meds I'd feel better."

"You know how she went on when I asked her about that." Holly adjusts the flower vase in the centre of the table, and straightens a picture on the wall, an abstract collage of newspaper cuttings, strips of lace, and paint streaks.

"Come on, she's looking at us."

"Thank you for being so safe and sensible, Izzy. I don't ever worry about you."

It never occurs to Izzy to be jealous of Abi, and of the attention Holly and Aidan, and everyone, give her because of her illness. Abi's her little sister and she loves her completely. Rash, reckless, angry Abi. Izzy knows that, compared with Abi, she is safe and sensible, and not a worry to her family. That doesn't mean I don't feel anything though, she wants to say to Holly, but her mother has squeezed back behind the counter, and Abi is jabbing her finger at her phone, texting Rick, no doubt.

~

Tansy feels as though the week is creeping and racing at the same time. It must be the craziness of it all, the sheer incredible luck of meeting Gareth in the bookshop. Five minutes either way and they'd have missed each other, and she would still never have experienced the gorgeous swooping of her heart that she feels now each day.

She buys a bottle of Chilean Merlot to take for him. She was surprised, when she told him about the years of her sobriety, that he seemed neither shocked nor impressed. She stays up late at night after the girls and her mother are asleep, and waits for the flare of red to light her mobile with a new message. He tells her he's been doing some casual work on a building site for a few days, and there might be more coming up. He tells her he can't wait to see her, that he wishes she were with him right now. She pours herself another tumbler of Shiraz, and, her inhibition blunted by the wine, asks him if he's going to fuck her at the weekend. He replies: *do you want me to? X.*

~

"It's embarrassing," Skye says. "I shouldn't be doing this."

"He said he'd love to see your work." Vicky clicks in her seat belt and fires the ignition. The radio flares into life. "Ivor wouldn't have said that if he didn't mean it. He's not that sort. He's dead straight."

"I don't have anything good to show him. I don't have enough."

"He was an art teacher once, you know. He'll remember what it's like."

Skye's black portfolio is in the back seat. She has selected the best of her school artwork and the drawings she does at home. There's a large mixed media still life of leeks and swedes, murky shades of khaki and green. There are pencil sketches of objects round the house: a teapot, plants, a pair of trainers, shells. A couple of quick portraits of Harry, who sat for her in a rare moment of helpfulness.

"Are you and Dad getting divorced?" Skye asks suddenly.

Vicky turns the radio down. "Nothing's happening at the moment."

"But you don't like each other. Anyone can see that. You don't even speak to each other. He forgot your birthday. You were ever so upset. Harry says –"

"What does Harry say?"

"He thinks you're waiting for me to finish school and then you'll split up. Is that it?"

Vicky swallows. Harry has pretty much voiced what's in her own head.

"I don't know, love. You're right. We don't get on very well. We seem to have drifted apart. I haven't said anything to your dad though. Has he said anything to you?"

"Nothing. But he doesn't speak to us much, does he? Does he love us? Me and Harry? Even if he doesn't like you?"

"Of course he does. Don't ever doubt that. We both love you two more than anything."

"That's like a line. What parents say when they get divorced."

"Well, in most cases I'm sure it's true. Look, my parents got divorced, you know that. They both loved me and my sisters. We all knew that. But not each other. They were both happier apart. You've only known them apart so you can't see the difference."

"And then if you do, you'll both marry other people, and they'll have kids, and suddenly me and Harry have to, like, get on with these kids we don't even know. Like what happened to Tasha when her mum married. And look what happened to Danielle, don't you remember? Her mum married that guy and he started fiddling with Danni."

"Hold on, hold on. No-one's marrying anyone. No-one's doing anything. I know things aren't great with your dad and me. OK? I know that, but I'm so bloody tired and I have so much to do, I can't think properly about it. I'd never hurt you and Harry, and neither would Kev. Please tell Harry that if you two talk about it."

"Don't you want to know what we think you should do?"

Vicky turns into Ivor's road. She's pretty sure she shouldn't have said half the things she's said, but she doesn't know what she should have said instead. She wasn't prepared for this. She didn't realise the situation was so obvious to Skye and Harry. Is this why Skye has been starving herself? She never thought of that.

"Well?" She parks in front of Ivor's bungalow. "What do you and Harry think?"

Skye shrugs. "He thinks you should do what you want. What's best for you guys."

"And you?" Vicky asks as gently as she can.

"I don't know."

Vicky squeezes Skye's knee. "Let's go and see Ivor. You show him your stuff and listen to what he says. I'll do a bit of cleaning and tidying while you two chat and then I'll get him washed and changed. Come on."

―

Carol often thinks of the night she met Ivor Martin, twenty years ago, when she was forty. About the age Tansy is now. At the time she and

Louis were living in a tiny terraced house in the backstreets of Penzance. She was working in a dress shop and doing cleaning on the side. It was hard work bringing up Louis alone, and working all hours. She had a few friends in town, parents of kids Louis was at school with. Her sister lived nearby with her two girls. Louis was often shipped out to these other houses while Carol was at work. Sometimes at the weekend he'd come with her to the cleaning jobs. If they were at a house he'd bring a book and sit quietly and politely, perhaps accepting a glass of orange juice from the homeowner, and when Carol worked at the holiday park, cleaning the chalets, he'd escape to the kids' playpark: the swings, the high slides, the wobbly wooden walkways. A couple of times Carol's sister and her girls went swimming at the holiday park pool and Louis went with them. And then suddenly, overnight, it seemed to Carol, he moved up to secondary school and he chose to stay at home alone, watching TV or doing homework, rather than traipse around her grotty jobs with her.

Louis wasn't with her the night she met Ivor. He was at her sister's. In her youth, before Louis was born, Carol had done a bit of drawing and painting. But life got in the way of art, and having Louis put an end to those dreams.

That Saturday night she went to a private view in a gallery in Chapel Street. Of course she knew the name Ivor Martin. Anyone in west Cornwall who knew anything about art knew Ivor Martin's work, his giant abstracts and his economical, atmospheric charcoal sketches. He was one of the artists exhibiting at the gallery that night. A couple Carol knew tugged her over to meet him. He was standing before a huge brooding painting of Lanyon Quoit, streaky black teardrops cascading down the canvas, chatting to a small group of people. At seventy-five, he was still straight-backed and muscular, with a shock of white crazy-professor hair. His eyes were the most incredible green, Carol noticed immediately. The green of sea-glass, somehow both hazy and clear. He offered his hand, and she shook it, glad he was not an air-kisser. And, in that moment, the whole trajectory of her life changed.

~

Vicky settles Ivor and Skye together with glasses of cordial and a packet of ginger biscuits, and retreats to the kitchen. She fills the sink with soapy water and starts washing down the worktops. She removes the filthy bottle of Baby Bio and the hard sliver of soap and wipes the windowsill clean. Ivor is saying something to Skye about using warm colour to bring the subject forward. Vicky's heart still races from the conversation in the car. People always see more than you give them credit for. Perhaps the time has come to speak to Kev, ask him what he wants to do. Vicky squirts Dettol onto the taps and rubs them till they gleam. She doesn't want to talk to Kev, because she's afraid he'll say they can sort it out, and she knows now, that is not what she wants. She wants to be free of him.

~

Emmeline is reading Ivor's shopping list to add to their internet order.
"Coffee, you know, the South American one."
Tansy jabs at her mobile phone.
"Mummy, can I see a Duggee film?" Amber tries to grab the phone.
"Not while I'm doing this, darling. Maybe after if I've got any battery."
"Coffee. You got that?"
"Yes."

"Small bananas. A brown sliced loaf. A bottle of cordial. Not orange or lemon, something more exciting. Elderflower perhaps."

"Mummy. Please. A Duggee video. The one where –"

"Not now, Amber."

A message flashes up at the top of Tansy's screen. Gareth Crane. She wants to tap on it, to abandon Sainsbury's a moment, but Emmeline is ticking off items on the pad in front of her quicker than Tansy can add them.

"Washing up liquid. Cheese."

"Mummy!"

"Amber." Scarlet appears in the doorway. "Come and make a birthday card for Daddy with me. Mummy, have we got any glue? We need glue to make a card."

"I'll get them glue while you add those." Emmeline stands up. "Two pints of semi-skimmed."

Tansy fumbles through mature cheddar and milk. Emmeline is still with the girls, so she taps open the message and smiles and remembers that kiss in the car park in the rainshine.

~

There's never anywhere to park in Charlie's street. Tansy pulls up outside his door and hoots the horn. She leaves the engine running and jumps out. It's Saturday morning and Charlie's young assistant is running the shop. He has all weekend with his daughters.

"Quickly, onto the pavement," she says to the girls as Charlie opens the front door straight onto the street.

"Daddy!" Scarlet throws herself at Charlie.

"Happy birthday," Amber mumbles.

"It's not till tomorrow, sweetheart." Charlie ruffles her bright hair.

Tansy hands over the girls' overnight bag and a cardboard box of presents.

"Now, you two have a lovely time with Daddy, and I'll see you tomorrow."

"You're welcome to have lunch with us," Charlie says. "Or do something in the afternoon?"

"I'm not quite sure what I'm doing," Tansy says. "I'll call you. Look, I must move. Bye girls, bye Charlie." A car hovers behind her Golf and she dives back behind the wheel.

She is very lucky, she thinks again, as she drives down the narrow road of terraced houses. She never worries when the girls stay with their father. She doesn't dread handing them over as so many mothers do. She knows, if there were a problem, or if one of the girls were ill or unhappy, he would be straight on to her. In some ways it was sad they couldn't make things work as a couple, but Tansy knows they – and the girls – are much happier now. And, if she were still with Charlie, she wouldn't be going to Hayle later to meet Gareth Crane.

She leaves Penzance behind and guns down the lanes back to Gerent's Cross. She has promised to call in at Ivor's on the way home, to check how he is, if his chest is still improving, and if he needs anything from the shop that he might have forgotten to give them for the internet order.

When she arrives at his house Mel's car is parked outside. Ivor is still at the table finishing a late breakfast of cereal and tea. Tansy drops a kiss on his head.

"Your chest seems better," she says. "And your gout."

His swollen finger joints have subsided and the skin is a more usual colour, not strained and shiny.

"Thought I heard you," Mel calls, coming out of the bedroom with her arms full of laundry. "Just been changing his bed."

"I forgot to tell you yesterday," Tansy says. "Lanyon House has asked me for a reference."

"Really? I thought I'd cocked up the interview. I was so nervous."

"I'll email you a copy before I send it," Tansy promises. "Grandad, when you've finished that tea, how about a quick game of crib? Shall I get the cards?"

Tansy can't concentrate. Her mind rushes ahead to the afternoon, to driving to Hayle, to finding his door and knocking, and whatever happens next. Ivor plays a two to her ace; she responds with a three, and knows, from the grin on his face, that he can make a run.

"So what are you doing this weekend then, without the girls?"

"They're with Charlie. It's his birthday tomorrow."

"I know. Are you doing anything interesting?" Ivor gathers the cards and shuffles, slowly, carefully. Even with his better joints he fumbles and a couple of cards flutter to the table.

"I'm meeting that guy I told you about," Tansy says, not meeting his eye. "The one I met in town."

"What's this?" Mel asks, grinning, coming back from the kitchen with a pile of clean socks. "Meeting a man?"

"This afternoon," Tansy says.

"You be careful." Ivor discards cards for the box. "You don't really know him at all, do you?"

~

The sky has gradually been darkening and by the time Tansy leaves her house the air is clotted with damp fog. She covers her hair with her hood.

The drive to Hayle seems to take no time at all, her wipers cutting anxious swathes across the windscreen. She knows the directions from

Google off by heart and finds the car park down a side street. She checks her face one last time in the driving mirror.

Gareth's building stands at a junction. Some old warehouse. Three stone steps to the front door. There's no shelter from the rain. The bottle of Merlot is cold in her hand. She rings the bell for his flat. She's here. He asked her; she's here. No going back now.

"Hi," his voice crackles through the intercom.

"Hi, it's me," she says, but of course he knows it's her.

The door unlocks with a click. She steps into a hall, with pigeon-holes on the right and a wide staircase on the left. On the back wall, under the stairs, is a door for the ground floor flats. It swings open on the fluffy pale carpet. Lamps come on automatically as she runs down a short flight of steps and into the back corridor. His door is the last on the right. She knocks, and finds she's holding her breath.

"Tansy, hi," he says.

His hair is loose. He's wearing a patchwork shirt over jeans. Some elaborate beaded necklace.

"This is for you." She hands him the bottle. She is surprised he hasn't kissed her, or even hugged her.

"Come in."

She follows him into the flat. There is a kitchen area with a lot of white and chrome and, beyond that, the living space. He has a sofa scattered with cushions, bookcases, a pile of sketchbooks, shoes thrown around. There's a window on the back wall, with a wide white sill which is crammed with junk: a fat cactus in a Mexican pot, his mobile phone charging, a pair of sunglasses, a handful of pebbles and shells, paperback books. Tansy takes off her jacket and throws it on the sofa.

"Would you like a glass?" Gareth asks.

"Better not, I'm driving."

She could have one, just one glass. But she couldn't. If she has one, she'll have another, and another, and somehow she thinks she should be sober anyway for this encounter, which is not going quite how she imagined at all.

"Tea would be good."

"Tea then. But I'm having some of this."

Tansy watches Gareth twist open the bottle and slop an inch or two into a chunky mug. He finds a second mug, chunky too but mismatched, and drops in a tea bag.

"Can you see the estuary from here?"

"Not this room. You can upstairs."

Tansy wanders back to the window, looks out. Rain is falling, needle-sharp onto the concrete ledge outside, onto the churned-up gravel of a building site behind the house. The roofs are grey, the sky is grey. Indian ink, she thinks irrelevantly, Indian ink, and lots of water. Tear tracks.

"Here," Gareth hands her a mug of tea. "Would you like to see the rest of the place?"

She follows him up the stairs, carpeted in the same soft shade as the corridor outside. In his bedroom upstairs there is a futon, with a purple duvet, more bookcases, a pile of clothes, another wide windowsill with more junk. She finds a space for her mug on it and squints out. Over the building site, over the roofs, she can see the steely dash of the estuary beyond. Still he has not touched her, and she wonders – oh fuck – if she has got this wrong, so terribly wrong, if the things she has been texting have been way off the mark, if she looks arrogant and foolish.

"Are you OK?" he asks her.

"I'm OK." She picks up a large chunk of amethyst from his windowsill, closes her fingers round its icy heart. A healing stone, one to ward off drunkenness. "I suppose I wondered, I mean, what, have I got things very wrong?"

Gareth drinks wine, and Tansy can smell its perfume in the air.

"You haven't got it wrong," he says.

~

Carol wonders what the hell they can have for dinner. It's raining, a slatey dark rain, and she doesn't want to go out again to buy food. Jeff is still in his chair by the hearth. He hasn't moved for hours, except to turn a page in the giant hardbacked autobiography he's reading. Or rather, a ghostwritten autobiography of some boxer Carol has never heard of. Each time she looks at Jeff, there is a thicker chunk of pages to the left of the book's spine. She doesn't think she's ever seen him read anything so enthusiastically. Carol checks her phone to see the rota Tansy has sent out. Yes, she's right. It's Izzy again tonight.

"You all right?" Jeff asks without looking up as Carol stands.

"I'm just going to see what we can eat tonight."

Jeff grunts and Carol leaves him to it.

Are you mad? Louis said to her when she told him she was marrying Jeff. *You? Marry him?*

Carol didn't think she was mad, not at the time. Now she wonders. It's not that there's anything terribly wrong with Jeff, except that he's boring, and he doesn't like Louis. Really, those are two pretty important things. He was willing to move away from his daughters in the South-East to come back to Cornwall with her. That was a big sacrifice. Or was it? He doesn't make much effort to keep in touch with them. They have their mother nearby who is more use for babysitting and the like. They don't seem to miss him. Carol misses Louis terribly. It's not even like she can ask him down to stay at the cottage. He'd have to stay somewhere else. Not here with Jeff.

She opens the freezer and peers in. A few ready meals, some oven chips, pizza.

She wishes she were going to Ivor's tonight. She could talk to him. Tell him she should never have married Jeff. Twice she has been offered marriage. She refused the right man and accepted the wrong one.

~

"Take a picture of me."

Tansy scrabbles a hand over the side of the futon, finds her jeans and tugs her mobile out of the pocket.

"A picture?"

"I want to keep this moment for ever. I'm so happy now. Whatever happens, I'll have this moment."

She hands him the phone. He slides his jeans back on and rakes back his hair. She watches him, astonished and shocked and overwhelmed at what has surged into her life. She wants a picture of her now, lying laughing in Gareth's bed, to keep this moment forever. He throws the phone down on the bedcover. Tansy stares down into her own face. Luminous eyes, dark hair everywhere and a smile more radiant than she's ever seen on herself. She clicks the image away because already it belongs in the past, the moment has gone, and suddenly there are tears in her eyes because she will never be that girl, caught in that picture, ever again.

~

"Have you ever modelled?" Ivor Martin asked Carol at the long ago private view.

"What, like clothes?" she asked, confused.

"No, no," he laughed. "For an artist. Because you have a wonderful profile. Here." He sketched a line before her cheeks with a finger. "I would love to paint you."

"I thought you were a landscape artist. That's the work of yours I know."

"Mostly, yes. But I do work with people. Portraits, life drawing. My granddaughter Tansy sits for me sometimes. Would you ever like me to draw you, paint you? I would like it very much."

When Carol left the private view she held a small square of card tightly in her hand. Ivor Martin's number.

~

They stand side-by-side at the window. Tansy finds her mug of cold tea and takes a swig. It's bitter in her throat. Rain cracks against the glass, turning the lights of Hayle into wet stars. The flat feels so warm and cosy, that bed behind her so inviting. She wants to fling off her clothes and dive down under the covers with Gareth again.

"I don't want to go," she says at last.

"I don't want you to."

I don't have to, she almost says. I could stay a little longer. I don't have to be anywhere.

She was taken aback, hurt, when he said to her ten minutes before, "Come on, I must get moving. Got to get some shopping."

Shopping?! she wanted to ask. On a rainy Saturday evening? What the hell do you need so badly?

But he had risen from the futon and found his shirt and suddenly Tansy felt odd and alone lying there, as if waiting for a man who would not return.

She puts down her mug with a clunk. She doesn't want to leave. She doesn't want to drive home through the storm.

"I've had a lovely time," Gareth says.

He tugs the blind cord, and Tansy's view of the amber lights outside squeezes to nothing. Purple bed cover, circle of lamplight, alarm clock, chunky mug, a red T-shirt thrown across the chair: Tansy fixes all these images in her head. She thinks she may never see them again.

Gareth runs down the stairs and she has to follow. Turning her back on that room feels insurmountable. In the little hall below Gareth is putting on his boots, unhooking his long coat from a peg. Tansy retrieves her own jacket from the sofa. The lower window is uncurtained, and she can identify a few of the starry street lights she saw from above. As she turns to Gareth her eyes slide to the bottle of Merlot on the counter: black wine in the green glass. *When I'm home. I'll have a drink when I get home.*

The wall lights click on silently as they walk back along the corridor, feet hushed on the soft pile. Up the steps, through the door and into the cavernous hall. Gareth unlocks the front door and a squall of rain blows in.

"I'm going to the Spar down there," he gestures.

"OK. I'm parked the other way."

He's not going to walk me to the car. This is where we part. Here in the dark and the rain.

"Would you like to meet up again?" he asks.

"Of course. I mean, yes, that'd be lovely. Yes."

"Drop me a line."

He opens his arms and she stumbles into him, inhales the scent of his skin and his hair. He kisses her quickly, intensely.

She plods through the puddles and turns once, but he has gone. The car park is very dark. There are only a couple of other cars there, all parked far from each other. She walks out of the shadows, keys in hand. When she gets into the familiar cocoon of the Golf, she finds the mirror still skewed from when she checked her face. From when she was a different Tansy Martin. She takes out her mobile. Yes, it did really happen. She was in that flat, in that bed, with that man. She gazes down at the other Tansy's wide joyful smile and wonders if she'll ever smile like that again.

~

"She's an idiot." Izzy soaps Ivor's legs with a clean cloth.

The kitchen smells of his tikka masala, which is warming up. Izzy reaches for a towel and dries Ivor carefully, noting a few cracks in his skin. She'll put extra cream on those areas.

"Over ninety years' experience has taught me that people rarely realise when they're being idiots."

"Sure it didn't take you ninety years to find that out." Izzy grins up at Ivor as she smooths emollient up his calf.

Ivor chuckles and braces himself with his Zimmer to stand up so Izzy can slide on his pyjama bottoms.

"There's something really wrong with him. Abi can't see it. Why's he going on like this? Storming off, then making up, then ignoring her, making up again? That's not normal. That's not a man with nothing to hide."

"No," Ivor agrees. "But she won't listen to you. She'll have to find out for herself. It's the only way. People don't want to hear things. Oww."

"You OK?" Izzy grabs him.

"Just a twinge in the knee. There. That's all right. What about you, Izzy? Have you got a boyfriend?"

"God no."

Tansy lets herself in quietly. Her hood blew off when she got out on the drive, and her hair is wet. She feels cold and shivery, happy and unhappy at the same time. Emmeline is watching TV.

"Good time?"

"Um. Yes. Yes." Thirty-eight and still embarrassed.

"I thought you might be later. Or…"

Or not home until morning, Tansy fills in. *I never got that choice.*

She goes out to the hall to hang up her soaking coat. A red dot glints at her from her phone.

Are you home safe? X

Yes, home now X

I'm sorry, I should have walked you to the car. X

Doesn't matter. X

Didn't mean to be rude. X

I know. X

Tansy helps herself to some chocolates from an open box of Milk Tray. She pours herself a tumbler of Merlot. She wonders what Gareth is doing. Is he reading or watching a film? Is he thinking of her? Does he miss her? Suddenly she misses the girls' warm bodies and sticky kisses. She'd give anything to hold them both in her arms, breathe in their sweaty smells, stroke their fine hair.

She showers quickly, tops up her glass, and goes to sit with her mother in front of the TV. Her mobile nestles beside her.

Thanks for this wine. I'm finishing it now. It's a really good one. X

I wish I were there with you, drinking it. She doesn't type this.

I love the pic of me. I look amazing. X

You are amazing. I'd love that pic on my wall. X

Ivor made tea for Carol and led her out the back door and along a path to his garden studio. She stopped and gazed in the doorway. There were two huge canvases on the walls. One brown and khaki, with splashes of yellow.

"Daffodil fields?" Carol asked.

"Yes," Ivor beamed.

"I could see it straight away."

"This is the moorland by Zennor." He indicated the second canvas, a giant square of red and black and rust.

There were other canvases and frames stashed against the walls. A stained sink. Shelves with paints; brushes and pens in jars. A stick of charcoal was shattered on the floor.

"Come and sit here." Ivor pulled out a chair.

Carol sat and stared round at the drawings tacked on the walls, the row of books on the shelf, the tools propped in the corner. Ivor fiddled with his easel and stool, with his drawing board and box of charcoal.

"Just look towards the bookcase," he said. "That's all there is to it."

~

Tansy wakes with a bruise on her sternum and an ache in her heart. She texts Charlie a quick happy birthday. There's nothing from Gareth. She checks his Facebook. Has he written something like *I had a wonderful day yesterday?* No. He put up a link for some singer-songwriter she hasn't heard of. She checks the time he posted it. About three in the morning. There are two likes under it. A guy and a girl. Not the blondes.

"I'm going to Dad's to have lunch with him." Emmeline says. "Do you want to come?"

"I'll head into town. Go to Charlie's. Spend a bit of time with him and the girls."

Emmeline leaves just after eleven. Tansy sees Gareth is on Facebook, having an exchange with another bloke under the link to the singer.

Hey, how are you? Would you like to meet up this week? X

She stares at the little grey dot, waiting for it to flare into his profile picture to show he has read it, but nothing happens. He is still online, she can see that. She makes a cup of tea, checks again. Still online and he still has not opened her message. Her heartbeat starts to rush a tiny bit.

Everything all right? X

She shouldn't have done that. She should have just left it. Now he doesn't appear to be online. So she doesn't text him as well, grabs her car keys and drives into Penzance.

"Hey, happy birthday," she says when Charlie opens the door, and kisses him on the cheek.

The girls are still in their pyjamas. Wrapping paper lies ragged on the floor.

"Shall we all go and have a bite?" Charlie asks. "How about Samarkand? That's the one your new carer works at, isn't it?"

"Yes, Izzy."

"OK, come on girls, get dressed and we'll go."

"Just going to the bathroom." Tansy runs upstairs and clicks the bathroom lock.

Still no reply to her messages. They are still unread and Gareth is back online again. She shoves the phone away. She's got to act normal with Charlie and the girls. There's no reason to think anything is awry with Gareth. He sent her lovely messages just twelve hours ago. Now she is being paranoid.

~

"Oh well, nice of you to turn up." Holly loads two cappuccinos onto a tray.

"I'm sorry," Abi says. "It's just, you know, things have been difficult, and now it all seems OK again, and Rick wanted to make me breakfast. I did call."

"Yeah, but I wanted a lie-in," Izzy says, taking the tray from Holly.

"You go home now, Izzy," Abi says.

Izzy glances at Holly, who nods. "Yes, you get off, love. Thanks."

As Izzy steps out into the rainy sunshine she almost collides with Tansy and her girls and that guy Charlie from the music shop in Chapel Street.

"Hi," Izzy says. "I'm just off. I had to cover for my sister for a while."

Tansy looks bloody tense, Izzy thinks. She wonders if Charlie is like Rick, blowing hot and cold with her. Don't think about Rick the Prick. Just go home and have a snooze.

~

Sunday afternoon in the hotel bar, and Stefan has a quiet moment. It's getting busier each week now as the season kicks off. The women in the bar are all with men, except for a group of three girls drinking bright cocktails at the table where Vicky sat. He polishes a glass absently and watches them: one swiping on her mobile, another applying a coat of lip gloss, the third dripping a stiletto off her toes. He imagines Nina inserted into the group and can't. She was too natural, too wholesome, too real. Her sun-faded hair, often unruly and never properly styled, was so much more beautiful to Stefan than the sleek cuts and highlights of the girls in the window. Perhaps it shouldn't matter who; perhaps he should just find a girl and talk to her and fuck her, and break this lonely cycle, this vigil, he's built for himself.

~

Sorry Tansy, just feeling crappy today. Hope all OK. X
   Are you ill? X
   Migraine. X
   Too much red? X
   Maybe. Going for a lie down. X
   OK, look after yourself. X

~

The girls are dancing round Emmeline, telling her all about their weekend with Charlie, the birthday presents, the lunch out. Their overnight bag is dumped in the hall. Tansy is about to empty it, put the laundry in the washing machine, dig out Scarlet's book and new hairbrush and Amber's Tiger and all the other junk, when she remembers Mel's reference.

She leaves the girls with Emmeline and opens up her laptop in her room. Lanyon House has sent her a form to fill in. The questions are short and easy. She sends a draft to Mel, and quickly opens up Facebook. Gareth comes up online. She checks her messages. He has not opened her last one. This is getting crazy. Just turn off the bloody laptop, and turn off the phone too. A pop-up jumps onto her screen. Mel is more than happy with the reference. OK, send the reference to Lanyon House and then turn it all off.

She slams the laptop lid down and kills her phone to a black screen. The girls need a bath and then she's got their lunches to make for the next day. Chopped tomatoes and strawberries, a little sandwich for Amber, crackers for Scarlet, cartons of juice. She will not check up on Gareth until bedtime.

~

When Izzy comes back from Ivor's on Monday morning the house is quiet. Too quiet. Holly and Aidan left early, before Izzy set off, but she expected Abi to be up by now, at least downstairs in the kitchen, as she is due at Samarkand.

"Abi," Izzy calls as she slams the front door shut.

She gathers up a sheaf of envelopes on the mat: a couple of flyers. Something for Aidan, a catalogue for Holly. No sign of Abi in the kitchen. No dirty mugs or breakfast leftovers.

Izzy drops the post and bounds upstairs. She knows, she instinctively knows, something is wrong. Abi's bedroom door is shut. Izzy shoves it open. Abi is curled on her bed, her long hair loose and all over the place.

In two strides Izzy is there. There is a streak of blood on the duvet cover.

"Abi."

Abi turns. Her face is red and blotchy. Izzy takes her hands, flinches at the blood on her arms.

"Abi, it's OK. I'm here." She holds her sister, strokes the knotted hair from her face.

"He's left me."

Izzy's breathing is calming. This day has been coming for so long. She knew Abi would hurt herself again, and she knew Rick would be the reason.

"I thought everything was good? He made you breakfast."

"He left me. Read it." Abi waves her hand towards her mobile on the nightstand.

"By text?"

"Email. It's *not working*. Read it."

"I don't want to. Not now anyway. Can I help you clean your arms? Get some plasters?"

At last Izzy sees what she's been searching for. A Stanley knife in the folds of the bedcovers. Its triangular blade looks black and dirty. It's the one from Aidan's tool box.

"And we'll give this a clean too and put it back, yes?"

Abi shrugs. She had a Stanley knife of her own. Holly threw it out after the last time.

"You need some iodine or something."

"I love him."

"I know, I know. I'm sure it'll blow over. Really."

"No. Not this time. You know what it's been like."

"Why has he left you? Did he say?"

"Read it."

"I don't want to."

"That it's *not working*. He's not *satisfied*. He wants more than I can give him."

"What does he want? Marriage?"

"I don't know. I tried to call him."

"Leave it for now. Let's just get these arms sorted out."

Izzy helps Abi to stand and holds her hand as they cross the landing. The cuts are not deep, but there are many. They cross over each other, where she drew the knife a second or third time. Izzy runs water in the bowl, gently washes Abi's arms. Abi flinches at the water on her broken skin.

"I'll pat them ever so carefully, then we'll wrap them up."

"Are you going to tell Mum?"

Izzy scrabbles in the cupboard for iodine and plasters.

"Not iodine. It hurts."

"The knife was dirty. You need something. Savlon then?"

"Savlon. Are you going to tell her?"

"About this or about Rick?"

"This. Both."

"I'll have to."

Gareth has still not opened Tansy's last message. She was about to ring him up, then thought better of it. How has it come to this so soon? On Saturday night he said he wanted her photo on his wall; now he isn't answering her. *Give him space*, Emmeline said. *You hardly know him? Far too soon to go rushing in like this.* Just what Ivor said too. Tansy is grateful that only Mel knew, and as she's got enough going on with the family and the guineas and the job application, hopefully she will have forgotten.

In the bathroom Tansy pulls up her T-shirt. The bruise is still there. She didn't imagine it. She still has the photo Gareth took. The photo to remind her she had been happy one day.

When she opens her Facebook again there is a message from Izzy in the group chat.

Sorry to be awkward, but my sister is pretty poorly. I may need cover for my shifts.

Carol has already responded.

I can cover pretty much any day. Hope things improve.

Tansy wonders what is wrong with Izzy's sister. Abi is younger than Izzy, can only be twenty-two or three. Not cancer, surely? She taps out a reply and opens up Gareth's profile. She doesn't realise until his picture comes up that she actually thought he might have deleted her. But no, he's still there.

The first person Mel calls is Joe at work.

"Fantastic," he says. "I knew you would."

"Well I didn't," Mel says. "I thought they'd want someone with more recent experience."

"Not necessarily. And you said Tansy wrote a great reference."

"I must tell her too."

Mel rings off and thinks she might get fish and chips for everyone's dinner as a celebration. She calls Tansy. When she speaks, she sounds distracted and vague.

"Have you heard from Izzy?" Mel asks.

"Nothing more. Carol said she could help out if necessary. I didn't want to ask too much."

"No, of course. Are you OK, Tansy?"

"Yeah fine. Just…tired."

"I'll tell Vicky I've got the job. Perhaps we could have a chat about the place."

"Good idea."

Definitely something wrong, Mel thinks. Tansy sounds sad and deflated. She seemed so happy the other morning at Ivor's. Buoyant even. Oh hell, she was going to meet some bloke at the weekend. That must be it. Bloody men.

"Vicky? It's Mel. Mel Atkins. I got the job."

"Hey, that's brilliant."

There's a lot of whooshing in the background. It sounds like Vicky is standing on the cliff in a gale.

"Are you at work?"

"Yeah. Just taking five outside. Pretty blowy up here."

"Could we have a chat before I start? It's been a while. I'm anxious."

"Of course. Later this week? Let's go for a drink."

"That'd be great. Where shall we go?"

Vicky doesn't answer for a moment, then says, "I know somewhere."

Tansy's phone rings and she jumps. It's Carol.

"Hi," Carol says. "I wanted to ask you: please could I do Ivor on his birthday?"

"Uh yes, of course."

"Either shift is fine. Or both. But I would like to see him that day."

"I'll make a note," Tansy says.

She hangs up, checks her texts and Facebook for messages.

Sorry Tansy, feeling really shitty at the moment. Nothing to do with you. X

Anything I can do? X

She watches the screen. He opens it. She waits still. He doesn't reply. She takes her diary off the shelf and pencils in Carol for Ivor's birthday. Carol's never said much about how she knew Ivor years ago. Tansy understands they met at private views and she thinks Carol may have modelled for him, though she's never seen the pictures. It was all a long time ago, twenty years or so. Then Carol and her son left Cornwall. That's pretty much all Tansy knows.

"Can I get you two another drink?" Stefan gathers up Mel's coffee cup and Vicky's tumbler.

"You got time for another?" Vicky asks. "I haven't got to do anything till the kids get back."

"Nor me," Mel says. "As long as I leave in time to collect the little ones."

"Thanks Stefan."

"Your two at school in St Ives?" Mel asks.

"Yes. Harry's at sixth form now. Yours at Gerent's Cross?"

"The girls, yes. The boys are at secondary. Why have I never been here before?" Mel gazes out of the long window at the aching blues of sea and sky. She loves St Ives in all seasons: the wind-blasted winter months and the blue and gold palette of summer. She's known about the hotel, of course, but she's never been inside.

"I came the other day to give Stefan his ring back."

Stefan appears at the table, with a fruit-filled tumbler for Vicky and a fresh pot of coffee. Mel glances at his hands, sees the flash of blue on his finger.

"And some more biscuits." He takes a plate of golden squares from the tray and places it between them.

"How did you have his ring?" Mel asks when he leaves the table.

"He left it at Ivor's. Tansy's girls nicked it. Luckily she found it. I brought it over for him as I'm the nearest." Vicky glances at Stefan, behind the bar, pulling a beer, and leans closer to Mel. "It's got his girlfriend's ashes in it. Really precious."

"Shit." Mel turns to Stefan, now taking a card from the customer at the bar.

"Tell you another time."

"We'll have plenty of other times at Lanyon."

"You'll be fine. Like I said, they're a nice bunch. So are most of the residents. Some are a bit tricky." Vicky drinks juice. "And there's no-one like Ivor."

"There's no-one like Ivor anywhere." Mel says. "D'you know, he's nearly ninety-six?"

"Lovely guy," Vicky says. "He looked at Skye's artwork for her."

"That's the sort of person he is." Mel adds a splash of milk to her coffee. "I so desperately want him to make a hundred."

"I'd say he has every chance. And we'll all be looking after him."

~

"We need to talk about the future," Emmeline says.

"Whose future?" Tansy asks, but she knows.

"I don't see how he can carry on living there on his own." Emmeline tugs out a chair and flops down at the table. She flicks through the sheaf of post Tansy left out for her. "But also I don't think we can do anything here. We don't have a room he could have, And he wouldn't want just a room. We know that."

Ivor wouldn't be content with a room. Not after the big bungalow he's lived in alone for years. Not after a garden to look out on, a garden drifting with daffodils and bluebells in spring, dusty roses in summer. Apple trees and a pear tree. The occasional hedgehog. A studio.

"What's the alternative?"

"Somewhere like Lanyon House."

"That's just a room."

"I know."

"And those other residents. And where would he paint? And he hated it there."

"I know, I know." Emmeline rubs her eyes. "Don't think I haven't gone over this. I lie awake worrying about it. We never seem to get the chance to talk, what with the girls, and you checking your messages every few minutes."

Tansy's face burns and she stares out of the window at the mossy terrace, the overgrown flower bed beyond.

"What do you think then?" she asks. "Have you spoken to him?"

"I can't. He's not well. The only other thing is we sell both the houses and find somewhere suitable for us all. But that could be impossible, selling both at the right time, and we'd need a downstairs annex kind of thing for him. I just don't know what to do."

"He thinks he can stay there. With his carers and us. And I get that he wants to. He doesn't want to leave his home."

"Of course not. Remember how sad he was when he handed in his driving licence?"

"All little losses of independence."

"I don't know what to do."

"If he carries on as he is he would be all right, wouldn't he?"

"I don't think it works like that," Emmeline says. "I think when people start to get frail they get more and more frail."

"We need to talk to him," Tansy suggests. "He's not stupid. And we can't do anything without him agreeing."

"He'll say he wants to stay at home."

"I know. But wouldn't you?"

"I would."

~

"Happy birthday." Carol kisses Ivor on his stubbly cheek. "I'll give you a shave later. Have you had a good day?"

She has made him a chocolate and vanilla cake, brought some lilies, and a couple of books. Jeff scowled at the lilies in their bowl in the kitchen, and scowled at Carol as she baked.

"I'm tired," Ivor says. "Stefan came to get me up. He brought me those." He gestures to a box of Ferrero Rocher on the table.

"Oh nice. Love those."

"Have one. Then Emmeline and Tansy brought the girls after school."

Carol smiles at the handmade cards from Scarlet and Amber. Scarlet has drawn a picture of Ivor with his Zimmer standing in a field of daffodils. Amber has made some abstract shapes and smudged some felt tip kisses inside.

"We had a cream tea," Ivor says. "So don't go making anything much for dinner."

"Just a sandwich perhaps. Come on, shall I give you a shave and a hair wash before we do your legs?"

"If you don't mind, that would be lovely, thank you."

"If I don't mind? Really."

"See, you never escaped looking after me." Ivor hauls himself to his feet and takes a heavy and tentative step.

"I enjoy it."

"I thought that was what you were running away from."

"Never that," Carol says.

She moves a chair out of his way and wonders again if she has told the complete truth.

—

Abi sits at the bottom of Izzy's bed. She is wearing a T-shirt and Izzy's eyes keep straying to the cuts on her arms, both the ones she helped clean up, and the fresh jagged ones, still knotty with dried blood.

"So he's come up with a reason then?" Izzy says. "It'd better be good. Have you told him how poorly you are?"

"Of course not."

"So, what's the reason?"

"I can't tell you."

"The other day you said I could read his message."

"Yeah, but you can't see this. It's…awful. It's…I love him, but I can't do this."

"Do what?" Izzy's head jerks up. "Do what?"

"Nothing."

"Is it drugs?"

"No. Nothing like that." Abi starts crying again.

Izzy's mind spins. Does Rick want Abi to kill herself or something?

"What? You're frightening me."

"Just stuff."

"Illegal stuff?"

"No. Please leave it."

Izzy reaches out and grabs Abi's hand to stop her tearing at the wounds.

"Look, I stuck up for you when Mum said you should see the doctor. I said to leave it and things would sort themselves out. You owe me one. Tell me what he wants you to do."

"Stuff," Abi says again. "Sex stuff. I can't do it."

~

It's some time after three in the morning. Tansy can't sleep. She pads into the kitchen, flicks on the light. The glare is hard in her eyes. Everything is harder, sharper: the rush of the tap in the kettle, the clunk of her mug on the worktop, her reflection in the dark window.

She is confused. Really confused. Gareth wanted her. That was real. She knows that was real. And yet, now he doesn't talk to her. Surely if he wanted to ditch her, he would delete her, but he hasn't.

He has even liked her posts and made the odd comment, but only on her public profile.

The kettle boils and she makes her tea, ignoring the half bottle of red left out from earlier. She sits at the table and drinks tea, and a plan falls into shape in her head. A plan so simple she cannot believe she didn't think of it before.

~

Izzy lies awake too. Fury wells up inside her like lava. Fury at the ghastly Rick and his demands on Abi. His blackmail. That if she won't do what he wants he will find someone else who will.

"I can't," Abi said to her over and over. "But I can't be without him."

Izzy doesn't want to betray Abi by telling Holly, but she thinks she will have to. She is frightened for Abi. Unable to give in to Rick's demands, and believing herself unable to live without him, would she find herself funnelled into a black hole? If anything happened to Abi and Izzy could have prevented it she would never find absolution.

Rick should be grateful to have a clever beautiful girl like Abi. He's nothing, Izzy thinks once more. Absolutely nothing but a bully. He's seen Abi's weakness, her lack of confidence. If he knows Abi at all he'll know there is no chance she would want what he wants: to fuck other men while he fucks other women, to have him watch her with girls.

"I can't do that," Abi sobbed in Izzy's arms. "I'm not even gay. It's yuck."

"It's nothing to do with being gay," Izzy said.

Tansy tells no-one of her plans. She chooses Easter Saturday in her head. The girls will be with Charlie on Good Friday, and coming home to her the following evening. She will have time to do what she needs to do. At night, when the girls and her mother are asleep, she takes clothes from her wardrobe and holds up tops and dresses in front of the mirror. She finds her box of earrings hidden away from Amber and roots through hoops and crystals, beads and silver.

Izzy has promised not to tell Holly and Aidan what Rick is asking of Abi. Holly tries to book Abi an appointment with the GP, but she refuses, screams, and takes a knife from the drawer. Holly, frightened, reads what's in Izzy's eyes: *leave it*. Izzy thinks, hopes, prays, that Abi will see herself that she needs help again, and will let someone book the appointment. Until Abi feels that, there is nothing they can do. Holly asks the other waiting staff to change some of their shifts so that Izzy can usually be off when Abi is. Strangely Abi doesn't seem to mind. Izzy thinks it's because she doesn't tell her not to hurt herself, only tells her to use antiseptic and plasters. Abi cuts her thighs instead of her arms so the diners in Samarkand can't see the crusty bloody lines.

One day, as Izzy takes a tray of dirties up to Jordan in the kitchen, she hears pounding feet racing up behind her. Abi's eyes are wild and she's holding her phone.

"He wants me back," she says, almost shouts. "He says it doesn't matter, all that stuff. It's me he wants."

And Izzy feels the weight of stones in her chest because just when it seemed Abi was imperceptibly inching away from Rick and his destructive cycle, there he is again, sucking her in, ready to spew her out.

"Not here," Izzy hisses. "Later."

"Whatever," Abi says. "But I'm going out tonight."

"Don't bring him to ours." Izzy mutters as Abi skips down to the café once more.

~

"Just going to town," Tansy says carefully.

"You meeting Charlie and the girls?" Emmeline asks.

"No. Might see if Jake's in the studio."

"Ring him first."

"It doesn't matter." Tansy has said too much. Keep it simple. Otherwise Emmeline will say she will come into Penzance too, and then the whole thing will collapse.

"OK, take a key, as I'm going up to Dad's today."

Tansy does not take the road for Penzance; she drives the other way, towards Hayle. It's a sunny blue spring morning. No rain today. She opens the window and cool air rushes in. She turns up the radio and sings along to steady her heart. There is no reason to be afraid. Gareth is not answering her messages, but he is still around online. He hasn't told her he doesn't want to see her. All she's doing is going to see how he is. And yet, she feels sick, and she arrives in Hayle far too soon.

She pulls a parking ticket from the meter and sticks it on the dashboard. There are people loitering in the car-park, and a couple of kids playing football in the corner. It's dry today, but in her mind she sees the wet street lamps from last time, the puddles underfoot, feels the sting of that other night's rain on her cheek.

She recognises his car parked in the side street by his flat, glances inside and hurries on by. She nips at her lip and tastes blood. The steps to the front door feel exposed and she wonders if he'll suddenly appear behind her coming back from Spar or town. She rings his bell and waits. A crackle and a whistle, and nothing more.

A delivery van roars past. A couple walking hand in hand. A bloke on his mobile. Tansy hovers and doesn't know what to do. She rings the bell again. Nothing. He must be out, on foot. Or with someone else. The front door opens with a scrape and a woman steps out, almost straight into Tansy.

"You looking for someone?" she asks.

She's older, forties probably, with a too-tight T-shirt. Tansy can't imagine her with Gareth.

"I was ringing Gareth's bell," she says.

"I think he's in," the woman says. "I saw him getting his post a while ago." She peers at Tansy, then adds, "Go on in, if you like."

Tansy can't refuse. The woman stands aside and she steps in. The outer door thuds shut. She could just wait a moment and run out. But she might encounter Gareth coming back to the flat. No, the woman said he was in. Whatever, she can't just loiter here. She starts down to the lower floor; the overhead lights come on soundlessly. She tiptoes the last few steps to Gareth's door and listens. She can't hear voices or music or anything. She knocks loudly.

He opens the door immediately, stares at her and grins.

"Hi, what are you doing here?"

"I rang the bell," she gabbles. "A woman came out, she let me in. How are you?"

He shrugs. "OK. Just very down. Haven't felt good lately."

"Can I come in a moment?"

"Sure, sure, but I've only got a minute. I'm meeting a friend."

Tansy goes into his tiny lobby. It looks familiar and different. His coat is there on the peg, and a pair of trainers kicked under it. There is a pile of newspapers and a couple of empty wine bottles.

"I'm sorry I can't offer you a drink."

"It doesn't matter." She glances round the room. The cactus on the windowsill. Books. Memories. "I wanted to see how you are. You've been quiet and I, uh, I wondered if it was because of, you know, me, what happened…"

"Don't be silly. Nothing like that. I get like this. I don't want to see people or whatever."

But you're seeing a friend, Tansy thinks. Unless it's just an excuse.

"Oh. Good. OK. I was worried."

"Don't worry. Really. I'm sorry. We'll do something soon, yes?"

"I'd love that. Maybe after Easter?"

"Yeah. Yeah, after Easter." He checks his watch and reties his ponytail. "Look, Tansy, I need to get ready now. I'm sorry I haven't got any time today. I didn't know you were coming."

"No. Of course."

He gives her a quick hug; she grazes his cheek with her mouth, but he doesn't turn into her kiss. He lets her go and opens the flat door.

Soft carpet, soft lighting, then into the echoey hall. She opens the street door and steps out into the sunshine, elated and deflated together.

Her tongue finds blood on her lip as she walks back. She hesitates a moment by Gareth's car, but he's not coming her way, with or without a companion. She can't hang about, she really can't, so she trudges back to her Golf. A glance in her mirror shows a gaping crack in her lip, and blood on her skin, and the edgy relief she felt at having found him bursts into overwhelming sadness.

Sometimes Ivor didn't draw Carol. Sometimes she worked beside him in the garden, pulling weeds and trimming the hedge. Sometimes he sat her down at the table with a pack of cards and the cribbage board, and explained over and over how to add together a double run, and when it was worth holding on to a flush. Once or twice he suggested she draw something herself, and handed her charcoal and pencils: a bowl of fruit, a twisted shell, a handful of his stained paintbrushes. And one afternoon he took her to bed in the room he'd slept in alone since his wife's death.

He listened as she told him about Louis and how quickly he was growing up. She made him laugh with stories of her beastly cleaning jobs. In turn he talked about his daughter Emmeline, a college lecturer, and granddaughter, Tansy. He showed her photographs of Tansy, a vivid dark-haired Modigliani girl, with long legs and almond eyes. Carol stiffened beside him at a sudden noise, but Ivor said the doors were locked and his family would not just arrive out of nowhere. Emmeline was teaching and Tansy was at college. They never surprised him with a visit in case he was working in the studio.

"What do you want, Carol?" Ivor asked one afternoon.

She was sitting on his sofa with a pile of bright cushions behind her, and he was sketching her with pastels. Short, sharp strokes, more colour than line.

"Want for what? For me?"

"For you and Louis. What do you want?"

"For us to be happy, I suppose." She fiddled with her bracelet. "It'd be nice to have more money, I suppose. I wish I had a better job. I want Louis to be happy. And healthy. And not sad that his father isn't in our lives."

"Will you stay in Cornwall?" Ivor's brown chalk snapped in a burst of dust.

"I hadn't thought. I suppose so. Yes, Louis is at secondary school. Where would we go otherwise?"

Ivor scrunched up the sketch, unsatisfied. "You could go anywhere."

"I don't want to."

It had never occurred to her that she could.

⁓

"Can you tell us what on earth is going on?" Holly looks tired after a long day in Samarkand.

"Apparently he wants her back."

"He's made her ill." Aidan says. "She was getting better till he showed up."

"Why did he leave her in the first place if he wants her so much now?"

Izzy hesitates, shuffles some papers on the kitchen table. "Oh, look, I don't know what his problem is."

"Is he seeing someone else?" Holly eyeballs Izzy. "Is that what he's doing? Stringing her along and someone else too? That'll destroy her. Oh Christ, why won't she go back on her meds?"

"It's not that. I don't think."

"You do know, don't you?"

"Look, Holly, don't put Izzy in this position."

"Is she in danger?" Holly shouts.

"Only from herself," Izzy says. But she doesn't think that's entirely true.

Mel has forgotten how tiring it is to work a full day in a care home. Before, she seemed to have hours to spare, but now it's like a huge vacuum has sucked away all her time. Sometimes she wonders if she's made the right choice. The boys don't seem to care, but should she be around every day for Megan and Sophie? On the schooldays that she works, they go to an after-school club until Joe's mother can collect them. Mel thinks she'll give it six months or so and then reassess things.

The residents have had lunch. Some eat in the dining room with its vast windows overlooking the bay, and a few take their meals in their rooms. Mel has walked one lady back up to bed and wheeled another to the downstairs cloakroom. She can take five minutes' break now. The door to the stairs swings open and Vicky comes through.

"Just going outside," Vicky says. "You free?"

"For a sec."

The automatic doors hiss open and they step out into the blustery car park. One of the residents is perched on a bench, cigarette in trembling hand, her Zimmer parked in front of her, its pockets stuffed with bags of salt and vinegar crisps.

"Don't you eat all those crisps now, Eva," Vicky says. "You've only just had lunch."

They walk across the gritty tarmac to where a fence separates the grounds of Lanyon House from the coast path. It's chilly in the wind, and Mel shivers in her short-sleeved tunic. Waves arch and break on the rocks below, the heartbeat of the ocean.

"I'm worried about Susan," Mel starts.

"I don't think she has long. We've been saying that for ages but I think this time it's true. Her son's coming down from up country."

"Hurts sometimes, doesn't it?"

"Mmm."

"You OK?" Mel asks. "Is it Susan or anything else? You seem really down."

"Just the usual. Kev. My life marching past. I'll be parked in front of the telly in that day room before I know it. Oh look, ignore me. I'm just being silly."

"Shall we go for a drink again?" Mel says. "One day when we're both awake enough."

"Yeah, that'd be good. Shall we go to Stefan's hotel?"

~

"I want to come down for a couple of weeks," Louis says to Carol on the phone.

"That'd be lovely," she says, then, "Where would you stay?"

"I dunno. I was hoping you might know somewhere. A caravan or something."

"I'll see what I can find," Carol promises. "I'll email you."

~

Abi doesn't bring Rick to the house any more. She sees him at his flat or in town.

"Hasn't he even noticed your arms and legs?" Izzy asks one day.

Abi shrugs, slides her eyes away. "He hasn't said anything."

"He hasn't said anything? Jesus."

~

Tansy plays with the girls in the Easter holidays. She takes them to the beach and to the swimming pool. They have a couple of days out as a family with Charlie. She sends messages to Gareth and, though he does read them, he doesn't read them immediately, and he stalls her suggestions that they should meet up. She should just walk away, but still she remembers a fierce kiss that came from nowhere, watching the rain streak down the pane of his window, the starry street lights in the gloom, and the overwhelming craziness of it all, of an obsession she's never felt before. That she doubts she'll feel again.

Mel breathes in pure blue air and lets her mind drift into nothingness. If she closes her eyes, her other senses become more acute: the smell of wild garlic and manure, the lingering taste of her earlier orange juice, the rise and fall of the kids' voices, and the soft scratchy texture of the grass beneath her hand.

"Hey, I need that."

"No, no, I'm using it. There's another green."

Mel snaps her eyes open. Two of Megan's friends are squabbling over an ice-cream box of pastels.

"Girls, girls." She scrambles up and brushes her jeans, but the grass stains don't budge.

"I had it first."

"Have my green." Megan holds out a lime stub to the nearest of the two. Mel grins quickly at her.

The class has come to the edge of the school field, where the grass grows long and ragged under a few scrubby trees. There is a stone wall, congealed with ivy and brambles, blackthorn and gorse. Bees whirr over the bluebells and wild garlic, and a Red Admiral spirals away to the field beyond.

Mel squats down beside the girls to look at their pictures. Megan is aloof, sitting in the next group, but Mel notices her daughter glancing towards her often, and smiling.

Jake Gregory strides over to Mel.

"Why don't you have a go? Plenty of boards and paper."

"Oh. I'm no good. I couldn't. Anyway, I'm supposed to be supervising."

"Miss is going to have a try." Jake nods towards Miss Hudson, the class teacher, who is taping paper to a drawing board.

"Go on, Megan's Mum," says one of the kids.

"I'll get you some kit."

Jake lopes away to the pile of boards and paper resting by a tree. Mel wanders over to Megan.

"Can I share your pastels?"

"Of course," Megan says, her earlier coolness dissolved. "You can share my sweeties too."

Jake reappears with a drawing board and paper, and hands them to Mel.

"Now, remember what I said to the kids?"

"Uh, look carefully?"

"He said to look at all the different colours that make up one colour," Megan supplies.

"That's it, Megs."

"And to not be frightened of making things bigger or smaller than they are."

"At least someone was listening. And why did I say those things?"

"Because we're going to make ab...ab...something art."

"Abstract art. That's it. So this afternoon, when we make our prints, we can change things even more, and then tomorrow, well tomorrow, is another day, and we'll do some really exciting things then."

"Jake, Jake!" yells one of the boys. "Come and see what I've done."

"See you later, ladies."

Mel watches him. Tansy's father. Tall and broad, with unruly grey hair. His jeans are faded to the palest slate-blue, streaked with lines and smudges of paint. The check shirt he wears over a T-shirt appears to be clean at the moment, but his red Converse are stiff with mud. He bends down to the group of lads, points at something on the wall. He's certainly attractive, Mel thinks. She's always had a thing for older men. Yes, definitely attractive.

"Mum, come on, I thought you were drawing too."

"I am, I am." Flustered now, Mel selects a blue pastel and starts shading in the top of her page for the sky.

"The sky's not just blue, you know. There's white and sort of yellow where the sun is, and that cloud right over there is darker."

That evening Mel arrives at Ivor's and sees Tansy's car parked outside. Anxiety flickers inside her for a moment and she runs into the house. Tansy is in the kitchen unloading shopping from carrier bags. Scarlet is jabbering away to Ivor.

"We're just on our way," Tansy calls out. "How did it go?"

"How did what go?" Mel drops her bag on a spare chair.

"The art group, of course. With my esteemed father."

"Oh good. Great. He got me to do a drawing too. It was awful. Then we made monoprints in the afternoon. The kids' were better than mine."

"I'm sure that's not true." Ivor interjects. "You are just more critical because you're an adult."

"Really, Ivor, there's no way I'd show you."

"You with him again tomorrow?" Tansy scrunches the carrier bags into each other.

"Yes, we're doing collage I think."

"Scarlet's class had Jason Stein. He just about managed to stay upright."

"Stay upright?"

Tansy mimes drinking. "She loved it though. He's sweet with the kids, just a bit…unpredictable. That right, Grandad?"

"He collapsed at one of my private views."

"Oh no."

"I think Miss Carey was hoping to get Jake. I reckon she fancies him. OK, Scarlet, let's get out of their way."

"Miss Carey fancies who?"

"Nothing, no-one. Come on, say goodbye to Grandad and Mel. Here Mel, say hello from me tomorrow, will you? Tell him I'll text. Have fun. Keep him safe from Miss Carey."

~

Vicky arrives ten minutes early and goes straight into the bar. She's disappointed to see a young woman with carefully highlighted hair behind the bar and glances round the room, but there's no sign of Stefan.

"Good evening, what can I get you?"

"Just a pineapple juice please. I don't know what my friend will have." It's not Stefan and Vicky feels a rushing need to explain herself, that she's not drinking alone, or looking for men or something, she is meeting a friend. "Is Stefan here today?" she asks, as the bartender drops a neon orange straw into the tumbler.

"He's not, I'm sorry. He was working tonight, but he's not feeling well, so I'm covering."

"Ah. OK, thanks." Vicky takes her drink to a table in the window. Not the one she likes best; that is occupied by three men in suits. She is sorry to have missed Stefan. The carers rarely get to catch up in real life, only on the Facebook chat, and that's not the same. That's why she enjoys meeting Mel like this. She'll text Stefan later and see if he's all right, if he needs anyone to cover shifts with Ivor.

"You were miles away," Mel says, sliding into the chair beside her with a sparkling glass of Diet Coke.

"I was. How are you? You've caught the sun."

"I have, I think. That was being outside with the art group yesterday." Mel touches her cheek, where the skin flares pink.

"Art group?"

"Art week at school. I was helping with Megan's class. Yesterday and today. With Jake, you know, Tansy's dad, Jake Gregory? He was one of the visiting artists."

"Ah, was that fun?"

"Yeah, it was great. How was work yesterday?"

"We lost Susan."

"Oh no."

"Her son was with her, but, you know, sad."

Mel gulps her drink.

"Stefan's not well," Vicky continues. "I asked her at the bar. I thought I'd text him or ring up later, make sure he's all right. He hasn't got anyone else to look after him."

"That's a good idea. If he's got a bug he needs to stay away from Ivor. Anyway, how are things with you at home?"

"Same old, same old. My daughter seems to be starving herself, my husband barely acknowledges my existence."

"I'm so sorry. What about Harry?"

"He's a teenage boy. He's fine, you know, but at that age."

"I've got that to come."

"Susan dying, you know, it brings it home, you only live once. What if you get to the end of that life and realise that most of the time you weren't happy? That you could have changed things but you didn't?"

"Is this about Kev?"

"Yes, that's it really. I don't see any point in it anymore. We've just grown apart."

"Don't you want to make some sort of effort to fix things? I don't know, a holiday without the kids or something? They're old enough, aren't they?"

"Stuck with Kev on my own? I wouldn't know what to talk to him about. He's not interested in anything I'm interested in. We'd just be sitting there in silence. You're lucky. Your Joe's decent, isn't he?"

"Yeah, pretty much so. I guess I'm lucky. Yes."

"Kev had a couple of affairs, you know. Not recently. Well, he might be at it again, I don't know. That's the thing. I don't think I even care now."

"Shit, that's bloody awful. I didn't know. And you stuck by him."

"For the kids. Joe would never do that, would he?"

Mel drinks again, and wonders. "I don't think so," she says at last. "I guess you never really know what someone might do."

"I'm sorry. I've upset you. Of course he wouldn't."

"I don't think he would."

~

Vicky waits until Mel has driven away then rings Stefan from her car.

"Vicky?"

"Hi, how are you?"

"Oh, er, not so great."

"I was at the hotel with Mel. The barmaid said you were ill. Is everything OK?"

"It's just a migraine. I get them every so often, but I can't work."

"Course not. Do you need any of us to cover for Ivor?"

"I'll be fine. It's getting better."

"OK, well, is there anything I can get for you? You got paracetamol or whatever?"

"I've got everything. Thanks Vicky. That's really kind of you."

It's only as Vicky turns on her ignition that she realises she wished Stefan had asked for something so she could go round and see him.

~

When Mel checks her Facebook just before bed she is surprised to find a friend request from Jake Gregory, and a message with it.

Hope you enjoyed the workshops. I've got one for adults coming up. Do you fancy helping out? J

I'd love to. As long as it fits in with everything else. Really enjoyed the last two days. Mel.

Surely he should be asking Tansy, or someone else who has a remote idea about art. Mel ruffles the guineas' fur and rearranges their hay for the night. Then she turns off the light and pads up to bed.

~

Whatever it is that Tansy is experiencing at the moment bubbles inside her like effervescent wine. She had almost given up hoping that, one day, Gareth would suggest meeting up, so when it came out of the blue, and signed off with a row of kisses, she almost lost her breath.

She drops the girls off hurriedly. Mel's husband, Joe, is in the school yard talking to another father. Joe waves at Tansy; she acknowledges him and runs back to her car before he can stop her to talk. She needs to get home and changed and be on the way as soon as possible.

Emmeline is already in the back garden weeding when Tansy returns from school, as though she's avoiding a conversation about the day.

The lanes, the main road, the car park once more. It seems to take only moments to get to Hayle. Tansy skips down the road, even remembering the jagged crack in a flagstone halfway along, and the house with butterfly transfers on the front window. Gareth's car is nearer his end of the street, squeezed into a tight parking spot. She rings his bell – happily this time, because he is expecting her, he invited her.

"Hi," he says, over the intercom, and she fancies she can feel warmth in his voice from that one word.

The lights pulse on softly as she walks down the passage, her feet silent on the carpet. There's a TV on in the flat next door; she can hear its tinny voice. Gareth opens his door to her knock. She's taken aback a moment, His hair is loose and all over the place, and he's wearing a shabby band T-shirt with a hole in the side, and she feels stupidly overdressed in her new skinny jeans, sparkly earrings, and what now feels like a thick slick of colour on her lips.

"Come in, I'll get you a drink," he says, "I thought we could go out somewhere. St Ives maybe?"

"Sure, yes," she says uncertainly, because she thought he'd be tugging her up that narrow staircase into his room, and she's lost now because he hasn't seen her for ages and hasn't even hugged her.

Just as she has never experienced such swooping peaks and lows before, she has never met anyone like Gareth Crane, who makes his own rules and probably breaks them all the time too. She is confused, has to let him lead her.

"I'm trying to tidy this place. Sorry about the mess. Actually I kind of overslept too, so I haven't had a chance to get ready. Tea or coffee?"

"Tea please."

She pads through piles of papers and abandoned shoes to the sofa and sits awkwardly. The kettle whistles and Gareth drops a teabag into a mug. Not the chunky one she had before, a blue and white striped one. He grins at her and she feels her heart soar. It's going to be OK. Whatever it may be, whatever happens, its going to be OK, because she is here with him, and he's happy to see her.

"Here, drink this, and I'll get myself sorted out." He hands her the mug and their fingers brush for a second, then he's loping up the stairs.

She hears him in the bedroom above, then he crosses to the bathroom and the door slams shut. There's nothing she can do but drink her tea and wait. It's too hot, so she leaves it and stands at the window, looking out on the grey jumble of roofs and chimneys, now bright in the sunlight. There's a rumbling noise from the building site as some kind of machine grinds through the earth, and a bloke yelling. It seems extraordinary to Tansy that here she is, in this tiny flat, one cell in a converted warehouse, looking out on a world which is just carrying on while she gazes through the glass wondering what the day will bring. But what is even more extraordinary is that at every window, in every house, in cars and offices, and on trains and in gardens there are millions of other people all thinking the same as her, wondering what the day will bring for them.

Footsteps on the stairs. Tansy swings round quickly. He's tied his hair up, put on a clean T-shirt.

"So, shall we go out?" he asks, and Tansy wonders for a moment if he doesn't want them to be stuck in this flat together, but no, of course not, he wants to enjoy the blue skies and sunshine with her.

"How am I supposed to have a relationship with anyone when you won't let them come here?" Abi flings open the fridge door, glances in, and slams it shut.

"It's not about having a relationship with anyone, it's about having one with him," Holly says.

"Well, that's nice, isn't it? You never used to mind."

"He hadn't made you ill then." Izzy waves at Abi's arms. "You were getting better, doing so well, we were all so pleased, then he comes along, and look at you. You're hurting yourself again. How can we like him?"

"Cutting myself is my choice, it's nothing to do with him. He didn't tell me to."

"He might as well have!" Izzy yells, suddenly so tired of this destructive situation. "He doesn't mind telling you what else he wants you to do, does he? What does he tell you to do?"

"Nothing. Nothing. I think the sooner I can move out of here the better. None of you want me here anyway. And I can't have a normal relationship with Rick if you won't let him come here. What am I supposed to say to him? Huh? Sorry Rick, they all suddenly say you can't come over?"

"Say what you like," Holly says. "I don't care. He has a place. You can see him there if you have to. But I'm not having anyone here who hurts you or Izzy, and makes you ill. That's it."

"If Dad were nearer I'd go and live with him."

Izzy glances at Holly. She knows that will hurt. Holly doesn't flinch. Instead she says, "Why don't you ask him then?"

"Because he's in fucking Plymouth. And Rick is here. Otherwise I would."

"Please, Abi," Izzy starts. "This is all getting out of hand. Please let's calm down."

"You just stay out of it. You've been telling her stuff you said you'd keep to yourself."

"She hasn't," Holly says. "I don't know what that creep's problem is. The more I hear the worse I feel. I can't stop you seeing him, Abi, but I wish you wouldn't. I really wish you wouldn't."

"So do I," Izzy says quietly.

"Oh you two just don't get it," Abi says, then turns to Izzy. "Just 'cos you're not interested in a relationship. What's wrong with you? You wouldn't like it if she started censoring who you could see, would you?"

"She wouldn't have to. I wouldn't get involved with anyone like that."

"Oh yeah, whatever. You don't even know him. Either of you. Is it Aidan who put you both up to this?"

"No, but he thinks the same. We all do. Abi, we love you. Don't you think we might be right?" Holly looks like she's about to cry. Izzy wants to hug her.

"Rick loves me too. Perhaps I should move in with him."

"Yeah, why not?" Izzy stands up. "I'm going to bed."

She trudges up the stairs and knocks on the spare-room door. It was her old bedroom before she moved in to the attic. Now its walls are solid with bookcases, there's Holly's old exercise bike, half folded in the corner, a couple of bin bags for the charity shop, and an old armchair where Aidan is reading with a tumbler of whisky.

"You heard all that, I suppose?" Izzy shuts the door behind her.

"Some of it."

"She won't move in with Rick. He won't want that."

"Neither would her father." Aidan drops his book. "Sorry Izzy, I didn't mean to bad-mouth your dad."

162

Izzy shrugs. "I don't care. He's a prick anyway. No, she won't do that either. She'll try to persuade you and Mum to let him here again."

"Won't work with me. We've got to get her back to the doctor. She was so much better on her tablets. If she'd take those again it might make her see things more clearly, you know, realise that she wants better than this. Can you talk to her?"

"Not tonight. She hates me at the moment. I'll try."

~

Scarlet can't sleep. Tansy feeds her a syringe of sticky pink Calpol and snuggles into bed beside her. Amber snores lightly in her cot, the covers thrown off, her hands in victory fists over her head. Tansy has left her mobile in the living room. Scarlet wraps sweaty arms around her so she can't move. Most of the evening Gareth has not been online.

~

They drove the few miles to St Ives. He talked a lot, quickly, about a couple of films he'd seen, some incident at university. A friend at the group where he models who already has an upcoming show. Tansy half-listened, trying to concentrate on the road, the tricky approach into St Ives, and parked by the station. They walked down into town, stopping to look in the windows of galleries and shops. The summer crowds were already about, pavements jammed, bars overspilling. The skim of water in the harbour was silver and filmy, the jetty a smudge of watercolour in that strange ethereal light found nowhere else. Tansy pressed closer to Gareth, willing him to take her hand, her arm, anything, but he didn't, and she stepped back, embarrassed and awkward once more.

They bought coffee at one of the bistros on the front, and sat on metal chairs outside, watching the visitors stumble by, the seagulls dive-bombing the pavement for scraps.

"We should go," Gareth said, draining his cup. "The parking will run out."

He had bought the ticket; Tansy didn't know how much time he'd paid for. She stood up heavily, sensing the day sliding out of her grasp. Back to the car, back to Hayle. And then what?

She pulled into the same parking spot she'd occupied that morning in Hayle and clicked out of her seatbelt.

"I like doing things with you," she started. "Perhaps we could do something another day?"

"Yeah, I'd like that. I like doing things with you too."

The sun was bright and hot through the windscreen. Tansy cracked open her door for some air.

"Send me a message," she said. "Any time. And we can sort out something."

He wasn't going to ask her in.

"Can I have a hug?" he asked suddenly.

"Yes, yes, of course."

His hug was fierce and he kissed her again and again, and Tansy's heart soared and relaxed, with delight and confusion and relief.

"So you are still interested?"

"I'm interested," he said, and kissed her again, and she was about to ask, *would you like me to come in*? when he broke apart from her.

"I must go. We'll talk later."

~

Scarlet's breathing has evened out. Tansy frees herself from her hold and slides out of the sweaty sheets. When she retrieves her phone she sees Gareth is not online. She flicks through his profile. No *wonderful day in St Ives with Tansy Martin*. No selfie of them together on the pier or outside the café. Suddenly she realises they didn't take any pictures. Not of St Ives or of themselves. The day might as well not have happened. There is no evidence that it did, except in her head.

~

Izzy is half asleep when she hears feet tiptoeing up to her floor. The door is open, to let in the landing light. Izzy sits up groggily. Abi wavers in the doorway.

"Can I come in?"

Izzy shrugs, shuffles across the bed.

"I'm sorry." Abi crumples down beside her. She's still wearing her clothes from before and, even in the grey gloom, Izzy can see the dark make-up smudges under her eyes.

"Sorry for which bit?"

"All of it. For yelling at you all. For saying I'd go to Dad. I'm so fucking stressed."

"He's making you stressed. This situation you're in. You're always frightened he's going to demand you do those things, aren't you?"

Abi gazes round Izzy's room. "The other day," she says, so quietly Izzy hardly hears, "when we were in the pub, he showed me a picture of this girl he knows and asked me if I fancied her and if I'd like to have sex with her."

"Christ, just get out of this."

"I said no, and he didn't say any more."

Izzy smooths down her duvet. When Abi is careering down one of her dark paths she can't see anything else. She can't see now that there is a world without Rick. A better, happier world.

"I'm so scared," Abi says. "I can't do what he wants and I can't live without him."

"You'll have to find a way to do one or the other."

~

The more Stefan thinks about moving on with his life the more he believes he must go to Amity and just spend an hour or so on his own in the place where Nina died. He can see the beach in his mind, can see the way through the low dunes, over the scree of pebbles and seaweed that marks the high-tide line, and down onto the sand. Past the giant outcrop of rocks, the beach shelves steeply into the water. He must go there. Must choose a quiet evening and drive up the coast and simply be there. He won't plan a day. He will know when the time is right. It is the first step.

~

Tansy feels her phone buzz and quickly checks the screen. It's Gareth.

Want to come sketching with me? X

I'd love to. Where and when? X

"Come on," Emmeline says. "Let's go now."

She pockets her phone and follows her mother out. That morning Stefan had called to say that Ivor's chest was bad again and his leg was inflamed, and that he might need some more antibiotics.

They find Ivor in his easy chair with his legs outstretched on a stool. Tansy smells the sweet breath of infection straight away. Ivor's face is pale. Emmeline rolls up his trouser-cuff. His leg is hugely swollen, red and shiny. The skin has cracked in places and blood seeps out.

"It's hot to touch." Emmeline looks up at Tansy. "We need to call the surgery."

"Give it another day," Ivor says, but his voice breaks into a cough.

"Stefan's right. You need antibiotics," Tansy says. "We'll sort it out. I'll make you a tea."

In the kitchen she selects a small mug because Ivor's hands shake too much these days for a big one. She half listens to her mother talking about infections and skin-cream and compression socks. Ivor can't seem to shake off the infections and fluid in his chest and legs. His kidneys aren't good, and haven't been for ages. He has to balance his diuretics carefully against his kidney function. Tansy splashes milk into his tea. When she puts it down beside him she notices the gout has flared up in his hands too. It seems no time since he was striding about on the cliff paths and the moors, sketchbook and charcoal in his rucksack, or kneeling for hours in his garden. Old age is like a black hole, Tansy thinks, the closer the end comes the more time speeds up. It really has become a countdown now. She will miss him desperately.

~

The art workshop is held in a studio in St Ives. Mel drives in early on Saturday morning. A haze smudges the sea's horizon; the water and the sky are pearlescent shades of grey and lilac and silver. Just the simple coastal palette of sea and sky; sand and lichen glows with its own luminosity in St Ives.

Jake's car is parked on the single strip of tarmac outside the studio. Wooden double doors are open to the lobby and Mel calls out to him as she steps into the building.

"In here!"

Mel runs a hand through her hair and straightens her back. Jake is in the inner studio: a vast room with high skylights and wooden floorboards splattered with paint of every colour.

"You seen that daughter of mine?" Jake asks as she hangs her jacket and bag on a hook next to his hoodie.

"I see her around a bit."

"Never has time for her old man." Jake waves a box of teabags at her.

"Kids take up a lot of time," Mel smiles. "I think the girls keep her busy."

"I wouldn't know. I was hardly around for any of mine." Jake grins and Mel can't help laughing.

"You got others then?"

"Yeah, but not down here. Right, I'll show you the set-up."

He plonks his mug down on the grubby kitchen unit by the sink and leads her back into the studio. There is a giant black printing press and a jumbled stack of easels, chests of drawers and jars of brushes. The walls are collaged with life studies in charcoal and pencil, watercolour and ink. Mel smells turpentine and something else, maybe the sour fumes of acrylic paint. There is a shrivelled pot-plant and a collection of sea shells on a folding table – abandoned remains of a still life – and a couple of silk screens propped against the walls. She gazes around her and suddenly wishes she were part of this world, this world of Jake and Ivor and Tansy, of so many artists who found their inspiration and passion in St Ives.

—

Carol watches Ivor spoon cereal into his mouth. His swollen hands are trembling badly, and the milk splatters off the spoon and onto the table and his knee.

"Don't forget your antibiotic."

She shoves the capsule towards him. He tries to pick it up, but his fingers are too clumsy. He can't grip the tiny bullet.

"Shall I get it for you?"

"No."

He uses two hands, one to sweep the capsule into his palm resting under the table edge. He raises his hand to his mouth, sucks the tablet straight from his hand.

"Your chest is getting better," Carol says brightly.

It hurts her to see him deteriorate this way. His spoon rattles against the china bowl as he scoops another tiny mouthful of cereal. His chest is improving, yes, but the cellulitis in his leg is unchanged, the skin stretched taut to cracking point, the limb heavy and swollen with excess fluid. Carol had to cut his sock down farther just to get it over his ankle, and it looks like even his slippers will be too tight soon.

"Look at me," Ivor says.

She turns to him.

"No, I mean look at me. Look what I've become. I'll never work again. You know that."

"I don't know that." She evades his eyes.

"Don't, Carol. Not you. You know. I won't even get into the studio again."

"You could try. I'd help you. Let's have a go. It's dry today. With the Zimmer and me you could do it."

Ivor drinks tea.

"And if you can't, it doesn't matter. We could ask Stefan to come and help too another day."

He drinks tea again, twists stiffly in his chair to look out at the garden. Carol follows his gaze. The seasons are turning now. Daffodils are crumpled and brown, and the bluebells froth under his fruit trees. The lawn needs mowing, but clumps of primroses have sprouted through the thick grass.

"We'll try," he says.

"Let your breakfast get down. I'll wash up. Then we'll try."

Carol gathers up the bowl and mug and takes them through to the kitchen. She washes them and puts them away, checks the fridge for milk and throws out a hard nugget of old cheese. The sounds of wheezing and the click of the Zimmer legs make her turn. Ivor has hauled himself up.

"Wait, wait, let me get the key." Carol grabs the studio key from its hook in the kitchen. The same place, the same hook, even the same key-fob, as before, when she was young, and Ivor held a brush with strength and confidence.

She opens the back door opens with a creak. Spring air floods into the house. The warmth of sunlight, unfiltered by glass, birdsong, the buzz of a lawnmower somewhere, a car's gears grinding. Ivor stands on the step, gazing out, breathing it in, drinking it in, absorbing it into his body.

The studio is only a few yards down the path. Ivor fumbles with his Zimmer, tries to lower it over the lip of the door. Carol is squashed between him and the wall. She tries to take his arm. He starts coughing, his lungs aroused by the clean air. The Zimmer leg is not even on the flagstone and Carol feels, rather than sees, the contraption buckle and slide from his grasp.

"Ivor!" She snatches at him, shuffles him against the wall, tries to hold him there with one hand while she reaches for the Zimmer with the other. He coughs again and his eyes water. She takes his knobbly hands and places them on the frame's handles. She notices a milk stain on his jumper. He breathes heavily, clears his throat.

"I can't. I'm sorry."

And Carol realises it's not the cough which is making his eyes water.

It's nothing like the primary-school workshop. Mel does not have to remind the adult artists to wash their brushes between colours, or to pick up the broken pastels on the floor. She drifts round the studio, glancing awkwardly over a few shoulders, and feels desperately out of place. She should not have come. This is not her world.

Jake seems oblivious to her discomfort. Sometimes he asks her to find some more paint in the cupboard or a knife for pencil sharpening. She doesn't know her way round the stores in this studio, and she has to check the labels again and again to make sure she has the right thickness of charcoal, the right shade of blue acrylic.

When one of the students asks her advice she panics and gabbles what she hopes sounds a sensible response. Jake is working with colour and shape; pure abstraction this time, as they haven't been out sketching in the countryside. In the morning they produce huge colourful mixed media pieces; after the lunch break they will cut them up for the next exercise.

"They don't know they're going to have to chop them up," Jake whispers to Mel by the paper drawers.

The students are unpacking lunches, queueing for the kettle in the kitchenette. A couple have gone out for a fag or a vape. Jake is drinking some kind of fruit infusion, heavy on blackcurrant, but he doesn't seem to be eating. Mel dithers, not knowing whether to open her own lunch or not. She hates people watching her eat. Eventually she takes out an apple and bites into its shiny red flank, but the flesh underneath is soggy and over-sweet, and she wishes she hadn't. When she's swallowed a few mouthfuls she chucks it in the bin, then checks her phone for messages, half-hoping Joe will have texted her with some silly story about the kids, or to ask how she is getting on, so she can feel the anchor of her home life tugging her back to safety, away from the dark edginess of Jake Gregory. Her screen is blank. No texts, no calls.

The studio door slams with a bang. The smokers and vapers are back. The group in the kitchen drift across to their easels.

"OK," Jake says. "You've all made some beautiful pieces this morning, and you're not going to like it, but we're going to cut them all up."

Mel puts her phone away and helps herself to a sheet of paper and some pastels. She's no help to Jake, has nothing to contribute, a part of her would like to walk out, go home, back to Joe and the children, and the guinea pigs. Or call in at Ivor's for a chat. He always makes her feel more grounded.

She absorbs herself in the lines and colours of her work, sitting alone, away from the students. She remembers what Jake told them that morning: to be free and uninhibited with mark-making and colour choices.

"Don't forget to spray it before you cut it up."

She jumps at Jake's voice. He's leaning over her shoulder with a can of fixative in his hand.

"I'm sorry. I didn't think I was being much help."

"I like it." He flicks off the spray lid and hisses the acetone vapour over her paper. The colours darken with the spray into wet patches. "You don't have to cut it. We'll be finishing up in half an hour." He perches on the wooden table beside her. "I'm sorry you haven't enjoyed today so much. Let me take you for a drink afterwards."

Before Mel can reply he has stalked away with the spray can. She picks up her paper and flaps it to dry the damp spots. A drink afterwards. It's only mid-afternoon. She has time for a quick one. She should go home. She has time for a drink.

She can't concentrate on art any more. She doesn't cut her drawing to abstract it to the next stage. Instead she starts gathering up stray pencils and brushes, rinses out the dirty tea mugs in the kitchen. At last the students pack up, put on their jackets and leave. The vast airy studio feels small with just her and Jake.

"Let's get all the crap cleared up and go," he says. "It wasn't very inspiring, was it? They weren't very inspiring. I've had some amazing workshops, where people have produced the most incredible stuff, stuff they never believed they could do, stuff I never believed they could do, but it wasn't today, huh?"

"I think they wondered what I was doing here. I wasn't much help."

"Ah don't worry. They probably thought you were my secret mistress."

Mel blushes as she shoves a handful of damp paintbrushes into a jar. Her hands are sore from the pastel dust and the cold water, and the skin has split in a couple of places.

Jake clatters a row of easels together and takes one last look round. "Come on, let's go."

He hasn't actually asked me if I can, or if I want to, Mel realises, as she gathers up her coat. *But I haven't told him I can't.*

Outside, the town is crowded with visitors clogging the narrow streets, dithering outside tiny shop doorways. Jake takes her to a wine bar on the front overlooking the harbour and Smeaton's Pier, made famous by so many artists from days long gone.

"Just fizzy water please. I'm driving."

He returns with a tall glass of sparkling water and a beer.

"I'm staying on in town," he tells her. "I expect you're going to head home soon, aren't you?"

"Yes, I'll have to." Mel gulps her water and the bubbles fizz in her nose.

"You're welcome to stay on with me, check out a couple of the galleries."

"I can't. I've left Joe with the kids all day."

"And you've left your drawing at the studio."

"It doesn't matter."

"I'll pick it up."

"Well, only if it's no trouble. Give it to Tansy perhaps."

"No, I'll give it to you."

Mel looks away, out of the window at the shiny sea-washed sand, the bright figures drifting along the pier, the gulls diving for chips.

"I'd like us to be friends, Mel. I'd like to see you again and talk to you."

"Oh. Well. Yes, of course we're friends." She drinks again. "Perhaps another workshop would be…"

"Not at a workshop. Like this. Or maybe you come to my studio or to my house. I live near St Buryan. You know it?"

"Sort of. Lovely out there. Yes."

"I'm in the middle of nowhere, in the valley. I've got a cottage. It's like the gingerbread house or something. All on its own in the woods, wildflowers, a stream, butterflies, moths, hedgehogs, all that stuff. So peaceful."

"Sounds amazing."

"Tansy found it spooky when she was little. You can't hear any traffic. Just the sounds of nature. You should come over."

"I'd love to." Mel doesn't even know she's said it. She swallows the last of her water. "I must go now."

She stops in the bar doorway and glances back. Jake is watching her; he waves and she runs out into the sunlight.

~

Tansy parks in a circle of gravel and mud, edged with stunted trees and blackthorn. A five-barred gate marks the wild track across the moors, trodden down into the semblance of a pathway. Across the lane is the high stone wall of a deconsecrated graveyard and the half-tumbled church tower beyond. She gets out of the car. The air is still, heavy with wild garlic; if she holds her breath she can almost feel the vibration, the hum, of the earth beneath her feet.

This landscape is ancient, humped with the raised shields of round barrows and stabbed with standing stones.

She shoulders her rucksack and gathers up her sketchbook. Gareth isn't late; she's early. She wanders over to the gate. The wood is rotting in places, dark and soft under her hand. There's lichen on the gatepost – ochre and lime and white – and the gate hangs crookedly. She follows the old road with her eye across the downs until it blurs into the tufts of golden grasses.

A rattle of gravel behind her, and she swings round. Gareth brakes erratically beside her car and leaps out.

"Isn't it wonderful?" he says. "Have you seen the church before?"

"Years ago." Tansy hovers, unsure whether to offer her arms for her hug, Burdened by the A3 pad she's carrying, she dithers and he opens the boot for his own gear. "I did my art A level piece on it," she says. "A big watercolour of the church door. I think it's all fallen down even more since then."

"Let's go."

He starts across the mud and shale to the lane. Tansy follows, still unsure, still confused, her heart still swooping at his nearness, but lost as to what to do.

She catches up with him at the lane and they cross together. Ahead, the churchyard wall rises up six feet from the road, roughly built from granite chunks. Four longer slabs stick out, forming a precarious stile.

"The lych gate is just along there," Tansy says, waving to her left, but Gareth has already thrown his rucksack into the long grasses at the top and is swinging up the wall.

He grins down at her and swipes his hair back from his face.

"It's sound. Give me your pad."

She hands it up, grabs what she hopes is a secure stone in the wall, and starts to climb. At the top Gareth takes her hand and tugs her gently into the churchyard.

There are tall trees overhanging the graves. The inscriptions are barely distinguishable, eroded by time and rain, and strangled with ivy. At the base of one leaning marker there is a straggly posy of dead flowers. A red and white warning sign hangs over the remains of the church door.

Tansy stops for a moment, remembering another visit when she was eighteen, when Ivor brought her to sketch and take photographs for her A-level project. They'd walked in through the lych gate but, when they left, Ivor scrambled down the stile effortlessly. Tears threaten her remembering that younger, fitter, vital man.

"You all right?"

"Just thinking."

"You've been before. Come and show me round. Can we get inside the church?"

"Yes. Some of the stained glass is still there."

"I might draw you in there," Gareth says, and his arm brushes hers as they wade through the long grasses to the church porch. The tower, squat and crumbling like a tooth, glowers down over their heads as they step inside.

~

I should have said no. It goes round Stefan's head over and over. *I should have said no.* He stares into the blue heart of his ring, at the tiny glittering shards of Nina. He couldn't have stopped her. There was no reason. No freak storms, no weather warnings. And she wouldn't have listened anyway. If she and George were on one of their adventures, their quests, their dares, they listened to no one. George was – and always will be – the person closest to Nina. They shared their mother's womb.

Stefan rolls over in bed and checks the clock. Half an hour until he needs to get up and shower and put on clean clothes to open up the bar. He slides the ring off his finger and turns his hand this way and that. When he first had the ring he imagined he would never be parted from it. He puts it back on again.

Stefan and George. Black-suited and black-tied, one on each side of Nina's heart as they carried her aloft in her willow coffin. Flowers and ribbons were woven into the willow; they tickled Stefan's cheek.

And later, in the pub, ties discarded, jackets flung on chairs. Too many beers for George, too much Shiraz for him, they sobbed on each other's shoulders, those same shoulders that had carried Nina.

~

Harry and Skye have left for college and school, and Kev is still hanging around in the kitchen in his boxers and grubby T-shirt.

"Aren't you working today?" Vicky asks at last.

She squeezes past him to put Harry's cereal bowl into the dishwasher, and is dismayed but unsurprised that her body recoils as their arms brush.

"It's been rescheduled." Kev clunks a mug down on the worktop and flicks the kettle switch.

Vicky isn't starting work at Lanyon until lunchtime. She has a morning with him here in the house, just the two of them.

"Christ, isn't there any milk in this house?"

"Harry had cereal."

"Is this all there is?" Kev waves a plastic milk bottle at her. There's only a skim of fluid at the bottom.

"Guess not then. I'll pick some up."

Kev splashes the milk in his tea and dumps the empty bottle beside the kettle.

Vicky gathers crumbs from the worktop, shoves an extra fork in the dishwasher, rinses her hands, and wonders how she can start this conversation.

"Can we talk?" she asks at last.

"Talk? What about? I was going back to bed."

"Please Kev." She immediately regrets the please.

"Are the kids OK?"

"The kids are fine. I think. I mean, yes. Skye's anxious though."

"What's she anxious about? Is that why she doesn't eat?"

"Maybe. Probably." Vicky stops herself adding *I'm surprised you even noticed her not eating*, then suddenly realises that it's not the kids Kev is sick of, it's just her.

"You want to talk about Skye?"

"No. I want to talk about us. What's going on? You never hug me or kiss me. We hardly speak."

"You never hug me or kiss me either," Kev says.

"No, I know. How has it come to this? That's what I want to talk about. Harry and Skye know it's not right. Is it…are you…are you seeing anyone else?"

"No, I'm not. I told you I wouldn't do that again. I'm not. Jesus. I gave my word."

"You gave your word before."

"Yes, well, the answer is no."

"So what is happening then? Do you want to break up?"

Vicky gulps down a treacherous pain in her throat. She doesn't like him anymore, she shouldn't care, but it's never that easy. She and Kev go back a long way, back to Redruth school. He was the year above her. She liked him then, but he had no time for her. And then she met him a couple of years later and there had never been anyone else for her from that day on.

Kev drinks tea and doesn't look at her.

"Hell of a hassle, that," he says at last.

"Hell of a hassle? And this isn't? Look, we can try to make things better if you're willing to try too…" Vicky trails off. She doesn't know what to do. She shares so many years with this man, two children, a house, memories. Despite this, the thought of her current lonely life stretching on until she finds herself in the dayroom of Lanyon House with an incontinence pad under her terrifies her.

"I'm tired, Vic," Kev says at last. "I had a shit night. I can't do this right now."

~

"You know that guy I was telling you about at the art group? The one who's really good?"

"Yeah." Tansy's perched on a fallen chunk of masonry, lying where once the nave would have led to the chancel. In her peripheral vision she sees Gareth's pencil striking his page.

"Sorry, your hand's a bit of a mess…I'm no good at hands. Anyway, yes, Ryan. He's got an exhibition coming up. There's a private view. D'you wanna come?"

This time Tansy turns to him.

"What? With you?"

"With me. You moved. Get back."

"I'd love to." He must see the jittering in her chest, she thinks, as she settles her hand back on her knee. "When is it?"

"I'll send you the date. He's invited everyone from the group."

"Will there be some pictures of you?"

"I don't know. OK, I'm done. Come on, let's check out the graveyard."

Tansy stands and stretches, picks up her bag. Sunlight flares through the broken stained-glass windows and onto the stony ground. Dandelions sprout amongst the pebbles and fallen bricks. A white butterfly skitters down the nave, followed by a second, spiralling above. Tansy turns her face to the open roof and the aching blue sky. She's hardly done any drawing, but she does n't care. She is here with him, and that is enough.

―

Every time Abi looks at her phone Izzy stiffens, almost holding her breath, waiting for the frozen face, the stabbing finger, the crumpled eyes. Hoping that Rick hasn't hurt her again.

It happens in Samarkand, of course. A busy lunchtime. Aidan is on the till, Izzy and Abi on tables. Holly isn't in. Abi shows a group of four to their table in the back room. She whisks away the reserved card, adjusts the flower vase, and hands the menus around. The customers shrug out of their jackets, place phones on the tabletop, shuffle shopping bags around their feet and, in the midst of this, as Abi is most likely saying something like *today's soup is carrot and coriander* or *can I get you some drinks?* Izzy sees her sister place a hand on the side pocket of her jeans. Izzy knows this means the buzz of a message, and that it will be from Rick, and that he will have dumped Abi once more.

A woman with huge tortoiseshell glasses waves Izzy across to the window table. She scribbles down an order for two more cappuccinos and a refill of Darjeeling. Aidan grins at her as she takes it to him: he's just sold four packets of speciality tea to a pair of tourists.

Izzy sees Abi flee up the stairs to the kitchen and private rooms.

"Aidan, I think there's a problem."

"What?" Aidan scans the room.

"Abi." Izzy gestures to the staircase. "I think she just had a message. I think it's that twat again."

"Jesus." Aidan places golden biscuits in a bowl to go with the refills. "Yeah, go and see. I'm OK for a minute."

Izzy plods up the stairs. Usually she runs up and down lightly in her Converse boots or ballet flats; now each footstep feels leaden. She knocks on the staff bathroom door.

"It's me."

The bolt draws back. Abi is hunched, crying.

"He says he means it this time. Says he's wasted too much time already. Wasted time on someone who can't give him what he needs."

"I thought things were better," Izzy improvises as she goes in, then locks the door behind her.

"They were, they were, everything was good, lovely." Abi stops.

No, Izzy thinks. It wasn't good or lovely. Rick just enjoyed having Abi begging him to stick around.

"Says he needs someone who understands what he needs…someone less "vanilla". I fucking hate that fucking word. Someone who wants to make him happy, instead of unhappy and frustrated and angry all the time, which he says I do, but I don't, we have fun. Had fun."

"Are you two OK?" It's Jordan from the kitchen. "I've got two bacon baguettes to go here."

"Coming." Izzy squeezes Abi to her. "Look, clean up your face, your eyes are all smudged. Just go down and finish this shift and we'll talk later."

"There's nothing to talk about. He says this is it. This relationship makes him unhappy and he deserves happiness and…"

"Izzy." Jordan again. "Please. Two baguettes."

Izzy snaps the bolt open and comes out onto the landing.

"Sorry," Jordan says. "But I need you here, you know."

"Yeah, I know. Sorry Jords."

Jordan looks relieved as she takes the plates from the kitchen service hatch and heads downstairs. Abi doesn't appear for another fifteen minutes. When she does, her make-up is still streaked. One finger is bleeding from where she has bitten the nail.

"Go home." Aidan says to Abi.

Izzy glances at him.

"Izzy, you stay. I can't manage without both of you."

Abi stumbles out the door with her black apron still tied at her waist. Izzy gathers up dirty plates and glasses from an empty table, and her heart thumps with dread, as she wonders what state Abi will be in later.

~

Mel keeps thinking about the gingerbread cottage in St Buryan. She drifts over the village on Google maps and even gets out an old Ordnance Survey. There are wooded valleys and tiny lanes, like threads, burrowing into the green, ending at a single dwelling. It could be any one of those hidden houses. Mel folds the map back together with a snap. It's nothing to her where Jake Gregory lives. She won't be going there.

~

He kissed me. Tansy hugs the three words to her heart as she drives home. *He kissed me.* But nothing else. He didn't ask her to go back to his. He didn't even suggest finding a secret spot in the churchyard. He kissed her, yes, many times, but that was it, and Tansy was too afraid of the answers to ask the questions.

When she gets home, Emmeline has just collected the girls. Tansy steps over the jumble of backpacks and lunchboxes, water bottles and abandoned muddy socks. She staggers as Amber mobs her, throws sticky arms around her legs.

"Where have you been?" Scarlet asks. "Why didn't you come for us?"

"I was out with a friend."

"What friend?"

"Mummy, Mummy, I didn't eat my tomatoes."

"What friend?"

"Just a friend. Someone I know."

"They were all squishy."

Tansy drops her own bag and drawing pad on the spare chair. Scarlet grabs the pad.

"You went drawing."

"Yes."

"I said, they were all squishy," Amber bellows.

"What were?"

"My TOMATOES. I told you."

"Where is this?" Scarlet asks.

"Let me have it, love, because your hands are grubby."

"I don't ever want tomatoes again."

"They're not grubby. I washed them after lunch."

"I SAID I don't want them again. Those tomatoes. Squishy."

"Come on, you two." Tansy says at last. "I'll run you a bath."

He kissed me, she thinks again as she chucks bubble bath into the tub, as she peels their muddy sweaty clothes off. *He kissed me*, as Scarlet and Amber throw handfuls of foam at each other and at her. *He kissed me*, as she squirts fruity shampoo on their heads. *He* kissed *me*. But why was that all?

Stefan slides the razor across Ivor's stubbly chin. The hairs are white and coarse and make Ivor itch. His skin is red and inflamed. Stefan has already nicked him once.

Ivor's dinner is in the oven and will be ready by the time Stefan has washed him and put him into his pyjamas.

"The things I can't do," Ivor says, as Stefan rinses the blade in the bowl. "Can't even shave myself. I shaved every day, you know. Tried to get outside with Carol. Couldn't do it."

"I didn't know that. Was it wise, just the two of you?"

"It was never going to happen. She wanted to try. I knew I couldn't. Bloody Zimmer skidded, nearly went over."

"You *must* be careful."

Ivor coughs and splutters into a tissue. Stefan pauses with the razor and glances quickly at the thick yellow sputum before Ivor can scrunch it up. He can't remember who was scheduled to come to Ivor that morning, but wonders if they also thought he was looking more frail, noticed he was still coughing despite the antibiotics.

"OK, we're done." He washes the razor again. A tiny swirl of blood mists in the soapy water. "I'll wash your legs, then that pie should be ready. Are you sure you don't want me to heat up some peas with it?"

"No peas. No appetite now. Everything's just packing up. Would you believe I used to eat T-bone steaks? Had teeth then."

Stefan squeezes Ivor's shoulder. Each time he comes, Ivor seems smaller and frailer. This gradual shrinking hurts Stefan. He's sure it hurts the others too. And as for Tansy and Emmeline, well, he can't imagine. His mother's death was swift, from cancer. He never had to see her becoming a tiny dot fading into the distance in this way.

Ivor stands, his swollen hands shaking on the Zimmer, and Stefan whisks down his trousers and underwear as quickly as possible. Ivor almost falls backwards, but regains his balance. Stefan gently washes his legs. One is large with fluid, the skin tight and cracking. The knee on the other leg is knobbly and twisted out of alignment. Stefan draws in his breath, wonders how Ivor even manages to shuffle around the house on his walking frame, and wonders how this decline can be happening so fast, so mercilessly.

˜

"You're definitely OK for Saturday night, to be with Ivor?" Tansy asks Carol.

"Definitely."

"It's just that I'm going out, so mum will have the girls and it'll be hard for her to cover if you can't make it."

"Tansy. Relax. I'll be there."

"Thank you."

Tansy ends the call and the screen dies. But her mind races. Nothing must stop her going to the private view with Gareth. Perhaps she should speak to one of the others too, make sure there's a back-up plan. After all, Carol can't *guarantee* she'll be there. She could be ill, or fall over, or Jeff could be in a car crash; anything could happen. She decides to call Mel.

˜

Mel hesitates before opening Jake's Facebook message. She can see the first few words: *So have you thought about when you…*

Might come over, she finishes the question in her head. Once she opens the message he'll know she has read it, and be waiting for a reply. She puts the phone down on the kitchen table, sets up the ironing board to prepare her uniform for Lanyon. She smooths the iron over the fabric, feeling the warmth through her fingers as she moves it across the board. The message is still there, still waiting. Jake is still there, still waiting.

She hangs her uniform on the back of the door. The air is warm and yeasty from the iron. She unplugs the flex and stands the iron upright to cool. She will read the message now. The repetitive action of the ironing has calmed her.

So have you thought about when you might like to come round?
I do a mean sparkling water.

Mel smiles. Her guess was spot on. The green light under his name tells her he is online. Online and waiting. Three dots pulsing. He has seen her open his message and is writing again.

Or something more interesting if you prefer?
No, sparkling water would be perfect :-)
So, when are you free?
Not sure just yet. I'll let you know.
Look forward to it.

Mel deletes the conversation and exits the app. Her heart is thudding unnervingly.

The phone rings shrilly in her hand and she jumps, thinking, for a stupid second, that it's Jake. *Tansy,* the screen says.

Mel's first thought is that somehow Tansy has read the exchange between her and Jake. In a nanosecond she dismisses the idea as ridiculous, paranoid, guilty. Ivor. It must be Ivor. *Jesus, no.* She stabs at the screen quickly to stop voicemail cutting in.

"Hi Mel, just asking a favour please."

Mel's darting pulse quietens. Ivor is fine.

Friday lunchtime. Tansy starts to feel uneasy. She hasn't heard anything from Gareth about the private view, not even a hello. She has texted him, left a voicemail, sent him a couple of Facebook messages. He hasn't opened them, but she can see he's been online. One of his blondes has shared a Facebook memory on his page: the two of them in a bar somewhere, cosied up on a settle, a lager bottle in front of him, a sparkly icy glass in front of her. Gareth has put a heart under the photo. No comment, so Tansy can't guess what the context was. Someone else must have been there to take the photo though. She enlarges the picture. Gareth in a black jacket and white shirt, his hair loose. The blonde's boobs spilling out of her top, a flower tattoo just visible on her collarbone, perfect black eyeliner flicks, a smug smile.

The day marches on towards school pick-up and the start of the weekend. At quarter to three, just as she's about to gather her keys and go for the girls, she gets a Facebook message.

Tansy, sorry, I'm not going tomorrow after all. Sorry to let you down like this.

What's the problem? I thought it was arranged. X

Yeah I know. Sorry. Just stuff.

Are you OK? Are you ill? X

I'm fine. Yeah. Good.

So what is it then? X

He does not open her message.

Gareth, what's going on? X

The green light is still there, smirking at her.

Please tell me what's the problem? I was looking forward to it. X

At last she finds her keys and trudges out to the car. The three o'clock news is starting on the radio. She's late. Scarlet will be anxious and angry, stuck in the classroom, Amber will be noisy and difficult, and when Emmeline gets home she'll have to tell her Gareth has stood her up. She negotiates the school traffic in the side road with tears burning her eyes.

Somehow she knows, she just *knows*, this is the end. If there was ever a beginning.

~

Later, Tansy is hunched on the sofa in the darkness with a tumbler of Shiraz. She shouldn't still be drinking. She has a thudding headache from coping with the girls' laughter and tantrums and squabbles with a rictus grin nailed on her face. It's now gone one in the morning, and Gareth still hasn't opened her messages. She started to text him, then deleted it. He knows she is trying to get in touch with him. He's been online all evening. He's ignoring her. This is the end.

The beginning was a rainy kiss in March's pale sunlight. It was the blurry sodium lamps of Hayle through a darkened window. Ephemeral moments, now gone. A single photo, some scratchy sketches in a ruined church to prove they had ever happened.

~

The girls wake her in the morning with the usual chorus of demands. Amber is wet and needs her nappy changed. Scarlet wants cereal, Amber wants a yoghurt; it quickly ends up on the carpet. Emmeline bangs the fridge and cupboard doors, writing a shopping list for the supermarket.

"When are you going out tonight?" Scarlet asks, slurping milk from her spoon.

Why, why the fuck, when she forgets so many things, does she have to remember this one quick remark.

"I'm not," Tansy tells her.

She wipes up the last of the yoghurt from the floor. Amber drops the spoon and it bounces off Tansy's sleeve, leaving a slimy white trail.

"No more news then?" Emmeline asks, as she gathers up a couple of mouldy apples from the fruit bowl and tips them in the bin.

"Nothing."

"Nothing what?" Scarlet demands. "I've finished. I don't want any more."

Tansy's eyes are dry and sore from wine and crying. She has looked online. The exhibition of Ryan Davenport's work is still happening. The private view is tonight. She flicked through the sample images: two life paintings of a voluptuous dark-skinned woman, an abstract of bright slashes. No drawings of Gareth.

"You're not going, are you?" Emmeline asks.

"What, on my own?"

"I wouldn't do that if I were you."

"Why not? He says he's not going. I could go on my own."

"What's the point of that? And what if he is there?"

"He said he couldn't go."

"Right. And he's ignored you since."

"What are you saying? He's going with someone else?"

"I don't know." Emmeline adds something to her list. "But whatever it is, he doesn't want you there."

Doesn't. Want. You. There. Four brutal words. Not new words. The same four brutal words that have been thudding in Tansy's head relentlessly. He doesn't want her there. He doesn't want her.

~

Izzy nudges open the bathroom doorway. Abi doesn't see or hear her. She's not looking at the door. She's not interested in the door. Izzy opens her mouth to speak, closes it again, watches in horror, grisly horror, as Abi slashes more black lines across her face with a marker pen. She's wearing a vest top; her arms and chest are already tattooed in black, the ink mixing with the blood from where she's gashed her forearms. She throws the marker down, capless, into the sink, and holds out a long long clump of her hair.

"No." Izzy lurches at Abi and grabs her before she can snatch up the scissors. "No, no, don't do that."

She holds Abi to her. Abi's face is hot and wet with tears. When they break apart there are black streaks on Izzy's T-shirt.

"He's not worth this," Izzy says, stroking Abi's head. "He's not worth anything."

She wishes she could think of original lines, not the tired old tropes from soap operas and magazines. She's frightened that she can't handle Abi alone, wonders if she should call her parents, ask one of them to come home. It's an early summer Saturday and the café will be heaving. There's a gig tonight. She can't ask them to leave. Not unless it's an emergency. Is this an emergency?

Abi stumbles out of her arms. Izzy looks at her sister, her little sister, who's made her laugh and swear for so many years. Ink and tears have made black streaks down Abi's face. Her chest and arms are black too, with crazy crosses and swirls and angry slashes. Some of the older cuts on her arms have reopened from the trauma. Abi rubs at blood and ink, and winces at the pain.

"Let me help you clean up," she says.

Abi doesn't speak. Izzy takes the marker pen out of the washbasin and runs some warm water. Abi cries silently, her tears snaking through the black and the grime. Izzy looks up a moment, studies their two faces in the mirror. Her own spray of freckles is startlingly bright across her white cheeks. Her jaunty chopped hair looks flat and squashed. Beside her, Abi trails long tendrils of strawberry blonde, tears and snot, with ink and blood congealing on her face. Her eyes are swollen to slits. Izzy shudders at the two faces, starts to gently wipe her sister's face. Still Abi does not speak.

~

Today. This will be the day. Stefan isn't at the hotel, isn't with Ivor. He has the whole day to himself, and is sure that today is the day he will finally face his fear and go to Amity. It's not planned. He just knew, when he woke, that the day had come. He feels a profound sense of peace as he envisions a quiet evening walking on the beach, kicking through shells and sea glass. He'll scramble up the rocky path to the clifftop then hunker down among the thrift plants and watch the waves breaking below. He'll remember and he'll cry. The spray will wash away the endless tears and he'll come home cleansed.

~

"What you looking at all the time?" Scarlet asks as Tansy pockets her mobile.
"Nothing."
"Can I play a game on it?"
"No."
Gareth has been online most of the day. That bright lime-green dot stares back unblinkingly at Tansy each time she checks. He doesn't open her messages. He doesn't post anything on his own page. What the hell is he doing? She searches for the exhibition artist, and finds one mutual friend: Gareth Crane. The artist has posted about the private view, has included one of the female nudes. Gareth is one of the people who liked the post.
"Are you going out tonight or not?" Scarlet asks.

"Not." Tansy thinks back to her conversation with Carol, demanding that she cover the shift for Ivor, and the back-up plan with Mel. All for nothing. What the fuck can she say if they ask her how her Saturday night went?

As the afternoon slides by she wonders whether she should go to the private view alone. If anyone questions her she could say she had made arrangements to meet Gareth there. But what if Gareth went anyway? With the blonde with the tattoo and the perfect eyeliner.

Scarlet is watching a musical on CBeebies and Emmeline is reading to Amber. Tansy sneaks into her room and flicks through the clothes hanging in her wardrobe. If she goes alone she'll wear something different to what she imagined she'd wear with Gareth.

"Don't do it."

Emmeline in the doorway, still holding one of Amber's gaudy pink books.

Tansy spins round, a short blue dress in her arms.

"Do what?"

"Go to the private view. I promise you, it'll be a mistake. Whatever's going on, whatever the story is, that would be a mistake."

Tansy drops the dress on her bed. She's been useless all day, ignoring the girls, letting Emmeline change Amber and pour juice for Scarlet. Her pulse is thudding erratically and she wants a drink.

"If only he'd tell me what's going on. I don't know what I've done. He asked me to come. I wouldn't have even known about it if he hadn't invited me."

"Perhaps some other people he knows are going and he doesn't want to have to explain who you are, but he didn't know they were going when he asked you."

"Maybe." *The blonde.*

"It's not like you'll never see him again. You know where he lives."

Tansy starts, thinking of the dark rain-streaked windows, the hazy street lamps, the soft carpet on the back corridor. She doesn't think she'll ever see any of those again.

"I'm not going," she says at last, and stuffs the dress through a hanger in the wardrobe.

"Come on, nearly time for the girls' tea. Shall we have pizzas?"

"Sure they'd like that. I'm not hungry."

"Granny! You were reading to me."

"Sorry darling. Just had to see Mummy a minute."

Emmeline goes back to Amber. Tansy checks her phone again. Nothing. It's almost time for the private view. She kicks off her slippers and fumbles her feet into Converse boots, grabs her denim jacket.

In the kitchen Scarlet is helping Emmeline place tomatoes on the pizza.

"I'm not having those," Amber grumbles. "They're squishy. I told you."

"It's a new packet, stupid." Scarlet pretends to lob a tomato at Amber

"We'll leave your bit without any," Emmeline says quickly. "Ah, here's Mummy."

"I'm going out," Tansy says.

"You said you weren't." Scarlet bites into a tomato and pips squirt out.

"Tansy. I thought you said…"

"I'm not going there. Look. I haven't done my face or anything." Tansy gestures at her scruffy boots, old jeans and T-shirt. "I just want to go for a drive. I won't be long."

"Be careful. Drive safely."

"I will."

In the hall Tansy swipes her phone again. Gareth is offline. Of course. He's on his way to the private view.

Izzy is so tired. It's been a long day at home with Abi. Her silent tattooing of her skin was almost more shocking, more painful, than the wrenching sobs that came afterwards. Izzy suggested they went for a walk together, but Abi refused. Now Izzy is feeling trapped and hot in the house. She opens the back door and breathes the warm clean air.

Holly texted several times and Izzy replied blandly. Abi was upset but they were OK. Abi had eaten some lunch. She hadn't but Izzy didn't want to worry her mother any more than necessary. Samarkand is so busy on Saturday lunchtimes. It would be far too unkind to give Holly any extra stress.

Abi has been in her room for the past half hour or so. Izzy closes the back door quietly. She'll creep upstairs and check on her. If she's asleep Izzy will have a quick shower. Her eyes are scratchy and her hair creeps with sweat. She'll feel more awake, more alive. Then she can wake Abi and try to get her to eat something.

Izzy jogs upstairs. No sounds of crying from Abi's room. She pushes the door open gently. Abi is curled on her bed, eyes closed, one hand flung out, loose hair dripping over the edge of the bed. There are still some dark patches on Abi's pale skin – her cheek, her chin, her cut forearm where Izzy didn't want to scrub too roughly because it made Abi wince.

"Abi," Izzy whispers.

Abi doesn't answer or stir. Izzy creeps out and shuts the door once more.

It doesn't hurt as much as Stefan imagined. He walks on the soft sand of Amity, and picks up a few shells and rounded nuggets of glass, blue and green, mauve and clear. He scrambles on the dark rocks, slimy with seaweed and rough with barnacles. He peers in the pools left by the tide, some in scooped-out hollows of rock, some in sandy basins, one – deeper, darker – under the cliff. Sometimes he sees the dart of a fish, and once the lilac bloom of a tiny jellyfish. When he agitates the water with his hand, the sand erupts up into a frenzy of gold sparkles, and the strands of weed swirl red and green.

He ignores the few other people on the beach. He walks with his head down, and his hands in his pockets. The sea pounds in his ears, his brain, sends his heart rocketing, but he doesn't look at it. His fingers sift the stones and glass in his pocket, and the tiny sand crystals that he knows will stay in the lining for months, if not for ever. It reminds him of the shards of Nina in his ring, that sand in his pocket. Microscopic glitter, fairy dust. He turns his hand, this way and that, watching the spark of the ring. He no longer hears the sea, the shouts of other people on the beach, a car on the road.

"We're here together," he tells Nina.

～

Izzy pads out of the bathroom wrapped in a pink fluffy towel. She glances at Abi's door. Still shut. Still quiet. She must still be sleeping. Izzy goes up to her attic to dress and rub her hair dry, and into its tufty spikes.

～

Tansy slams the car door shut and scrabbles the keys into the ignition. For a second she feels like she could vomit with relief, just to be away from her mother and children, from Emmeline's suspicious gaze, from the girls' constant demands.

As her breathing calms and her nausea subsides a little, she tugs out the seatbelt and starts the engine. She has no idea where she's going, except that she's not going to that gallery. Or to Gareth's flat.

She turns up the radio and the songs that are the soundtrack to this evening of loss and sadness. The sky is a clear blue-mauve with skeins of cloud over the moorland. Tansy turns to the rocky spine of Cornwall, its inner core of granite. The bleak uplands of red and gold and umber, the stunted trees and half-forgotten standing stones. She finds herself on a moorland road she knows well, and the landscape opens up either side of her. A dark knot of conifers to her left, the undulating humps of round barrows, a few lonely horses grazing the tough grass. A narrow lane on the right. She indicates, though there is no traffic around, and rumbles over the ragged tarmac. The flash of a stream darting under the road, then the layby, tangled with grasses and bracken. She stumbles out of the car.

It's so quiet. A few whickers and rustles. The gate that leads onto the moorland is almost stuck in the overgrown foliage, but she forces it open enough to squeeze through. The grasses are long, licking at her legs; under her feet the ground is springy from the nearby watercourse.

She came here with Charlie. Many years ago, before Scarlet. They scrambled past this same thicket, where he kissed her long and hard, and yanked her knickers down under her skirt. Tansy pauses. It was this tree where Charlie fucked her, surely, or that one next to it, the mossy one. It doesn't even matter anymore.

The grass and heather turn to churned-up mud. Hoofprints. Puddles of viscous water. She jumps from one dry ridge to another, slides, and her foot goes into a puddle. Ahead the stream crosses the bridleway, and a haze of dragonflies blurs before her eyes. Turquoise and gold, iridescent and gauzy, they hover over the shallow water and half-submerged stones.

Charlie brought her here to show her the dragonflies. She never asked him how he knew of the place, if he'd brought another girl, fucked another girl up against a mossy tree under a vacant blue sky.

~

Izzy feels her heart rate rising. On some visceral level, her body is aware that all is not right. She throws her hair-towel on the bed, careless of the damp, and runs barefoot down the stairs. Abi's door is still shut. Izzy bursts into her sister's room. There is no one there. Izzy gulps. She thought, in those crazy seconds, she might find Abi lying in a blood-stained bed as her life leached from her wrists, or hanging from some makeshift gallows.

The bedcover is thrown aside. Abi's phone is on the bedside cabinet. She must have woken and gone down for a drink.

"Abi," Izzy calls as she flies down to the ground floor.

The house is too quiet, too empty. Abi is not in the kitchen making tea, or in the living room lying on the sofa, clutching a cushion to her chest. Izzy whirls in panic and suddenly glances out of the front window. The slash of yellow that should be there is not. Abi has taken the car.

~

Stefan scrambles up the scree of rocks to the cliff path and starts walking. Amity Cove is below, to his right. From here he can see the swirls of colour making up the sea and its currents, the jumbled footprints on the sand. The path clings close to the edge, where bluebells drift in a mauve stain, and sea thrift bobs in the crevices of lichen-gold rocks. He walks on, higher and higher, to a rugged outcrop on the edge of the world. There's a hollow beside it, edged with bluebells and wild garlic. He slides down into the nest and inhales the garlic, and the bluebells, th e sand and the salt.

—

Tansy returns to her car, her eyes blurry with tears. She must get back. They will be worrying about her. She checks the time. The private view is still going on. Gareth is still offline. She turns the car clumsily and heads back along the lane. On the main road across the moors a yellow car careens past her. She can't see the driver, but it's Izzy's car, going at a hell of a pace.

—

Izzy doesn't know what to do. Abi has gone out in the car and left her phone behind. Holly and Aidan are at Samarkand. It's Saturday night and there's a gig on. She just doesn't know what to do.

—

Stefan doesn't immediately understand or acknowledge what he's feeling. Then he realises he's at peace. He is here at Amity – with Nina in his ring – and he feels calm and rested. The gentle folding and breaking of the waves below is now like a soothing heartbeat, slowing his own pulse. He doesn't want to get up. He could stay here all night in this sheltered hollow, as the evening sky darkens to amethyst, and ships' lights sparkle on the horizon. He could sleep here, he thinks, his dreams lapped by the sea and the breeze, and he would wake to a new day and a new life, knowing at last he had found the absolution he needs.

    He starts. He is not alone.

Nina?

He scrabbles round in the hollow to see who is there.

It's a young girl. She has long red-gold hair in knotty tresses. She's wearing jeans and a grubby T-shirt. She's hovering on the edge of the cliff just beyond the outcrop of rocks. She's too close to the edge.

Stefan stands stiffly. He does not dare call to her. It may frighten her.

The girl wavers on the edge. Stefan knows the cliff crumbles to a ledge, overhanging the boiling surf and eddies round the rocks below. He climbs out of his hollow as the girl takes a step, then another. She squats down, puts her hand to the ragged turf and slides over. Stefan catches his breath, even though he knows the narrow shelf of rock is there. She straightens on the lower level, catches her flyaway hair with a hand at her neck. He moves quickly towards the cliff edge.

There's no one else about. He glances behind him and along the cliff path. It's just him and her on the edge of the world.

The breaking waves sound louder again, angrier. The soothing heartbeat has become a jagged fibrillation.

"Are you OK?" he calls out.

It sounds feeble, anodyne. He just knows he must say something, make her turn before whatever it is she intends to do. The girl doesn't turn. She holds her hair in one hand, stares out to sea. Her shoulders are hunched and he thinks she may be crying.

"I said, are you OK?" he calls louder. "Can I help you back up?"

She turns this time. He can see her head and upper body above the broken cliff. Her face is blotchy, her eyes swollen.

"What d'you want?" she shouts.

"I thought you were stuck and might need a hand up."

"No."

She turns away from him.

Please don't jump, he thinks. Almost says it aloud.

"It's not safe there. Please let me help you up." He walks towards her, focussing on her bright hair, and not the crumbling cliff edge, the crash of the breakers, the wind in his face.

"I don't want to be safe."

"What do you want then?"

"Fuck off."

Stefan stops. He could almost reach her, but he'd never be able to haul her up at this angle, not without her co-operation. He doesn't want her to fight him. He watches her, her tense spine, her tangled hair. He knows she knows he is still there.

"Go away," she calls. "Fuck off. Leave me alone."

Stefan twists his ring. Of course. He should ring 999. He scrabbles his phone out of his pocket. The girl staggers and turns back to face him.

"What are you doing?"

"I'm calling…" Who does he ask for? Police? Coastguard?

"You put that down."

"You need help."

"You hang up or I'll jump now. I mean it."

A gust snatches her hair. He hesitates, his finger on the 9. Leaving the number undialled on the screen, he puts the phone in his pocket, raises his hands.

"OK. I've put it away."

"Now fuck off. This is private. I have to do this on my own."

"Do what?"

The girl gestures to the edge of the rocky shelf, the sea, blue and mauve to the horizon. The light is falling.

"My girlfriend died here." Stefan is shocked at the words that leave his mouth.

"She jump?"

"No. Surfing. Rip current. The sea's vicious down there."

"Yeah, they'll never find me. I could end up anywhere. Hawaii. Tahiti. The North Pole."

"You been to any of those places?"

"Of course not."

"Nina, my girlfriend. She wanted to go to Hawaii to surf. And Tahiti."

"Perhaps she's there now then."

"They found her body."

"She even fucked that up then."

"She didn't fuck anything up. She didn't want to die. She wanted to live."

"Lucky her."

"Not really. Not now. Look." Stefan holds up his hand. "This is all I have of her."

"What?"

"This ring. Look at it. Come closer. It's got her ashes in it. That's all that's left of her. Of a person. When they're dead. Dust. Bits of dust in glass."

The girl doesn't answer, doesn't come closer to look at the ring.

"What's your name?" Stefan asks. "I'm Stefan."

"What's it to you?"

"Well, if you jump, I will have to tell people. I need to know who you are."

"Abi."

Long red hair. Abi.

"Are you Izzy's sister?"

She starts. "You know Izzy?"

"Yeah. She looks after Ivor. So do I."

"Ah fuck. Stefan. Of course. Dead girlfriend."

"I won't call 999. Can I call Izzy?"

Abi shrugs, defeated.

"How did you get here? Did you drive?"

She nods. "Car's down there."

"Does anyone know you're here?"

"Of course not. I'd be fucking dead now if you hadn't turned up."

"I didn't turn up. I was already here."

"You know what I mean."

"OK. I know what you mean. Can I call Izzy? Please?"

She wavers. She takes a tiny step towards the grassy ridge.

"Give me your hand."

"I don't want to be here any more."

"You didn't. I think you might now. I think you're thinking of Izzy and your family. I think you want to see them again."

"I never wanted to get away from them. Just him. I can't live without him."

"Come on, Abi." Stefan holds out his hand. The left one, the one with the ring glittering on his finger.

"I can't."

"You can. I'm not leaving until you come."

She stands, shivering in the dusk. A wave breaks below; spume flies up.

"Please," Stefan says. "Just come to me. Let me call Izzy. I'll drive you home. Or wherever you want to go. You can stay on my sofa if you want. Please just take my hand."

Her fingers are bony and icy in his. He grasps her hand, puts his other arm around her shoulders and heaves her up onto the tufty grass. She's shaking. So is he. His throat is dry, so dry. He thinks he might shit himself. Keeping his arm around her he guides her to the path. When she is safely away from the cliff he tugs off his jumper and wrestles it onto her. That's when he sees the scabbed cuts on her arms. Cuts and dark ink stains.

"Come down to the car and I'll call Izzy," he says.

Abi stumbles beside him, exhausted. She must not drive herself anywhere, he thinks. He bundles her into the passenger seat of his car, gets in beside her.

"Christ Abi, you scared me to death."

"I'm sorry. I'm so sorry." She chokes on her tears.

He squeezes her arm gently, lets her cry and cry. The number 999 is still on the screen when he gets out his mobile. He deletes it, and scrolls for Izzy in his contacts.

She answers immediately.

"Stefan?"

"I'm with Abi."

"What? Abi? What? Is that her crying?"

"Yeah. I…bumped into her up at Amity. She's…upset. I'll bring her home. You'll have to come and get the car tomorrow."

"Is she all right?"

"She's all right."

"Can I speak to her?"

"Sure."

He hands the phone to Abi.

"Izzy?" she asks thickly. "I'm sorry. I'm so fucking sorry."

Abi shoves the mobile back to him.

"She's very cold and upset, but she's all right," Stefan says. "I'll bring her over now, OK?"

It sounds like Izzy is crying at the other end. She knows damn well what Abi was planning.

"Stefan, thank you."

"It's all OK. We'll see you soon."

Stefan's feet shake as he engages gear. The car is moving. She can't escape now. Surely she won't fling open the door and leap out? He glances across. Her seat belt is fastened. Her hands are in her lap. He can't see her face because of her hair.

"What about the car?" Abi says.

"Get it tomorrow. It'll be alright."

Stefan is calmer now they are speeding towards Penzance.

"You were really brave," he says.

"They say it's what cowards do."

"I don't think so. You were really brave to get up there, but even braver to come back."

"I'm sorry about your girlfriend."

"It was horrible. Awful."

"Izzy said something about her once."

"Do you want to tell me why you're so unhappy? Would it help?"

"It'll sound so stupid…after what happened to you. This guy. He wanted me to do things I didn't want…couldn't do. Said if I wouldn't he'd leave me. He fucked around with me, ending it and coming back, then he left me because I couldn't do what he wanted."

Stefan wants to ask what this guy, this arsehole, demanded, but he can't. Instead he says, "You must never do things you don't want to do. Not for anyone. If he cared about you he wouldn't be pressuring you like that. But you know that, don't you?"

"I know that," Abi whispers.

~

Tansy flicks open a bottle of lager. The gold cap skitters across the worktop. She picks it up, turns it over and over in her spare hand as she drinks. Emmeline and the girls are making a lot of noise in the living room, reading stories, acting out the voices. She can't bring herself to walk in, to have to smile and laugh at their antics, to gasp at the wicked witch or the wolf, to point out details in the illustrations. She hopes the girls will go to bed soon. It's been such a long and painful day. She has had to pretend to be strong, and she has failed.

The private view is over now. Night is falling, that dark green dusk of early summer. Gareth is back online. Her messages are still unopened. She does not dare send any more. She drains her bottle and immediately opens the fridge for another. With a twist of her wrist the gold top flies off. She realises she still has the first in her pocket. She rubs the two tiny discs together as she drinks, as the girls shriek. It's almost as if they have become souvenirs, amulets, of this night. She'll put them on her shelf. Not that she needs reminders.

~

Izzy just holds Abi and lets her sob and sob.

"I'm sorry, I'm sorry," Abi gasps over and over.

Izzy strokes her messy hair. "It's OK," she says. "You're safe now. Let me run you a bath."

Abi nods distractedly. "You'll tell them, won't you?"

"I have to," Izzy says gently. "And the car's not here."

Abi nods again.

"And, Abi? You need to see the doctor again. First thing next week. Please. Get yourself some tablets again. Please."

"Will you come with me?"

~

Stefan doesn't realise how his legs are trembling until he parks and scrambles out. Abi still has his jumper, and he is freezing. His feet feel like the circulation has died. He stumbles down the road, his heart juddering uneasily under his sternum. He almost saw someone die. And not just anyone. Izzy's little sister.

The flat is dark and unwelcoming. He flicks on the lights, grabs a hoodie from the sofa and zips it up tightly. He's scared and spooked, and doesn't want to be alone.

~

Vicky is about to start washing up when her mobile rings. *Stefan*, says the screen. She glances round the kitchen. No one there. Well, there wouldn't be. Kev and Skye are watching TV. Harry is out with friends. She presses green.

"Vic, hi."

"Hi," she says, momentarily confused by his use of Kev's shortening. "Everything OK?"

"You know you said I could talk to you and that? Do you have a moment?"

"Sure." She kicks the kitchen door closed. "Is everything OK?"

"Yes. No. I just feel fucking weird. I think I just stopped a girl from killing herself."

"What? What?"

"Izzy's sister. I was up at Amity."

The line crackles.

"Stefan, the signal's terrible. Are you at home? Can I come over? You can tell me about it."

"Ah, you don't want to bother with that."

"You said Izzy's sister nearly killed herself?! Let me come over. I can be at yours in fifteen."

Kev is grumbling to Skye about something in the living room. Vicky runs softly to the bathroom, gives her hair a quick brush and swipes on some lipstick.

"Just popping out," she calls, her hand on the front door latch. "One of the carers wants a friend to talk to."

She thinks Skye calls something back, but she doesn't wait to be sure.

~

Stefan gathers up the pile of clothes and books and junk on the sofa and dumps it all on his bed. The place is a tip. There are dirty mugs and plates to be washed, and the bin is overflowing with cartons and tins. He just doesn't have the energy to clean up. He never expected Vicky to come round. Or did he hope, with some dark corner of his heart, that she would?

He fills the kettle with fresh water and waits.

~

The warm day has faded to a chilly evening and Vicky zips up her jacket as she walks along Stefan's street.

"Hi," he calls down from the upstairs window. "I'll buzz you in."

He is waiting for her on the upper landing.

"I didn't mean you to come out."

"It's fine. No trouble. Please tell me what on earth's happening."

"Come in. Let me get you a drink."

He ushers her to the sofa. She shrugs out of her coat. He makes tea, offers her chocolate biscuits. He stands at the window, his back to her.

"I went up to Amity. I've been meaning to go for ages, you know, to find closure or whatever they call it. Today seemed the right day. I was up on the cliff, just sitting on the grass watching the evening and the sea, and I was feeling it. At peace. OK about being there. OK about Nina. Then this girl appeared. Like out of nowhere. She was on the edge and I asked if she needed help and she told me to fuck off and that if I called 999 she'd jump. I was so fucking scared. I didn't know what to do. To call 999 or not. What I should say to her."

"You say it was Izzy's sister? I didn't know you knew her."

"I don't. I was talking to her. Just trying to get her to talk, take her mind off, no that's stupid, I don't mean that. You know. I asked her name and she said Abi, and she had red hair like Izzy and I told her my name and then I guessed. Her arms were all cut up, like she'd taken a knife to them."

"Christ. It must have been awful."

Stefan slides down beside her on the sofa. "Of all the places…I told her about Nina. I tried to show her the ring. She wasn't interested."

Vicky glances down at the blue stone on Stefan's finger. "You were trying to get her in a conversation. Any kind of conversation."

"Yeah, yeah, that's it." He bites a biscuit, swallows awkwardly. "God, I feel sick. So shaky. It's worse now."

"You got her down though."

"I don't know how. I don't really remember. I got her down and into my car. I asked if I could call Izzy. She, Abi, she was like all deflated, given up, didn't care. I drove her back home to Izzy. Her car's still up at Amity."

"You've done something incredible." Vicky reaches out and takes his wrist in her hand. "You saved her life."

"I don't think…she probably wouldn't have done it."

"She might. But she didn't. Because of you."

"I feel weird. Awful. Like, imagine if I hadn't been there and she had meant to do it. D'you think Nina was helping me?"

"I don't know. She may well have."

Vicky spots a bottle of whisky by the toaster.

"Let me get you a nightcap."

"What? Oh, thanks. Yes. Have one yourself."

"Better not. Where are the glasses?"

Stefan points to the wall cupboard. She finds a tumbler, and sloshes whisky into it. She inhales the peaty fragrance for a second, then replaces the stopper.

"Thanks, Vic." He takes the glass. "I'm sorry. I just wanted to tell someone. Not to be congratulated or anything. Just to tell someone, to share it with someone. I didn't know who to tell."

"I'm glad you called me." She squeezes his hand, the one holding the glass. "We're friends, aren't we?"

"We are. Thank you. Thank you for coming. I'm not much company."

"You don't have to be." Vicky drinks tea. "You're better company than my family tonight. Harry's out. Skye and Kev are watching some reality show on telly."

"What did you tell them?"

"I said one of the carers needed someone to talk to. Could have been someone from Lanyon. They didn't ask. Whatever. I think Kev and I have reached the end of the road."

"I'm sorry."

Vicky shrugs. She honestly doesn't know if she's sorry or not.

"I don't know if am," she says at last.

"Well, if you ever need a friend to talk to, I'm here."

Stefan finishes his whisky, sets the tumbler down on the floor with a clunk. He shifts on the sofa, so he's facing her.

"Kev's a twat."

Vicky smiles and shakes her head.

"He's a twat."

"We probably both are…but these things happen."

"You're not. You're a lovely person."

Vicky feels the blush stain her face, and something else, something deeper, darker, more visceral. It's like that moment, that ephemeral moment on the top of the tide, before the answering surge. They face each other, then the current pulls, and Vicky does not know if it is him kissing her or her kissing him, but either way she doesn't care.

—

Tansy wakes early. The house is quiet. It takes a few seconds for her to recall why she is feeling so wretched. Gareth. The private view. The dragonflies on the downs. Two beer bottle lids rubbed together between her fingers like amulets.

There's nothing on Gareth's Facebook and he's offline. Still dazed from sleep she sends another message.

Hi, how are you? Please talk to me. X

She imagines him waking, reaching for his phone on the bedside cupboard, seeing a new message. He knows he has ignored her other ones. Will he open them now the private view has been and gone? Or will he simply delete them? He may already have deleted the others. She wouldn't even know.

—

Stefan arrives early at Ivor's. He parks on the drive and waits a moment. The last twenty-four hours – less than that really – have been crazy. Amity, Abi, Vicky. He intended his evening visit to the cove to be a peaceful reconciliation with himself, with the memory of Nina. He half imagined calling George, but he can't now. Not after what happened with Vicky. His pulse jumps at the memory. She didn't pull away or shout at him or anything. She kissed him back, and slid her arms round him and, when they drew apart, she smiled at him, and stroked his face, and kissed him again, harder, deeper.

Nothing more. Nothing more than kisses. Not last night. Stefan woke terrified that Vicky would have texted him to say it was a mistake and must never happen again. There were messages on his phone. The first from Izzy, thanking him again for looking after Abi, and thanking him for offering to wake Ivor up this morning for her. The second was from Vicky and Stefan felt sick clicking on it.

Hope you're OK this morning. I'm at Lanyon. Will text or call. X

Before he gets out of the car he reads it again. He hasn't replied. He doesn't want her to think he's pressuring her. But if she hasn't sent him a message by lunchtime he'll send her one.

He gets out of the car. The morning is beautiful. A washed-out blue sky. That lovely cool-warm air. Ivor's clematis nods huge purple blooms. Stefan brushes the rosemary bush by the front door, and the smell rises, medicinal and pungent.

~

It's all Vicky can think about. She washes the residents at Lanyon House, carries breakfast trays, rubs cream onto sore legs, administers eye drops. She wheels people into the day room after breakfast, and lends an arm to those on walking sticks. She smiles and jokes with residents and staff, but all she can think about is kissing Stefan, and whether that had been in her mind all along when she said she would go round to his flat.

~

The pictures appear by the middle of the morning. Ryan Davenport has tagged Gareth, along with a host of other people, so the photos come up on Gareth's Facebook page. He's not in many of the shots. In one he's talking to an older couple, a glass of red in his hand. In another all Tansy can see is his back as he stands in front of a huge abstract canvas. She can't see that busty blonde with him anywhere;

he does seem to have gone alone. But he went. And he went without her. And he obviously doesn't care that Tansy can see these pictures, because he's put likes and commented: *Great show, Ryan. Well done.*

And, of course, her messages remain unopened.

~

The electric doors hiss open and Vicky steps outside, inhaling deeply. The sun is warm on her bare arms, and the breakers must be gentle below as she can hardly hear them. She takes her phone out. No reply from Stefan. He must have had a change of heart. Stupid woman, she berates herself. He had gone to Amity to sort his head out about Nina, then he rescued Abi from the cliff edge, and then she had the audacity to kiss him.

Ignoring two of the residents perched on a bench with their walking frames parked before them, she starts across the asphalt towards the stiff pale grass of the cliff. The horizon is clear, a sharp watercolour line with only a drift of cloud. She stops and turns back to Lanyon, gazes up at the giant cream building, its many windows, the spiral iron fire escape – how many residents could attempt that? – and the turret at its heart.

Vicky's phone jumps in her hand. She squints at the screen. It's hard to read in the sunlight. She cups her hand. A message from Stefan.

Hi, how are you? X

Vicky quickly hits his number. He answers immediately.

"I was just outside," she rushes. "I was about to text you. It's been so busy today." She stops.

"Are you all right?" he asks.

"I'm all right."

"I mean, you know…yesterday…last night…are you OK about that?"

Vicky grins into the blue horizon. "I'm very very OK about that. But I thought you might have had second thoughts."

"I did have second thoughts," he says, but she can hear his smile. "And third and fourth. And they were all really good thoughts."

"Stefan! I'll have to get back in a minute. I'm here till this evening."

"Can I see you again? I mean, you know…would you like to come round or something? I know it's hard for you."

"I'd love to."

"I'll let you go then."

Vicky hangs up and almost skips back to the electric doors. One of the guys on the bench calls out to her and she waves and grins, and the rest of the long day of commodes and ulcers and false teeth doesn't seem daunting at all.

~

Tansy doesn't even understand what has happened for a few moments. She clicks on her conversation with Gareth, sees her messages are still unread, and then sees that Gareth is no longer available to chat. She tries to go through to his profile and it has disappeared. He simply doesn't exist any more. And then she understands that he has completely blocked her, severed her from his life, without any words.

~

On Monday Izzy calls the surgery and gets an emergency appointment for Abi. She goes with her, assuring Holly and Aidan that she will let them know how it goes, and sits quietly in the corner by a box of Lego and plastic toys, while Abi explains brokenly how she needs help again.

Izzy drifts her eyes round the little room, reading the titles on the doctor's bookshelf, examining the model of the cervical spine, trying to trace her height and weight on the loudly coloured BMI chart. Abi mutters about a man who hurt her, her struggle to cope without him, the thoughts that led her to the cliff on Saturday night.

"It was Izzy's friend who found me," she says. "He talked to me. Stopped me doing it."

"Doing it meaning what?" the GP asks gently.

"Jumping over."

"Would you have done that if Izzy's friend hadn't been there?"

"Yes," Abi says.

Ten minutes later they leave with a prescription for the tablets Abi took before. They go to the pharmacy and cash it in. As soon as they get home Abi punches one of the blue and white bullets out of the blister pack and gulps it down with water. She seems like an empty cloth sack, Izzy thinks. The fight, the fierce desperate fight inside her, has simply gone, evaporated into nothing.

~

Tansy answers the phone to Charlie.

"Hello stranger," he says.

"Stranger?"

"Well, I dunno. You haven't spoken to me for ages. I haven't seen the girls for ages. You seemed so distracted last time we spoke I thought I'd give you some space."

"Oh. Right. Distracted."

"Tansy, what's wrong?"

"Nothing."

"D'you want to meet up sometime? Drink?"

"Uh. Yeah, sure. Would you like the girls this weekend?"

"I'd love to. If it's not a problem for you."

"It's not. I'm sorry. It's been...oh I dunno."

"You can tell me."

"It's nothing."

And yet, Tansy knows the one person she could tell, the one person she could share her impetuous obsession with, and her sudden jagged heartbreak, is Charlie. But she cannot.

~

Izzy takes Abi to Ivor's with her on Monday night. Abi hunches into the passenger seat, tells Izzy she is scared to drive again. She reaches out a finger to touch the gearstick, the handbrake, the radio dial.

"I don't think I'll be able to drive again."

"I think you will," Izzy says. "One day it will just happen."

Like Stefan choosing to go to Amity that evening. Izzy shivers again at the sheer luck, the coincidence, whatever it was, that made Stefan decide to climb the cliff and watch the sinking sun.

Abi has never met Ivor before. Izzy suggests they have a chat while she starts on some vegetables for Ivor's dinner. Then Abi can take over the cooking while she washes Ivor's legs and dresses him for bed. Izzy glances up from the sink, where she is scrubbing new potatoes. Abi is smiling at Ivor as he tells some story. She is still deathly pale and strained and fragile, but she is listening and smiling and, once, she laughs.

~

"I start work at twelve tomorrow," Stefan says.

He can hear the rush of wind behind Vicky's voice. She must be out in that car park again.

"Would you like me to come over?" she asks.

"I'd love to see you. When could you be here?"

"When the others have all gone out."

—

The dark is soft and soothing on Tansy's face. She pulls the front door to behind her but doesn't let is shut. A tiny moth buzzes round the porch light. Tansy steps over a snail on the path and drops down to the lawn. Sounds and scents are more acute after dark. The leaves and blooms in the garden are all shades of silver and grey. The headlights of a passing car pick out a beam of more tiny moths and gnats.

Tansy inhales the scents of summer. She hoped she would share nights like this with Gareth, walking under the moon, sitting out late on the terrace drinking as the light fell and the moths came out.

She walks on, over the damp grass, to the wall. Three tall foxgloves, spectral in the moonlight. She thinks of the wild paths and tracks of the far west, her fantasies of walking the ancient ways with Gareth, finding a sheltered hollow behind a cairn, somewhere by Zennor or Morvah.

A large soft moth swoops down from the boughs of the apple tree. A hawk of some kind, she thinks distractedly. Poplar perhaps, or Eyed.

Voices of two or three people approaching along the path. The bobbing of a torch. Life is striding on, people are weaving home from the pub, moths are gliding the air currents by moonlight. None of them care that a man she hardly knew has cut her out of his life.

—

"Marry me."

Carol stared at Ivor. She must have misheard.

"I said, marry me," he repeated.

"I...I can't," she stammered, and drank quickly from her tea to give her hands something to do, her mouth something to do.

"You can," Ivor said gently. "If you want to. Perhaps you don't want to. And that's fine. We're fine as we are, aren't we?"

"It's not I don't want to...just...I've got a son, and you've got a family, and they don't even know about me."

"They know you model for me," Ivor said. "At least, I think they do."

"They've never met me. You've never introduced me to them. You've met Louis. But I don't know Emmeline and Tansy at all. They wouldn't like you to marry me."

"It's not up to them."

"No, but you don't want to upset them. They're your family. They're important."

"So are you, Carol. I love you." He sighs. "I'm just being stupid. Of course you don't want to marry me. You're a young woman still. You can do anything, marry anyone. You don't want an old codger."

"It's nothing to do with age," Carol flares.

But it was, in a way. Ivor was healthy and fit, yes, but nothing could change the immense difference in their ages. One day he would fall ill and she would still be young. One day he would die and she would be left alone. And his daughter and granddaughter would condemn her as a gold digger. Carol couldn't even think about things like Ivor's house and paintings, his legacy, and who would inherit them if she married him. Certainly she and Louis wouldn't struggle financially if she said yes, but that wasn't the right reason, and it wasn't enough.

"I'm sorry," Ivor said. "I've upset you, made you feel awkward."

"No, I'm sorry. I should say sorry. You surprised me. Thank you. Thank you for asking me. I just don't think I want to marry anyone."

Carol stood up, and the room tilted.

"Do you want to go home?" Ivor said.

"I think I will, if you don't mind. I feel wrong staying here."

Carol snatched up her coat and keys and ran to her car. Ivor stood in the doorway watching her reverse out. She waved once, awkwardly, through tears.

She didn't see him again for twenty years.

~

"I thought they'd never go," Vicky says as Stefan shuts the flat door behind her. "I was going nuts. They weren't any later than usual really. You know what it's like, when you're waiting, when you want people to go, and they don't, it takes for ever."

"Vic," Stefan says softly. "Calm down. It's OK. You're here."

"Sorry. Yes, I'm here. I'm anxious. I suppose. I haven't…" She stops, unable to find the words, the words that will make it real.

"Haven't been unfaithful to Kev?"

"Yes. That. But I want to be here."

"Shall we go to the bedroom?"

"Let's."

"It's been a while for me."

"I know. It's been a while for me too."

"So we're equal then."

"We're equal."

They're not, of course, Vicky thinks, as he takes her hand and leads her to his bed. He's young and free. She has a husband and two teenage children. It is completely unequal. It's crazy, probably stupid. It can only end badly. But, at last, after so long in the dark and the cold, she feels alive and vibrant; her blood pulses with new energy, and her heart is full.

Mel almost misses the tiny side road under its canopy of trees. She brakes harshly, without checking her rear-view mirror first, and swings into the lane. Grasses and thorns brush the sides of the car as she rolls gently down. There's a scrubby passing place in front of a gate, and she memorises it in case she meets anything coming the other way. At the bottom of the hill the car rumbles across a stone bridge that looks like it's been there since forever. She catches a steely flash of the stream, and beside it a half-crumbled stile and a finger post showing a footpath into no man's land.

So far she hasn't seen any houses or cars, any signs of human life. The road curves to the left under another awning of trees and there, in front of her, is a cottage, with Jake's car parked in the yard. The road continues on, under the trees, with grasses sprouting along its spine, and Mel wonders where on earth it might end. She pulls into the tiny yard of the cottage and gets out.

Jake's right. It is like the cottage in a fairy tale, the home of a witch or an enchanted woodcutter. There are purple foxgloves growing against a stone wall and fat hairy poppy buds ready to burst into gossamer petals. Tiny blue flowers and dandelions grow amongst the flagstones under her feet.

She feels eyes on her back and turns. Jake is standing in the doorway, hands in the pockets of his jeans.

"You like it?"

"I love it."

She picks a sprig or two of lavender and rubs the oil on her hands. A couple of white butterflies whirl over the cottage roof.

"Once when Tansy was little there were hundreds of Hummingbird Hawk moths here. She kept trying to catch them."

His careless reference to Tansy, to Tansy being here as a little girl, makes Mel's head swim for a second.

"Come in, have some coffee...or sparkling water." He grins at her and she relaxes.

"Sparkling water please."

She follows him into the cottage. The ground floor is one room, with a couple of sofas and overflowing bookcases on the left, a mosaic-tiled kitchen to the right. Narrow wooden stairs spiral up from the back wall. Mel glances at the postcards propped up on the fireplace, the photographs of Tansy, none of them recent.

"You don't have any paintings up," she says as he hands her a tumbler of water.

"No," he says. "Not here. Not mine. Not anyone's. Although I do have a very modern and experimental piece by Mel Atkins to return to her."

Mel smiles. "Surely you haven't really kept that? It was horrible."

"It's not horrible. Of course I kept it for you. I'll get it later. Here, sit down."

She sinks down onto a sofa. Jake takes the other, places a bright patterned mug on the table.

"Do you have a studio here?"

"Not really. I have an outbuilding where I can do a bit of stuff, but I try to keep that side of my life in town and this is home. A place for chilling, reading, gardening, music, cooking, you know, being on my own."

"Does Tansy come much?"

"Not as much as I'd like. I usually see her at my studio. She does come sometimes and brings the girls, they love it. Tansy doesn't like driving down the lane."

"It is a bit horrific. Does the road go on anywhere?"

"It meets up with another lane. There are a couple of houses farther up that way. Nice footpaths round here, very old ones, you know. D'you fancy a walk?"

Mel gestures at her ballet flats. "I haven't got the shoes."

"Boots next time then."

"Next time?" she asks.

"Yes. Next time. Boots."

~

"I must get ready. I'm sorry." Stefan puts his watch back on the bedside cupboard.

Vicky smiles up at him from the pillow. Her hair is dishevelled, and her mascara smudged under one eye.

"What are you doing the rest of the day?" he asks her.

"Housework. Getting my uniform ready for tomorrow. Boring married-woman stuff."

Stefan laughs. "You're never boring, Vic. You're wonderful."

He sits up, runs his hands through his hair. He jumps when Vicky traces a finger down his spine.

"Can I see you again?" he asks.

"Yes please. I don't know how or when, but yes."

"Here."

"Here's safe."

He shuffles round to face her. "The last few days…my life has turned upside down. That awful night with Abi and now you. I could never have imagined it."

"And you made your peace at Amity, yes?"

"I did. Despite the rest of it, yes." He glances down at his hand. "Oh shit, I'm so sorry. I should have taken this off."

"It doesn't matter. I wasn't thinking about it."

"It was wrong. It is wrong." He tugs Nina's ring off and holds it, unsure whether to put it on the cupboard or stash it away somewhere. He takes Vicky's left hand. "You're not wearing a wedding ring."

She laughs. "I lost it years ago."

"What really?"

"Yes. Really."

Stefan puts his ring down beside his watch.

"It's OK to wear it," Vicky says. "I don't mind. It's been part of you for so long."

"It was sort of what brought you to me."

"Sort of."

"I won't wear it with you. I might wear it sometimes, just out of habit, it feels weird without it, but never with you. I promise." He leans down and kisses her. "I have to get on."

Vicky grabs the pile of her clothes. "Shall I leave first?"

"Good idea," he says. "Just in case."

—

Tansy arrives at the wine bar. The darkness inside disorients her for a moment after the sunshine. She glances about her, can't see Charlie anywhere. He's often late. Sometimes his assistant covers the shop if he needs to go out; sometimes he simply closes with a handwritten sign on the door, but he won't rush a customer if there is one.

She wants a proper drink but she orders tonic water, and takes it to a table, checks her phone to see if Charlie has sent a message. She goes onto Facebook again and tries to open Gareth's page and still it won't let her. She doesn't realise Charlie has arrived until she hears his voice.

"You OK for drinks?"

"Fine thanks."

"I'll just grab one."

He returns with a bottle of lager and throws himself into the easy chair opposite her.

"So what's going on? Girls all right?"

"Girls are great. Driving me nuts at times, you know." She drinks the bitter tonic water and knows how false she sounds.

Charlie watches her a moment. "Something's happened? Is it Ivor? You would tell me?"

"No, he's fine too."

It's an effort to speak to anyone after this betrayal. The girls, her mother, Charlie. It's all too much.

"I've known you long enough to know when something's upset you. Or someone. Is it a man? Is that why you've been distracted?"

"Ah fuck it. Yeah, there was someone. I met him here. I mean in town. It was all good, great…" Tansy trails off. It wasn't all good, all great. She was constantly looking to see if her messages had been read, if he had responded, if the blondes had written anything on his Facebook. He never met her family. He lied to her. He blocked her.

"And then it went tits up?"

"Tits up. Pretty much." She's speaking in half sentences, but she wants the dam to split and the words to rush out. There isn't anyone else she could tell. No one knows her like Charlie.

"I'm sorry," he says, reaches over and squeezes her hand. "There's nothing I can say, but I am. Sorry, I mean."

"He asked me to go to a private view with him, then he told me it was cancelled when it wasn't, and he went anyway without me."

"How do you know?"

"It was all over Facebook. And then I tried to message him and he blocked me."

"That's shit." Charlie drinks beer, looks round the room, raises a hand to a guy standing at the bar. "One of my regulars," he says to Tansy.

"What?"

"That bloke. Nothing. Doesn't matter. Well, look, this guy of yours, he doesn't deserve you, you know. What did the girls think of him?"

"They never met him"

"What about Emmeline?"

"He didn't meet any of them. It wasn't like that." It sounds pathetic, Tansy realises, spoken aloud in these staccato words. She thinks she can't stand Charlie's sympathy, yet suddenly she just wants him to hold her and say he still loves her and that they must be together again.

"This is going to sound pretty crass after what you've said," Charlie starts, and Tansy wishes she could cover his mouth, stop whatever words are about to come. "It's that, well, I've been seeing someone too, and I like her a lot, and I hoped the girls could meet her soon. She knows all about them. And you."

Tansy slams down her cold glass onto the table. She's going to cry. In public, in front of Charlie. She's going to cry.

"I wanted to tell you," Charlie says. "I didn't know how you'd feel. About the girls meeting her, I mean. I didn't know this thing had happened to you. I'm sorry."

This thing. That is all it is. Was. A thing. A no-thing. A nothing. She hardly knew Gareth Crane. It shouldn't hurt so much. It hurts more than when she and Charlie split up.

"I'm going." Tansy stands and the room wobbles as if she'd been drinking gin. "I want to go now."

Charlie drains his bottle. "Let me –"

"I want to be on my own."

She stumbles out onto the bright street. She wants to be on her own. She wants Charlie to spin her round and say this new woman doesn't mean anything, she wants Gareth to appear out of the crowd and tell her it's all been a dreadful mistake and he wants to be with her and meet her family and be part of her life always.

But Charlie doesn't follow her – if he does she doesn't know it – and the crowd doesn't part for Gareth to stride over and take her in his arms. She hurries down Market Jew Street past Boots and Superdrug, past Smiths and the undertakers, and there's the signboard for Samarkand where she went with Gareth the day they met, when she felt those first stirrings of this ridiculous poisonous passion.

She stops walking, and a man behind cannons into her. She barely acknowledges his apology. If Gareth won't speak to her, she can go to him. She knows where his flat is. A new pain squeezes her heart: the rain-streaked window, the murky street lamps, the soft carpet and her silent footsteps.

Vicky tugs absently at her tangled hair as she drives home and wonders if Kev felt like this when he left his lovers: elated and slightly otherworldly, but not guilty. Her eyes feel gritty and she knows her make-up has smudged, that she probably looks like a girl out all night partying. This makes her laugh. She can't even remember an all-night party.

She will make another appointment at the surgery and get a new implant inserted. She stops jaggedly, reverses, heads towards the pharmacy. She's pretty sure everything is OK but she'd better be sure. For a moment, as she negotiates the traffic, she imagines holding another baby in her arms, her child and Stefan's. Oh for fuck's sake, she thinks. He'll probably dump you in a few weeks.

When Mel gets home she can't meet her eyes in any of the mirrors. She takes off her clothes and throws them into the washing machine in case they bear any scent of Jake's house, of the garden flowers, or of deceit. They only sat and talked, he showed her his tiny shed-studio, walked her round the garden. He pointed to a couple of footpaths, barely discernible tracks stitched into the fields, marked only by rocky stiles and half-leaning finger posts.

He didn't even kiss her goodbye.

Boots, he said, as she unlocked her car door. Boots next time.

There will be a next time.

—

"What's up with you?" Skye asks Vicky that evening.

She pauses in folding the washing from the laundry basket. "Nothing."

"You won some money or something?"

"No such luck." Sheets, pillowcases, towels, jeans, underwear, school skirts. "You going to help with this? These are yours."

Skye shuffles over reluctantly and holds her arms out for a pile of uniform and socks. Vicky feels her daughter watching her.

"You were kinda weird this morning," Skye says. "And now you're really different. Something's going on." Suddenly she drops the pile on the table, grabs Vicky's arm. "Is it you and Dad? Are you getting a divorce?"

"No, love," Vicky says, looking at her properly. "It's nothing to do with Dad."

But it's everything and nothing to do with him.

The next day Tansy drops the girls off at school and nursery. Mel is waving goodbye to Megan and Sophie.

"Hi," Tansy says as she passes her.

"Oh. Hi."

Mel's face looks awkward and closed. Tansy doesn't want to stay and chat anyway. She tries to smile at Mel and walks on to her car. She told her mother she was going into Penzance, but takes the road out of Gerent's Cross that leads to Hayle.

It's a silver and blue summer morning, so far from that dark rainy night with the blurred sodium lamps and iodine puddles. She has imagined, over and over, that view from Gareth's flat in all seasons and times: the cold grey bluster of a winter morning, a hot blue afternoon, a bloody sunset. Whatever the weather, still those lights.

She parks in the usual car park. It's only when she gets out that she realises how shaky her legs are. Whatever, she thinks once more, whatever is going on she needs to know, she needs to know why Gareth lied to her and cut her off.

She runs lightly along the street, as if by taking quiet steps Gareth won't hear or sense her near by. Seeing his car makes her heart judder. He is real. He is still here. He is only yards away from her. She stops on the corner and glances all around. Just a few people walking by, a postman on a bike, a delivery van. There's a wall opposite Gareth's building. This is where she will wait. He has no front windows; he won't see her there.

The wall is rough under her bottom. She feels like everyone is staring at her. She keeps looking over to the front door of the old warehouse. After a few moments the door opens. She springs up as an older man steps out, mobile phone to his ear. He strides away and she crumples down on the wall again.

Gareth might not leave the building all day. He might leave with one of his blondes, or some other girl. Tansy has been through all these thoughts over and over again. She dare not ring the bell. He would never respond to her.

It seems as though she's been waiting there for hours when the front door opens again. This time Gareth comes out. He's alone. He's wearing a bright T-shirt and jeans. He flicks open a pair of sunglasses and puts them on. Not once does he look across the road.

Tansy unpeels herself from the wall. It is now. She has to do this now. She checks quickly for traffic and runs across the road.

"Gareth."

He stops. She can't see his eyes because of the shades.

"Tansy. What are you doing?"

"I came to find you. I'm sorry. I think I've done something to upset you and I'm sorry. Can we just…start again?"

"You don't owe me an apology." He takes the shades off. Green eyes. Cold as mint.

"I…I think I do. I really wanted to go to the private view and –"

"I told you I wasn't going. I was knackered, overwhelmed with stuff."

"You did go. I saw it on your Facebook. Ryan tagged you. There were photos."

"A last-minute decision. I wasn't going to go. Look, Tansy, I have to get a few things done before the life class."

"Just give me a moment please. Why have you blocked me?"

"Oh. That. I block loads of people. It doesn't mean anything. I need space, you know."

"No, I don't know. We were getting on so well. I thought we were. We had fun. If you didn't want me to go to the private view you should have just said."

"It's not about the private view."

"What is it about then? Come on, Gareth. We've had some great times, haven't we? Please, let's forget the past week. Will you unblock me so we can talk?"

He folds and unfolds the glasses in his hand. He doesn't look at her.

"I'll send you a friend request," he says at last.

Tansy feels the breath she's been holding pour out of her chest.

"Thank you," she says.

"I'll do it when I get back from the shop."

"Thanks," she says again, then, "Can I have a hug?"

He holds her stiffly, for a moment. She inhales the scent that is Gareth, as though she will never smell it again. But that's stupid because he said he will sort out Facebook. He steps away and lets her go.

"I must get on," he says.

"You won't forget?"

"I won't forget."

He slides the dark glasses on and starts walking. Tansy stands there, still, watching him. He doesn't look back. She should feel happy, relieved, elated, but she feels empty and strange.

—

Vicky arrives home from her long day at Lanyon House. Harry is in the kitchen hacking up a pizza.

"D'you want some, Mum?"

"No thanks."

"Skye?"

Skye wrinkles her nose. "It's disgusting. It's all fat and grease and stodge."

"Is it pepperoni?" Kev slouches into the kitchen, doesn't greet Vicky.

"Yeah."

"I'll have some then. Bloody starving."

Oh God, oh fuck, Vicky thinks. Why is my family so dysfunctional? So disjointed? Why can't we even eat the same food? She's about to yell why *can't we eat the same food?* but then remembers the messages she's exchanged with Stefan, ducks her head, smiles to herself, and kicks off her black work shoes.

"Have you eaten?" she asks Skye, as she unpacks the Tupperware containers from her lunchbox.

"I was waiting for you."

Vicky looks up and smiles at her. "Fancy some chilli when I've had a wash? There's some in the freezer."

"Yeah, that'd be good."

"Won't be long."

Vicky dumps her uniform in the laundry basket and showers quickly. When she comes down to the kitchen in her pyjamas, wet hair hanging down her back, Kev is scraping the burnt pizza crusts into the bin.

"Shit."

"What's happened?" Vicky asks.

"Knife. Gone in the bin."

"Here's the chilli." Skye waves a plastic tub at Vicky. "Shall I get it in a pan?"

"I'll do that, love. You grab the rice when Dad's out of the corner."

Kev thumps the bin bag down on the tiles and dunks his arm in.

"Jeez, gone right to the bottom."

The bin bag is too full and rubbish spills across the floor. Banana skin, soggy teabags, wet kitchen paper, the pizza wrapper, a small cardboard box.

"Here it is." Kev says. "Yuck."

Vicky is heating the chilli and not looking at Kev as he chucks the spilt waste into the sack.

"What's this?" Kev asks.

"Here's the rice." Skye thumps a bag of basmati next to the stove.

"Skye. What's this?"

Something in Kev's voice. Vicky turns. Kev is still crouched on the kitchen floor holding a small cardboard box. A cardboard box stained red-brown from tomato sauce or tea or something. A cardboard box labelled *emergency contraception*.

"Skye? I can read, you know. Emergency contraception? You're fourteen, for Christ's sake!"

Vicky's insides swoop up and down. She thought the kitchen bin was safe. She should have taken it to a public bin. Kev is staring up at Skye, and Skye is staring down at Kev, and Vicky is doing nothing, and she should be, she should be telling her husband this is nothing, nothing at all, to do with their daughter. The chilli bubbles and the smell makes her nauseous.

"Kev, listen," she starts, not knowing how to say what needs to be said.

"You keep out of this, Vic. Skye, I'm waiting. What are you playing at?"

Skye glances at Vicky. "I'm sorry, Dad. It was a mistake."

"I'll say it was a bloody mistake. Who is it?"

"Kev, please, Skye, listen, I –"

"I said I'm sorry."

"Vic, did you know about this? Did you get this for her?"

"She doesn't know," Skye yells. "No one knows. I thought I was doing the right thing. Better than having a baby."

"Better than having a baby," Vicky whispers. The chilli still bubbles, and her stomach still heaves, and she still hasn't said the right words. She is letting her daughter, her fourteen-year-old daughter, take the blame for her adultery.

Kev stands up, the knife in one hand, the packet in the other. It looks like it's been sprayed with blood.

"Look, I'm sorry," Skye says. "I won't do it again."

"Damn right you won't." Kev throws the dirty box back into the bin, washes his hands at the sink. "What the hell do you think you're doing? Who is it?"

"Who's what?" Harry dumps his greasy pizza plate on the worktop.

"Nothing," says Vicky.

"Nothing? Your sister, Harry, is having sex at fourteen. That's not exactly nothing, is it?"

"So what? Everyone does. Mum, we got any ice cream?"

"Everyone does? I doubt that. Were you, Harry?"

"Were you?" Skye asks.

"Well, no, I'm a boring geek. But loads of people do, Dad, just chill. Don't yell at her."

"I want to know who he is," Kev demands. "Or is it more than one?"

"Stop it!" Vicky cries. "All of you, just stop it. Skye and I are going to eat in peace."

"You haven't heard the last of this." Kev takes a beer out of the fridge and shoves past Vicky.

Harry puts his arm round Skye. "Look, has someone forced you into it? Just tell them to fuck off."

"No one forced me into anything." Skye rubs her eyes.

Vicky wants to run to her, hold her, hug her, kiss her, but she stands at the stove, stirring the chilli and measuring out the rice.

"How did he find out anyway? Was it Facebook?"

"Harry, let's leave it," Vicky says.

"Just wondered how he knew. Not like he's interested in any of our lives really, is it?"

"It was a morning-after pill box in the bin," Skye mutters.

"Christ, he went through the bin to catch you out?"

"No, he just found it. Look, Mum, sorry, can I take my dinner to my room please?"

"Of course." Vicky cracks bowls down, can't look at her daughter.

"Bring yours too," Skye says, gathering up the forks.

Vicky nods, and wonders how she will be able to swallow anything.

~

Tansy throws down her phone. Gareth said he would add her again and he hasn't. He has had hours to do it. She still can't find his page or reply to him. He won't have forgotten their meeting.

When she left Hayle she felt strange. He hadn't shouted at her or ignored her, or told her to fuck off, which were all things she had imagined could happen. He'd stopped and spoken to her, and said he would be friends again. As soon as she got home she checked her phone. He'd have got back from the shop by then. Maybe he meant after the life class. Throughout the day, even waiting in the school yard where the sun was so bright she could barely see the screen, she checked.

Now it is dark outside. There has been no friend request. She sends him a text.

Please will you sort out Facebook? You said you'd be friends again. X

She doesn't even know if it reaches him. He may have blocked her number as well.

Skye is hunkered on her bed, against a pile of cushions. Vicky perches on the end as though she were a hospital visitor. She shoves the chilli round the bowl, takes a couple of mouthfuls. It's hard to swallow.

"Why did you do that?" she asks Skye at last.

Skye shrugs, eats, drinks water from the pink tumbler beside her.

"Skye? Why did you say it was yours?"

"I didn't actually say it was mine. He assumed."

"OK. Why did you let him blame you?"

"It was easier."

"Easier?" Vicky dumps her bowl on the floor. The chilli tastes dirty in her mouth.

"He'll get over it. Harry's right. Lots of people do it. It's no big deal. I didn't want things to be worse between you and him."

"But, love, you realise what it means?"

"It means you needed a morning-after pill. And obviously it's nothing to do with Dad."

Colour stains Vicky's face at Skye's words.

"Aren't you furious with me? Don't you hate me?"

"He did it too. You think I don't know but I do." Skye pecks another forkful of rice. "I said you were different. Now I know what it is. Are you happy? Who is he?"

"Am I happy? I don't know." Vicky rakes fingers through her damp hair. When she's with Stefan she feels alive, hopeful, wanted, happy. All the clichés. Her carelessness has had dreadful repercussions. She looks straight at Skye. "I can't let you take the rap for this. It was mine, and I should come clean. What the hell sort of mother am I, letting a fourteen-year-old-girl –"

"He'll get over it. Just leave it. It'll be worse now if you start fussing. He'll want to know why I covered for you, did I know you were shagging someone, who is it and all that."

Vicky is defeated. Skye is fourteen. And Skye is right.

"I'm sorry," she whispers. "I never meant it to happen."

"Who is it? Someone at Lanyon? Actually, no, I don't want to know."

"OK. I don't think you should know."

Skye hands her half-eaten bowl of food to Vicky. She puts it beside her own on the floor.

"Can I get in with you?" Vicky asks.

Skye shuffles over and moves some pillows. Vicky stretches out beside her, strokes her hair.

"I love you so much."

"I know. I love you too."

"Things are a mess."

"They already were."

"Yeah, they already were."

Vicky closes her eyes. Next to her, she listens to Skye's breathing evening out. She takes her daughter's hand.

When she wakes, her mouth is foul from the chilli and dehydration. Her pyjamas are sticking to her back, and her damp hair has dried into a knot. She must have let go of Skye's hand while they slept.

Skye hardly stirs as Vicky sits up and gulps from the water glass. She turns off the bedside lamp and snuggles beside Skye again.

~

Tansy scuffs her feet in the school yard. She's early, which she didn't want to be. The metal gates are still closed and padlocked. Parents arrive one by one and loiter around her. Some nod, and she nods back, but she averts her eyes to stop them coming to her, asking after her, after Ivor. It hurts too much to speak to people now. The man she thought was going to want her, love her, save her, has turned out to be flimsy and cruel. She hasn't heard a word from him. He hasn't added her on Facebook. He has not responded to any of her texts. And all she can think about, all she can go over and over in her mind, are the times they spent together, those few times, whose sum was even less than their parts. Lunch in Samarkand, a kiss in the wet spring sunshine, the dark evening rain in Hayle, walking in St Ives, the ruined church. They run unchecked again and again in her mind, and she picks and bites at them trying to guess what on earth she did to make him turn on her. Because it must be her fault.

At last one of the teaching assistants grinds open the two gates and secures them back with weighted plant pots. The parents surge forward. Tansy glides on the current, but her mind is stuck in the rain in Hayle as she ran back to the darkened car park. Someone taps her arm, says hello, and she recognises Mel's mother-in-law.

Children stumble out of glass doors, dropping books and bags and water bottles. Shoelaces trail and plaits unravel. At last Scarlet appears, her ponytail askew. Despite her pain, Tansy's heart squeezes. She hasn't seen the girls for twenty-four hours. Charlie collected them the day before to spend the night with him.

Tansy squats down and Scarlet rushes over, hugging her.

"How are you, darling? Have you had a good day? Was it fun with Daddy last night? Did you get chip shop chips like he said? Did you watch *Frozen*?"

"We had chip shop chips." Scarlet says, taking Tansy's hand. "And we saw *Frozen*. And Mia was there. Mia's cool."

"Who's Mia?" Tansy asks, but she knows already.

"She's Daddy's friend. She's got really, really black hair. It's curly. And she brought us chocolate. And she came with us to school this morning. She met Jo-Jo and Savannah."

"She came to school with you?"

"Can you hold my bag for me? I need to take my jumper off. I'm hot. Look, this jumper's got ketchup on it from last night."

"Daddy picked her up on the way to school then?"

"No, she had a sleepover with us and Daddy."

Tansy hardly realises she is dragging Scarlet to the nursery door. Not only did Charlie introduce the girls to this woman without telling her, he let her stay over when the girls were at his. Tansy feels so queasy she leans against the pebble-dashed wall.

Amber barrels out of the nursery, a painted egg box in her hand.

"Mia did my hair this morning," Scarlet says. "She did a fancy plait thing but it came out at break so I had to do my own ponytail. Mumma. Are you listening?"

"Mummy!" Amber shrieks. "I've missed you. I cried for you at lunchtime."

Tansy hates the way her heart soars to hear her daughter cried for her. She cuddles Amber, ruffles her bright head.

"I'm here now."

"Amber. I was telling Mumma about Mia."

"I like Mia," Amber says. "When can we see her?"

~

Carol pulls out a chair and sits down beside Ivor. She has cooked him a chicken breast and cut it into small pieces. He said he only wanted a bit of salad with it, but she put a potato in the microwave as well.

"I'm sorry to ask," he says. "Could you get me a drink?"

"How could I forget? Elderflower or orange?"

"Elderflower please."

Carol makes up a glass of cordial and returns to the table. Ivor's hands are shaking as he pushes the knife and fork around the chicken pieces. Carol sets the drink on a coaster.

"Are we going to try to get out again?" she asks.

"No."

"To the studio?"

"No."

"We could ask Stefan to help. Or even Louis when he comes down. He won't be long now."

Ivor drops his knife and fork to the plate and reaches out to take her hand. His fingers are hot from gout as he strokes hers, lingering on Jeff's wedding ring.

"It's not going to happen. I won't be going out again. I won't be going to the studio again. Ever." He coughs and snatches his hand away to grab the cordial.

Carol blinks away tears. "You could try," she says. "Even if you don't paint, can't paint, wouldn't you like to go in the studio? So many memories there. So many memories of us…"

"That's partly why I'm not going to try. I'm not that man any more. I'm not the man lying with you on the studio floor…my painty hands leaving marks on your skin. I read you poetry in there, remember? Auden and Yeats and –"

"Housman."

"Yes. Blue remembered hills…that's the studio to me."

Carol turns away. One of the reasons she turned him down so many years ago was because she saw a future of nursing an old, ill man. And here she is doing it anyway. She sniffs and swallows.

"Can't we pretend we're young again? Just for a day. Like we were?"

Ivor shakes his head and stabs at a slice of tomato.

"It's too late for that, too late for me now. We both know I haven't got long. You get the key, go to the studio, and take what you'd like. The pictures of you, anything else you'd like. You should do it soon."

~

This time Mel finds the lane straight away. The hedges are even more overgrown, and valerian and foxgloves tap the car windows as she nudges her way down. Jake's cottage appears out of the greenery like a fairy story. His back wall is a riot of flowers and butterflies. She recognises Red Admirals, Painted Ladies, and Orange Tips.

"I hope you brought your boots."

She turns round, smiles. "My boots are in the boot."

"Best get them out then. I'm showing you the sights."

Mel takes out her old Doc Martens and slams the boot down. The sound is too loud in the quiet of the secret valley.

"Come and have a drink," Jake says. "I thought we could throw together a picnic."

"Sounds lovely." Mel drops the boots on the floor and follows him to the kitchen.

Sunlight pousr through the window and onto a pile of scattered sea glass on the sill. There's a giant round cactus in a Mexican pot and a stack of faded postcards, an antique green bottle and a snowglobe. Mel picks up the snowglobe and shakes it. Tiny sparkling flakes fizz round a fairy castle.

"From Scarlet and Amber," Jake smiles, handing her a glass of water.

"Does Tansy know?" Mel asks. "That I've been here, I mean?"

"No." He watches her.

"I don't think she should."

"Probably best."

Mel drinks icy water. She hasn't really done anything. She's just visited Jake at his house, and today they are going for a walk. They haven't done anything. They haven't even kissed. Mel sifts her hand through the sea glass at that thought. She shouldn't want him to.

"Ivor seemed a bit down this morning," Izzy says to Tansy on the phone.

She didn't know whether to tell her or not. She was probably over-reacting. Just oversensitive because of Abi.

"What, sad?"

Tansy herself seems to be dreadfully unhappy. Izzy doesn't like to ask what's wrong.

"Yes, just quiet and down. I asked if he felt ill, and he said no. I think he's sad about not getting in the studio."

"Yes, yes. I'll go and see him later."

"Let me know, would you? I'm just off to the café now."

"Of course yes. Oh, I should have asked. How's Abi?"

"She's getting there, thanks." Izzy glances to the stairs to make sure Abi isn't listening on the landing. "I feel able to leave her for a while now."

"Good. That's good."

"Are you OK? You sound very down."

Don't get involved with anyone else's troubles, Izzy screams silently to herself, but she can't help it. If someone is unhappy or worried she wants to help.

"It's nothing. Really."

"OK, look, I'd better get to Samarkand now."

"Izzy, before you go, do you ever see…Gareth Crane in there? In Samarkand? That guy I came in with once? You knew him."

"Oh. Gareth. No. I think he's only been in once since while I was there."

"Ah. OK. And..."

"He was on his own." Izzy immediately sees the lie of the land.

"He just had a coffee or something and left. I didn't speak to him much."

Izzy ends the call and runs upstairs to check on Abi. She's in bed, reading.

"Anything you need?"

"No. Thank you, Izzy. For everything."

Izzy gives her a hug and tells her she'll be calling to check up on her later. Aidan will be home in a few hours.

"I'm all right," Abi says. "Really. The tablets. I just don't feel anything any more. I won't do anything again. I promise."

~

Vicky is glad to be busy at Lanyon so she can't think too much about what's happening at home. Kev and Skye have made an uneasy peace, and Skye has promised him nothing like that will ever happen again until she's over the age of consent.

"That's easy enough to promise," Skye said to her. "I don't want to sleep with any of those twats at school anyway."

"You shouldn't be doing this for me," Vicky said to her. "What the hell kind of mother am I?"

"You're the best mother. If you're happier, then that's got to be good. You said you and Dad didn't like each other any more, and you know, you could hardly pretend you did. We can see you don't. But I sort of want to know who this guy is at Lanyon. And I sort of don't."

"Don't ask," Vicky said, not correcting her about Lanyon. "Don't know these things."

Vicky is leaving work early today to go to the surgery to get an implant fitted. She will never, ever, compromise Skye again. As it is, she doesn't know how she can ever repay her for that loyalty. Skye risked Kev's fury for her, knowing she was doing something she should not be doing. Stefan is not working at the hotel today and Vicky is going to see him straight after her appointment, and before he goes to Ivor's. She checks the time. She can't wait to see him.

Tansy and Emmeline arrive home after visiting Ivor. He was sad, depressed, but didn't appear ill. He wasn't coughing excessively, and his legs were no more swollen than usual. Emmeline opened the window and let scented summer air into the house. Tansy promised to bring the girls to see him at half-term next week.

"I don't really get it," Emmeline says as they walk to their front door. "You hardly knew the man. Just put it down to experience, and don't get so involved so quickly next time."

Tansy marches away onto the lawn. She can't make her mother understand because she can't understand it herself. She can't help wondering, silently to herself, that if she had stayed off alcohol she wouldn't have become so obsessed about Gareth. Obsessed. She hates that word. Emmeline has used it several times. It didn't feel like obsession. It felt like two people meeting and sharing happy times, and yet, and yet, under all that was her constant anxiety and jealousy, his secrecy and refusal to disclose anything about himself. It was all an illusion, and it has shattered, but Tansy still wants to gather the broken shards and try to mend it.

There are foxgloves and poppies, irises and roses in the flowerbed, a summer palette of pink and purple and blue, but it all looks grey to her. She imagines that flowers will always be monochrome to her now, she will never look at them and feel the warm joy of early summer, smell their intoxicating perfumes with anything other than despair and desolation.

~

They walk together up the lane to the bridge. Mel runs her hands along the stones. There are dips and bumps, ochre lichen and moss. She wonders how many hands have rested here over the centuries. The stream slides darkly underneath, eddying around a jutting rock. Jake leaps up the stile and holds a hand out for Mel. His palm is rough on hers, cracked and worn from paint and water and wood. She looks only at her feet as he helps her up, at the scuffed-up toes of her boots.

Beyond the stile, the footpath is hemmed onto the edge of the field. It's only discernible by the different shade of grass. It looks like no one has walked this way for months. The bushes grow thickly to the right of the track, brightened with splashes of valerian and foxglove, trails of ivy and sprays of feathered grasses.

A pair of Red Admirals skitter away ahead of them. Jake points to a rabbit bounding through the tussocks.

"It's lovely," Mel whispers. "I had no idea there was anywhere like this."

"No one walks this path any more," Jake says. "I think it's a very old one. It comes out at a farm a mile or so farther on, then on to the church. It's probably a corpse road."

"A corpse road?"

"The paths they used to carry the dead, way back, Middle Ages and before. I was thinking about doing some paintings of this path. When we get back I'll show you the sketches and photos. Something different, something more enclosed."

"I could imagine Ivor doing something with this path."

"Yes," Jake smiles. "He'd love it. How is he?"

Mel shrugs. "Not good. Not strong. I don't know if he'll ever paint again."

"Ah fuck. I should go and see him."

"I'm sure he'd like that."

"Yeah. Decent guy, Ivor. After the way I was with Emmeline he could have told me to fuck off, but he never has…come on."

Again he takes her hand and pulls her gently along. At the far end of the field is another stile.

"Mel." Jake stops, turns back to her.

This time she looks up to his face.

"Mel. I like you very much."

"I like you," Mel says.

There's a snail sliding up a tree trunk beside her. She watches the snail stretching and pulling, stretching and pulling.

"And I know you have…a family and all that, and obviously I'm not asking you to compromise anything…just that I would like to spend time with you and get to know you."

Jake traces the side of her face with his hand, his rough artist's hand. Mel closes her eyes, tries to dredge up images of Tansy and Emmeline, but they won't come, and when he bends down to kiss her, in that moment when she should pull away gently but definitely, she doesn't. She doesn't pull away.

~

Vicky shifts her arm. Her new implant stings under its bandage. There's a tiny smear of blood seeping through. It's smudged onto Stefan's sheet.

He comes back into the bedroom with two mugs of tea.

"I'm so glad you could be here today." Vicky says.

"Kate's pretty easy going," he says. "I can cover for her one day."

"Thanks for asking her."

"No problem." Stefan leans down to kiss her.

"I don't think I've ever asked you how you came to look after Ivor."

"It was a Facebook ad. I wanted a bit more work. Yeah, it just sort of happened. Me and Carol and Mel, we were the first ones."

"And then Ivor fell and needed more people."

"I don't know how long he should stay living there," Stefan says. "The place is too big and the garden is beyond him now. Which reminds me, I'll talk to him tonight about mowing the lawn and tidying up a bit. Hey, why don't we see if we have a free day and I can do his lawn and you can do the weeding and stuff, get it nice for him, and give us some time together. What do you say?"

"I'd love to. Ivor won't think anything, will he?"

"Course not. Before you go, let's work out when we could do it."

He drinks tea and Vicky snuggles against him. She feels lightheaded, as though she has been drinking. She doesn't want to get up and go home, which she'll have to do soon so that Stefan can get to Ivor's.

"What scares me," Stefan says, "is arriving there one day, probably in the morning, and finding he's gone."

"I know."

"You must get that at Lanyon a lot."

"Yes, but you never get used to it. You're never really prepared. Years ago I was self-employed when the kids were small. I had this lady I went to. One morning I got there and she'd tried to get herself up and into her stairlift and she was dead."

"Oh sweetheart, how awful. You were on your own?"

"Yes. I panicked. I ran over the road and got a guy there to come back and...well...agree with me that she was dead. He helped me sort it all out."

"Must have been so upsetting."

"It's easier at Lanyon, for sure. But you go to someone's house and you don't know what you might find. Another lady I was looking after…I got to her place and there was a terrible water leak…I had to stay and sort that out, get a plumber and so on. So I was late for the chap after her, and he'd soiled the bed by the time I got there. The things we have to do."

"I think Ivor would prefer to die at home and have one of us find him than to be in hospital or even Lanyon, don't you?"

"I think so, yes."

Vicky reaches for Stefan's hand and strokes the pale band on his finger, the spot where Nina's ring once rested.

~

"Give that to me. NOW."

"Get off, Amber. It's my book."

"*My* book. Give it to me."

"You can't even read. Oww! Mumma, Amber hit me. Amber hit me, I said."

"You give me that!"

"Mumma! Oww! Get off, you horrible baby. I shall kill Tiger."

"Mummy! Scarlet's going to kill Tiger."

"I'll throw him in the bin and the binmen will take him."

"No! Mummy! He's mine."

"Oww! Mumma, she hit me again."

"Please stop it, both of you. As soon as I've done this I'll get your tea."

"Where's Granny?" Amber stuffs Tiger under her T-shirt.

"Out. Seeing a friend. I told you. Now give me five minutes to finish this. Please, girls. Just play nicely or watch telly."

Tansy rubs her eyes and goes back to her pad and diary. The carers tell her which shifts they can't work each week, or which shifts they'd prefer and she writes the rota. What with Mel and Vicky at Lanyon, Stefan in the bar, and Izzy at Samarkand, it can get very tricky organising the shifts. Today she can't seem to work it out. It's half-term next week too, so Mel wants time off.

Tansy drops her pen and flicks back though her lined pad. Rough copies of rota after rota, going back to before she even met Gareth Crane. She pauses at one particular page, and rests her hand on the grid of names and crossings out. That was the week she met him. She wrote this rota, unaware, oblivious, of what was to unfold.

She turns back to the half-term week to come. Charlie wants the girls for some days. Days Tansy could have been spending with Gareth. Instead, she'll be alone, and her daughters will be having their hair styled by Mia.

Tansy grabs her phone and finds Mia's profile again. Charlie is a mutual friend. Tansy glares at the profile picture. Mia is younger than her and Charlie. Long curly black hair, huge smoky eyes. Sometimes Tansy wants to smash her mobile with a hammer, or kill off her Facebook or something. Blondes, brunettes, they all smirk at her from behind that screen.

~

"What am I doing, girls?" Mel whispers to Maggie and Ruby.

The guineas squeak up at her, hoping for a handful of leaves or some strawberries. Mel trails her hand into their hutch. Maggie bounds over to sniff her fingers. Mel strokes the soft ears. In the corner Ruby is shifting a clump of hay by burrowing under it.

"What *am* I doing?" Mel whispers again and gathers up half-chewed discs of cucumber, shredded spinach, and a chuck of carrot, gone hard.

The girls have gone to bed, quietly for once. Joe is doing something on the computer with the boys. She chucks the old veg away, rinses her hands, and wonders what night-time creatures are flitting and bounding in the secret meadow behind Jake's cottage. Moths and bats flickering through the trees, rabbits darting in the undergrowth. Spiders and snails and other tiny creatures crawling out from the leaves into the cool of the night. And what ghosts walk the old corpse road, that ancient track of the dead? Can they see the imprint of her and Jake, two figures from another time, reaching to each other and kissing under a summer sky?

—

"Ivor!" Izzy calls as she closes the front door behind her.

The morning sun has not reached the back of the house and, despite the huge windows, the room is chilly. Izzy shivers suddenly. The house feels different. Some mornings Ivor calls out in response to her. He doesn't always hear her but he often wakes with the dawn, waiting in bed for whoever is coming. Izzy's heart races and she runs through into his bedroom.

It smells musty. She can see the dome of Ivor's head on the pillow and hear the wheeze of his breathing. Just asleep then. She exhales in relief and draws the curtains open.

"Hey, Ivor, wake up, sleepyhead. You're always awake when I get here."

Ivor mumbles something and blinks sticky eyes.

"You all right? It's only me, Izzy."

She helps him sit against the pillows. He hacks phlegm from his chest and she hands him the beaker of water from the bedside cabinet. His hand trembles as he drinks, and droplets fall on the duvet.

Izzy takes his overnight urine bottle to the bathroom, empties and cleans it. When she returns to Ivor, he is swinging his swollen legs over the side of the bed to stand.

"Would you mind giving me a hand, Izzy? In the bathroom? I don't feel so good today."

"Of course," Izzy says, as he takes her arm. "Can I get you any paracetamol or anything? Do you need the doctor?"

"No, no, girl, just wear and tear."

Together they shuffle to the bathroom. Izzy helps him take down his trousers, wash his face and clean his teeth.

"I can stay on for a bit if you like." Izzy offers. "I can do some cleaning or washing or whatever. You tell me what needs doing."

"Keeping an eye on the old buffer, huh?"

"Yeah, that too."

Back in the bedroom Izzy dresses Ivor and tugs on his compression socks. His leg is bloated again, and flushed pink, warm to the touch. The cellulitis never seems to fully leave him, even with antibiotics. Izzy places his Zimmer in front of him.

"I'll make a start on breakfast," she says, and gathers the dirty clothes from the laundry basket. "Then I can change your bed. That'd be nice, yes, fresh sheets?"

She shoves the laundry into the washing machine. There isn't room for bedding too, so she pours in detergent and starts it off. Ivor's walking frame clicks through the house with its staccato tattoo, to the dining table. Izzy puts teabags into mugs, shakes out cereal, and chops the only decent banana left.

"You need bananas," she calls out. "And some more milk. Looks like you're low on butter too."

"I'll get Emmeline and Tansy to put them on their internet order."

"I can go to the shop for you when you've had breakfast."

"You sure, Izzy?"

"No problem. I'm glad to be out, you know. Change of scene. Look. Let me see what else you might need. Who's coming tonight?"

"Carol, I think."

"Are you having this chicken breast for dinner?"

"Oh, I don't know. Whatever Carol gives me."

Izzy grabs a Biro and an old envelope and starts to write a shopping list.

~

Gareth may have blocked Tansy on Facebook but she knows it's his birthday soon. She memorised that date as she memorised his address. Surely if she sends him something for his birthday he won't still ignore her? He'll have to say something, acknowledge the gift, and then she can talk to him and find out whatever it is that has gone so badly wrong, and put it right. It must be her, her fault, something she's done, but whatever it is, she will put it right. Whatever it takes.

A standard birthday gift is not enough. It must be unique, special, something to remind him of the days he spent with her, something to make him want those times again. She relates their brief tale to herself, from the start in the bookshop to the end on the street in Hayle.

She could get him the Ivor Martin book he was looking at. She could get Ivor to sign it. And it has drawings of her in there, the ones she showed him. Each time he flicks through the book, his gaze will pause on those drawings.

"I'm going into town," Tansy calls to Emmeline.

"What for?"

"Nothing. Just need to buy a few things. I won't be long."

Before Emmeline can say that she'll come too, Tansy flings open the door. She'll go to the bookshop where she and Gareth met, and buy the book there. It might even be the same copy he held that day.

~

Izzy dumps the shopping in the kitchen and flicks the kettle on to make Ivor another drink. She unloads bananas, milk, butter, tomatoes, tins of soup, a small loaf, lemonade, two baking potatoes. The washing machine has stopped and she tugs the wet bundle of clothes into the basket. She will change Ivor's bed as she promised, but first she'll have a tea with him and see how he's feeling.

"That's kind of you, Izzy. Thanks."

"I'm not in a hurry to get back today." She puts two mugs on the table. "I don't have to watch Abi all the time now. The tablets are really helping her. I don't think she can manage without them. Especially when she has these awful, destructive relationships. That Rick, he was the absolute pits."

"Sounds a thoroughly nasty man." Ivor sips his tea, watches Izzy with his green eyes, which have lost none of their colour to age. "What about you, Izzy? Is there a young man in your life? I'm being nosy. A privilege of the elderly."

Izzy smiles, looks away. "No. No young man for me."

"Ah, just you wait. One will pop up when you least expect it."

"No," Izzy says again.

Her heart is thudding and she feels sweat on her back. She wants to finally get the words out that she has buried for years, to tell Ivor, because he is a kind and decent man. But she hasn't even said them to her own family. There's never been a time, never the right time. And always Abi being ill, cutting herself, getting muddled up with dangerous people. Never a moment for Izzy to find herself, it sometimes seems.

"There won't be," Izzy says, carefully. "Because I'm not like that. I'm not into men." She looks up again and meets Ivor's green gaze. "I've never said this to anyone. Not even my own family. Ivor, I'm gay."

Ivor reaches for her hand and squeezes it as hard as his gout will let him. Tears prickle Izzy's eyes at the same time as her whole body relaxes.

She has said it. She has said it to someone she loves and the sky hasn't fallen in.

—

Tansy is surprised to see Izzy's car outside Ivor's house. She grabs her phone and checks for messages – nothing – so she guesses perhaps Izzy has broken down or had to come back for something. It's almost lunchtime.

"Hi, it's me," she calls as she goes in.

Izzy and Ivor are sitting together at the table, eating sandwiches, smiling and laughing.

"Everything O K?" Tansy asks, the book held to her chest.

"Absolutely. Izzy did a bit of shopping for me and I asked her to stay for lunch."

"Oh. Right." Tansy feels a quick surge of guilt. She hasn't been checking on Ivor's supplies lately, hasn't asked him what he needs added to the internet order.

"Not Samarkand standard," Izzy gestures at the sandwiches.

"They're lovely," Ivor says. "I just can't eat much."

Tansy hovers. She feels like the odd one out.

"Would you sign this for me?" she asks awkwardly.

Ivor wipes his fingers on a tissue. "You know my writing's not up to much. Is it for a present?"

"Yes." Tansy avoids Izzy's eyes, wishes she had never asked about Gareth coming into Samarkand.

"So who's it for?" Ivor tugs the cap off a pen, and grasps it in his swollen shiny fingers.

"If you could just sign it, that would be great. Don't worry about anything else. I know your hands are poorly."

Tansy gazes out of the window. The garden has grown rampant, with constellations of daisies and dandelions amongst the straggling grass.

"It's like a jungle out there."

"All done."

She turns back to Ivor and glances at his trembly signature. Suddenly she's no longer sure she even wants to send the book to Gareth. Those two spidery words – *Ivor Martin* – show a vulnerability and she doesn't know if she can share that with a man so careless of others' feelings.

"Stefan's going to mow the lawn tomorrow," Ivor says. "Vicky's coming too, to help out in the garden."

Tansy picks up the book, blows on the drying ink. She feels even more out of place. Izzy eating lunch, Stefan and Vicky coming to garden. While she has been chasing an illusion, these other people have grown closer to Ivor. They are more his family than she is.

"Thanks." She kisses him on his soft head. "I'll leave you two to finish."

As she pulls the door to behind her, the tears start, and she is unsure if she is crying about Gareth or about Ivor, or both, somehow woven together in this bitter summer of joy and pain, this wonderful disaster.

Izzy has shed such a load. She drives fast with the windows down and music blaring. For so long, for so very long, she has chewed over the words to use to tell her family, and never been able to utter them. All she needs is one simple sentence. She will speak to them all tonight. Ivor must have been the missing piece. All she needed was the right person to tell first.

She told Ivor first. She will remember this day for the rest of her life.

The unearthly feeling she had when she arrived, how she feared the worst, but no, it was monumental in another way. The trip to the village shops, making sandwiches, Tansy arriving looking wild and strange, clutching a copy of Ivor's book for him to sign.

Will that be the last time Ivor signs a book?

I will remember him and this day for the rest of my life, Izzy affirms. Because she will never forget who she first told. They are bound together, her and Ivor.

Stefan wipes sweat from his brow with his forearm. The mower splutters as it chews up the grass and dandelions. Vicky is crouching in a flower bed, tugging up scraggy weeds and chucking them in a bucket beside her. Stefan watches her a moment. She stretches for a woody stem and her ponytail falls over one shoulder. Stefan wants to creep up behind her and hold her to him, their sticky damp bodies together. He turns the mower towards the bottom of the garden, towards the pear and apple trees, the spears of violet and white foxgloves in the shade of the back wall.

He can't really explain how he has ended up in this place with Vicky. He no longer misses the ring of glass and ashes on his finger. His first and last thoughts of the day are of Vicky, and not Nina.

Vicky is married, she is older than him, she has two teenage children. They are at different points on their journey. He should be finding a girl he can move in with and have children with, but he doesn't want that. Right now, all he wants is Vicky. Even if she never leaves Kev, he doesn't care. She is the girl he wants.

He turns the mower towards the house. Vicky straightens and shakes out her shoulders. Her hands are muddy and her jeans stained at the knee. She is beautiful. Stefan stops the mower and walks over to her.

"I want to kiss you," he says.

"You can't," she laughs. "Ivor's sitting in the window."

"Ivor would keep a secret."

"Later," she says, and touches him quickly on the arm. His skin jumps under her fingers.

"Shall we see if Ivor wants to try coming out?" Stefan asks her.

"With us both here?"

"We'll ask him. Just to stand in the garden would be good for him."

"We could put a chair out for him."

Stefan grins at her; she looks puzzled.

"What?"

"Nothing."

He goes back to the mower, smiling. Even for just a moment, they were a *we*, him and Vicky.

"No," Ivor says.

Vicky brings the tray of tea to the table. Stefan glances up at her.

"Thank you both, but no," Ivor repeats. "I've resigned myself to it. I won't get out again. I won't go in the studio again. I won't paint again. Really, I'd prefer it if you all stopped asking and talking about it."

"Of course," Vicky says quickly and offers him a chocolate digestive.

Ivor takes the biscuit, snaps it uncertainly, and a quarter chunk falls to the floor.

"I'm sorry. I can't even break a bloody biscuit."

Stefan leans down and grabs the shard from the floor. "It's fine, don't worry. Anyway, the garden's looking tidier now, isn't it? Vicky's a good weeder. You should make her do it more often."

Stefan grins at her and she smiles back. She's not a good weeder. She's not confident what should be pulled up and what should stay. She dreads finding snails and slugs and caterpillars amongst the leaves. Her back and hamstrings ache from the bending.

"Thank you both. I do appreciate it. I'm a very lucky man. I have some wonderful people who look after me." Ivor drinks tea; the mug shakes in his hand and droplets spill from his chin. "Izzy did the shopping for me the other day. You're all so kind."

"Ivor, we love you," Vicky cries. "We want to help. We –" She stops, about to say *we all feel so sorry for you stuck in the house* but that's not what Ivor wants to hear.

"I'll come again and do the lawn. Perhaps Vicky can help too?"

"I'm sure I can."

"I may be old, but I'm not completely stupid." Ivor takes a second biscuit, looks from Stefan to Vicky.

"Of course you're not stupid," she starts, unsure what he's getting at.

"Vicky. What are you doing with that husband? Are you leaving him?"

Vicky flushes at the mention of Kev. "I don't know, I mean, it's difficult."

"I've known Stefan for a while now and he's a thoroughly decent young man. Been through a lot. Don't hurt him, Vicky. Please. I doubt I'll be here to see how this all ends up, but please don't hurt him."

"Ivor, you've misunderstood," Stefan interrupts.

"No, I haven't. I'm not stupid. Vicky's a lovely girl, I know that. Very pretty, very kind, all that. I would be delighted if you two were happy together after I've gone."

Ivor gasps and coughs. Biscuit crumbs fly from his mouth. Vicky unscrews the cap on his water bottle and hands it to him. His larynx wobbles as he gulps.

"Crumbs went down the wrong way," he splutters, and hands the bottle back.

Vicky smiles and brushes down the front of his shirt. She can't meet Stefan's eyes.

"So. Yes. It's because of me you've met. That's lovely. I like that. I've done some good in the world."

~

Ten minutes later Stefan unlocks the passenger door for Vicky.

"Would you like to get a drink somewhere?" he asks. "Not the hotel."

"How did he know?"

"About us?"

"Of course about us."

"As he said, he's not stupid. He won't say anything."

"But if he worked it out, so might other people."

"I don't care." Stefan kisses away Vicky's retort. "I know. I'm sorry. It's much harder for you. Of course I care. Let's go to a pub. How about the White Rabbit? Not much off the way home."

He knows she's thinking of anyone she knows who might be in the pub.

"We've been helping Ivor in the garden. That's all," he says.

"I know. Yes, let's go."

"Oh, let me show you something." Stefan swipes his phone open. "I had a message from Abi. Saying thank you and all that. Probably Izzy made her do it." He hands the mobile over to Vicky, watches her read the Facebook message.

"She's the sort of girl you should be with," Vicky says quietly. "Young, pretty, single."

"She's also suicidal. Or has been."

"I'm sorry. I didn't think. I'm hurting you. Doing what Ivor told me not to do."

"You're not hurting me. You've made my life a million times better."

He fires the ignition and flicks open his sunglasses. It's true. She has. He doesn't think too far ahead. He has learnt the hardest way that it is a dangerous thing to do.

—

Tansy has torn out one of her drawings of the ruined church. She's added some strokes of colour and collage, folded it into a card. It's more of a painting than a card. It's probably too much. She should have just bought a crap card from Tesco.

Wishing you a very happy birthday
Love from Tansy xxx

That's all she has written – in her best careful writing and with a fountain pen. She suddenly realises she has never seen Gareth's handwriting. She's seen his drawings, yes, but not his writing. He has never sent her a card, she's not seen him write a shopping list, or sign anything. She will probably spend the rest of her life not knowing what his writing is like.

She stops a moment and considers. Italic with a drawing pen, or scrabbly as spider legs? Perhaps he only uses an expensive pen and coloured ink. Or maybe any old Biro will do. Maybe it's small and tight writing. Mean writing.

She paperclips the card to the front of the Ivor Martin book and wraps the whole parcel in geometric patterned paper. She'll stop at the Post Office on her way to collect the girls from Charlie's. *Oh hell, don't let that Mia bitch be there.* Tansy snaps the tape in her teeth.

~

Vicky can't relax in the pub. The White Rabbit is a thatched inn just outside Gerent's Cross. It's cool and dark inside the bar and she shrinks into the settle. Stefan sits opposite her on a stool.

"I can't be long," she says, glancing at her phone.

Kev had left for work early that morning. Harry and Skye were sleeping in as usual in school holidays. Vicky had left a note saying she was going to Ivor's to do some gardening and housework. She'd taken her car and met Stefan as they'd arranged so they could travel to Ivor's together. Now she's panicking that the silence on her mobile means that Skye has told Harry about her affair, the truth about the contraceptive box in the bin, that they're talking about her right now.

"All right, drink up, and we'll be off." Stefan downs the last of his beer. "I'll see you soon, won't I?"

"Of course."

Vicky glances around the bar. No one is looking at them. She doesn't recognise anyone. She grabs Stefan's hand and kisses him quickly, while the lights on the fruit machine run red, white, gold, red, white, gold, behind his head.

~

Tansy parks in Charlie's road and walks to his house. She feels sick, sick at the thought of the parcel which she has handed over at the Post Office, and sick at the thought of Mia being at Charlie's. Young, glamorous Mia touching her girls, plaiting their hair, kissing Charlie in front of them.

Her angry footsteps have led her to the door. Charlie opens it almost immediately.

"Scarlet! Amber! Mummy's here." He steps back into the hall. "Coming in?"

Tansy hovers. Surely he wouldn't ask her in if Mia were there?

"No, it's OK. You say goodbye to them. I'll wait on the street."

"Tansy," he starts, but then Scarlet is barrelling into her, and Charlie turns back into the house, calling for Amber, gathering up a dropped raincoat.

"I've missed you, Mumma."

"I've missed you too, darling," Tansy gasps through Scarlet's kisses. "You had fun, though?"

"Yes, but I always miss you, Mumma. You're the best. Better than Amber, better than Daddy."

"Ssh now." Tansy straightens up and swallows the tears.

Charlie adjusts Amber's backpack on her little shoulders. They wouldn't have heard. She squeezes Scarlet's hand. Whatever shit is going on with Gareth, she has these two little ones to look after and love. It should be enough.

"Where've you been?" Skye asks.

"I was at Ivor's."

"What, all this time? Yeah right. You've been with him."

"I was doing some gardening for Ivor. With one of the other carers. Stefan."

"Stefan. Is that who it is?"

"You said you didn't want to know anything about it. And I don't want you to. I don't want to talk about it. I've got so much to think about, sort out." Vicky covers her face with her hands.

"Were you really gardening at Ivor's?"

"Yes."

"OK," says Skye.

―

I can't. It's half term.

OK, sure. I don't know these things. Next week?

Yes, next week.

Mel deletes the messages immediately, as though clearing them will clear the suggestion, the intent. She leans against the cooker, gazing out of the kitchen window, while the voices of her four children rise and fall around her. And suddenly she can't wait for Joe to come home. Surely seeing him will make this stop, make her fully realise what she is risking, and for what? A kiss in a field?

Joe is a good man, a decent man. He always has been. He's looked after her and the children, he's worked hard to build his business. His mother is one of Mel's best friends. But. But. Jake Gregory. Bloody Jake Gregory. If she hadn't been caring for Ivor she would never have met Tansy, and then she would never have met Jake. Somewhere in a parallel universe, she did not answer Tansy's Facebook request for carers, or she did but felt ill the day of the school art workshop, or something, or something. There have been a million crossroads where she could have chosen another path, where she does not end up in a field in Penwith kissing an artist she cannot stop thinking about.

~

On Saturday night Vicky arrives home after a long shift at Lanyon. She's had a difficult day. One patient fell in her room. Another had to be taken to hospital in an ambulance after having a stroke in the breakfast room. Two members of staff went home ill. It's raining and her shoes are leaking. She is dehydrated, but with a bursting bladder, and hasn't been able to speak to Stefan because she's been so busy and he's been working too.

She dumps her bag in the hall. Hears Kev's voice in the kitchen, saying, "Bathroom and kitchen. Whole place sounds pretty ropey." A pause. "Yeah, couple of weeks' work at least. St Ives."

He's on the phone to someone. Vicky kicks off her shoes. Kev looms in the kitchen doorway, mobile to ear. Before he speaks again Vicky somehow knows what his words will be, where in St Ives the ropey bathroom and kitchen are. She ducks her head as he gives the name of Stefan's road.

"Number er…33, I think. Look Vic's here. Going to clear off now." He swipes the screen. "Good day?"

Vicky hovers. Kev has got several weeks' work in Stefan's road. If it's number 33, it's pretty much opposite his flat.

"I'm tired," she mumbles.

"Harry's gone to Jonathan's."

"Right."

Vicky snatches her mobile and takes it into the bathroom with her. She turns on the shower but before she tugs off her sweaty uniform she texts Stefan about Kev's job.

He'll be right there.

How can I see you?

As she steps under the warm jet of water, she's crying. She can't bear the thought of not being able to see Stefan.

~

"So, I have some news for you," Louis says as he slides onto the bench opposite Carol.

"I'm going to be a granny?" she asks, breathlessly.

"Sorry. Not that, I don't think." He drinks his coffee, grins at her.

He's let his hair grow long since she saw him last, and it skims his shoulders in dark blond waves. He's wearing a T-shirt that shows off arm muscles hardened from hours in the gym.

Rain drums on the roof of the caravan. Night is unfurling behind the clouds. Carol watches a family scuttling into the next-door van. Lights snap on inside.

"What then?"

"Leaving London."

"What? Where you going? When?"

"Now. Put all my stuff in storage. Found another tenant to share with Lars."

"But where are you going? What are you going to do? Are you going abroad again?"

"Is Cornwall abroad?"

"You're moving here?"

Louis shrugs, drinks coffee. "Hope so. I've got this place for a month. Got to look for somewhere proper. A job too. But hell, there are plenty of galleries here. More per square inch than anywhere…perhaps Ivor could write me a reference? How is he anyway?"

Carol untangles a stray hair from her earring. "Not great. Getting very frail."

"You were a monumental twat not to marry him."

"I had you to think of!"

"You didn't think of me when you married that arsehole Jeff."

"You were a kid when Ivor asked me to marry him. It's completely different. And lay off Jeff. You don't have to ever encounter him. Even if you move down here."

"Good." Louis drains his mug. "Could I come and see Ivor with you one day?"

"What, for a reference?"

"No. Just to say hello."

"OK."

"And to tell him how stupid you were to turn him down. Do you realise how big he is these days? Just think what you could have inherited."

"Stop it," Carol cries. "He's not dead yet. Far from it." She wishes she were that certain.

~

Tansy bows her head as she hurries the girls into the yard. There are parents, mostly mothers, in twos and threes, loitering over buggies and yapping dogs on strings. An older kid whizzes crazily through the gate on a scooter. The sky is the blue of a St Ives summer and the air is already hot. This summer is passing her by, and she wonders what she will have to show from it other than endless trips to and from school, and silence from Gareth Crane.

She kisses Scarlet, adjusts her backpack, makes sure the cap on her water bottle is secure, and watches her scamper through the glass door. A mother walking away smiles and says hello, and Tansy forces a reply before urging Amber towards the nursery. There's a huddle of little kids and mothers and one father, outside the nursery door. Amber bounces up and down waving her lunchbox wildly, shouting at one of her friends watching behind the window.

At last the queue moves forwards. Tansy hands over Amber and all her kit, and exhales with relief as she starts back to her car. As soon as she slams the door she checks her phone. It's Gareth's birthday and he will have received the present by now. Still she cannot see his profile, still there is no reply. She imagines all the *Happy Birthday*s on his Facebook page, the messages and hearts from the blondes, the memories of birthdays long past: *great evening, do you remember, must do it again.* She wonders who he will be sharing his birthday with. Surely, surely, even he could not open a present from her and do nothing? Surely he would write somehow and say thank you. But, as she discards her phone on the passenger seat, and twists the ignition key, she knows that he's more than capable of ignoring her.

~

"I've brought someone to see you," Carol calls from the hall. She hesitates as she hears Ivor coughing from the living room.

Louis crowds in behind her. Ivor coughs again.

"Ivor." Carol marches in, dumps her bag on the table. "Here's Louis. Long time no see, hey?"

Ivor coughs into a handkerchief. Carol glances at Louis and wonders what he's thinking, whether he still thinks she made a mistake not marrying Ivor.

"Louis," Ivor croaks at last. "Yes, it has been a long time."

"I'll make a start on dinner," Carol says, "then I'll do your legs. Louis, don't wear him out. That cough doesn't sound good."

She hurries away to the kitchen and checks the fridge. There's a packet of ham, some tomatoes, a couple of eggs. She'll hard-boil one of those and make a ham salad. There are a few strawberries and an unopened punnet of raspberries. She strains her ears as she peels cucumber and chops tomatoes. Louis is talking about moving down, the caravan he's staying in, how he's relieved to leave London. Ivor says the odd word, makes the odd affirmation, and coughs. Carol doesn't like that cough. She hopes Louis will have the sense to stay in the living room when she peels off Ivor's compression stockings and washes his legs, when she smooths cream into the taut skin and eases him into his pyjamas. Ivor wouldn't want anyone watching that.

—

Jake lifts his arm from Mel's shoulders.

"I'm not rushing you." He runs a finger down her cheek and she gulps silently. "I know this is difficult. It's like I said. I like you enormously, I love spending time with you. And if anything more should happen…" He shrugs. "That would be wonderful."

"And if it didn't?" Mel asks quietly. "If I just can't?"

"That's fine," Jake says. "But I hope you will."

Mel rubs her eyes. Too late she remembers the eyeliner she put on in the car. A glance at her palms shows smoky smudges. She and Jake are side by side on the sofa in his cottage. She knows he was hoping to take her hand and lead her to his bed today, and she did want to, does want to, but it really isn't that easy. Such a cliché, but true. Sometimes what you want is not easy. She knows the moment has broken, for her at least, and it will not happen today. And yet, if she keeps coming over, if she keeps meeting him, it will, one day. That is a certainty.

~

"I'm going to see Dad soon," Emmeline says. "Do you want to come? I thought I'd stay and have lunch with him."

Tansy wavers. She would like to see Ivor. Of course she would, but he might ask her who the book was for. She doesn't want her mother knowing about that.

"You go today," she says eventually. "I'll go another time. I think I might be getting a sore throat."

"OK, well, best to stay away from him then."

"Give him my love. Tell him I'll call."

As soon as Emmeline's car has gone, Tansy gathers up her keys and phone. This is a crazy decision, a stupid dangerous decision. Nothing right will come of this, but she has to do it. She's angry now. Hurt, betrayed, and angry.

It's a clear run to Hayle. She parks in the usual car park, shoves coins into the meter, rips out the ticket. This really might be the last time she comes here. She walks along the street, now so familiar. The broken paving slab, the butterfly transfers. She notices that a pale blue peeling front door has been repainted in a smart navy. There's a Costa takeaway cup skittering in the gutter, an old receipt. No sign of Gareth's car.

She strides straight up to the building.

Did you get your birthday present? Did you like your present? You could have said thank you. Why won't you talk to me?

She has no idea which, if any, of these she will say. She will probably say something completely different. She rings the bell. Static, nothing else. She waits, heart squeezing with fear, then rings again. The same static.

She steps away from the door, glances up at the front panes. There's no way she could get round the back to see Gareth's windows. She's not sure she could even work out which they were. His car isn't in the street. Maybe he's simply gone out. She could wait where she waited before.

As she starts away from the door a young guy comes towards her. He has spiky brown hair and glasses. He's carrying a plastic shopping bag. He's coming to the door.

"All right?" he says as he taps in the key code.

"Do you know if Gareth's in? Gareth Crane? I've been trying his bell."

The guy stops half in, half out of the door. Tansy stands on tiptoes to see beyond his head, to the pigeonholes, the door at the back of the hall.

"He's gone, hasn't he?" the guy says.

Tansy thuds back onto her heels. "Gone? Gone where?"

"Truro, I think. He said he was moving. Think he's gone now. Haven't seen him."

"But." Tansy stops. This guy just wants to get in with his shopping. "I sent him a parcel the other day. Can I see if it's in there?"

"I'll have a look."

The guy checks the pigeonholes, without asking her in.

"No parcel for him. Just some junk. Look, he probably came to pick up the last bits and took it then."

"Have you got his new address?"

"Nah. I didn't really know him. He's on Facebook though. Send him a message."

The door shuts with a hard click. The guy has gone. The pigeonholes have gone. The back stairs have gone. And Gareth has gone. Tansy has no way of finding him.

She stands there a moment, heart skipping, stunned. A group of girls walks past, then a couple, talking, heads bent together. She stands there waiting. Waiting for what? The door to open? Gareth to come out or arrive, to tell her the guy was lying or confused or something. No. That isn't going to happen.

Her throat is dry and tastes thick and sweet. She takes her first step away from the building. She will not come here again. After a few hesitant steps she turns back to the door. It's still closed. She walks back to her car, down the street she knows so well. A tiny terraced backstreet in Hayle she would never have gone to if it weren't for Gareth. It would not even be a name on a map for her; an insignificant strip of road. An unknown cracked flagstone, unknown stickers on windows, an unknown freshly painted door.

She's exhausted when she arrives at her car. Her mind spools on decades ahead as she wonders if there will ever be some occasion where she has to walk along that street, even go to Gareth's building, for some other reason, some other person. And, if she does, will the memory of this summer still be so jagged, so acute, or will it take her a moment to realise that this was the car park she ran from in such excitement that wet afternoon, and this terrace was the street where Gareth once parked. Will the paving stone be mended? The butterfly house will have changed hands and the stickers long gone. Old sash windows will be replaced with modern white frames, and the doors will be a rainbow of new colours.

Vicky checks that Ivor has everything he needs for the evening. He's in his chair in front of the TV. He has a plate of fruit and biscuits to hand, and a glass of cordial. Fresh water in all his drinking bottles. He coughs and coughs into a handkerchief, shoulders heaving.

She's uneasy. Ivor hardly ate anything for dinner. She cooked him an omelette and some toast. He shoved the eggs around his plate and ate a few bites of toast. He didn't want any pudding, even though she offered him raspberries, ice cream, or simply a few squares of chocolate. His legs were swollen and red, hot to the touch, when she washed him, with cracks in the skin. He had a job moving about because his legs were so painful.

"Ivor, I think you might need the doctor in the morning."

"I'm fine."

Talking starts off his cough again. Vicky hovers beside him. He doesn't look well. He's pale, grey-blue. He isn't even trying to watch the screen. Vicky hands him his phone.

"If you feel ill, call me. Please. Or any of the others. I know it's hard for your family with the girls. We can help too."

Ivor nods, but she isn't sure he has even taken it in. She wishes she didn't have to leave him. Outside, she sits in her car and brings up Stefan's number. Then she remembers he's working in the bar. Instead she goes to the Facebook group for Ivor's carers. No one's used it in a while. She taps out a message.

Whoever has sent her a message is just being cruel, Tansy thinks, watching the little red dot on her screen. That is ridiculous: no one else even knows how she's spent weeks of her life waiting for Gareth to talk to her. She clicks the message open. It's probably Charlie.

"Mum," she shouts.

Emmeline is washing up in the kitchen, and doesn't hear her above the girls' squabbling, and the rush of the taps. Tansy scrambles up off the sofa, her pulse rising.

"Mum, listen."

"What?" Emmeline turns off the water.

"And wheeeeeeee he goes!" Amber throws Tiger across the room.

"Hey, you wouldn't let me wheeeeeeee him."

"He's my Tiger. Not your Tiger. He doesn't want you to touch him. Ever. Ever."

"Girls, ssh please," Tansy shouts. "Message from Vicky."

"What?" Emmeline spins round, gloved hands dripping bubbles.

"Says he's not at all well tonight. Wouldn't eat. Vague. Legs and chest bad. She thinks he needs antibiotics. We should call a doctor in the morning."

"I should go up now."

"Or me."

"You'll be over the limit." Emmeline says shortly.

"I only had one glass."

Tansy slouches away, embarrassed once more. She must stop this. She *must*. The summer has been so painful, so sad, she can't imagine how much worse it would have been without a drink. Suddenly she remembers a night, long ago, only a few months ago. The night Ivor fell. The night she opened a bottle. The night everything seemed to change.

Vicky can't sleep. She wants to talk to Stefan, but she doesn't dare make a call, even though everyone else is asleep, and it's gone two in the morning. She runs through the messages in the conversation group. Emmeline went up to see Ivor. He was subdued but all right. She offered him Paracetamol and he refused. She helped him into bed. Carol has promised to be there early in the morning.

Vicky can't help feeling she should have done more. Should she have called an emergency doctor? An ambulance? For what exactly? The same problems Ivor has all the time. But she is sure this is something else. Like smelling rain in the air, she knows this is a warning.

You did everything right, Stefan had texted her earlier when he finished his shift. *Carol will update us all tomorrow.*

Will Carol be too late? Vicky wonders in this lonely dark hour. Will any of them ever see Ivor again?

Tansy stumbles from the bathroom back to bed. She has another half hour before she has to get up, get the girls ready for school. She stops. It's not worth going back to bed. She might as well make tea. She and Emmeline will sort out a doctor once the girls are safe at school. Tansy's mind is jumbled with the thoughts that consume her, but she still wonders in moments of clarity: how long can Ivor live alone?

The landline rings, jarring her thoughts. Too early for Carol surely. She swipes to answer the call.

She can hardly hear Ivor. His voice is so high and broken.

"I'm very ill," he gasps.

"What's wrong?" She turns, aware of her mother appearing beside her in tatty checked pyjamas. Emmeline is pulling faces; Tansy turns her thumb down. Emmeline crowds nearer.

"...know."

"What?" Tansy asks, trying to keep her own voice calm.

"I...don't...know."

"OK look, one of us will come right away," Tansy says. "I'll call Carol too. Just stay where you are."

"You go." Emmeline says. "You're better in emergencies."

"Not true."

"Please. I can't bear...I'll get the girls to school."

"I'll get dressed...I'll call Carol."

Tansy holds her mobile to her ear as she gathers clean knickers and socks.

"Carol, can you come as soon as possible please? He's not well. No, I don't know. He called us...he sounded terrible. Thanks. Thanks. See you."

―

Vicky opens sticky eyes, disorientated. Her neck aches. And her back. She's on the sofa in the living room, and something is jabbing into her thigh. Her mobile. She grabs it. No messages in the conversation group. Surely if something awful had happened in the night Tansy or Emmeline would have told everyone? But how would they even know? Vicky's heart rate skitters as she hauls herself up off the sofa.

―

Tansy fumbles with the lock and barges into Ivor's house. She can hear his breathing as she approaches the bedroom.

"I'm here," she says. "Grandad. I'm here."

"Uh…uh…"

Ivor's eyes are unfocused. It's like he can't see her or does not recognise her. She reaches out to his hand lying on top of the covers. It's frozen.

"You're so cold."

"So cold." That squeaking whistle again.

She pulls the duvet away from his neck. His face is icy too, and blue-grey.

"Tansy…I…"

"What is it? How do you feel?"

"Terrible. Terrible. I'm dying. Tansy…I can't…"

"I'm calling an ambulance."

Tansy runs out into the living room where the reception is better. As she dials 999, the front door swings open and Carol rushes in. Tansy has never seen Carol so dishevelled, without her make-up, without her jangling earrings and beads.

"Ambulance," Tansy says, pointing to her phone, and waves Carol towards the bedroom.

—

"Carol. You're early."

"Ivor, darling, you've got us all so worried. Tansy's calling an ambulance."

Carol takes Ivor's hand, and almost recoils at the cold. His face is waxen; he looks more dead than alive. Carol's heart shudders. This might really be the moment she has dreaded.

"Carol?"

What the hell is wrong with his voice?

"Yes, I'm here."

"Remember what I said...the studio...the paintings. Take what you like...need."

"I'm not going into that studio until you're better, OK?"

"Carol. I think this is goodbye."

"Ring them again," Carol says to Tansy. "Now."

Tansy glances back to Ivor. He's shuddering under the quilt, no longer talking. His breathing is harsh in his chest. Carol lifts the bedcover up, sees swollen red legs and recoils.

"OK." Tansy calls 999 again, and is told the ambulance is on the way.

She watches out the kitchen window for the neon green, the spinning blue lights. Her ears strain for the siren. Ivor's riotous garden has never looked more lovely, more summery, she thinks. Huge roses, as tall as she is. are weighed down with blowsy flowers in peach and pink, lemon and white. The honeysuckle shades the kitchen window with its spidery blooms, and tiny apples are swelling on the tree. The cruel everlasting cycle of life and death.

Emmeline's car shoots past the gate and a moment later, she jogs onto the drive. As Tansy opens the door for her mother, the ambulance arrives – no sirens, no lights – and Tansy has no time to tell Emmeline anything further before the two burly paramedics stride in with their gear.

—

Vicky doesn't like to call Tansy, just in case. Just in case of what? Just in case the unthinkable has happened. She types a message in the chat group and waits. Mel replies.

I'm at Lanyon today.

Please let me know. Love to Ivor.

Tansy doesn't appear to be online. Nor Emmeline.

Once Kev, Harry, and Skye have left she calls Stefan.

"Come round," he says sleepily. "I've got a couple of hours."

"What about Ivor?"

"Well, we'll get any news together."

Five minutes later she's in the car. They still haven't worked out how and where they can meet while Kev is working in Stefan's road. They can't meet at Vicky's, even in the daytime. Booking a Travelodge room is insanely expensive. They'll just have to find somewhere quiet in the car.

The alternative – not seeing Stefan for a few weeks – isn't an option.

~

Tansy and Emmeline have driven separately to the hospital. By early afternoon Ivor is still in a cubicle in A and E. He's been started on some antibiotics, but is still glazed and incoherent. Tansy jerks the stained curtains aside and glances up and down the room. Cursors blink from a bank of screens. Ivor's name is among many on a whiteboard. Two fat nurses are chatting, going nowhere quickly.

Tansy tugs her T-shirt away from her skin. It's hot and airless. In her hurry to get to Ivor she forgot to put on deodorant and her underarms are sticky and unpleasant. She's sent a few texts to Carol.

Just been seen by a Dr, He didn't seem to know anything, Antibiotics. Don't say anything to the others yet.

Now her battery is almost dead.

"I'll have to go soon for the girls," she says.

"I'll wait here," says Emmeline. "I think we should tell the others now. Izzy needs to know not to come tonight. And I should tell Jake."

Tansy nods, distracted by a porter shoving a comatose woman in a wheelchair.

"I'll tell them all what's happening." Emmeline taps her phone into life.

Tansy kisses Ivor's bristly cheek. "I'll see you soon," she whispers fiercely, willing it to be true.

~

When Emmeline arrives home it's almost evening. Tansy is spooning boiled egg into Amber's mouth. Scarlet has left her egg and toast and helped herself to crisps. Tansy has showered and changed and answered the messages from her father and the carers, but she hasn't had a drink. She might have to drive.

"He's on a ward now." Emmeline kicks off her shoes and crumples down at the table. "I would have called you but I was running out of juice too."

"Granny, Granny." Amber flicks the spoon away. Gold egg-yolk streaks the tablecloth.

"I'm here, darling," Emmeline opens her arms.

"And Savannah didn't even know that," shrieks Scarlet. "Are you listening? She didn't even know that two and two are four."

"How is he?" Tansy asks.

Emmeline shrugs. "They don't seem to know. They said he might have had a stroke. But they don't seem convinced."

"A stroke? He doesn't seem like that."

"I think it's sepsis. From his chest and his leg. He's on antibiotics. They should help."

Tansy nods, and gathers up the remains of the eggs. For the first time in weeks she hasn't spent the entire day thinking about Gareth Crane. She wishes, wishes, wishes, it hadn't taken this to give her that respite.

Later, when the girls are finally asleep, Tansy calls the ward for an update.

"Hold the line," says a surly voice.

A sinister electronic *Fur Elise* plays on repeat. She remembers Charlie once telling her about Numbers Stations, codes broadcast by spies on shortwave, and the tinny notes remind her of the recordings he played for her, and dread swells in her chest.

When Ivor's nurse finally comes on the line, all she can tell Tansy is that Ivor is sleeping, and asks her to ring again in the morning after the ward round.

She hangs up, reports back to Emmeline, and opens up the chat. Her eyes pluck the text from all the kisses, hearts, and emojis.

Tansy: Just spoke to the nurse. No real news. Ward round tomorrow.

Carol: Can I go and see him tomorrow or next day if OK with you?

Tansy: Of course.

Mel: I'd love to see him too. Poor Ivor. I've just got home, but I have been thinking about him.

Izzy: Send him my love, please. And how are you all doing?

Tansy: Oh well, you know, stressed.

Carol: Have they done anything yet?

Tansy: Antibios. They don't seem to know what's wrong. He's asleep.

Mel: Rest will be good for him.

Stefan: Anything I can do to help? Just ask.

Vicky: I should have called an ambulance last night.

Tansy: Vicky, stop beating yourself up.

Izzy: Yes, stop it.

Vicky: I knew something was wrong.

Carol: He was definitely poorly this morning.

Mel: I can have the girls if you need me to. I can probably change shifts.

Vicky: We can swap if necessary.

Stefan: Tansy, get some rest yourself.

Tansy: Thanks all. I'm going to bed. Tomorrow I'll give your names to the ward so you can ring up yourselves for news.

Izzy: Thanks Tansy. Hope you get some sleep.

Stefan: Take care and let us know anything we can do.

Vicky: Yes anything. Lots of love.

Carol: I'm always here.

Mel: Night night Tansy. Hope there is good news in the morning. Does your dad know?

Tansy logs off before she can be dragged back into the conversation. Yes, Jake does know. Fuck, she should probably ring or text him again. She just wants to sleep.

~

In the morning Scarlet refuses her usual yoghurt for breakfast, and hunches over her abdomen.

"I've got tummy ache, Mumma. I want to stay at home."

Tansy looks at Emmeline in despair.

"Easier for her to be with us than getting sent home," Emmeline says.

"OK," Tansy agrees. "Take off your uniform then, and have a lie down. I'll take Amber and see you soon." She kisses Scarlet and gathers together Amber's lunch and water bottle.

Amber chatters away in the back seat as Tansy drives to the nursery. Tansy zones out. If anything has happened to Ivor in the night, surely the ward staff would have called. No news is good news. It must be.

She drops off Amber at the nursery door. Amber scampers in, her huge backpack like a tortoise shell. As Tansy turns away to walk back to the car someone catches her elbow.

"Any news?" Mel asks.

"Nothing yet. The ward round is about now I think. They said to call after ten."

"Let me know please."

"Of course."

"Did you tell Jake?"

"Yeah, he knows."

"Ah. Good. Yes, that's good."

"Scarlet's poorly, so I've got to go."

Tansy scrabbles for her keys in her pocket. Of course, Mel did those workshops with Jake. That's why she's concerned that he knows.

~

Fur Elise sounds just as creepy in daylight. The nurse – a man, this time – tells Tansy that Ivor is vague and confused, but that the ward is open for visitors any time.

"I'll go now," Tansy tells her mother, "and you stay with Scarlet. Then you can go this evening."

When she arrives on the ward the nurse she spoke to directs her to Ivor's cubicle.

"He's not making a lot of sense today," the nurse says. "His kidney function is pretty bad but we're hoping that will right itself. See how you get on. He refused breakfast. Next time you come if there's something he might eat…"

Tansy nods vaguely. "Yes, some fruit or something. Of course."

The nurse wanders off with a bulky folder of notes. Tansy walks over to Ivor's cubicle. His is the middle bed of three, the side curtains closed to his neighbours.

"Hi, it's me."

She takes his thin cold hand and squeezes it.

"Ah you," Ivor says. "I tell you, no one here understands about what happened in Japan."

Tansy flinches.

"I explained how I got on the wrong flight. And I think a lot of the staff here were also in that place...that place...in Japan."

"You're in hospital," Tansy says.

Ivor's voice is stronger, and he carries on over her. "Last night...there was a drugs bust in this ward. Come here. I don't want to shout."

Tansy leans in, nausea spreading through her guts.

"The junior doctors, they let in some blokes with guns and stuff. Looking for drugs. It was so noisy, I tell you. Then this morning there was some kind of inspection going on. Everyone lined up. Some VIP I think."

"Grandad, I think your medicine is making you muddled."

"Well, you know whose fault that is? Kathy Haywood. She was sorting that out."

"Grandad. Kathy Haywood died about ten years ago, remember?"

"No, no." Ivor has exerted himself; he coughs and phlegm slides down his chin. "She's not dead. She's here doing the breakfasts."

~

Tansy sits a moment behind the wheel, unable to even think about driving. Ivor did recognise her, she is sure, but it's like his eyes are seeing another world, his ears hearing other sounds and voices. Wearily she swipes open her mobile. She no longer expects anything from Gareth, but she can't say it has stopped hurting. Before she calls home she drifts through her photographs. It's still there, that tiny thumbnail hidden amongst the girls' smiles: the image of her in Gareth's bed, the luminous eyes, the ragged sensual hair, that smile. That smile. She holds eye contact with that other Tansy a moment. That Tansy who knew, even then, that by the time the camera clicked, the moment had gone. And now here she is, staring back at her past, and Ivor lies alone and confused, possibly dying, in the hospital. Driving home feels beyond her but she throws down her phone and starts the ignition. Her throat is dry and she doesn't have the energy to talk to her mother at the moment.

The next day Carol visits Ivor. At Tansy's request she has prepared some strawberries and raspberries for him, and has a new bottle of fruit cordial. She hates hospitals, always has. She keeps her eyes ahead of her as she walks down the corridor to the far end, as the man on reception told her to do. She passes a shop and a café. There are groups of people loitering and chatting. A couple of blokes in theatre blues. Someone pushing a laundry trolley. Carol keeps walking firmly, wondering if she should have asked Louis to come with her after all.

The last door on the right. She stops, gulps at the foetid institutional air. Tansy and Emmeline have told her that Ivor is confused, that he keeps talking about strange impossible events happening on the wards, recent flights he's been on. The doctors thought he might have had a stroke but now believe him to have sepsis. Sepsis causes hallucinations and confusion, Carol knows this. Surely the antibiotics must be kicking in by now.

The ward clerk directs her to the cubicle. Ivor is propped up at what looks like an uncomfortable angle, and a healthcare in a tight lavender tunic is spooning some sort of slop into his mouth. It snakes out of the corner and down his chin. The healthcare ignores it and shovels in another mouthful. Ivor flaps his arm to say stop.

"Ivor!" Carol calls, trying to paint a smile on her face.

What she sees makes her heart thunder and her legs tremble, but she strides forward, rummaging for a tissue to wipe his face. His chin is hairy and scratchy because no one has shaved him. His green eyes, those startling green eyes, focus on her a moment.

"Carol."

Carol almost sobs with relief that he knows her.

"I've brought you some fruit," she says.

Ivor nods, ignoring the spoon being jabbed towards him.

"I'll see what I can get him to eat," Carol says to the healthcare worker.

"Right you are then." The bored-looking woman heaves up, tugs the tunic over her vast arse and ambles away to the nurses' station.

Carol dumps the remains of Ivor's meal on the floor. She's not surprised he didn't want it. Some kind of brown mashed up mince and then the ghastly pudding. She puts the tray on the floor and notices a *soft diet* notice above his bed.

"You can manage these?" She opens the Tupperware box, and the aroma of strawberries wafts up to kill the stink of hospital food and wounds.

Ivor opens his mouth and she pops in half a strawberry.

"What's the news?" he asks.

"Not much. We all miss you. Louis is still here. Stefan and Vicky said something about going round to yours to do some gardening, keep the place looking nice. We all want you home as soon as possible."

"Emmeline…Tansy…they don't have to come every day."

"We've told them we want to visit you too, but of course they want to see you."

"Don't want the little ones to see me like this."

"No," Carol says softly. "No, I wouldn't want them in a hospital either."

"Just want to get home."

"Have you seen the doctors today?"

"I saw some girl…" Ivor drifts off for a moment. "On the plane."

Carol's hand wavers with a raspberry. Just when she thought Ivor was back to normal. She was hoping, hoping so hard, she could report back to everyone that his delirium had passed.

"She seemed to think I'd been to Japan before, but I told her categorically it was my first visit. No one listens."

"I'm listening."

"These are nice." Ivor opens his mouth for another berry.

~

I'm leaving work early tomorrow to visit Ivor. Tansy says it's fine. Do you want to come?

When?

I'll leave about 5.

I'm at Lanyon. I can't do it.

Damn. OK. Never mind. I'll tell him I'll cut the lawn. You still up for some gardening?

Definitely. Give him my love.

Will do.

Vicky would love to go with Stefan to see Ivor, but it's too late to ask anyone to change shifts with her and anyway they shouldn't be seen together by too many people. They still haven't worked out where they can go when Kev is in St Ives.

~

"He's really poorly," Tansy tells Jake on the phone.

"I'll get up and see him in a few days."

"You may not have a few days," Tansy snaps. "He's delirious. He's got sepsis. They don't seem to know what else he may or may not have. Oh yes and kidney problems."

"I'm sorry," Jake says. "How's your mum?"

"How d'you think? And, you know, I haven't…haven't been myself lately and I should have spent more time with him and now…I don't know if I'll get that chance."

"You have been preoccupied. I've hardly seen you either."

"I know. I'm sorry."

"Or the girls."

"Yes. I'll make it up to you. I promise. When this is all…"

"Sorted out."

"Yeah. Sorted out."

"Perhaps he'd benefit from another stay in Lanyon before he goes home."

"I can't think that far ahead."

~

"Tansy said you'd like some strawberries." Stefan digs the box out of his backpack. "And here are some grapes."

"Thanks Stefan."

"How are you now?"

"The same. I just want to get out. Home again. I can't walk, you know. Lost the use of my legs."

"Have you had any physio?"

"No."

Stefan glances around the ward to see if there's anyone he can speak to. Ivor doesn't sound at all deluded or confused. He's angry and depressed, and he needs some physio to get him back on his feet. If he's left here in this miserable ward of old men he will fade away.

"Hang on, I'm going to see if I can find a nurse."

Stefan strides out of the cubicle and down to the nurses' station. There's a gaggle of three there. One is fiddling with a patient's folder. Another young one – probably a student – wanders off. The third eventually looks up at Stefan.

"Can I speak to Ivor Martin's nurse please?"

"That's me," she says. "Are you family?"

"I'm one of his carers. The family gave permission for us to talk to you."

"Oh. Well. I haven't heard about that."

"Yes, they have," the one with the folder interrupts. She scrabbles for a piece of paper. "Here's a list of the carers."

"Stefan Rose," Stefan says.

"All right," Ivor's nurse says grudgingly. "What do you want to know?"

"Is he getting any physio soon? He says he can't walk. I know he wants to go home as soon as possible, but he lives alone and he must be able to get about."

"I think a physio is coming to assess him in the next day or so. The physios are terribly understaffed and –"

Stefan balls his fist in irritation. "The longer he's off his legs the harder it will be. He really wants to go home."

"We're looking at moving Ivor either to a community hospital or a care home."

"He was at Lanyon before. He has friends there. Two of his carers work there."

"It depends on vacancies. We'll be talking to his family later."

Stefan drifts back to Ivor. He is plucking at the grapes, trying to break one off.

"Here, let me." Stefan tugs off a sprig, and hands Ivor a grape. "I have news. They're talking about moving you out of here."

"I can't go home. I can't walk."

"They're talking about a home or a community hospital. I said Lanyon would be best because of Vicky and Mel."

"That would be much better." Ivor sucks a grape and swallows. "And how is Vicky?"

"She's going to help me with your garden again. If that's OK?"

"Of course it's OK. Give her my love."

When Stefan leaves the ward he sees Emmeline coming in. Her hair is in a scruffy ponytail, and she's carrying a big holdall.

"Give it to me," Stefan says. "He's really good today."

"Really?"

"Not confused at all. Wants to go home. They're talking about moving him out, possibly back to Lanyon."

"That's good then."

"Back again, Ivor." Stefan drops the holdall by the bed, and gives Emmeline's shoulder a quick squeeze. "I'll leave you both now."

Moving Ivor to Lanyon would be the best thing, he thinks as the electric doors hiss open. He squints in the bright sunlight. Between them Vicky and Mel would look after him, get him moving again. They know him better than anyone here, and Ivor would be so much happier there.

Izzy takes Abi with her to visit Ivor at the weekend. It seems like Abi is balanced on a tightrope, walking ahead, tiny steps, one foot at a time, but there's that chasm beneath her all the time, and the slightest breath of wind could send her tumbling. She hasn't even mentioned Rick for days, weeks. It's been so long Izzy can't even remember the last time. It's as though she has had him wiped from her brain.

"You said you always knew," Abi says, as Izzy guns up the A30, overtaking a trembling van, and a motorhome.

"Always knew?"

"About being gay."

"Well, yes."

Izzy flicks her eyes to the rear mirror. An Audi is gaining on her; she slips back into the inner lane.

"So what about the boys you went out with? Were you pretending?"

"Not pretending as such. Just trying to fit in, wondering if there was some way I could be like other people. It's still what's expected, you know. And then…"

"And then what?"

"Oh nothing."

"What? Tell me."

"Then you were poorly so it wasn't the time and then you got better and life calmed down and I just wanted to enjoy the peace, and then you got ill again this year."

"I'm sorry." Abi reaches over to Izzy's hand on the gear stick.

"Don't be sorry. It's not your fault. I'm just so happy to see you getting stronger."

"I don't think about him any more. These tablets…it's like they've washed my brain clear. Washed all the shit out."

"That's great. I had noticed. I mean, I didn't know you weren't thinking about him, but I knew you hadn't mentioned him."

"The things he gave me. I shoved them into a box and put it in the loft, marked *toxic waste*. There was very little. I realised he'd never given me anything special like a lovely necklace or anything like that. Just bits and bobs. But I didn't want to throw it all out yet."

"You'll know when to. Or not to. Just take it like you are."

"I'm glad Stefan found me."

"Jesus, so am I. Would you have jumped?"

"I don't know. I think so."

~

"Mumma, Amber's being mean to me because I said I like Elsa best and she says I have to like Anna best because she does, but why can't we like Elsa and Anna?"

"Anna! You have to like Anna!"

Tansy strains to hear Emmeline on the phone in the kitchen. She hears words like *physio* and *walking*, *support* and *Lanyon House*.

"Why do I have to like Anna? Anna's the stupid little sister."

"ANNA. Because I SAY SO."

"Ssh, please," Tansy hisses.

"You're a stupid little sister too."

"Oww. Mummy, she hit me."

"Scarlet, why d'you do that?"

"Because she's so stupid and – oww, hey, Mumma, Amber poked me."

"Stop it, both of you. I'll be glad to hand you over to Daddy tonight."

"Yes, yes, we would prefer that," Emmeline says. "If you could let me know as soon as possible."

"What's going on?" Tansy asks, as Emmeline hangs up.

"They're sending someone from Lanyon to assess him. Obviously they want to boot him out as soon as possible. I don't think he's ready, but is he going to get any help there? I doubt it. It's never even the same staff one day to the next. At least at Lanyon Mel and Vicky can keep an eye on him. I know they'd help him get on his feet."

Tansy tugs at her hair absently. "What if Lanyon can't take him? They're not going to send him home?"

"Well they can't. He can't go to the bathroom. Can't even stand up at the moment. He needs more than what our gang can do. It's absolutely not going to happen. We just have to hope Lanyon has a room. It's nicer than many, and so handy, and the girls are there. That's the most important thing. If they thought he was going downhill they could make the right noises, get him back to hospital."

"The nurse or whoever…did she say how he is today?"

"Said he was alright. Lucid, alert. Had some lunch. Still needs two people to take him to the bathroom. She was more or less saying it's wear and tear and there's nothing they are going to do for him. Oh, his gout is bad again, she said, and she's going to get the doctors to put him back on colchicine."

Gout, chest, cellulitis, sepsis. Poor Ivor, Tansy thinks, fighting off old age on all sides without any weapons. Fighting his own mortality.

~

Vicky parks in the far corner of the car park and waits until Stefan drives in before she gets out. She locks the door without rushing and walks over to where he's pulled his car over. She doesn't have to feel guilty, she tries to convince herself. She's sharing a lift to Ivor's house with another of his carers. Stefan is going to mow the lawn and she'll do some cleaning inside, and maybe help in the garden if there's time.

The grass will still be growing and the dust settling while Ivor is in hospital. They are simply looking after his home.

Stefan kisses her quickly when she gets in and roars off before she can click her seatbelt into place.

"It's so beautiful," Vicky breathes as he turns into Ivor's drive. "He should be here to see it."

The tiny apples on the tree have swollen into bright marbles of green. White butterflies flutter and land on the lavender. The front of the house is half hidden with honeysuckle and giant roses.

"It's like *Sleeping Beauty*," she says as she gets out.

"You know Ivor would want some order in it."

"I know, but I love gardens like this, at this time of year, all roses and daisies and drifts of colour. Half wild."

"Yeah, it's lovely, but the lawn'll be a jungle if I don't keep on top of it. Come on."

Stefan digs out his key and opens the door. There's a fan of mail on the hall floor. He picks it up, casts his eyes quickly over the envelopes.

"We'll leave these on the table, and Tansy and Emmeline can decide if he needs any of it. Hey, you haven't heard anything from Lanyon's side, have you? About him moving there?"

"Nothing. They wouldn't tell me anyway."

"Come here." Stefan holds out his arms to her, and she slides into him. "Next week, isn't it? Kev in my street?"

"Yes. Where can we go?"

"We'll find somewhere." He kisses her again, runs a hand through her ponytail, and smiles. "Stop worrying. I'll work it out. OK, I'll make a start on the lawn."

"I'll hoover."

Vicky watches Stefan trundle the mower out of the little shed. The lawn has sprouted like a wild meadow again. There are long tufty grasses, dandelions, daisies, buttercups, some tiny mauve plant she doesn't recognise – maybe thyme. He glances up to the window and waves at her. She blows him a kiss from the safety of the living room, then turns away to get the hoover out of the cupboard.

Once she's done the living room she drags the vacuum down to Ivor's room. She stops in the doorway. This was where he last was in the house, where Tansy and Carol found him blue and barely responsive. She sits on the bed and inhales his scent from the duvet cover: his leg cream, his soap. She should strip the bed and wash the covers, but she won't without asking Tansy or Emmeline. They must have been in here to get clothes for him, but there is still so much of Ivor there. His alarm clock and torch on the bedside table. An old pair of scuffed slippers. A half bottle of colchicine and a tube of emollient. The curtains are half drawn and she can see the dusky pink and cream roses just beyond the glass.

Stefan comes in as she is stashing the hoover away.

"I need some water. It's boiling."

She watches him splash water on his face at the kitchen sink, run a glass under the tap.

"Should we check the studio?" Vicky asks.

Stefan gulps water. "Probably no need. We could though."

"Have you ever been in?"

"Yes, before he had the fall. Have you?"

"Never."

Stefan grins. "You want to look?"

Vicky blushes. "Well, yes, I mean, I'd love to see in there. I never liked to ask him, especially as he couldn't get out there any more. It seemed too unfair."

"He wouldn't mind. I know where the key is."

"You sure about this?"

"Really. Ivor won't mind you having a look. And no one will see."

"What if Tansy or her mum come?"

"They know we're up here. I told them it was today. I don't think they'd come while we were here."

Stefan takes Vicky's hand. He smells of sweat and grass and summer air. He unhooks a key and leads her into the garden. Bees buzz up from the lavender. There are butterflies – whites, an Admiral, something small and brown – swooping round the buddleia's purple spikes. Stefan unlocks the studio door and stands aside for her to enter.

"He hasn't been in since he fell." Vicky whispers as though she were in church. "Is that what he was working on?"

There's a huge canvas streaked with powerful strokes of green and white, grey and brown. Brushes in a jar. Tubs and tubes of paint, stained and cracked. A dirty rag, dried to a stiff frill with old acrylic pigment.

Vicky moves forward to the canvas, reaches out a finger to it. The clotted paint is shiny and hard. She can see where he layered the colours, where he washed on a stain with a wet brush underneath, where he scratched green away to reveal an earthy ochre.

Stefan's arms slide around her and he rests his head on hers.

"I don't think he'll ever finish it."

"That's so sad." Vicky can feel tears stinging her throat. "We must find a way to get him here. Or the painting inside."

"No," Stefan says softly. "It's not what he wants. You heard him the other day. This is where he wants to sign off."

"It's so cruel, so fucking cruel."

Vicky wriggles in Stefan's arms and buries her face in his sweaty T-shirt.

"It is, sweetheart," he says. "Life is. Come and look at his drawings down here."

There are sketchbooks and loose sheets shoved into an ancient chest of drawers. There are prints tacked up on the walls. Broken stems of charcoal on the floor. A few paperback books. A sticky tube of cough sweets. A pile of blankets and cushions in the corner.

"Don't cry." Stefan kisses away her tears. "If Ivor wanted to get back out here we'd find a way. You know that. It's his choice."

Vicky nods. "I know, I know. I just feel like we're losing him."

"I feel like that sometimes."

"He is old."

"He is."

"And I don't think I could handle that as well as everything else."

"Sssh now." Stefan eases her down onto the pile of tattered and stained cushions and tugs the band from her ponytail.

~

What once seemed impossible has happened. Tansy realises there have been whole minutes when she hasn't been thinking about Gareth Crane. Yes, she does still check her Facebook to see if he has unblocked her or thanked her for the gift. As she expects, he has done neither, so there is no shock, no nasty surprise.

She dumps the bags of shopping down on the step and unlocks the door.

"I couldn't get any leeks, but I got some berries for Grandad, and some smoothie." She stops as she hears the low murmur of Emmeline talking on the phone, and carries the bags into the kitchen.

"The infection really has cleared up then?"

Tansy glances at her mother, who grimaces back at her.

"Yes. Lanyon would be best. OK, give me her name and I'll call her shortly. Thanks."

"Moving to Lanyon?" Tansy asks as Emmeline hangs up.

"Yes. Never thought he'd get the assessment so quickly, but someone came first thing. They're happy to have him. They've got a room."

"Hope it's that lovely room at the front." Tansy stops, a bag of bananas in her hand.

So long ago, and yet only a heartbeat. Ivor watching the waves from the huge bay window. Before her heart broke again.

~

"God, Stefan, we shouldn't have. Not here, not in the studio."

"It's OK. I'm sure it's OK. Ivor's not some maiden aunt, you know that. He knows about you and me."

Vicky fiddles with her clothes, and tries to scrunch her hair up again.

"Shall I help?"

Stefan runs his fingers through her long hair and scoops it up. There's a knot he can't remove without a brush, so he twists the scrunchie on anyway.

"Meeting here?" Vicky looks at him. "Is that what you're thinking?"

"Here," he says.

~

Two days later Mel runs up the stairs to the first floor of Lanyon House and knocks on the door. When there's no reply she edges the door open.

"Hello you."

Ivor turns awkwardly from the chair in front of the TV.

"Mel. Lovely to see you."

"How are you?"

"Seen better days. Don't think much of this room, I have to say."

Mel grins. "I know. It's the only spare at the moment."

The room is small and awkward. The window is too high for Ivor to see out of easily from the chair or the bed. Even if he could, the view is only of the car park, and the scrubland behind it. Heavy pink curtains are secured back and hot afternoon sun streaks in.

"I'll close those for you," Mel says. "It's so hot. And you can't see the TV with the sun."

She squeezes past him and draws the curtains. In the cooler darker light she can see his face properly. He has lost weight, looks gaunt round the cheekbones. His wispy hair seems thinner. There's coffee or food splashed down his shirt. She knows how he hates that.

"Shall I get you a new shirt?"

"Thanks. Emmeline brought some things this morning. In the…the…you know…"

"Cupboard."

She finds a clean polo shirt and eases off the dirty one.

"How was lunch?"

"I'm not hungry these days." He gestures to the box of grapes, the banana, the pack of digestives on the table. "That's all I need."

"You must eat more. You look thin. I'm not surprised. The food in the hospital is horrible."

Before she leaves she checks his walking frame is near him, although she knows he can't rise without assistance. She tucks the red call cord under his leg.

"There. If you need anything, just ring it. Whatever."

"Mel."

She stops at the door, her hand on the knob.

"I don't think I'll leave this place. I don't think I'll see my home again."

Mel strides back to him and squats down. "Now come on. It's early days. We'll get you mobile again and then you'll be fine to go home."

She drops her eyes, wishing she could believe her words. "I'll come back in a bit and let's have a go at getting you moving."

Ivor doesn't answer, and Mel sees his eyelids have dropped. His chest is still raspy. She thought the antibiotics had cleared any infection he had. She'll tell the others to keep an eye on his breathing.

Quietly she creeps out and runs back down to the day room. Her bun is falling down and strands of hair are stuck to her neck with sweat. Many of the residents are swaddled in jumpers and cardigans, thick trousers and woolly socks. Mel fans her face with her hand. As she walks through the day room, glassy eyes turn to her and away again. One of the women is nursing a baby doll on her knee, crooning gently to it. Another is trying to unpick the stitching in a piece of material. A man is shouting aloud to anyone and no one.

The electric doors buzz open and Mel goes out into the car park. The sun is white and hot on the tarmac. She starts walking away from the building and turns back to face it. There's the fire escape, and there's a small pinched first-floor window with pink curtains closed. That's Ivor's room.

She takes out her phone and messages Jake.

Just seen Ivor at Lanyon. He doesn't look too good. Not sure he should have left hospital.

As she is about to go back inside her phone buzzes.

That's rotten. But good that you are there with him. Can we meet up soon?

She stands there a second, listening to the faint breaking of the sea, feeling the heat of the sun on her neck, the institutional smell of food and urine pulsing out of the dayroom.

Yes.

Tansy is boiling in Ivor's room. The sun has moved round, but the radiator is on, the door and windows are closed and the thick air clots in her throat. Ivor muted the TV when she arrived; now the silent people with open stretched mouths seem sinister in the falling summer light.

She has brought him strawberries and biscuits, cordial and chocolates, clean clothes and a sheaf of mail from his house, but he brushed the envelopes aside when she handed them over.

"Let me open them for you," she says again.

He pulls a face, shrugs. "How are the girls?"

"With Mum."

"She came this morning."

"Yes."

"Don't bring the girls."

"I won't. Not yet."

"I don't know when I last saw them."

"It was –" Tansy stops. She can't remember either. "I saw Mel when I arrived. She was almost off home."

"If I go home…"

"Yes?"

"Who will be there with me?"

"The same people. Mel, Stefan, Carol, Izzy, Vicky."

"They can't."

"They can."

"Not enough."

"We'll make sure you don't leave here till you're ready. Mel said she got you up out of the chair."

"I vomited."

"Oh no. Are you all right now?"

"Do I look all right?" Ivor throws out a hand, sweeps the bleak little room.

A stained commode on wheels, half a jug of tepid water, broken biscuits on a plate.

"Do you feel poorly?" Tansy asks.

Ivor doesn't answer. She leans forward. He has sagged in the chair, eyelids shut, breathing uneven. Tansy watches a moment, and a trail of spittle slides from his mouth. She gazes round the room sadly. She feels helpless. There is no way Ivor can come home yet, not for weeks, months, and this place is so barren, soulless, unhappy. There's none of the colour and vibrancy that has filled Ivor's life. The thought that he might end his days here cracks her heart.

"Grandad."

Ivor's head drops a little more. Tansy gathers up the carrier bag of dirty washing.

"I'll see you soon."

Mel is on the landing, writing in a folder outside another room.

"He's not good," Tansy says.

"I know."

"His chest is wheezy. He's very depressed. D'you think the doctor could come and give him something to make him feel a bit happier?"

"I can ask Beth. It has to go through her."

"Are you in tomorrow?"

"No, but Vicky is, I think."

"I'll come up with Mum together when the girls are at school. It's like…he's slipping faster than I can catch him."

Mel squeezes her shoulder. "He isn't young any more. He's had a tough few months."

Tansy nods, rubs away her tears. "I'll get off home."

In the morning Vicky is serving breakfasts in the dining room downstairs. One of the other carers has told her that Ivor refused to eat any of the breakfast that was taken up to him, and that his chest was whistling and crackling again. Vicky is anxious to get to him, but a resident soiled herself in the dining room, and another got lost wandering in the staff quarters, and she doesn't get up to the first floor until the middle of the morning.

She stands outside the door a moment. In three days' time Kev starts work in Stefan's road, and she and Stefan are meeting at Ivor's. She wants to ask Ivor if this is all right, but that's ridiculous because it's not all right at all, but her time with Stefan is the thing that gives her the greatest happiness and she cannot contemplate weeks without him.

She hears voices inside Ivor's room. Tansy and Emmeline. She opens the door. Stale air hits her in the face. Ivor is in his chair – someone must have got him up, but he is still in his pyjamas. A memory jars her mind: easing Ivor into the same blue-and-grey striped pair in his house.

"Hi," she says to Tansy and Emmeline. "How are you, Ivor?"

"He's not well," Emmeline says. "His chest. His leg's swollen too. He needs more antibiotics."

"I believe he's on the list for the GP."

Emmeline and Tansy glance at each other in relief.

"Thanks," Emmeline says. "Should we wait on?"

"I don't know when it'll be. I'm here till evening. I can call you."

Vicky touches Ivor gently on the arm. "Ivor? The doctor's coming to see you later. How are you doing? I heard you didn't want any breakfast. Would you like some tea?"

Ivor's green eyes flick to her face, then close. Vicky takes a tissue from the box beside the bed and wipes his mouth and nose.

"He's hardly spoken," Tansy says, and her voice is tight and strung, like she is about to cry or scream or crumple to the floor.

"I'll keep an eye on him," Vicky promises.

~

Tansy scuffs the dry white grit by the school gates. She's early for the girls. Savannah's mother comes up to her and asks after Ivor, says she can have Scarlet and Amber if necessary. Tansy thanks her automatically and exhales with relief when another woman peels her away.

She jumps when her phone rings. *Vicky* says the screen. She hits green, and watches the teaching assistant crank open the gates.

"The doctor came," Vicky says. "More antibiotics."

"Did he say anything else? Like why he's not talking, not eating?"

"That's the infection."

"OK, thanks." Tansy starts towards the open gates. "At least something's been done about it."

~

Summer rain splatters on Carol's windscreen as she parks behind Lanyon House. The clouds are thick and gnarly, heavy with more rain. It could thunder. Certainly it feels ominous. The whole atmosphere is ominous. Carol stumbles out the car – it's parked on a slope and the door won't stay open – and glances up at the pale edifice. She knows Ivor is in a different room, one facing this way, and she checks each window for any sign of him, but there's nothing. The damp on her face and hair feels more like sweat than rain and, as she crosses the glistening tarmac, she hears a low growl from the clouds.

Through the electric doors and she's into the day room. A row of blank faces gaze at her from wheelchairs and recliners. She almost jumps when she sees Ivor at the end of the row.

He's dressed in baggy tracksuit trousers she does not recognise and a grey-green polo shirt she does, which matches the colour of his eyes. His swollen right leg is propped up before him. He stares back at her, hardly acknowledging her.

"Ivor." Carol takes his hands in hers. They're red and shiny with gout. "Let me sign in and I'll be right back."

She crosses to the big reception desk and scribbles her name and registration number in the visitors' book. As she walks back to Ivor she sees his fluffy hair is standing up like the stalk of a turnip; no one has brushed it.

There's a spare plastic chair and she draws it up beside him. His eyes flick to her face and away again. Unintentionally she follows his gaze as though he were watching something far away that she should seek too.

"Carol."

"Yes?"

"Get the paintings."

"Ivor."

"In the studio. Your paintings. Get them. I don't want anyone else having them. They're yours. Ours."

"We can talk about this when you go home."

"Stop it!"

The woman opposite shrieks at Ivor's shout. Carol strokes his hand.

"OK, OK, I'm sorry."

"I'm not going home. I know that. You know that. They know that here. Everyone knows it, but they won't say it."

Carol squeezes Ivor's hand; he winces and she lets go.

"I'll take them," she says, and the words are heavy as mercury. "I'll take them tomorrow."

"Good girl."

—

The lawn doesn't need mowing again, despite the rain of the day before. Stefan and Vicky stand together at Ivor's window, looking out at the garden.

"Is he there?" Vicky asks at last.

"Yeah, saw his van. Right opposite."

Sometimes Stefan wants to grab Vicky and say *leave him, come to me*, and has to ball his fists or take deep breaths to calm himself. He has no right to ask Vicky to leave Kev, even though she is unhappy at home. If this is all he has of Vicky, it will have to do. So easily he could have had nothing of her.

"Shall we go?" Already he has the studio key in his pocket.

Vicky nods, perhaps a little uncertainly, and follows him to the garden.

The grass is damp and lush. There's a snail on the path to the studio. He kicks it aside, knowing how Vicky hates them. She stiffens as it contracts its slimy body back into its shell.

The huge canvas faces them as he swings the door aside. He wishes he could move it, cover it with a sheet, wonders which is the very last brushstroke.

—

"This is a stupid idea," Louis says as he gets into the passenger seat of Carol's car. "Give it another day, sort somewhere out."

"I've told you. I will when I've got them. They'll be fine at yours for a day or so. How hard is it getting a storage unit?"

"It's a fucking caravan. You can't keep paintings in a caravan."

"It's just for a day or two. I can't take them home, you know that."

"They'll be wrecked. Look, let me sort out the storage. You'll never do it."

"All right then. Whatever." Carol changes down to enter the village of Gerent's Cross.

Louis peers over his shoulder at the flattened back seat. "Will they even fit?"

"I think so."

"Do you know how many there are?"

"Not exactly."

"Jeez."

"Pack it in, Louis. The whole thing is so upsetting for me. Can't you see that? Ivor doesn't think he'll ever leave that place. All he talks about is that he'll never get home and that I must take the paintings. He doesn't want his family finding them. So please, just shut up and help me, or I'll take you back and do it on my own."

"I'm sorry. Of course I'll help. Don't listen to me."

Carol flicks on her left indicator to pull into Ivor's drive.

"Who the fuck's that?" Louis asks. "The family?"

Carol stalls the car half into the drive. There's a car parked there. It is vaguely familiar.

"I think it's Stefan," she says at last. "He must be doing the lawn."

"Well, Ivor gave you permission to get the pictures."

"I don't know," Carol fumbles with the ignition, her feet, the gear stick.

"Come on. You nearly married the man. You can't be scared off by some…some carer."

"I didn't marry him. I'm just some carer too."

Jake is outside his cottage, dropping weeds onto a pile, when Mel arrives. He stands back to let her drive in. Mel wishes twining roses would snake over her car, hide it from nosy eyes. She gets out, feeling Jake's gaze on her. She's in a long floaty dress she hasn't worn yet this summer, and has added an inch of jangling bangles to one arm.

"You look beautiful," Jake says.

Mel blushes. "Thank you."

She tries to pocket her car keys, but the unfamiliar dress has no pockets, and she's left clutching them awkwardly as he leans down to kiss her. He smells of earth and turpentine.

"You are beautiful. I want to paint you."

"You don't paint people."

"Doesn't mean I can't."

He waves her through the door into the cottage, and Mel knows that today is the day, and it was painted in the stars so long ago, she would not be able to retrace her steps and change the course of her life even if she wanted to.

~

The landline is ringing as Tansy and Emmeline come into the house. Emmeline scoops up the receiver and Tansy knows, in a heartbeat, that it is Lanyon House, and that the news is bad.

"Yes, yes, right, "Emmeline says. She is turned away from Tansy. Tansy wants to spin her round, but she doesn't really need to as it's all in her mother's voice. "OK, we'll be here. Let us know please. Is Vicky in today? Or Mel? Oh. Right. Thanks then."

"What's happened?"

"He's bad. Chest very bad. Hardly there. They're going to call a doctor. Let us know."

"Shouldn't we go there?"

"Let's wait and see what the doctor says. We don't want to get in the way or have them think we're dealing with it and send the doctor away or something."

Vicky lies curled up on the cushions and rugs, still sticky from sex and uncomfortable about being in Ivor's studio. Stefan's pulled his jeans back on, but not his shirt, and is carefully sifting through canvases stacked against the wall.

"I thought you said Ivor had shown you his stuff."

"Hmmm. Some of it."

She watches him slide out a canvas and hold it before him. She shifts position to see what he's looking at.

It's a life painting of a woman with dark curls caught in a red scarf, and full white breasts. She has big gold hoops in her ears and a bead necklace bright against her collarbone. Her eyes are dark and haunting. Vicky stands up, tugging her dress over her head.

"That's good."

"Yes, but…no, I must be going mad."

"What?"

"Look. Look at it."

Vicky looks at it.

"The eyes…don't you think? Can you see it?"

"It's someone I know," Vicky replies at last.

"It's Carol."

"Carol?"

"I knew they were friends, her and Ivor…look, that's Carol all right."

"Put it away, Stefan. I feel awkward. She wouldn't want…Ivor wouldn't want…"

"Ivor wouldn't want what?"

Vicky and Stefan spin round. Carol is standing in the doorway with a young man. Carol looks furious, hostile. She pushes into the studio. Stefan props the painting against a stack of other canvases.

"No, he wouldn't want you two poking through his stuff. What the hell are you doing in the studio? Stealing paintings? He's not dead yet, you know."

"We saw it by accident," Vicky starts. "We were just…"

"Trespassing," says the man beside Carol. "Mum, shall I call the police?"

"It's not what you think," Stefan says. "We've been coming up to do a bit of gardening, a bit of cleaning for Ivor. He showed me round the studio once, and I asked Vicky if she'd been in and she said no, and stupidly I offered to show her."

"You took the key?"

"Yes, Ivor showed me where it was. I was out of order. Shouldn't have done it."

The man with Carol is smirking. "Looks like there's a life class going on here, doesn't it?"

"Oh…I was hot mowing the lawn."

Vicky lifts a cushion with her foot and tries to slide Stefan's shirt under it.

"Lawn doesn't look mown to me."

"This is Ivor's studio!" Carol cries. "What is going on here?"

"Jesus, Mum. Let me call the police."

"Leave it, Louis." Carol strides farther into the studio, stares round with her hands on her hips. "Have you stolen anything? Even just a paintbrush? A pencil?"

"No!" Vicky and Stefan cry together.

"Why don't you put your shirt on, mate?" Carol's son, Louis, leans down beside Vicky, scoops up the shirt and tosses it across to Stefan. "Looks more dignified."

Stefan fumbles the catch.

"You've been using this studio as a…as a…"

"Shagging den," Louis supplies.

"Carol please," Vicky says. "It's so difficult, and…"

"But why are you going through his paintings?" Carol demands.

"I wanted to see his work. You and Stefan have known him so much longer."

"Well I certainly have."

"Mum, are we taking the paintings?"

"You don't have to do that." Stefan buttons up his shirt. "Just take the key. We won't come in here again."

Where else can we go? Vicky screams silently, then *is this the end?*

—

They've been waiting for the call and it comes much sooner than they ever expected. Emmeline is unloading the washing machine; Tansy answers.

"It's Beth from Lanyon. I think you should come in as soon as possible."

"What did the doctor say?"

"Doctor hasn't been yet. As I said: I think you need to come in now."

Something is making a noise, and it takes Carol a moment to realise that it's her mobile in her bag. She's about to let it go to voicemail then snatches it.

"Tansy," she says aloud.

Stefan puts his arm round Vicky. Carol keeps her eyes on them as she answers the call.

"Tansy?"

"Carol, you must come to Lanyon. They've called us in. He's so poorly. We're on the way now. I know you'd want to see him."

"I'll come now."

"Could you ring some of the others for me please? I can't do it all."

"I'm with Stefan and Vicky anyway. I'll ring Mel and Izzy."

"What? With them?"

"Don't worry about it. Just get to Ivor."

Carol hangs up.

"That was Tansy. She says Lanyon have told them to go in. Ivor's really ill."

"Come on, Mum."

"You two," Carol says to Stefan and Vicky. "You'll want to come too, yes?"

"Yes," Stefan says.

"OK. Let's get this studio locked up."

She watches Stefan lock the door. He offers her the key. She shakes her head, and tears slide from her eyes. "Put it back where it lives."

Izzy's phone rings as she hands a customer his change. He drops a few coins in the tip box and she smiles her thanks as she takes the phone out of her pocket.

Carol.

"Hi Carol."

"Is that Izzy?" asks a man.

"Yes, is that Jeff? Is Carol OK?"

"It's her son, Louis. We're just on the way to Lanyon House. Apparently Ivor is very ill and anyone who wants to see him should come now."

Izzy glances round the café. Aidan is at a doctor's appointment. Holly and Abi could manage alone until he comes back, surely.

"I'm coming."

Mel grabs her bag from the floor as Jake pulls her up off the sofa. She's a mother of four. Just because she's about to go to bed with her lover, she can't change her habits. Someone might need her.

Jake's bedroom walls are a bright turquoise, the colour of the ocean at Porthcurno. The white bedding is splashed with bright cushions: sun-yellow, scarlet, purple. Mel drops her bag on the floor and turns to Jake.

"Jesus, Mel, sometimes I thought this would never happen."

"Nor me," she breathes, as he unhooks the straps of her floaty, frivolous dress.

The ring of her mobile is harsh as Indian ink spilt on watercolours. Jake steps back.

"You want to get that?"

"I should…the kids."

Heat floods Mel's face as she scrabbles in her abandoned bag. Her car keys fall out – she stuffed them in there in the end – and a tissue blotted with lipstick.

"It's Carol." She answers the call, flicks the dress straps back on.

"Is that Mel? This is Carol's son, Louis."

As Mel listens to Louis, her desire shrivels inside her. She's already calculating how long it will take her to get to Lanyon from Jake's cottage, whether to take the main road or the back lanes.

"It's Ivor," she says faintly, dropping the phone on the bed. "I think he's dying."

"Let me drive you."

"No, no." Mel gathers her phone and keys, adjusts her dress. "You can't. We can't be seen."

"Is he really dying?"

"I don't know, do I? That was Carol's son. Tansy and Emmeline have been called in. They want everyone to go and see him. If we're not too late." She runs out of the bedroom.

"I'd like to see him too. I've known him forty-odd years."

Mel stops and faces Jake on the landing.

"How would you know about him? I mean, no one's called you."

"No. No one's called me. What a fucking surprise."

"You must go. Not with me. Let me go. You follow in five minutes."

"And how am I supposed to know if no one's told me?"

"I don't think anyone will be thinking that through right now, and so what if they do? You're right. You've known him years longer than any of us. I'm going now."

She runs out to her car and reverses awkwardly onto the lane. Jake stands by the cottage door, raises one hand in a salute as she judders up the lane.

"What the hell can we say?" Vicky is crying.

"Today it's about Ivor. We'll worry about that when…when…"

"Even if Carol doesn't say anything that ghastly son will."

"Not today he won't, if he's got any sense. Please Vic, let's just go and see Ivor."

"Is it over? You and me?"

"What? I bloody hope not."

Vicky's heart rate subsides and she tugs her nails with her teeth.

~

Izzy turns up the radio to match her anxiety. It's summer and the roads are heavy with holiday traffic as well as the usual tractors, vans, and buses. She taps her hand on the wheel angrily. *Don't let me be too late.*

Whatever happens today, or tonight, tomorrow, or some day in the future, Izzy will never forget Ivor. The first person she was truly honest to.

~

"You should let me call the police."

"Just leave it, Louis."

"At the very least they were breaking and entering."

"Look, right now I don't care what they were doing. This is the man I should have married. The man I love. The man I love is dying. And I may be too late."

Mel roars out onto the main road. What the fuck was she thinking about, going to bed with Jake Gregory? She loves Joe. She loves her children. She doesn't want to be some fling, some throwaway lover, to a man with pretty words and prettier paintings.

She checks her rear-view mirror to see if Jake is behind her, but the road is empty.

~

Tansy's eyes are hot and bloated with crying. Her head thumps and burns. She's drunk a bottle of Shiraz and her throat is dry and her stomach raw because she needs food but she hasn't had a chance to eat, what with Ivor and picking up the girls, and then…and then…

Everyone came to see Ivor. All his carers. Carol with her son, Vicky and Stefan. Izzy. Mel. Everyone crept into his darkened room for a few moments, said whatever words they had in their hearts, and crept out again. And still Ivor's rattling chest rose and fell. At last the doctor came. The carers scattered back to their cars, back to their lives, leaving just Tansy and Emmeline with Ivor.

Emmeline stayed with Ivor while Tansy picked up the girls. Mel was in the school yard in that long gauzy dress, and Tansy told her about the new antibiotics the doctor prescribed. Mel said she would send a round robin to the other carers and Tansy was overwhelmed with gratitude that she didn't have to do it.

~

Summer rain, warm summer rain, and a faraway rumble of thunder. A tight crescent of figures around the long hole in the earth. Old words from the priest, old comforting words, words infused with the power of the ages.

Tansy and Emmeline cling to each other as the coffin descends. An artist returning to his earthly pigments. Tansy's eyes are stretched and wild, raw from tears; Emmeline stares ahead. Scarlet and Amber are hiding behind other headstones. No-one is watching them.

Tansy raises her eyes at last. Charlie, black-suited with a new sharp haircut. Mel gulping and swallowing into a mangled tissue, Vicky stroking her arm.

Izzy moves close to Tansy.

"He'll live on," she whispers. "Through you and your beautiful girls," and she nods to the two bright heads, dampened by rain, as they run to Charlie.

Tansy nods, speechless.

The coffin has gone down, down to the cool and the warmth of the earth.

Stefan hands his black umbrella to Carol, and guides the wheelchair over the sticky grass and mud. Someone holds a bowl before Ivor. He claws a tiny handful of earth, flings it with unexpected force towards the grave.

He would have liked to see Jake one last time.

Acknowledgements

I'd like to thank Sarah Hembrow at Vulpine Press for giving me a chance and believing in me and my books. Thanks also to my editor Robin Ash for his help with the manuscript, and lots of laughs along the way.

Lucinda Hart lives in Cornwall and has been writing fiction since the age of three. She divides her time between writing, raising two daughters, re-learning how to swim, and falling over in martial arts classes. For further information, follow Lucinda on X @Lucinda_Author, or find her on Facebook and Instagram.

Printed in Great Britain
by Amazon